International be

Graham

&

Jane Porter

present

The Sheikh's Woman

Two dramatic, red-hot, seductive stories of passion in a far-away land.

Also available

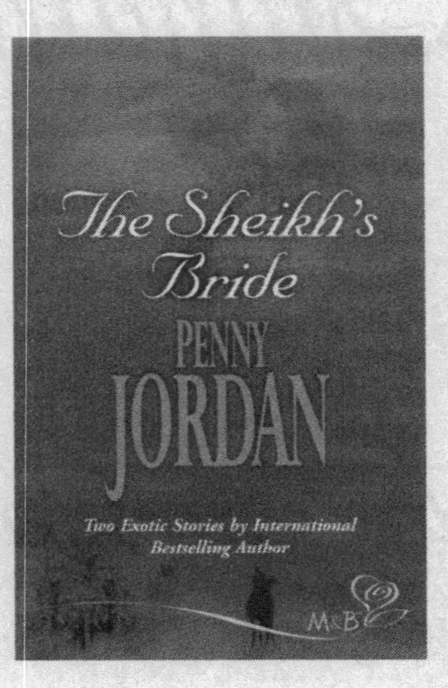

featuring

The Sheikh's Virgin Bride & One Night with the Sheikh

The Sheikh's Woman

Containing

The Arabian Mistress
by Lynne Graham

&

The Sheikh's Wife
by Jane Porter

*Harlequin Mills & Boon Limited, Eton House,
18-24 Paradise Road,
Richmond, Surrey TW9 1SR*

The Sheikh's Wife and *The Arabian Mistress* were first published in Great Britain by Harlequin Mills & Boon Limited in separate, single volumes.

ISBN 13: 978 0 263 85078 9
IISBN 10: 0 263 85078 1

108-1006

*Printed and bound in Spain
by Litografia Rosés S.A., Barcelona*

THE ARABIAN MISTRESS

by

Lynne Graham

Lynne Graham was born in Northern Ireland and has been a keen Mills & Boon reader since her teens. She is very happily married with an understanding husband, who has learned to cook since she started to write! Her five children keep her on her toes. She has a very large dog, which knocks everything over, a very small terrier which barks a lot and two cats. When time allows, Lynne is a keen gardener.

Lynne Graham has fabulous new novels available in September and December 2006. Look for *Mistress Bought and Paid For* and *Reluctant Mistress, Blackmailed Wife* in Mills & Boon Modern Romance®.

CHAPTER ONE

IN HIS villa in the South of France, Prince Tariq Shazad ibn Zachir, paramount sheikh and ruler of the oil-rich Gulf state of Jumar, tossed aside the cellular phone and turned his attention to his most trusted aide, Latif.

Shrewd at reading others, Tariq noted the strain etched on the older man's face. 'Something wrong?'

'I regret that I should have to disturb you with this matter…' Latif settled a folder down on the desk with an air of profound apology '…but I felt it should be drawn to your attention.'

Surprised by the other man's discomfiture, Tariq swept up the folder. The opening document was a detailed report from Jumar's chief of police. Tariq scanned the name of the foreign national, who had been imprisoned for bad debts. He froze, his superb bone structure clenching, narrowed dark eyes hardening with angry incredulity. It was Adrian Lawson, Faye's elder brother!

Yet *another* Lawson guilty of dishonesty and deception! As he read the explanation of the events which had led to Adrian's arrest his lean, strong face hardened in disgust. How could Faye's brother have dared to set up a construction firm in Jumar and rob the very citizens that he, Tariq ibn Zachir was sworn to protect?

Powerful memories were stirring, disturbing memories which Tariq had spent twelve months endeavouring to forget. What male wished to recall his own worst mistake? Faye with her fake innocence, who had laid a snare to entrap him as surely as any seasoned gold-digger. The bait? Her beautiful self. The threat after the trap had snapped shut? *Scandal!* The paramount sheikh of Jumar might exercise feudal power over his subjects. But, even in the twenty-first century, Tariq ibn Zachir accepted that it was his duty to maintain a conservative lifestyle. And a year ago his choices had been few for his father, Hamza, had been dying…

Snapping back to the present, pale with bitter anger beneath his tawny skin, Tariq slowly breathed in deep. Unlike many other scions of Middle Eastern royal families, he had not been educated in the West. Tariq had been raised much like his ancestral forefathers. Military school, tutors, desert survival exercises with the British special forces. At the age of twenty-two, a pilot and an expert in every possible form of combat, Tariq had finally convinced his father that, while the ability to lead his future people into battle was naturally important, one hundred years of peace within their borders *and* with their neighbours might suggest that a business degree could be of rather more imminent use to his son.

Tariq had duly discovered a natural talent for the business world and had enriched the swollen coffers of a state already so fabulously wealthy that he and his people made the highest per capita charitable contributions of any country in the world. And with his entrance into the more liberal culture of Europe, Tariq had also received an unparalleled education on the ways of Western women. Yet even in the grip of his subsequent cynicism, he had *still* been slaughtered like a sitting duck when he'd met Faye Lawson…

'How do you wish me to act in this matter?' Latif enquired.

Tariq flashed him a questioning glance. 'There is no action to be taken. Let the process of law take its course.'

Latif studied his feet. 'It seems unlikely that Adrian Lawson will be able to produce the money necessary to obtain his own release.'

'He may rot.'

After a very long and tense silence, Latif cleared his throat with deprecatory hesitance.

Tariq sent him a look of grim amusement. 'Yes, I *know* what I do…'

Uneasy though he was with that response, the older man bowed and departed again. Well aware of the source of Latif's anxiety, Tariq considered his own position with grim disfavour. Realities he had sidestepped now confronted him. His fierce pride, his fury at being set up and trapped, had come between him and common sense. But it was time to sever his connection with Faye Lawson and move on.

It *should* have been done a year ago. It was not a situation which could be left unresolved. Particularly not when he now had the responsibility of bringing up three young children, orphaned by the plane crash which had decimated his own family circle. He needed a wife, a warm, maternal woman. It was his duty to marry such a woman, he reminded himself. However, it could not be said that he was eager to embrace that duty.

Thrusting aside the folder on Adrian Lawson, unread beyond that first enlightening page, Tariq lounged back in his chair like a restive tiger, brooding dark golden eyes hard as iron. The Lawson siblings and their boorish stepfather, Percy, were a sly and greedy trio, who allowed no moral scruple to come between themselves and financial profit. How many other men had Faye played for a sucker? How many lives had Percy ruined with blackmail and dishonest business practices? And now it was evident that even Adrian, the only one of the trio whom Tariq had believed to be decent, was equally corrupt. Such people *should* be punished.

Tariq pictured the hawk that was the emblem of his family soaring high above the desert in search of tender prey. A chilling smile formed on his well-shaped mouth. There was no reason why he should not strike a blow for natural justice. Indeed there was no reason why *he* should not take advantage of the situation and have a little fun at the same time…

Faye sat beside her stepfather in the back of the taxi in total silence. Small and slight of build, she was dwarfed by the bulk of the man beside her.

It was only mid-morning but it was hot and, after the long night flight from London, she was exhausted. The cab speeding them through the wide pristine streets of Jumar city was taking them to the prison where her brother, Adrian, was being held. Had she not been so worried about Adrian and had money not been so tight, she would have refused to share even a cab with Percy Smythe.

It still shook Faye that she could feel such intense dislike for any living person. Family loyalty had always been very important to her but she knew she would never forgive Percy for dragging her down into the dirt with him and utterly destroying any faith that Prince Tariq ibn Zachir had ever had in her. Nor could she forgive herself for being so infatuated that she had refused to allow herself to question Tariq's sudden unexpected proposal of marriage twelve months earlier.

'This is a waste of time.' Percy's plump, perspiring face was full of exasperated impatience. 'You've got to go and see Prince Tariq and ask him to have Adrian released!'

Beneath the pale blonde hair which merely served to accentuate her present lack of colour, Faye's delicate profile froze. 'I *couldn't*—'

'Well, how are you going to feel if Adrian picks up some ghastly Middle Eastern infection and pops his clogs?' Percy demanded with brutal bluntness. 'You know he's never been strong!'

Her sensitive stomach churned for there was more truth

in that melodramatic warning than she liked to credit. As a child, Adrian had had leukaemia and, although he had recovered, he still tended to catch every passing bug. His uncertain health had finally destroyed the army career he'd loved, forcing him to rethink his future and plunge into the business venture which had led to his current plight.

'The Foreign Office assured us that he was being well treated,' Faye reminded the older man tautly.

'Insofar as he's been locked up indefinitely! If I was a superstitious man, I would believe that your desert warrior put a hex on us *all* last year,' Percy complained bitterly. 'I was riding high then, making money hand over fist and look at me now—I'm practically broke!'

Just as he deserved to be, Faye reflected heavily. Her stepfather would walk over anyone and do anything to feather his own nest. But there was one surprising exception to that rule: Adrian had somehow become as dear to Percy as any flesh-and-blood son. It was ironic that Percy should have sacrificed his own security in trying and failing to keep her brother's business afloat.

The prison lay well outside the city limits, housed in a grim fortress surrounded by high walls and lookout towers. They had to wait for some time before they were shown into a room where a line of seats sat in front of a sturdy glass partition. Faye only then appreciated that neither privacy nor physical contact were allowed between inmates and visitors.

But a bigger shock was in store for her when Adrian appeared. He had lost a lot of weight and his prison clothes hung loose on his thin frame. The drawn pallor of his features alarmed her: her brother looked far from well. His bloodshot eyes were strained and reluctant to meet hers.

'You shouldn't have come, sis,' Adrian groaned on the phone provided for communication. 'This is *my* mess. I got too cocky and over-extended myself. I let Lizzie spend like there was no tomorrow. It's the way people live here…you go a bit mad trying to keep up—'

Percy snatched the receiver from Faye and growled, 'I'll go to the press back home and kick up such a *stink* they'll let you out of this hell hole!'

Adrian studied his stepfather in open horror. 'Are you crazy?' he mouthed silently through the glass barrier.

Faye retrieved the phone, her violet-blue eyes full of anxiety. 'We can't raise the kind of money you need to get out of here. Your lawyer met us off our flight but he said that he could no longer act for you and that the case was closed. You have to tell us what else we can do to fight this.'

Adrian gave her a bleak defeated look. 'There *is* nothing. Didn't my lawyer tell you that there is no right of appeal in a case like mine? How are Lizzie and the kids holding up?'

At that reference to his wife, Faye tensed for she had no good news to offer. After the experience of having her luxurious home in Jumar repossessed and being deported with her twin toddlers because she no longer had any means of support, her sister-in-law, Lizzie, was feeling very sorry for herself.

'Like that, is it?' Adrian read his sister's evasive gaze. 'Lizzie didn't even send me a letter?'

'She's pretty down…' Faye hated adding to his misery with that admission. 'She asked me to tell you that she loves you but that right now she's having a problem just coping with being back home without you.'

Adrian's eyes filled with moisture and he twisted his head away, swallowing hard to get himself back under control.

Faye blinked back tears at her brother's distress and hurried to change the subject. 'How are you managing?'

'Fine…' her brother mumbled curtly.

'Are you being treated all right?' Faye was intimidated by the suspicious appraisal of the two armed officers watching their every move.

'I have no cause for complaint…just that it's hell because I hate the food, speak rotten Arabic and keep on getting sick.' Her brother's jerky voice faltered. 'But whatever you do, don't let Percy go screaming to the media because that will make me a marked man in here. The locals see any criticism of Jumar as criticism of their lousy womanising ruler, Prince Tariq—'

In an abrupt movement, one of the armed officers strode forward looking outraged and wrenched the phone from Adrian's grasp.

'What's wrong…what's happening?' Faye surged upright in a panic.

But on their side of the restrictive glass, she and her stepfather might as well have been invisible. Adrian was escorted back to the doorway through which he had earlier entered and vanished from view.

'I bet those thugs are taking him away to beat him up!' Percy was as aghast as Faye at what had happened.

'But neither of those men put a hand on Adrian—'

'Not in front of *us*…but how do you know what they're doing to him now?'

They waited ten minutes to see if Adrian would reappear but he did not. Instead a severe-looking older man in uniform came in to speak to them.

'I want to know what's going on here,' Percy demanded aggressively.

'Visits are a privilege we extend to relatives, not a right in law. Your visit was terminated because we will not allow our most honoured ruler to be referred to in offensive terms.' As Percy swelled like a ripe red fruit ready to burst in messy rage, the senior prison officer added loftily, 'Let me also assure you that we do not abuse our prisoners.

Jumar is a civilised and humane country. You may request another visit later this week.'

Registering then that every word spoken during such visits appeared to be monitored and that Adrian must have been equally unaware of that reality, Faye hurried her stepfather out of the room before he could add to her brother's offence.

Percy raved in frustrated fury all the way back to their small hotel in the suburbs. Faye was grateful that the taxi driver did not seem to understand a word of Percy's vitriolic diatribe against Jumar and all things Jumarian. Taking Tariq's name in vain in a public place might well be tantamount to inviting a physical assault. As her stepfather headed straight for the residents' bar on the ground floor, Faye got into the lift and went back up to her hotel room.

In her mind's eye, all she could see was the look of naked despair on her brother's haggard face. Just six short months ago, Adrian had believed he would make his fortune in a city reputed to be a building boomtown. Faye sat at the foot of the bed staring at the challenging reflection of the telephone in the dressing mirror facing her.

'The number is easy to remember,' Tariq had told her once. 'We owned the first telephone in Jumar. You just dial *one* for the palace switchboard!'

Momentarily Faye shut her swimming eyes, pain and regret and bitterness tearing at her. However, like it or not, Prince Tariq ibn Zachir seemed to be the only option they had left. In most other countries, Adrian would have been declared bankrupt, not imprisoned for debt as if he were a criminal. She had no choice but to approach Tariq and plead her brother's case. Tariq was all powerful here within his own country. Tariq could surely do *anything* he wanted to do…

So what if the prospect of crawling to Tariq made her cringe? How could she value her pride more than her brother's welfare? Tense as a cat on hot bricks, Faye paced the room. Would Tariq even agree to see her? How did she beg such a massive favour from a male who despised both her and her stepfather? She was out of her depth here in Jumar where the very air seemed to smell of high-powered money and privilege, she thought bitterly. A year ago, she had been even more out of her depth with a male as exotic and sophisticated as Tariq ibn Zachir. And bone-deep foolish to imagine that anything lasting might come of such an inequal relationship. But, no matter what Tariq had chosen to believe, she had played *no* part in Percy's sordid attempt to blackmail him!

Reminding herself of that essential truth, Faye reached for the phone. Dialling that single digit to be connected to the palace was easy. However, in the minutes that followed, she discovered that the palace switchboard was tended by personnel who spoke only Arabic. Breaking off the call in frustration, Faye reached for the purse in her bag. From the central compartment, she withdrew a slender gold ring etched with worn hieroglyphic symbols.

Her hand shook. For a split second, memory took her back to the instant when Tariq had slid that ring onto her finger in the Embassy of Jumar in London. She shivered, assailed by a tide of choking humiliation. How stupid she had been to believe that that was a *real* wedding ceremony! It had been a farce staged solely to combat Percy's threat to plunge Tariq into a sleazy media scandal. But only when that cruel farce was over had Faye realised what a complete clown Tariq had made of her.

Making use of the hotel stationery, Faye dropped the ring into an envelope and dashed off a note requesting a meeting with Tariq. She went down to Reception and asked how to have an urgent letter delivered. The receptionist studied the name on the envelope with widened eyes and extended her interest to the additional words, 'PERSONAL, PRIVATE,

CONFIDENTIAL' taking up half of the space. 'This…it is for Prince Tariq?'

Faye reddened and nodded.

''One of our drivers will deliver it, Miss Lawson.'

Back in her room, Faye went for a shower and changed. Then she lay down on the bed. A loud knock, recognisable as Percy's calling card, sounded on the door. She ignored it. He thumped again so loudly she was afraid that the hotel staff would come to investigate. She opened the door.

'Right…' Her stepfather pushed his way in, his heavy face aggressive and flushed by alcohol. 'You get on that phone now and contact Tariq. Hopefully he'll get a kick out of you grovelling at his feet. And if that's not enough to please His Royal Highness, warn him that you can *still* go to the newspapers and give them a story about what it's like getting married and divorced all in the space of the same day!'

Faye was horrified. 'Do you really think that wild nasty threats are likely to persuade Tariq to help Adrian?'

'Look, I may have miscalculated with Tariq last year but I know how that bloke ticks now. He's a real tough nut to crack—all that SAS training—but he's also an officer and a gentleman and he prides himself on the fact. So first you try licking boots and looking pathetic…' Percy subjected her navy blouse, cotton trousers and her clipped-back long hair to a withering appraisal. 'Look pathetic *and* beautiful!'

The light rap that sounded on her door at that point provided a merciful interruption. It was the hotel manager, who had greeted them on their arrival. He bowed as if she had suddenly become a most important guest.

'A limousine has arrived to take you to the Haja place, Miss Lawson.'

Faye swallowed hard. She had not expected so speedy a response to her request for a meeting.

'Don't you worry…she'll be down in two minutes.'

Percy turned back to his stepdaughter to say appreciatively, 'Why didn't you just *tell* me you'd already started the ball rolling?'

Keen to escape her stepfather's loathsome company, Faye went straight down in the lift. She settled into the luxurious limousine, feeling like a fish out of water in her plain, inexpensive clothes. And she was, wasn't she?

She had lived in a quiet country house all her life, rarely meeting anyone outside her late mother's restricted social circle. Percy had married Sarah Lawson when Faye was five. Disabled by the same car accident in which her first husband had died, Faye's mother had been confined to a wheelchair and desperately lonely. She had also been a well-to-do widow. After their marriage, Percy had continued to use a city apartment as his base and, pleading pressure of work, had spent only occasional weekends with his new family.

Faye had never gone to school like other children. Both she and her brother had initially been taught at home by their mother, but once Adrian had overcome leukaemia Percy had persuaded his wife that her son should complete his education with other boys. At eleven years old, hungry for friends her own age, Faye had finally worked up the courage to tell her stepfather that she too wanted to attend school.

'And what's your mother going to do with herself all day?' Percy's accusing fury had shaken her rigid. 'How can you be so selfish? Your mother needs you for company…she's got nothing else in her life!'

Faye had been devastated at eighteen when her gentle mother had died. But only then had she appreciated that some people believed she had led an unnaturally sheltered life for a teenager. Indeed, at the interview for the nursing course she was hoping to begin in the autumn, several critical comments had been made about her lack of experience of the *real* world. Had she felt like baring her soul, she might have told them that, with Percy Smythe in the starring role of stepfather, she had had ample experience of life's nastier realities…

Having traversed the wide, busy streets of the city to a gracious tree-lined square, the limo pulled up in front of a vast old sandstone building with an imposing entrance. Spick and span soldiers stood on guard outside. Faye clambered out, flustered and unsure of herself.

Climbing the steps, she entered a vast and imposing hall crowded with people coming and going. Frowning, she hesitated. A young man in a suit approached her and with a low bow said, 'Miss Lawson? I will take you to Prince Tariq.'

'Thank you. Is this the royal palace?'

'No, indeed, Miss Lawson. Although the Haja fortress still belongs to the royal family, His Royal Highness allows it to be used as a public building,' her companion informed her. 'The Haja houses the law courts and the audience rooms, also conference and banqueting facilities for visiting dignitaries and businessmen. While retaining offices here, Prince Tariq lives in the Muraaba palace.'

So this was *not* Tariq's home and he had chosen a more impersonal setting for their meeting. Her eyes skimmed over the fluted stone pillars that punctuated the echoing hall and the wonderful mosaic tiled floor which gleamed beneath the passage of so many feet. The Haja was a hive of activity. An elderly tribesman was sitting on a stone bench with, of all things, a *goat* on a string. She saw women veiled in black from head to toe, other women in elegant western clothing, their lovely faces serene, clusters of older men wearing the traditional male headdress, the *kaffiyeh*, sharply suited younger ones bare-headed and carrying files and attaché cases.

'Miss Lawson…?'

Forced to quicken her steps, she followed her escort under an archway. Tribal guards armed with both guns and ornate swords stood outside the door which was being spread wide for her entrance. She forced her feet onward, heart thundering, throat tightening. Perhaps what she least expected was to find herself standing alone in a beautiful inner courtyard, lush with islands of exotic greenery and embellished with a tranquil central pool. She blinked. Hearing the sound of footsteps, she turned and saw Tariq coming down a flight of steps about twenty feet away.

To disconcert her yet further, Tariq was clad in riding gear, a white polo shirt open at his throat, skintight beige breeches outlining his narrow hips and long powerful length of leg, polished brown boots on his feet.

Her tummy muscles clenched. She had forgotten quite how tall Tariq ibn Zachir was and how dynamic his presence. He stilled like a lion on the prowl. Magnificent, hugely confident, his silent grace of movement one of his most noticeable physical attributes. In the sunlight he was a golden feast of vibrant masculinity. His luxuriant black hair shone. His tawny skin glowed with health and his stunning bronze eyes gleamed like precious metal, both brilliant and unreadable. Indeed, he was quite staggeringly beautiful and it was an appalling challenge for Faye not to stare at him. Her mouth ran dry, a slow, painful tide of pink creeping up to dispense her pallor. Her heart hammered against her breastbone so hard she could barely catch her breath.

'I appreciate your agreeing to see me so quickly,' Faye muttered dry-mouthed.

'Unfortunately, I haven't much time to spare. I have a charity polo match to play in an hour's time.'

Tariq came to a halt at the stone table by the pool and leant back against it. He angled his arrogant head back and studied her with a bold, all-male intensity that made her feel horribly self-conscious. His expressive mouth quirked.

'Surely Percy did not advise you to wear trousers to this meeting? Or is that sad outfit supposed to be a plea for the sympathy vote?'

At that all too accurate crack about her stepfather, Faye turned as red as a beetroot and stammered. 'I c-can't imagine why you should think that.'

'Don't play innocent.' Tariq gave her that advice in a tone as smooth as glass. 'I had a surfeit of the blushing virgin act last year. I should have smelt a rat the instant you ditched it and appeared in a plunging neckline but, like most men, I was too busy looking to *be* cautious.'

Writhing with chagrin under such fire, some of which she knew to be justified, Faye snatched in a stark breath of the hot, still air. 'Tariq…I *very* much regret what happened between us.'

Tariq dealt her a slow smile which chilled her to the marrow for it was not at all the charismatic smile she recalled. 'I'm sure you do. It could not have occurred to you *then* that your precious brother would soon be locked up in a prison cell in Jumar.'

'Of course, it didn't.' Faye took that comment at face value, striving to be grateful that he had rushed them straight to the crux of the matter. She curled her hands together. 'But you like Adrian. You know that he's been gaoled through no fault of his own—'

'Do I?' Tariq broke in softly. 'Is our legal system so unjust? I had not thought so.'

Recognising her error in appearing to criticise that system, Faye said hastily, 'I didn't mean that. I was only pointing out that Adrian hasn't done anything criminal—'

'Has he not? Here in Jumar it *is* a crime to leave employees and tradesmen unpaid and clients with buildings that have not been completed according to contract. However, we are wonderfully practical in such cases.' His shimmering smile was no warmer than its predecessor. 'To regain his freedom, Adrian has only to satisfy his creditors.'

'But he's not able to do that...' As she was forced to make that admission, Faye's discomfiture leapt higher still. 'Adrian sold his home to start up the construction firm. He plunged *everything* he had into the venture—'

'And then lived like a king while he was here in my country. Yes, I am familiar with the circumstances in which your brother's business failed. Adrian himself was foolish and extravagant.'

As Tariq completed that brief but damning indictment, Faye lost colour. 'He made mistakes...*yes*, but not with any bad or deliberate intent—'

'Surely you have heard of the principle of criminal irresponsibility?' Indolent as a sleek jungle cat sunning himself in the sweltering heat that she was finding unbearable, Tariq surveyed her. 'Tell me, why did you send me *this*?'

That switch of subject disconcerted Faye almost as much as his complete lack of emotion. The last time she had seen Tariq he had been hot with dark fury and outrage. Now she focused on the ring in the extended palm of his lean brown hand and her tummy twisted. He tossed the ring into the air where it caught the sun and glittered, exercising the strangest fascination over her. Catching it again with deft fingers, he then tossed the ring with speaking carelessness down onto the stone table where it finally rattled into stillness.

'Were you hoping that I might have some sentimental memory of the day I put that ring on your finger?' Tariq asked with cold derision.

Faye studied his superb riding boots until they blurred beneath the fierceness of her gaze. A wave of deep shame enveloped her and roused a terrifying lump in her throat. How very hard it was to accept that he had caused her such immense pain yet deprived her of any real right of complaint. True, he had misjudged her, but he could hardly be blamed for that when her own stepfather had tried to blackmail him. Nonetheless, unjust as it might be, Faye hated Tariq for believing that she was as calculating and mercenary as Percy Smythe.

'Tell me…' Tariq continued with awesome casualness, '…do you think of yourself as my wife or as my ex-wife?'

Reacting to that light and, to her, inappropriate question as if it was the cruellest of taunts, Faye's pale head flew up and mortified pink warmed her cheeks afresh. 'Hardly. At the time you made it very clear that that wedding ceremony was a charade! I know all too well that I was *never* your wife.'

His dense black spiky lashes lowered over dark deep-set eyes for once unlit by any lighter hue. 'I was curious to find out how you regarded yourself.'

'I'm only here to discuss Adrian's position—'

'Adrian doesn't have a position,' Tariq interposed without hesitation. 'The law has already dealt with him and only repayment of his debts can free him.'

He was like a stranger. Neither courteous nor sympathetic, neither interested nor perturbed. This was Tariq as she had never known him. Hard, distant, forbidding. Terrifyingly impersonal. A male whose cool authority of command was so engrained that it blazed from him even in casual clothing. Faye's slim hands closed in tight on themselves. 'But surely *you* could do something…if you wanted to…'

'I am not above the law,' Tariq stated, ice entering his rich dark drawl.

Her desperation grew. 'But, even so, you can do exactly as you wish…isn't that what being a feudal ruler is all about?'

'I would not interfere with the laws of my country. It is a grave insult for you to even *suggest* that I would abuse the trust of my people in such a way!' Hard golden eyes struck hers in a look of strong censure.

Faye tore her shaken gaze from his and tried not to cringe. She fully understood that message but did not want to accept it. Even though she was standing in partial shade, she was perspiring and wilting in the suffocating heat that he seemed to flourish in. But knowing that she undoubtedly only had this one chance to speak up on her brother's behalf, she persisted. 'Adrian can't work to pay off his creditors from inside a prison cell—'

'No, indeed, but how is it that you and your stepfather find yourself so poor that you cannot rescue him?'

'Percy used up all his surplus cash trying to *save* Adrian's business. And don't tell me that you weren't aware of that.' Faye could not conceal her bitterness at the brick-wall reception she was receiving. It was now clear that, even before she'd approached him, Tariq had known all the facts of her brother's case but had already decided not to interfere. 'I'm only here begging you to find some way to help my brother because I have nowhere else to turn.'

'You have yet to explain *why* I should wish to help Adrian.'

'Common decency…humanity…' Faye muttered shakily. 'Officer and a gentleman?'

Tariq elevated an aristocratic dark brow. 'Not where your self-seeking, dishonourable family is concerned.'

'What can I *say* to convince you that—?'

'Nothing. You can say nothing that will convince me. Tell me, were you always this obtuse? Or was I so busy looking at your angelic face and divine body that I failed to notice a pronounced absence of brain cells?'

His ruthless mockery lashed red into her tense, confused face. 'I don't know what you're getting at—'

'Why don't you just ask me under what terms you might persuade *me* to settle Adrian's debts?'

'*You* settle them?' Faye studied Tariq in bewilderment. 'That idea never even occurred to me—'

That disclaimer fired an even more sardonic light in his level gaze. 'We're running out of time. So I shall use plain words. Give yourself to me and I will buy your brother out of trouble. There…it is very simple, is it not?'

Her lips parted. *Give yourself to me.* Her dark blue eyes huge, she stared back at him in disbelief.

Tariq absorbed her reaction with a cynical cool that sent her shock level into overdrive. 'Sex in return for money. What you once used as a bait to set a trap for me but *failed* to deliver.'

Hot, sticky and stunned by that blunt condemnation, Faye raised her hand to tug at the constricting collar of her blouse. A trickle of perspiration ran down between her breasts. His keen gaze rested there and then whipped up to connect with her shaken eyes. The charged sexuality of that knowing look scorched her sensitive skin like a taunting flame. A helpless flare of response gripped her taut body without warning. Thought had nothing to do with the sudden ache in her breasts, the throbbing tautness of her nipples or the curl of dark secret heat darting up between her thighs.

Appalled self-loathing trammelling through her, Faye dropped her head, fighting and denying the physical sensations which threatened to tear her inside out. She needed to think, she *had* to concentrate for Tariq could not possibly mean what he was saying. This could only be a cruel power play at her expense. At the same time as he let her know that he would not lift a finger to help Adrian, he was trying to punish her for the past. Punish her with humiliation.

At that energising thought, Faye lifted her head high again. Her fine-boned features were pink but stiff with angry, injured pride. 'Obviously it was a mistake to ask you for this meeting.' Struggling to keep her voice level, she thrust up her chin. 'Whatever you may think of me, I don't deserve what you just said to me.'

A caustic smile slashed Tariq's lean, powerful face. 'What a loss you have been to the film world! That look of mortally offended reproach is quite superb.'

'You ought to be ashamed of yourself!' Undaunted by the incredulous blaze that flamed in his spectacular eyes, Faye gave him a scornful glance. Spinning on her heel, she stalked back out of the courtyard without lowering herself to say another word.

CHAPTER TWO

FAYE shot like a bullet back into the crowded concourse again, cannoned off someone with a startled apology and backed away into one of the pillars.

She was in shock. She knew she was. But she was furious to find that her eyes were awash with tears and she couldn't see where she was going. Gulping back the thickness in her throat, she whirled round to the back of the pillar and struggled to get a grip on herself again. What was she? Some wishy-washy wimp all of a sudden?

'Allow me to offer you refreshment…' an anxious male voice proffered.

Frowning in surprise because she recognised that voice, Faye parted her clogged eyelashes and focused on the polished shoes of the little man standing in front of her. Latif, Tariq's most senior aide, whom she had met in passing on several occasions the year before. Slowly she lifted her bent head. Latif bowed so low that she got a great view of his bald patch. Indeed she honestly thought he was trying to touch his toes and could not immediately grasp what on earth he was doing until it occurred to her that the older man might well be granting her a tactful moment in which to compose herself.

'Latif…'

'Please come this way…'

Latif led her through a door and across a hall into a charming reception room furnished in European style. Grateful for the blessed cool of the air-conditioning there, Faye collapsed down on a silk-upholstered sofa and dug into her bag in search of a tissue.

The reserved older man stayed by the door at a respectful distance and Faye averted her attention from him. Latif was kind. He had seen her distress and brought her here to recover in privacy and, unfortunately for him, good manners forbade leaving her alone.

Jingling with jewellery and barefoot, a procession of maids carrying trays entered the room. One by one they knelt at her feet to serve her with coffee and proffer cakes and sticky confectionery. Beneath her astonished scrutiny, they then backed away across the whole depth of the room with downbent heads before exiting again. Presumably all visitors, many of whom would naturally be VIPs, were treated with such exaggerated attention and servility but it made Faye feel extremely uncomfortable.

'I believe the heat may have made you feel unwell.' As Faye finished the bittersweet coffee in the tiny china cup, Latif broke the silence with exquisite tact. 'I hope you are feeling better now.'

'Yes, thank you…' Faye bit at her lower lip and then took the plunge for she had not the slightest doubt that the discreet older man knew all about Adrian's predicament. 'Have you any idea how I can help my brother?'

'I would suggest that a second approach might be made to Prince Tariq tomorrow.'

So much for inspired advice from an inside source! Faye tried not to release a humourless laugh. Surely Latif could not have the foggiest clue of what had passed between her and Tariq? *Give yourself to me.* Pretty basic, that. No room for misunderstanding there. She was still shattered that Tariq could have made such a suggestion to her. It was barbaric.

Yet no sooner had she made that judgement than an unwelcome little voice spoke up from her conscience. Hadn't she once offered herself to Tariq in no uncertain terms? Hadn't she once made it quite clear that she'd been willing to sleep with him? And hadn't she then got cold feet when she'd seen how that unwise invitation had altered his attitude to her? Without a doubt, Tariq now saw her as the most shameless tease! Tears lashed the back of her eyes again. Wasn't it awful how one mistake could just lead to another and another? From the instant she had departed from the values she had been raised to respect, she had learnt nothing *but* hard lessons.

Eager now to leave the Haja, Faye rose to her feet. 'Thank you for the coffee, Latif.'

'I will send a car again for you tomorrow, if I may.'

'I'd be wasting my time coming again.'

'The car will remain at your disposal for the whole day.'

Latif evidently wanted her brother released from prison, Faye decided. Why else was he getting involved behind the scenes? She returned to the hotel in the same style in which she had departed. As she crossed the foyer, slight shoulders bowed with exhaustion, Percy emerged from the bar to intercept her.

'Well?' he demanded abrasively.

'All I got was…was an improper proposition.' Faye could not bring herself to look at her stepfather as she admitted that but she hoped that that honesty would satisfy him and save her from an interrogation. Percy was a bully. He had always been a bully. Just then, she did not feel equal to the challenge of standing up to him.

'So what?' Percy snapped without hesitation. 'You've got to do whatever it takes to get Adrian home!'

Once again, Faye was shocked. But as she hurried into the lift and left her stepfather fuming, she asked herself why. Percy had never had much time for her. It had been naïve of her to believe that he might be angry on her behalf. For Percy, the bottom line was Adrian. And shouldn't that be *her* bottom line as well?

Knowing it was past time that she ate something, Faye

rang room service and ordered the cheapest snack on the menu. Then she made herself face facts. But for her, Adrian would not have got to know Tariq and would never had thought of setting up business in Jumar. It was also her fault that Tariq now regarded her and her brother in the same light as their stepfather. Like it or not, *she* had put Tariq into a compromising position where Percy was able to threaten him. Her foolish infatuation, her lies and her immaturity had led to that development. Adrian was suffering now because Tariq despised and distrusted all of them. Who could ever have imagined that from one seemingly small lie, so much grief could have flowed?

Faye swallowed hard. When she had first met Tariq, she had pretended to be twenty-three years old, sooner than own up to being a month short of her nineteenth birthday. Tariq's subsequent outrage at the lies she had told had been extreme and succinct. She might as well have set out to trap him for the end result had been the same. Retreating from recollections that still made her writhe with guilt, Faye returned to the present and the grim prospect of what she ought to try to do next to help her brother…

That evening, her stepfather came to her hotel room again but she opened the door on the chain and said she wasn't well. It wasn't a lie: she was so tired, she felt queasy. In her bed she lay listening to the evocative call of the muezzin calling the faithful to prayer at the mosque at the end of the street. With her conscience tormenting her, she got little sleep.

At half-past eight the following morning, wearing a loose dress in a pale lilac print, Faye climbed into the limousine which Latif had promised would be waiting. The day before she had made serious errors with Tariq, she now conceded, newly appraised humility weighing her down. She had tried to save face by talking only about Adrian. But, mortifying as it was to acknowledge, Tariq had good reason to think she was a brazen hussy, who had set him up for a sleazy blackmail attempt. Perhaps an open acknowledgement of that reality, a long overdue explanation and a sincere and heartfelt apology would take the edge off Tariq's animosity. Maybe he would then consider *loaning* Adrian the money he needed to settle his debts and let bygones be bygones…

This time the limo whisked her round to a side entrance at the Haja fortress where Latif greeted her in person. Quiet approval emanated from the older man.

Ushered straight into a large contemporary office, Faye breathed in deep and straightened her shoulders. Sleek and sophisticated in a pale grey business suit of exquisite cut that moulded his broad shoulders, lean hips and long powerful legs, Tariq was standing by the window talking on a portable phone. He acknowledged her arrival with the merest dip of his handsome dark head.

Taking the seat indicated by Latif, who then withdrew, Faye focused on Tariq. His classic profile stood out in strong relief. She watched the long, elegant fingers of his free hand spread a little and then curl with silent eloquence as he spoke. Memories that hurt assailed her and she dragged her attention from him and folded her hands together on her lap to stop them trembling.

But she remained so aware of his disturbing presence that she was in an agony of discomfiture. She knew that lean bronzed face almost as well as her own. The slight imperious slant of his ebony brows, the spectacular tawny eyes that had such amazing clarity, the narrow bridge of his aristocratic nose dissecting hard high Berber cheekbones, the strong stubborn jawline, the passionate but stern mouth.

Only the day before, she had felt the humiliating pull of his magnetic physical attraction. Her soft full mouth compressed. That had unnerved and embarrassed her. But he had caught her at a weak moment. That was all. She was no longer an infatuated teenager, helpless in the grip of her own emotions and at the mercy of galloping hormones and foolish fantasies. She had got over him *fast*. She might not have dated anyone since but that was only because he had truly soured her outlook on men.

'Why are you here?'

Shot from her teeming thoughts without due warning, Faye jerked. Then she lifted her head and tilted it back. 'I believe I owe you an explanation for the way I behaved last year.'

'I need no explanation.' Derision glittered in Tariq's steady appraisal. 'Indeed I will listen to no explanation. If you think I'm fool enough to give you a platform for more lies and self-justification, you seriously underestimate me—'

In one sentence thus deprived of her entire script, Faye breathed, *'But—'*

'It's very rude to interrupt me when I'm speaking.'

Faye flushed but she was already so tense that her temper sparked. 'Maybe you would just like me to lie down like a carpet for you to walk on!'

'A carpet is inanimate. I prefer energy and movement in my women.'

Her humble and penitent frame of mind was already taking a hard beating. Cheeks scarlet at that comeback, Faye nonetheless tried afresh. 'Tariq…I need to explain and apologise. You wouldn't give me the chance to explain at the time.'

'If that is your only reason for being here, I suggest you leave. Sly words and crocodile tears won't move me. The very thought of your shameless deceit rouses my temper.'

Faye swallowed hard. 'OK…you have the right to be angry—'

'Grovelling insincerity makes me angry too,' Tariq incised even more drily. 'Cut the phony regrets. I made you an offer yesterday and that's why you're here now. Only a tramp would accept a proposition of that nature, so stop pretending to be a sweet, misunderstood innocent!'

Faye, who usually had the mildest temper in the world, was appalled to feel a river of wrath surge like hot lava inside her. She rose from her seat in an abrupt movement. 'I won't tolerate being called a tramp! What do you call a man who *makes* such an offer to a woman?'

'A man with no illusions…a man who disdains hypocrisy.'

Faye trembled. 'My goodness, you insult me with a proposition no decent woman would even consider and then you turn round and you flatter yourself from your pinnacle of perfection—'

'You are *not* a decent woman. You lie and you cheat and there is nothing you would not do for money.'

'That is not true…it all started because I told a few stupid white lies and I know it was wrong but I was crazy about you—'

'Crazy about me?' Tariq flung back his arrogant dark head and laughed out loud, the sound discordant in the thrumming atmosphere. 'You let me go for a mere half million pounds. You were so blinded by greed, you were content to settle for whatever you could get!'

Almost light-headed with the force of rage powering her, Faye now fell back a step and gaped at him. 'I let you go…for half a million pounds? What the heck are you trying to accuse me of doing now?'

Tariq centred his brilliant golden eyes on her, his beautiful mouth hard as granite. 'You were a cheap bride, I'll give you that. You may have come with no dowry but I was able to shed you again for a pittance.'

Faye was no longer sure her wobbling knees would hold her upright and she dropped down into the chair again, all temper quenched. Evidently, Tariq had handed over money to somebody, money she knew nothing about. She did not have to think very hard to come up with the name of the most likely culprit. 'You gave money to Percy...?' She swallowed back a wail of reproach at that appalling revelation.

'I gave it to *you*.'

And like a flash in the darkness, Faye finally recalled the envelope which Tariq had flung at her feet after their fake wedding that dreadful day. Did he recall that he had been talking in Arabic at the time? Didn't he realise that she had naively assumed that their marriage certificate had been in that envelope? And when she had finally stumbled out of the Embassy of Jumar, heartbroken and with her pride in tatters, she had thrust the envelope at Percy in revulsion and condemnation. 'Are you satisfied now that you've wrecked my life? Burn it...I don't want to ever be reminded of this day again!'

How many weeks had it been before she'd finally forced herself to see her stepfather again and ask for the certificate in the hope that he had not after all destroyed it? She had believed that she might need that certificate to apply for an annulment in case the extraordinary ease of Jumarian divorce was not actually recognised by English law. But Percy had laughed in her face when she'd mentioned that fear.

'Don't be more dumb than you can help, Faye,' her stepfather had sneered. 'That wasn't a legal marriage! It wasn't consummated and he repudiated you straight after the ceremony. Your desert warrior was just saving face and trying to protect himself with some mumbo-jumbo. Why else did he insist it took place in private in the embassy?'

Percy had followed that up with the explanation that embassies fell under the legal jurisdiction of the countries they belonged to, rather than that of the host country. Faye had felt too mortified by her own obvious ignorance to counter his charge of 'mumbo-jumbo'. An Arab gentleman dressed just like a Christian vicar *had* presided over the first part of that ceremony but he had spoken only in Arabic and there was no denying that Tariq himself had called their wedding a complete charade.

Repressing that slew of memories, Faye focused her bemused thoughts back on the cheque which Tariq had said was in that envelope she had blithely surrendered. She closed her eyes in stricken acknowledgement of yet another insane act of foolishness on her part. She had handed a cheque for half a million pounds to Percy Smythe! But if the cheque had been made out to her, how on earth had he cashed it? For she had not the slightest doubt that it *must* have been cashed!

'Tariq…I didn't know that envelope had a cheque in it.' Her taut temples were pounding out her rising stress level. 'I don't know why you would have chosen to give me money either.'

The silence stretched and stretched.

Overwhelmed by guilty self-loathing and the most drowning sense of sheer inadequacy, Faye stared into space. No wonder Tariq ibn Zachir thought she was a trollop. No wonder he believed that she had conspired with her stepfather to set him up for blackmail. No wonder he was so certain that she was greedy for money. What had Percy done with that half million pounds? Percy, who had been outmanoeuvred in his blackmail attempt by Tariq's announcement that he would *marry* Faye. Whatever, that huge sum of money was evidently long gone.

'I can't believe that you would want a woman with such low moral standards,' Faye said finally.

'You'll be a novelty.'

'A woman who doesn't *want* you?' Faye was past caring about how she sounded. Here she was guilty as charged it seemed on every count. Guilty of serial stupidity. Guilty of being a teenager madly in love and doing all the wrong things in her efforts to make him love her back. She had done a marvellous job on him, hadn't she? Thanks to her own lies, he thought she was the most dishonest brazen hussy he had ever met!

'Is that a challenge?'

Faye gave him a dulled look. Tariq gazed back at her with a sizzling force that penetrated her veil of numb defeat. 'No!'

'You will be my mistress for as long as I want you.' Tariq surveyed her as if he had just stamped a brand of ownership on her, his male satisfaction unconcealed.

Seriously unnerved by that statement of intent, Faye leapt back out of her seat again, her hands clenched into fists. 'You can't *still* want me…you never wanted me that much to begin with! This is just a giant ego-trip. It's mindless revenge—'

'*Not* mindless. I never act without forethought.' Tariq stretched out an imperious hand. 'Come here…'

Faye went into retreat rather than advance. Shark-infested water might as well have separated them. 'I didn't say I agreed.'

'Then make your mind up.'

Faye folded her arms in a defensive movement. 'Adrian?'

'He goes home to England on the first available flight.'

Faye shook her head, tried to still the nervous tremor in her lower limbs. 'I'm not what you think I am. I can't imagine being any man's mistress. I won't fit the bill—'

'You underestimate yourself.'

Tariq extended his hand again, glittering golden eyes fixed to her with intimidating cool and expectancy.

'If you think I'm going to come running every time you snap your imperious fingers—'

'Sooner or later, you will. I have immense patience.'

That quiet confidence took Faye wholly aback and froze her to the spot. 'You're crazy…'

A slight smile curved his lips. 'You're scared.'

'Like heck I am…I'm just fed up with all this nonsense!'

The smile acquired amusement, veiled eyes resting on her slight, taut frame with an intimate intensity she could feel as surely as if he had touched her. 'I didn't sleep last night. I *couldn't* sleep, not even after a couple of cold showers. I knew you were mine then.'

'But you…you hate me!' Faye slung back at him in vehement protest.

'Hate? Too strong a word.' Tariq strolled closer like a hunter set on closing in for the kill but doing so at his own leisure. 'Is that why you look sick with fright? Is that fertile imagination of yours throwing up images of gothic whips and chains? Do you really think I would inflict a single bruise on that perfect skin of yours? You'll cry out with pleasure, not pain, in my bed.'

Faye was so mortified by that assurance, she whirled away from him. It was a mistake. He closed his arms round her and turned her back to him. With one hand, he loosened the clasp at the nape of her neck and cast it aside. Gazing down at her with scorching golden eyes, he threaded long fingers through her long pale blonde hair and tugged her head back in a gentle motion.

'Tariq—'

'You *want* me.' A lean hand pressed to the shallow indentation of her rigid spine and curved her into intimate contact with his long muscular thighs.

Suddenly it was a challenge to talk and breathe at the same time. She stared up at him, trying to hold herself rigid but awesomely conscious of the all-pervasive strength of his powerful physique. *'No—'*

'You're trembling—'

'I'm cold!' Faye scarcely knew what she was saying any

more. That close to Tariq, her mind was a sea of confusion and her own physical reactions took over.

'Cold?' Tariq lowered his proud dark head, his breath fanning her cheek, the evocative timbre of his low-pitched drawl sentencing her to stillness. 'Who are you trying to fool?'

Feeling weak as water, Faye mumbled, 'Please…'

'Please what?' Tariq brought his wide sensual mouth within inches of hers and somehow made her lips part in invitation, her very breath catching in her throat, her slender length instinctively stretching up to his to get still closer. 'Tell me, please, what?'

The scent of him enveloped her like a sneak invasion by an aphrodisiac. So familiar, so special, so…*him*. Her nostrils flared, head spinning on a released flood of sensuous recall from the past, heat forming in her pelvis, breasts lifting and swelling within the constriction of her cotton bra. It was as if her whole body were burning and melting from inside out, a blind sense of fevered anticipation enthralling her, pitching her high.

'What?' Tariq prompted soft and low, even his dark sexy voice sending a darting quiver of hot response through her.

'Kiss me…' The instant she actually yielded and formed the words, Tariq released his hold on her.

She staggered back on cotton-wool legs, ill-prepared for staying upright without his support. She blinked like a woman wakening from a disorientating dream.

'As a people we prefer to keep intimacy behind closed doors,' Tariq murmured smooth as silk. 'This office is too public but there is no greater privacy available than that within the harem quarters at Muraaba.'

Faye pressed an unsteady hand against her tingling lips as if she might quiet the sheer craving which still held her taut. 'Harem quarters—?'

'To be a mistress in Jumar is no sinecure and no ticket

to freedom or excess. To be *my* mistress is, above all, to be an invisible woman,' Tariq said with a regretful sigh. 'To live behind high walls and locked doors and centre your whole being and your every thought on the man in your life because he truly will be *all* that is in your life. Say goodbye to the world that you know for the foreseeable future.'

Faye was slower to recover from that near embrace than he had been. She had only just reached the point of dying a thousand deaths over the recollection of how she had swayed against him, reached up to him on tiptoes of yearning, begged for his kiss like a brainless programmed doll. He had *made* her want him. With effortless ease and within seconds. She was devastated by that discovery.

'On the other hand, since an aversion to me would not appear to be a sticking point…' Tariq surveyed her with the predatory gaze of a hawk '…you may well be inconsolable when I get tired of you.'

'Harem…you think you're going to put *me* in a harem?' Faye parroted in a wobbly voice. 'Are you out of your mind to suggest such a thing?'

Tariq lounged back against his polished desk. 'Very much in it. Furthermore, since I cannot trust you, your brother will *not* walk free from his prison cell until you have moved in—'

'Tariq—'

He made an unapologetic play of studying the slim gold watch on his wrist. 'I'm afraid your time is up. Unfortunately, I have other people waiting to see me. A car will now convey you to my home—'

'Now?' Frowning in absolute disbelief, Faye just gaped at him.

'Your hotel room was cleared within minutes of your departure from it. Having been informed that your brother may soon be released, your stepfather is already waiting at the prison. You will see neither of your relatives again until our arrangement comes to an end.'

Faye attempted to swallow but the lead weight of incredulity sat like a giant rock at the foot of her throat. 'You're not serious...you can't be serious about *any* of this stuff—'

Tariq strode past her and opened the door for her departure. He gave her a lethal smile that tied a cold hard knot inside her. 'How much of a gambler are you?'

Faye turned pale.

'And how well do you think you ever knew me?'

CHAPTER THREE

FAYE saw a stone bench sited near the side entrance. From there, she could see the now familiar limousine waiting outside. To take her to the Muraaba palace? Or to the airport? Her choice, wasn't it? Essentially, she was free as a bird. Sitting down, she tried to calm her seething thoughts.

How well do you think you ever knew me? A body-blow of a put-down from the male who had almost destroyed her. In spite of her attempts to suppress it, angry bitterness welled up inside Faye and she laced her trembling hands together. Was it *her* fault that her stepfather was a con artist? Her own mother had died penniless but for the roof over her head. Within weeks of Tariq's defection, Adrian had decided their childhood home should also be sold.

'OK, sis?' It had been a rhetorical question.

Adrian had had no desire to hear that his sister's heart had been breaking at the prospect of losing her home. Nor had he wanted to be reminded that she had hoped to set up a riding school there or that, deprived of both stables and paddock, she would have to sell her beloved horse as well.

But then Faye was not used to putting herself first. Growing up, she had not been encouraged to think her needs or wishes should carry the same weight as other people's. But that didn't necessarily mean she was a doormat, did it? How *could* she have argued about the sale of their family home? Her clerical job had not paid enough to cover her share of the maintenance costs. So Adrian had sold house, contents and land to raise capital for his construction firm. He had promised that she would share in the fruits of his success, would undeniably have shared those profits generously had there been any…

And what had Percy done with that half million pounds from Tariq? Pocketed it by forging her signature? Or had Tariq made it even more simple for Percy by making out that cheque in her stepfather's name? Tariq, who thought all women leant on the nearest man for financial support. A 'goodbye and get lost and keep quiet' payment.

Was that what that cheque had been, on his terms? Faye shuddered. Compensation for the wedding that had filled her with pathetic joy and then concluded in the cruellest farce? She folded her arms tightly round herself. She could not bear to think of that day at the embassy. She had truly believed it was her wedding day. But after the ceremony Tariq had turned on her as though she were the lowest form of human life, stamping on her pride, her hopes, her love, devastating her.

'Divorce is easy in my culture,' Tariq had delivered. 'I say in Arabic, ''I divorce thee'' three times and circle as I say it. Do you want to *watch* me reclaim my freedom again? Do you want me to demonstrate what a sham this ceremony was?'

The savage hurt and humiliation of that day would never leave Faye. The unwilling bridegroom, the arrogant and autocratic prince, outraged even by a wedding that *was* a charade. He had just stomped all over her feelings as if she were nothing, nobody worthy of any consideration. Was it any wonder she hated him?

Yes, she hated Prince Tariq Shazad ibn Zachir. Yet the same frightening physical longing which had deprived her of her wits before still lingered like a bad hangover. Why? She refused to think about that. However, she had not the slightest intention of taking up residence in any harem! Thought that was a good joke, did he? Well, she wasn't quite as wet as she had once been.

Adrian had to be freed from prison before he fell seriously ill. No choice on that count, she told herself. No matter what the cost? And then her strained eyes widened on a sudden realisation: the instant Adrian was on his flight back to London, he would be safe! Tariq had called her a liar and a cheat. So why should she act any differently? Tariq deserved to be double-crossed. Tariq *deserved* to be cheated. For the sin of having the stepfather from hell, she had already paid a high enough price.

'May I be of assistance?'

Faye glanced up to see Latif and she stood up. 'I'd like to make a phone call.'

The little man looked uneasy.

'Even a criminal usually gets one phone call...but maybe not in the civilised and humane country of Jumar,' Faye conceded in a bitter undertone.

Latif flushed and bowed his head. 'Come this way, please.'

He left her alone in an office a few doors down the corridor. She called her stepfather on his portable phone.

'Faye?' Percy demanded loudly. 'Whatever stunt you've pulled, it's working! I haven't had the final word yet but it looks like our Adrian may be walking free this afternoon—'

'Just answer one question for me,' Faye interrupted in a flat little voice. 'The day of the wedding, I gave you an envelope. What did you do with the cheque inside?'

Total silence buzzed on the line.

Percy cleared his throat.

'You took the money, *didn't* you?' Faye pressed in disgust. 'You let Tariq think he could buy me off as if I was a blackmailer too!'

'Adrian's had most of the money without knowing where it came from and stop talking about blackmail, Faye. All I did was try to protect your interests and, if Tariq wanted to pay us off to keep us quiet, why shouldn't I have accepted the money?' her stepfather protested. 'It's all in the family—'

'You're a con man and a thief. You robbed my mother and you ripped off me. Don't insult my intelligence by talking about family!' Faye sent the receiver crashing down again.

Slowly she retraced her steps and walked head held high out into the hot sunshine to climb into the limousine. 'How well do you think you ever knew me?' Tariq had asked. Well, some day soon he might be asking himself just how well *he* had ever known *her*!

The drive out to the Muraaba place took much longer than Faye had expected. Once the city limits were behind them, the desert took over for miles. It was the emptiness that fascinated Faye, then the rise of the rolling shadowed dunes baking below the remorseless heat of mid-morning. Sand and more sand…what a thrill! Had she really been so crazy about Tariq once that she had fondly imagined she could live with all that sand?

In the distance she saw a massive sprawling building surrounded by fortified walls that got higher the closer they got. As the limo approached, a cluster of tribesmen squatting in the shade jumped up to open the gates. Two sets of solid iron gates, Faye noted, one shorter inner pair, the outer so tall they could have kept the sun trapped, she thought fancifully.

Within the walls, terraced gardens of breathtaking beauty stretched up the hillside in every direction. She was blind to them. She was noting the number of guards on duty and reckoning that Tariq's desert palace appeared braced to withstand both imminent seige and invasion. Her heart sank. Her nebulous plan to stage an escape within the next twenty-four hours would be more of a challenge than she had naively hoped.

Shoulders straight, chin tilted, ignoring the curious eyes

and the whispers that accompanied her passage, Faye entered the palace. On her way past, soldiers snapped to attention, presented arms and saluted. She drifted on. It would be so easy to develop delusions of grandeur in Jumar, she decided. The Muraaba was a really ancient building, she registered with a grudging stirring of interest. Fantastic mosaic panels in glorious turquoise, green and gold covered every inch of the walls in the great hall that echoed from her footsteps.

A startling cry of pain followed by the shout of a child smashed the tranquillity and made Faye first freeze and then hurry on in search of the source. If a child had been hurt…

Faye came to a halt on the threshold of a room. So appalled was she by the scene which met her gaze, she could not initially accept what she was seeing. Three servants were huddled by the wall wailing and a fourth, a woman, was down on her knees while a small boy struck at her back with a switch. For an instant, Faye waited for one of the staff to intervene and then she realised that nobody was going to intervene and that the victim seemed too scared to protest such treatment.

Faye stalked forward. 'Stop that!'

The little boy in his miniature robes stopped for an instant in surprise and then started again.

'Stop it right this minute!' Faye ordered icily.

The next thing the little horror rushed at *her* with the switch! She bent down and gathered him to her. The switch fell from his hand. Then she held him at a distance from her to let him kick out his tantrum without hurting her or anyone else. He was very young but his little face was screwed up in a mask of uncontrollable rage. 'Let go of me!' he bawled at her. 'Let go, or I will whip you too!'

'I'll put you down when you stop shouting.'

'I am a prince…I am a prince of the blood royal of Jumar!'

'You're a little boy.' But Faye stiffened, now picking up on the stricken silence surrounding her. She studied the exquisite silk embroidery on the clothing the child wore. He spat at her and she grimaced. '*No* prince of the blood royal would behave like that,' she told him without hesitation.

His bottom lip came out. His big brown eyes suddenly filled with tears. 'I am an ibn Zachir. I am a prince. You do what I tell you...why you not do what I tell you?'

And in that instant he went from being a little monster to being a child, and a distressed and frightened child at that. As he went limp, Faye slowly released her breath in relief that she had won the battle and drew him close. He could not have been more than five years old, maybe not even that. 'Does the prince have a name?'

'Rafi...'

Belatedly conscious that an outraged parent might descend on her at any minute, that she was in a foreign country with a very different culture and that for all she knew even the tiniest royal children were encouraged to beat servants all the time, Faye attempted to set the boy down again. Disconcertingly, he clung like a limpet.

Faye felt something touch her toes. She peered down over Prince Rafi's back. His female victim was sobbing at Faye's feet. The other servants were now lying face down on the floor as if they were waiting on a bomb dropping or someone shouting, 'Off with their heads!' She felt like an alien set down without warning in very dangerous territory.

'Sleepy...' Rafi told her round his thumb.

'Will someone put Rafi...I mean, His Royal Highness down for a nap?' Faye asked with the weak hope that someone spoke some English.

'Nurse...I am nurse.' It was the lady cowering at her ankles.

'It is wrong and unkind to hurt people, Rafi.' Faye sighed.

'He no mean hurt,' his nursemaid muttered fearfully.

'Rafi sleepy…' He snuggled his silky dark head under her chin. 'Lady take Rafi to bed?'

Well, hopefully that would get everybody up and moving again, Faye decided.

'My horse flies faster than the wind,' Rafi told her sleepily as she carried him from the room.

She resisted the urge to ask if he beat the horse too. 'I love horses.'

'I show you my horse.'

It was a long trek through passageways, a positive procession for they seemed to gather servants and grow into a crowd on the way. And with every covert marvelling look that came her way, every awestruck appraisal that suggested she was doing something extraordinary, Faye's frown grew. It was one weird household. She might possess the stepfather from hell but Tariq had got nothing to boast about on his *own* home front. Did he beat his servants too? Her tummy turned over at that image.

Finally they arrived in Rafi's bedroom which was just stuffed with every imaginable toy and indulgence. Spoilt little brat, Faye thought, refusing to be softened by the child's sweet innocence asleep. But some adult must surely first have taught such brutality by example, she conceded heavily. A parent? Evidently, Tariq shared his huge palace with his extended family. No wonder he was talking about stashing her like a guilty secret in a harem! No way was she staying in the Muraaba palace!

With that conviction in mind and ignoring the servants following never more than a dozen feet from her, Faye explored until she found a room literally walled with packed bookshelves. Her search took some time but eventually she found a map of Jumar which had the airport clearly marked. Noticing that the airport appeared to be a much greater distance from the city than it actually was, she assumed that it was an older map for the city had grown much larger in more recent times.

Concealing the map in her bag, she settled down in a magnificent reception room on a low traditional divan. Refreshments were brought to her there. More grovelling, all the staff seeming so scared and desperate to please. At the same time, her dazed eyes roamed over the spectacular exoticism of her surroundings. Rich geometrical patterns of faience tiles adorned the walls, some of which were even studded with what appeared to be precious stones, and the elaborate domed ceiling far above appeared to be composed of tiny coloured glittering mirror-glass mosaics. Superb Persian rugs lay on the pale marble floor. The divan on which she sat was covered with hand-painted precious silk. This was where Tariq had grown up, she found herself thinking, against a fantastic and opulent backdrop so dissimilar to hers, it took her breath away.

A wave of what appeared to be collective anxiety sent the maids into retreat a mere minute before Faye heard a man's footsteps echoing in the main hall. Seconds later, Tariq strode in and stilled to view her.

His lean, strong face was taut. 'Latif has informed me that there had been some incident between you and Rafi—'

Eyes flaring with anger as she recalled the shocking episode she had witnessed earlier, Faye shot to her feet in full defensive mode. 'So someone has complained about my behaviour, have they? Well, let me tell you, you had better get me on a plane home because I have no plans to stand by and watch any child or indeed any adult beating servants!'

His superb bone structure clenched hard. 'Say that again—'

'You mean once wasn't enough? What sort of primitive

country is this? What kind of a society allows a small child to behave like that?'

Pale with anger beneath his bronze skin, Tariq breathed. 'Are you telling me that Rafi struck one of the household staff?'

Breathing in deep, Faye described the scene she had interrupted in a few pithy words.

'Rafi is mine to deal with,' Tariq growled, the darkening of outrage accentuating his bold cheekbones. 'We are *not* a primitive country. I will have you know that assault is assault in Jumar, no matter who the victim or who the perpetrator. I am very grateful that you intervened but do not judge a whole people by the behaviour of my obnoxious little brother!'

'L-little brother?' Her cheeks were now glowing red as fire. 'Rafi is your little brother? But if what you are saying is true, why didn't someone step in to assert control over him?'

'*Who?* My father died when he was three. His mother died six months ago. She was an evil-tempered woman from another Gulf state.' His stunning dark eyes had a grim light. 'She taught Rafi to behave as he does. The servants who look after him were *hers* and the spirit was knocked out of them long before they accompanied their mistress to Jumar. They would never dare to try and restrain Rafi. It is an offence to lay hands on anyone of royal blood—'

'Is it?'

'That law was not made to allow a child to rampage out of control! I was reluctant to deprive Rafi of the nursemaids who have looked after him since he was a baby but I see now, it must be done. He *has* to be taught how to behave.'

'What age is he?'

'Four…old enough and bright enough to know better. I shall deal with him.' Tariq headed for the door like a male with a target and a definite purpose in mind.

Faye rushed after him. 'What are you going to do?'

'I can see what you *think* I'm going to do but you're wrong,' Tariq spelt out in impatient reproof as he read her anxious expression. 'I may know little about children but I hope I know enough not to repay violence with violence. I will talk to him and remove certain privileges as a punishment.'

'I'm sorry about what I said a moment ago. It's just I was upset about the whole thing…but Rafi's awfully young and, having lost both his parents, probably very unhappy—'

'I know these things but I also fear that he has his mother's cruelty in him.'

Left standing, Faye chewed at her lower lip, wondering why she felt so troubled and why on earth she should feel so involved. It was nothing to do with her and she was certainly no authority on childcare. However, she was terribly relieved that Tariq had been furious about the episode which she had witnessed. At least, she hadn't been *totally* wrong about his character the year before when she had honestly believed that, with very little effort, he might walk on water…

Fourteen months ago, Adrian had been invited to his commanding officer's wedding at which Tariq had been the guest of honour. Heavily pregnant at the time, Lizzie had decided to stay home and Adrian had asked Faye to accompany him instead.

'Come on, sis,' Adrian reproved when she tried to turn him down. 'Since Mum died, all you've done is hang out with horses. I *know* you're shy but you need to get out occasionally.'

The day of the wedding, Adrian's car refused to start and, much to his dismay, they had to use Faye's ancient little hatchback instead. A poor passenger, her brother honed her nerves to screaming point during that drive. Her less than pleasant day out then got going with a real bang when, stressed beyond belief in her efforts to find a parking space at the church, she reversed her car into Tariq's stretch limo.

As aghast as if she had killed somebody, Adrian leapt out and started shouting at her. 'What do you mean you didn't *see* it? It's as big as the blasted *Titanic*!'

Welded to the bonnet of her car to stay upright and shaking with reaction, Faye stared in even greater horror at the dark-skinned excitable men erupting out of the limo. Then the passenger door opened and Tariq climbed out with unhurried grace. Silencing his bodyguards, he strolled across the tarmac to where her brother, who had his back turned to him, was still ranting.

'How could you do something so stupid?' Adrian was seething.

But Faye's attention had already been captured by the tall, dark, incredibly handsome male smiling at her. A smile that literally *talked*. Sympathetic, concerned, charming. Her heart started beating very fast. From his wonderful smile, her gaze travelled upward to encounter spectacular lion gold eyes that made her feel breathless, boneless and pretty much mindless too. Within seconds of first seeing Prince Tariq Shazad ibn Zachir, Faye was mesmerised.

Ignoring Adrian, Tariq strode straight to her side. 'You're suffering from shock. You *must* sit down.'

'B-but...but your car—'

'It is nothing. Please do not consider it.'

He urged her back to his limo where a guard already had a door open. Guiding her down on to the edge of the leather seat, he murmured something in his own language in aside and then said to her, 'Try to calm yourself. Nothing that need concern you has happened.'

'Your Royal Highness...er...' Adrian began in a strained and apologetic undertone from behind him '...Prince

Tariq…my sister…er…well, I'll see to her, no need for you to be bothered…'

'Thank you but I am not easily bothered.' Tariq passed a crystal tumbler of iced mineral water into Faye's hand. He gazed down into her eyes and her heartbeat went so far into earthquake mode she felt literally dizzy. He smiled again. Straightening, he then turned to extend a hand to her brother and speak to him.

It was Adrian who then hurried Faye back out of the limo. Walking away from Tariq, all Faye was able to think about was whether she would ever get to speak to him again. She felt…*sent*, no longer grounded on solid earth. Butterflies in her tummy and excitement pulsing through her in a crazy flood.

'I've never thought about it before but I suppose you *are* quite beautiful.' Her brother treated her to a frowning appraisal inside the church. 'Nothing like looks saving your skin, sis! You reversed into a giant stationary vehicle that a blind man could have avoided. Yet His Royal Highness chose to insist that *his* limo was parked in the wrong place, that non-existent sunlight must have reflected off your mirror and that *he* will pay for the repairs to your car!'

'Oh…is he…is he really a prince?' she muttered.

'About as real as they come,' Adrian said drily. 'Commander-in-chief of his own army and acting feudal ruler of the Gulf state of Jumar. Hamza, his father, is supposed to be on his last legs and Prince Tariq has already taken on all of the old man's public engagements abroad.'

Her heart sank at that dismaying confirmation for even the smallest spark of common sense warned that a male of that status was out of her reach, but still curiosity had to be quenched. 'Married?'

'No. What's that to you?'

'I was just wondering. He's awfully nice—'

'Nice?' Adrian grimaced. 'Look, I may not have actually

spoken to the chap before today but, according to what I've heard, he's faster than a jump jet with women! Thankfully, you're far too young to interest him.'

'Too young? I'm nineteen next month!'

'Oh, wow…' Adrian rolled his eyes, unimpressed. 'Well, you're still safe as houses. I doubt that Prince Tariq is the kind of creep who takes advantage of starry-eyed kids!'

A fateful and unfortunate conversation which within the space of hours led to the first outright lie which Faye had told since she had outgrown childish fibbing. At the reception, Adrian soon abandoned her for the more convivial company of his fellow officers and Tariq strolled over to speak to her. 'May I join you?'

And even a year on, Faye had to admit that lying never came so easily or so naturally to her again. For the first time in her life she wanted to impress a man and *not* with the image of some starry-eyed kid, and she knew she had only that one chance for there was little likelihood that they would ever meet again.

'Hardly anybody knows you here but one who does referred to you as a teenager.' Tariq made that lazy comment only after asking her if she was fully recovered from the episode in the church car park.

'People really do lose track of the passage of time when they don't see you for a few years.' Hugely aware of his lustrous dark golden eyes resting on her, she ran far from idle fingers through the glossy fall of her silvery fair hair. She knew he could barely drag his admiring attention from her crowning glory and she gave him what she hoped was a mature and yet teasing smile. 'I may not be that tall but I'm actually twenty-three years old.'

'You don't look it,' he murmured frankly.

'That's the fresh country girl bloom,' she told him, batting her eyelashes.

And that was it, that was how easy it had been. Her sole

objective had been that she should not be excluded from attracting his interest by her age alone. She had not thought further than that, had foreseen no potential problems in the future because at that point, before he'd even asked her out, it had not occurred to her that they might *have* a future of any kind.

'I would like to see you again,' he said then.

'When?' she prompted, ditching her attempt at older woman cool.

Tariq stilled in surprise and then the beginnings of an amused smile tugged at the corners of his beautiful mouth. 'Wait and see.'

And the roses began arriving the next day. White roses every day, white roses that filled the house with their rich perfume. No card but she knew, of course she knew, they were from him and she dreamed away every hour, leapt every time the phone rang, but it took him a week to call her.

'Tell him you're booked up!' Lizzie printed on the phone pad when she realised Faye was speaking to Tariq.

Faye gave her sister-in-law an agonised look. At the shortest possible notice, she would have walked barefoot all the way to London in a thunderstorm to see Tariq!

'I'm sorry, I can't make it…'

Perhaps another time, Lizzie mouthed at her to repeat and made shocking faces at her until she did so.

'You've got a lot to learn, kiddo.' Her sister-in-law groaned when Faye was in tears after Tariq rang off without having suggested an alternative. 'If you want to be kissed off after one date, go ahead and show him how keen you are!'

Only four years older than Faye, Lizzie thought it was all a terrific laugh. When Tariq called Adrian and invited the entire family out to dinner instead, it was also Lizzie who took her husband aside before they went out the following evening to warn Adrian not to drop Faye in it with Tariq about her age.

'I don't like the fact you've lied at all.' Adrian looked at his hot-faced sister with surprise and strong disapproval.

'Give it a rest, Adrian.' Percy backed Faye up and startled her. 'It's not like this little flirtation is likely to go anywhere, is it? Not with him being a *royal* prince. Let your sister enjoy herself. If a squeaky clean night out for the whole flippin' family is this bloke's idea of a hot date, what have you got to worry about?'

In the weeks which followed, Faye worked very hard at telling herself that there was no future in any relationship with Tariq but it did not stop her falling head over heels in love with him. Indeed, realising just how *much* she loved him soon made her feel very vulnerable and increasingly desperate. Once his father died, she was convinced that she would be ditched and forgotten about because Tariq would be spending more time in Jumar than abroad. Believing that her time with him was running out, believing she was never going to love anyone the way she loved him, she reached an impulsive decision that subsequently proved to be the biggest mistake of her life.

It was so ironic, Faye reflected in mortification as she returned to the present in the tranquil beauty of the Muraaba palace: a year ago, Tariq had sounded so utterly shocked when she'd invited him to spend the night at her home and made it clear that they would be quite alone there. But it was really his own fault that her stupid and unwise invitation had not led to *any* actual intimacy.

Nervous as she had been, she had tried to create a special ambience for a romantic evening with the man she had loved. The very last thing she had wanted was a guy who showed up late and crushed her tender naïve expectations by saying things like, 'I won't be staying all night. I never do when I am with a woman.'

Or: 'Why must we eat now? I am more likely to be hungry *after* sex than before it.'

And finally: 'How many *other* men have you done this with?'

At what had to have been the ultimate put-down for a virgin, Faye had spilled wine all over herself, burst into floods of tears and raced upstairs. Sticky and reeking of alcohol, she had got into the shower to wash. When she had returned to her bedroom, wrapped only in a bath towel, Tariq had been waiting there. Mere minutes later, Percy had walked in on them and the trap as such had snapped shut without her even appreciating the fact for she had fled back to the bathroom in embarrassment and Tariq had left the house by the time she'd emerged again.

Faye closed her eyes and literally flinched from her memories. What a total idiot she had been to throw herself at Tariq like that! Carried away by her own imagination, she had begun behaving as if she were involved in some great tragic love affair. She had refused to see that that affair as such had existed only in her own head. The humiliating truth was that, in spite of a series of incredibly romantic outings, Tariq had never mentioned love. Indeed, apart from a few light kisses and a little discreet hand-holding, she might well have been a platonic friend. So it was hardly surprising that, after such minor flirtation, Tariq had been pretty taken aback when she'd suddenly chosen to surrender to her own far more passionate inclinations and asked him to spend the night with her! Resting back against the comfortable cushions, Faye slowly drifted to sleep on uneasy acknowledgements that still filled her with pain and deep, deep chagrin.

Faye woke up, dimly conscious of motion, of being too warm, yet of feeling strangely secure in the arms that held her. *Arms?*

'Be still…' As she stirred Tariq's dark deep-timbred drawl sounded, commanding even when quiet, she noted without surprise.

'What…wh-where?' Her eyes opened in the same instant as he laid her down on a comfortable yielding surface. She had a hazy impression of a big sunlit room but the recognition of the reality that she was on a huge canopied bed hit her with more striking effect. At incredible speed, she reared up off the pillows and flipped backwards off the bed again, landing upright like a trained gymnast.

From the far side of the mattress, Tariq surveyed her with transfixed golden eyes. Then he shook his dark head slightly as if he was questioning what he had just witnessed.

'Lucky fall…' Faye was furious and embarrassed by her own instinctive and childish reaction. The couple who had looked after her late mother had at one time been circus performers. As a child, with a brother who was frequently ill and a parent who had bad days too, Faye had spent a lot of time with Pearl and Stan. To keep her amused, the kindly couple had taught her some of their skills.

His aristocratic brows drew together. 'How…and why did you do that?'

How? She didn't want to answer that for there was nothing very cool or sophisticated about circus tricks in the bedroom. But her heart hammered, her mouth running dry on that second question. *Why?* Why did he have to be so gorgeous? Why did her rebellious brain throw up a mental image of them entwined in loverlike intimacy on that silk-draped decadent bed? Lust, her conscience told her in reproof, while her gaze rested on his lean, powerful face and, without her seeming volition, widened to take in inch by appreciative inch his long, lithe, muscular physique. The heat she despised sparked a licking, taunting flame in her pelvis. She reddened, shifted her feet, pressed her thighs together in a desperate effort to quench that treacherous response.

'You frightened me,' she condemned on a sudden brainwave, hoping to shift the focus of the dialogue from her acrobatic talents.

'How did I frighten you?' Tariq threw his proud dark head back, a level challenge etched in his darkly handsome features.

He was fairly leaping for the red herring she had proffered. But, in a sense, it was true that he frightened her, Faye acknowledged ruefully. However, it was her own lack of control she feared and his power over her. She just looked at him and he sent her traitorous body haywire. Intelligence didn't get a look-in. She did not need to ask herself why she had turned herself into a lying pushover a year ago!

'Under no circumstances would I ever hurt a woman.' As Tariq made that declaration, feverish colour scored his hard cheekbones.

It was extraordinary but he made her feel guilty. Faye backed away from the bed and moved her hands in a rueful dismissive motion. 'I don't want to be here and you know that—'

Tariq now viewed her with steady cool. 'You made the choice.'

'Between a rock and a hard place?'

'Welcome to how I felt on the day of our wedding. Trapped like an animal!' Tariq spelt out, shocking her with that allusion. 'No choice but to accede to the *lesser* evil of marrying you. My father was dying. You knew that. What a comfort it would have been for him to learn in his last week of life that his son and heir had been exposed in some English tabloid as the sordid seducer of a teenage girl!'

Her lashes lowered, her lovely face bled free of colour. 'But you *didn't*—'

'I need no reminder of that fact.' Venting a derisive laugh, Tariq strolled forward to capture both her hands in his. He tugged her to him as easily as if she had been a doll. 'What are the odds of my letting you go untouched a second time? A billion to one?'

The atmosphere sizzled. Tension curled her every nerve-ending. 'Tariq…'

He released her hands and framed her flushed cheekbones with splayed fingers instead. Molten gold eyes inspected her with hungry precision. His intense gaze enthralled her. She breathed in brief rapid bursts. Excitement was shivering through her in delicious little waves. Excitement was rising in her as fast as her body temperature. Excitement that literally consumed every rational thought.

One hand pushing into her hair, he ran a sensual forefinger along the line of her full lower lip, watched her pupils dilate, her moist pink lips part. And then he met that invitation with the hot devouring hunger of his mouth. For her, the effect was instant conflagration. Every skin cell charged up on the passion he had never shown her before and just went wild. Her hands slid beneath his suit jacket, found silk shirt, clawed it away, finally reached skin, warm, smooth skin covering hard whipcord muscles. She felt him shudder against her, all potent male power and promise, and she melted with liquid longing.

Tariq moulded his hands to the feminine curve of her hips and hauled her closer still, crushing her sensitised breasts to the hard wall of his chest. Low in her throat she moaned acquiescence to the plunging penetration of his tongue. On fire, she gasped, shivering violently, out of control, mindless…*ecstatic.* With a driven groan, Tariq dragged her back from him.

'I can't stay…' He breathed thickly.

She swayed, passion-glazed eyes locked to him. 'You can't stay?'

'I found you asleep and carried you to bed but I only came home to change. I have *Majilis* to attend this afternoon.' Stunning eyes fully screened by his lush black lashes, he was already endeavouring to straighten the clothing she had disarranged and smooth his tousled black hair.

Faye breathed in so deep she thought the top of her head might fly off to release the surplus air. Disbelief held her fast but she didn't even know what he was talking about. 'You...you have *Majilis*...you're going out?'

Tariq flashed her a rather sardonic look of amusement. He shrugged back his wide shoulders with sensual cool. His slow-burning smile mocked her. 'Only minutes ago you told me you didn't want to be here. You change direction like the wind. Even I did not expect a single kiss to win the battle...'

Faye might as well have been turned to stone by that speech. She closed her eyes: she dared not look at him lest he saw her raging mortification. She was drowning in self-loathing but still she could feel the pulsing ache of the hunger he had roused in her. How dared he speak to her like that? How dared he gloat?

'So you think you're irresistible?'

'No...*you* make me feel irresistible. Small distinction,' Tariq contradicted on his fluid passage to the door. 'You're hot for me. I'm sure other men have enjoyed the same response. But, right now, you're mine alone.'

'Do you know how much I hate you?' Faye snapped, her hands knotting into defensive fists.

'Why would I care? What is that to me?' Arrogant head thrown back, his dark deep-set gaze pierced her like an ice dagger. 'I want to possess you. I want to lie with you all through the night and make love to you as and when I want. But that is *all* I want from you.'

CHAPTER FOUR

LONG after Tariq had gone, Faye stared at the door, her fingernails still biting sharp crescents into her palms. His honesty had devastated her. Sex was all he wanted. For goodness' sake, had she expected him to confess to a tortured longing to know her heart and her mind instead? And why on earth did she feel so hurt by that admission of his? It was not as if she still *cared* about him. In fact, it was ridiculous for her to still be so sensitive!

A light knock sounded on a door at the other side of the room and she spun round. A pair of smiling young girls, who bore little resemblance to the crushed individuals in little Prince Rafi's retinue, entered.

'We are Shiran and Meyla. Your lunch is ready, my lady,' one of them informed her shyly.

Faye discovered that through that second door lay a whole host of other apartments, each as exquisitely appointed as the next. Was she in the harem? It scarcely mattered. Now that her adrenalin was leaping again, all she could think about was escape. Presented with a fabulous array of dishes all laid out on a low table in a superb reception room next door, Faye sat down to eat. Checking her watch and seeing that it was almost two in the afternoon, she then asked for a phone.

Once again, she dialled the number of her stepfather's portable phone.

'Faye? Adrian's out!' Percy sounded immensely cheerful. 'We're at the airport—'

'Good. How soon will you be on a flight home?'

'Another half-hour. Look, I can't talk long. Adrian's in

a shop but he'll be back in a minute. I told him that you flew back home this morning. He wouldn't agree to leave Jumar if he knew the truth,' Percy admitted without a shred of embarrassment.

'You're really worried about me, aren't you?' Helpless bitterness tinged Faye's unusually sarcastic response.

'Come on, Faye. It's my bet you're in the lap of luxury right now and it's not like His Royal Highness is some bloke you don't fancy! Let's face it, you've been a right wet weekend ever since he dumped you—'

Faye closed her eyes and said, 'I just don't believe I'm hearing this—'

'Well, now you finally got your prince, so I don't see why you should be complaining or feeling sorry for yourself.' Percy was warming to his theme, having rationalised events to his own satisfaction. 'I think our Adrian has done you a favour.'

'Thanks…thanks a bundle!' Riven with resentment, Faye slung aside the phone in disgust.

Escaping from the Muraaba palace would be a challenge. She had two options, neither of which struck her as that promising. Borrow a horse and try to sneak out in disguise or conceal herself in a car that was about to leave. First, she asked Shiran if the palace had stables and where they were and then she made a series of requests. The maids' eyes widened in surprise and confusion at the items she asked to be brought to her but they went off to do her bidding.

Her suitcase arrived, along with the food and bottled mineral water she had requested and the set of male robes and the headdress. Those last two demands were fulfilled with a great deal of giggling curiosity. Maybe the maids thought she was going to try and dress up as a man and spring some stupid childish prank on Tariq, not to mention a less than inviting midnight feast of bread and water.

Finally alone, Faye changed into trousers and a shirt and crammed the supplies along with her passport into her capacious backpack. A courtyard lay outside her bedroom. Using the elaborate wall fountain there as a foothold, Faye climbed the perimeter wall. Never having had the slightest fear of heights, she could have walked the wall blindfold. Traversing it, she continued along the walls of the eerily empty courtyards next to her own. Forced to climb higher at one point, she crossed a balcony so that she could ease herself down onto the flat parapet surrounding a giant domed roof.

Progress was slow but only twice did she have to risk touching ground level again to cross between buildings. Perched on the low sloping stable roof, she watched a couple of grooms leading a magnificent black horse out into a big flashy motorised horsebox. Bingo! She dropped down onto the cobbles in a shadowy corner and donned the robes she had in her backpack. Then she waited for a chance to board the horsebox.

When the men paused to talk, she made a run for it. Hurrying up the ramp into the box, she saw there was only that one horse on board. Startled by her entrance, the stallion threw up his head, his hooves clattering and banging on the boards. Faye dived into the furthest stall and crouched down to hide herself as best she could.

The ramp went up with a hydraulic hiss and minutes later doors slammed and the engine fired. The horsebox rocked over the cobbles, making the stallion fuss even more. Halting, presumably for the gates to be opened, the vehicle then turned, not towards the city as she had hoped, but in the other direction. Oh, great, she thought in exasperation. So now she would most probably have to take the horse as well. No way would she try hitching a lift in a country where, outside of the city, absolutely nobody seemed to walk.

How far would Tariq go in an effort to retrieve her? Might he simply shrug with fatalistic acceptance and just let her go? Faye recalled the look on his face when he'd mentioned those cold showers and felt hot all over. No, Tariq would not be cool about her vanishing act. All over again, she would be damning herself in his eyes. Refusing to concede that she was welching on their agreement, she grimaced at the noisy fretful movements of the stallion. Arabians were highly strung and *this* was the horse she was planning to steal and ride if need be?

The horsebox ground to a slow, jolting halt. Of course, they were stopping; the stallion was becoming frantic. Standing up, she approached his stall, talking in a low, soothing voice, calming him with confident hands. He was very responsive. She heard the ramp being unbolted. Holding the stallion's reins with one hand, she undid the gate of his stall. Was she *mad* to take such a risk? But the stallion was already surging forward, eager to leave a confinement he clearly hated, and without further hesitation Faye threw herself up into the magnificent leather saddle.

What happened next was just a blur. The hydraulic ramp went down and full daylight flooded in, momentarily blinding her. She had a fleeting impression of startled dark faces but by that stage the stallion was already plunging out past them, heading like a bullet for the flat salt plain that bounded the layby in which the horsebox had parked.

Faye gave the beautiful animal his head and let him gallop. It wasn't as if she didn't know where she was for she had studied that map in detail. Basically all she had to do was stay out of sight of the road and skirt the edge of the desert until she reached the city limits. At some stage she would have to pass the horse over to someone to be returned to the palace but that was really her only source of concern.

She was surprised by the strength of the breeze that blew

her hair back from her face. However, it felt wonderful after the claustrophobic interior of the horsebox. Even so, it was still incredibly hot and she stopped to open her backpack and, disdaining the male head covering, she covered her head with a scarf. She noticed then that there was a faint haze over the sun.

Within the first sweltering hour, the salt plain gave way to sand and their pace slowed, but that was only what she had expected. However, when the landscape began changing again from sand and scrub to dunes that began to build from almost imperceptible rises in ground level into gradually steeper gradients, Faye's brow pleated in dismay. She had not been prepared to see deep dunes on the careful route she had traced for the simple reason that there was none close to Jumar City. Obviously she had drifted too far out into the desert.

Stark unease assailed Faye. But for the rushing sound of the wind that was getting steadily stronger, the silence beat at her ears. The light seemed to be fading, only it couldn't be, she told herself, for it was barely five in the evening. She had at least three more hours of daylight, plenty of time in which to complete her journey. However, the sun now lay behind a peculiar reddish haze and dark clouds were gathering in a sky as grey as a stormy sea.

So it was going to rain, she thought, possibly even a full thunder and lightning job. The stallion snorted and jerked, a nervous ripple running through his powerful haunches. Of his own volition, he broke into a canter, resisting her efforts to pull him back. He was far too strong for her to hold and he plunged wildly up the side of a steep dune. That was when she heard the thwack-thwack sound of an approaching helicopter above the wind.

'Calm down, boy…' she urged as the horse began to buck.

She tried to hang on but she was thrown and she hit the

sand like a stone. The silky soft grains provided an unexpectedly hard surface and she was winded. By the time she caught her breath, removed the backpack which was digging into her spine and began to rise to her feet, the helicopter had landed and a male figure was striding towards her.

It was Tariq, but Tariq as she had never seen him before. She had the momentary sense of time having slipped back for before her stood a male who was every inch an Arabian prince in his regal splendour. He was sheathed in black gold-edged robes, worn over a pristine cream undershirt, a *kaffiyeh* covering his proud head, his clothing flowed back from his hard, muscular physique in the teeth of the buffeting wind. She collided with blazing golden eyes that had an electrifying effect on her already leaping nerves. Behind him, obedient as a pet dog and now infuriatingly calm, trotted the black stallion.

'Are you insane to run into the desert in a sandstorm?' Tariq roared at her with raw force. 'But you will suffer now too for I will not leave Omeir here to die—'

'Sandstorm…d-die?' Faye stammered in shock.

Tariq was already swinging round and vaulting up onto the stallion's back. Omeir was the *horse*, she worked out. Leaning down, Tariq hauled her up in front of him in a manoeuvre that made her awesomely aware of his masculine strength, not to mention his superior horsemanship. His sense of balance was superb.

'Tariq…how did you—?'

'Keep quiet!' he bit out above her head. 'Don't you realise how much danger we're in?'

As he sent the stallion leaping forward at a breakneck speed, she caught a last glimpse of the helicopter sitting abandoned on the sand. Danger? Yet he had come for her alone. Sandstorm? The sky *was* beginning to glow the most spooky red. Involuntarily, she shivered, clutching her backpack beneath her arm. Omeir galloped full spate along a *wadi* between the dunes. The wind lashed her cheeks, carrying grit that stung and dust that made breathing a choking challenge. She bent her head, closed her eyes. *He's* not getting away with doing that, so why should you? Guilt almost ate her alive at that point.

A little while later, she squinted from beneath the scarf she had pulled down over her brow. A whirling terrifying wall of sand the height of the sky was folding in. The sand already borne on the wind was fast reducing visibility but she saw the big dark irregular shape of a rocky outcrop looming ahead. Shelter? Barely thirty seconds later, Tariq swept her up and dropped her down onto the sand and, for a stricken moment, she honestly thought he had decided to dump her because her weight was slowing him and Omeir down too much.

Plunged into craven panic, trying to stay upright in a gale threatening to blast her off her feet, she cried, *'Tariq?'*

'Move!' Tariq was already behind her and only as he thrust her forward did she register that the mouth of a cave lay directly ahead of them.

Faye stumbled into the sandy interior on legs as weak as paper straws. Omeir surged deeper into the cave to stand sweating and shivering. Faye turned round just in time to see an uprooted date palm pitch into view and land only a few yards outside the cave. She fought to catch her breath in the sand-laden air, eyes huge, shaken face pale. Until that moment, she had not appreciated just how violent and destructive a sandstorm could be.

'You might have killed us both…you might have killed Omeir. Though he knows this oasis well, he was too frightened to find his way here on his own!' Closing a hand over her taut shoulder to steady her, Tariq pressed her through a break in the rock walls. 'The ground falls steeply here…watch your step.'

The passage opened out into another cave. The first thing Faye noticed with relief was the improved quality of the air and then she recognised the unmistakable sound of flowing water.

But for the pale linen of his undershirt glimmering in the darkness, she could hardly see Tariq. Feeling her way along the rough wall with a trembling hand, she dropped her backpack and slowly sank down onto the sandy floor. The last thing she expected and probably the last thing she wanted just then was for Tariq to strike a match and light an oil lamp.

She blinked in disconcertion. Flickering light illuminated soaring pillars of ancient rock and the glimmering pool of water refreshed by an underground stream. It also showed her a sight which at any other moment would have struck her as pure comedy: Omeir virtually squeezing his girth through the same passage by which they had entered and trotting over for a noisy drink at the rock pool.

With pronounced reluctance, Faye focused on Tariq. 'Obviously you and wonder horse have been here before.'

Tariq slung aside his gold-bound *kaffiyeh*, luxuriant black hair tousled above his hard, bronzed, dusty features. She literally saw his even white teeth grit. He dropped down lithely by the edge of the water and splashed his face, using the cloth he had flung down as a towel. 'So it amuses you to be sarcastic and flippant when you have done wrong…that is no surprise to me.'

This time, it was Faye's teeth that gritted. It had been an incredibly long day and she ached in places she had not known she could ache. More galling still, that exhausting ride into the desert had been a *total* waste of time and effort. Emotions already high after what she had endured, hot temper now bolted through her at the speed of light. His tone was so outrageously pious and superior, she leapt upright again with clenched fists. 'Go on…call me a cheat and a liar for trying to—'

'Run away?'

'I wasn't running away!' Faye launched at him even louder, pride stung by that label. 'You gave me no choice. You forced me—'

'I forced nothing. You agreed to my terms.'

Soft, full mouth tightening, Faye ignored that succinct and unwelcome reminder. 'My *departure* was my way of letting you know that, just like you, I won't surrender to blackmail—'

'I did not employ blackmail in any form.' Rising to his full imposing height, fabulous cheekbones taut, Tariq subjected her to a scorching appraisal. 'Give me one good reason why I should have agreed to settle your brother's debts and demanded nothing in return!'

At that blunt invitation, Faye simply saw red. Percy's smug words on the phone earlier had stung her pride like acid. In speedy succession, she recalled every piece of hurt and humiliation she had suffered since first meeting Prince Tariq ibn Zachir. Then she breathed in so deep, she trembled and gave him on her terms what she considered to be one very good reason. 'After what you did to me a year ago, I don't think it would have been such a big deal for you to give me one free favour!'

Tariq elevated an imperious brow. 'What *I* did to *you*?'

'You turned what should have been the happiest day of my life into a nightmare! You don't even know what I'm talking about, do you?' Faye's voice shook on that realisation. 'I'm talking about my wedding day. You asked me to marry you. You let me put on a wedding dress and wear something blue—'

'Something blue?' Tariq questioned with frowning bewilderment. 'What is this "something blue"?'

'And all the time you knew that you were going to turn

right round and divorce me straight after the ceremony. Not because you'd had a change of heart but because you had planned it that way from the start!' Faye's long-repressed sense of injustice was now rising as fast as her voice pitch. 'You asked me to marry you but you didn't *mean* one word of that proposal. I trusted you but you betrayed my trust.'

In receipt of that condemnation, Tariq strode forward, his gaze flaming molten gold. 'How you can accuse me of betrayal when you conspired with your stepfather to set me up for blackmail?'

'I just did accuse you, didn't I?' Finally getting to stage the confrontation her pride had demanded but been denied on the day of that wedding, Faye stood her ground. She had no intention of getting dragged down into the murky waters of Percy's opportunistic blackmail attempt because, no matter what Tariq believed, she had had nothing to do with that development. 'I married you in good faith—'

'Yet you made *no* attempt to dissuade me from divorcing you.'

'I beg your pardon?' Faye was totally taken aback by that statement.

'Did you even ask me to forgive you?'

'F-f-forgive me?' Faye got out with the greatest of difficulty, so shattered was she by the nature of that question. He had twisted the whole topic round and now he was throwing it back to her in an unrecognisable guise. Why would she have attempted to persuade him not to divorce her when divorcing her had so evidently been his intent all along?

'No, far from hanging your head in shame and admitting the truth of your greedy deception, you fled at supersonic speed with a cheque clutched in your hot little hand!' His lean, strong face was rigid with icy contempt and hauteur.

'Hanging my head in shame?' Faye enunciated in ringing tones of revulsion.

'You *had* no shame. You protest that you married me in good faith.' Tariq curled his lip. 'But a true wife, a true bride would never have left the embassy. A true wife would ultimately have followed me home.'

'What on earth are you talking about?' Faye was really struggling to comprehend but still failing to follow his reasoning. 'Why would I have followed you home? I was *never* really your wife…where do you get off saying that to me? You divorced me—'

'I did not divorce you.' Tariq's dark, deep drawl rose not one iota above freezing point.

'You didn't?' That declaration really shook Faye, who had always assumed that the dark deed of divorcing her had been done right there in front of her that same day.

'Not then,' Tariq extended with harsh clarity, wide, sensual mouth compressing into a hard, awesomely stubborn line.

Faye folded her arms, striving to look supremely unconcerned by the news that she had not been cast off by divorce quite as immediately as she had believed. 'Well, how would I have known what you were doing that day when you were striding up and down in a roaring rage and ranting mostly in Arabic?'

Tariq froze even more. In fact an ice statue might have revealed more expression than his hard bronzed features did at that moment. 'I did lose my temper to some extent—'

Omeir kept on walking between them, getting in the way of her view of Tariq. Faye circled round the stallion to hiss in retaliation, 'You lit up like Guy Fawkes' night!'

'Now I am seeing the real character you were once so careful to hide from me.' Tariq dealt her a contemptuous appraisal that served merely to heap nourishing coals on her inner fire. 'You are attacking me like a shrew.'

'If I was a shrew, you would have indelible teeth marks

all over you and instead you got away *scot-free* with what you did to me!'

'We will not discuss this matter further. Control your temper before I lose mine.'

'I like you better when you lose your temper!'

Having now imposed himself halfway between them like a large clumsy buffer, Omeir snorted, threw up his handsome head and pawed the ground.

'What's the matter with him?' Faye demanded involuntarily.

'All animals react to tension. Omeir has been with me since he was a colt. He knows my every mood and at this moment...my mood is not good,' Tariq spelt out.

'Well, I only have one thing left to say to you.' Angry resentment and pain still licked along Faye's every nerve-ending but she was already regretting hurling revealing recriminations about the marriage that had not been a proper marriage. Now all she cared about was conserving her own pride. 'I was really, really glad when I thought you divorced me. In fact I wasn't out of that embassy an hour before I appreciated what a lucky escape I had had! I can imagine no greater misery than to be married to a pious, judgmental louse like you!'

Electrified tension written into every taut line of his stance, Tariq studied her. The atmosphere sizzled hot as coals. 'Is that a fact?'

Faye flung back her head, shimmering pale hair rippling back from her pink cheeks. 'Does that hurt your ego, Tariq?'

'Not at all.' Tariq strolled forward like a prowling predator, his spectacular eyes smouldering gold in his hard-boned features. 'You are mine any time I want you and I do *not* wish to retain you as my wife.'

'Any time you want me—?' Her infuriated repetition of that bold assertion broke off in a startled squawk as Tariq caught her hands in his and pulled her to him, clamping her into intimate contact with his lean, powerful frame with easy strength.

'Yes…'

Raising her to him, he brought his demanding mouth down on hers with explosive force. Heat that had nothing to do with her temper set her alight. Shock shrilled through her quivering length, the kind of sensual shock her treacherous body exulted in. She closed her arms round his neck, let her fingers surge up into the silky black hair she loved. And all the time, stoked by the raw eroticism of every plundering passionate kiss, her excitement built higher and higher. She pushed helplessly against him to ease the throbbing sensitivity of her breasts, the taunting ache low in her belly.

With an abruptness that startled her, Tariq wrenched her back from him, breathing thickly. 'This is neither the time nor the place for such self-indulgence.'

Plunged into appalled embarrassment by her own response, Faye pulled free of him. She spun away, face hot as hell-fire. Her mind was a whirl in which stricken self-loathing rose uppermost. He had told her she was *his* any time he wanted her. Had she had to bend over backwards to prove his point for him?

'Tell me, when you ran away, where did you think you were going?' Tariq demanded.

Taken aback by that question but cravenly relieved by his choice of subject, Faye frowned. 'The airport…where else?'

'The airport is many miles from here.'

'It can't be…' Faye was glad of the excuse to go into her backpack and dig out the map. Eyes evasive, she turned back to extend the map to him. 'At least not according to this.'

'This map is more than half a century out of date. It is also written in Arabic—'

'I don't need to be able to read Arabic to recognise the symbol for an airport!'

'In this case, that symbol is for an airfield built during the Second World War and long since abandoned.'

'That's not possible,' Faye drew closer to study the map again. 'There's the city—'

'We have more than one city,' Tariq delivered in a raw driven undertone. 'And that is *not* Jumar City. That is Kabeer which is on the Gulf coast. Allah be praised that I found you before the sandstorm—'

'Well, you saved Omeir the wonder horse.' Cheeks burning with huge mortification at the news that she had totally misread the map, Faye whirled away again.

A lean hand snapped round her wrist and turned her back, unwillingly, to face him again. 'This is too serious a matter to be dismissed with a facetious comment as if it is nothing. All my life I have been trained to accept responsibility yet, in the space of a moment this afternoon, I forgot my duty.'

Releasing her again as if there was now something rather distasteful about a such personal contact with her, Tariq raked her dismayed face with brooding dark eyes. 'I was in the Haja when I was told of your flight into the desert. Hearing of your acrobatics on the various roofs and walls of the Muraaba would have greatly amused me had not a severe weather warning just been announced. In defiance of all common sense, I resisted the pleas of my companions and took up a helicopter. *Why?* In such dangerous flying conditions, I would not ask any man to risk his life to save yours!'

As he spoke, a forbidding darkness clenching his taut features, Faye fell back a step, colour receding, facial muscles tightening, sudden shame at the crisis she had caused engulfing her.

'It was not a risk I should have taken, I, who have no heir other than a four-year-old brother!' Pale now beneath his bronzed skin and rigid with tension, Tariq produced a portable phone and said with savage force. 'Even worse, I've been wasting time with you while my country, to whom I owe my first duty, is in a state of emergency!'

Recognising the depth of self-blame now assailing Tariq, Faye felt terrible. Rescuing her had demanded too high a price from him. For possibly the first time she recognised that, unlike her, he had to live *two* lives, both public and private, and naturally the responsibilities of being the ruler of his country counted way above other more personal inclinations. 'I'm really sorry…'

'Not one half as sorry as *I* am to have failed in my duty…' Grave and stern as only he could be, Tariq strode back into the outer cave. Within the space of a minute, she heard the faint echo of his voice speaking on the phone. The storm had ended and the wind had dropped without either of them noticing.

Faye stooped down to splash her face as he had done earlier, a great solid wodge of conflict and guilt attacking her. She grabbed up the *kaffiyeh* he had left lying and patted her skin dry. She could smell the evocative scent of him on the cloth. Sandalwood and just *him*. Male and warm and exotically sexy. In the wake of what he had admitted to her with such haunting, seering honesty, she was even ashamed of that last utterly inappropriate thought.

From somewhere she could hear a low throbbing drone. Engines of some kind? The childish part of her just wanted to scream that she had not meant to cause so much trouble. Omeir was squeezing back through the gap so that he could stay close to his lord and master. Faye's eyes prickled with hot, hurting tears. Omeir *was* pretty special and, just then, she didn't much care if she rated much lower than the horse in Tariq's estimation.

Picking up her backpack, she slunk back out of the caves. The bright blue sky was full of military and airforce helicopters. In the distance a trio of jets flashed past leaving trailing silver paths in their wake.

'You *see* what I have caused?' Tariq gritted out in a raw undertone. 'An all-out search for me is being staged when these resources should have been concentrated on those injured by the storm!'

'I'm really…desperately sorry,' Faye mumbled chokily. 'I honestly never realised how serious a sandstorm could be. I thought they just shifted the sand around a little—'

'Close your mouth before I strangle you.' Tariq groaned.

'Where was Omeir being taken?'

'At this season the tribal sheikhs meet at a gathering in the eastern territory. Omeir would have been collected on the road and taken into the desert in advance of my arrival. Now we will both be late,' he completed half under his breath.

'I really didn't mean to cause all this trouble for you—'

'Lust brings its own punishment.'

Compressing her lips on that grim announcement, Faye backed into the shadowy depths of the cave again. From there she watched the helicopters descend to land, one after another, sand flurrying up all around them.

Without warning, Tariq turned his imperious dark head to look at her again. A slashing smile that was purebred primitive momentarily lightened his brooding tension. 'On the other hand, perhaps I have finally paid the full price for desiring you and may hope to now enjoy the rewards.'

At the sound of raised voices nearby, he swung away again, having plunged her into flushed disconcertion with that concluding statement. A surge of anxious pilots and a whole bunch of less agile older men, who had clearly come along as passengers, were now converging on Tariq. As they approached, they fell down on their knees and began to offer loud and fervent prayers of gratitude for his safety. Never would she have witnessed such an unashamed and charged display of emotion in the West but, once she got over the drama of the scene, what she saw touched her to the heart.

They were so relieved that Tariq was unharmed. He wasn't only respected, he was genuinely loved and valued. Before Adrian had turned against Tariq under the mistaken impression that Tariq had attempted to seduce his kid sister, her brother had told her how very well-liked Tariq was and, indeed, that everyone he heard speak of him believed he was a terrific guy. She too had once held the same opinion. But then Percy had intervened and, overnight, Tariq had become a stranger. A stranger with a dark, volatile side to his character that she had never dreamt existed. She had lost the man she loved beyond all reason, lost him for ever, she recognized in sudden stark pain.

Yes, she *had* loved him, she acknowledged dully. After Tariq had, without question, risked his own life to save hers, it was beneath her to continue pretending that she had only been infatuated with him. Pride and pain had made her buy into that lie. He might never had loved her but he had liked and respected her. That was what she had truly lost and her bitterness had grown out of the reality that she had connived in her own downfall…

For loving Tariq as she had a year ago, she had wanted him at *any* price. The day he had asked her to marry him, she might not have known about Percy's blackmail attempt, but she had suspected that Tariq might only have been proposing because Percy had surprised them in each other's arms in her bedroom. Nevertheless, she had *still* accepted that proposal, hadn't she? What did that say about her principles? In her own eyes, it sunk her beyond reclaim.

CHAPTER FIVE

FAYE shifted sleepily and turned over, wincing at the stiffness of her muscles.

It was reasonably cool which told her it was still early morning. She had only the haziest recollection of boarding a helicopter the night before and none at all of being removed from it again. Bone-deep exhaustion and stress had wiped out the last of her energy reserves. Perhaps the final straw had been hearing that the helicopter in which Tariq had flown to find her had been buried right up to the rotor blades by a collapsing dune during the storm. What would have happened to Tariq had he still been inside it? She suppressed a shudder. Why was it that her every mistake seemed to rebound on him?

Pushing her tumbled hair back from her troubled brow, she finally opened her eyes. Soft, billowing folds of heavily embroidered fabric met her astonished scrutiny. The whole bed was shrouded in curtains. No such bed had featured in the room she had briefly occupied in the Muraaba palace. Wondering where on earth she was, she sat up with a start.

'You are awake, my lady?' With a gentle hand, Shiran brushed back one of the curtains several inches. '*Sidi* Latif is waiting to speak to you—'

'But I'm in bed—'

'Please excuse the interruption.' Latif's quiet intervention sounded from somewhere close by but out of view. 'I am standing outside your bedroom and, with your agreement, may address you from here.'

Already engaged in gaping at what lay beyond her bed, Faye blinked. Latif said he was standing outside her bedroom but she was in a *tent*! It might be an incredibly opulent, large and well-furnished tent, but it was still a tent! Evidently, Tariq had decided to take her to his tribal gathering in the desert, rather than return her to the Muraaba palace as she had assumed he would.

'Yes…' Faye faltered, her attention resting on the exquisite tapestries screening all canvas from view, the Persian rug covering the floor and the beautiful suite of satinwood furniture inlaid with intricate mother-of-pearl scrolls.

Shiran backed out through a curtained exit and Latif spoke up again. 'Prince Tariq has gone without sleep for many hours. Throughout the night he visited those hurt during the sandstorm—'

'Were there many hurt?' Faye had paled at that news and the awareness that Tariq had been up all night.

'It pleases me that you should wish to know.' Latif's response exuded warmth and approval. 'The storm struck hardest in the desert but in the city some were injured by falling masonry and flying debris. There were also several traffic accidents. In all, only three deaths which was a much lower number than we had feared might result. However, for the sake of his good health, His Royal Highness should now rest. I would be most grateful if you would make this suggestion.'

'If I see Prince Tariq, I'll do my best.'

'You will most assuredly see him.' Latif sounded slightly strained in his delivery.

She was to urge Tariq to go to bed? She was truly disconcerted that Latif should approach her with his concern. But, most of all, she was mortified by his clear acceptance that her relationship with Tariq was one of intimacy. Yet how *could* Tariq flaunt a woman as a lover without fear of censure? Surely standards of public propriety were too strict for such displays in Jumar? Surely even her presence in a tent at a tribal gathering was pretty reckless? Or was it a case of the old double standard? Her troubled face stiffened. Maybe people weren't too concerned about what their ruling prince did as long as the woman he did it with was a foreigner.

Not that they had yet done *anything*, Faye conceded ruefully, but that situation was unlikely to last. It was time she faced facts: she was stuck in Jumar for the foreseeable future. At the mercy of a male who knew exactly how weak she was in terms of physical self-restraint. No sooner had that reflection touched her cheeks with even warmer pink than she heard a rustle of movement and voices beyond the cloth partitions of her enclosed and private space, followed by Tariq's familiar dark, deep drawl speaking in a tone of command.

A split second later, the bed drapes were thrust back and Tariq himself appeared. 'Your maids are keen to keep you hidden from all male eyes…apparently even mine!'

'Yours?' Looking up, Faye collided with stunning tawny eyes that snarled the breath up in her throat and sent her nervous tension leaping.

'It has taken me ten minutes to find you.' Although Tariq looked exhausted, his bronzed skin ashen, strain etched in the taut line of his wide sensual mouth, his gaze was as brilliant as ever, the high voltage energy that charged him still in the ascendant over the tiredness.

'You're not wearing traditional dress…' She stared at him, her heartbeat quickening and her mouth running dry. Sheathed in a dark formal business suit of superb fit, Tariq looked sensational.

'Robes were only worn for ceremonial occasions and often in the desert, for in truth they are more practical than Western clothing. Yesterday at the Haja, I was in *Majilis*, holding open court for my people to approach me as I do every week. They bring their disputes for me to settle, they come to seek redress for injustice. I stand in the place of a judge.'

Resting one lean hand on the canopy of the bed, he gazed down at her with smouldering eyes that skimmed over her hot face, glided across the smooth fair skin of slim shoulders crossed only by the straps of her nightdress, and then extended with flashing mockery to the sheet she still hugged beneath her arms. The atmosphere throbbed with the undertones of sensual threat he emanated.

'You said you couldn't find me but this is a tent...' Faye mumbled, desperate to break the build of that pulsing silence.

'A tent that covers several acres.' Thrusting a wayward curtain out of his path, Tariq came down with lithe elegance on the side of the bed in a movement that stopped her breathing altogether. 'A tent palace no less and often in use. We are a desert people and the need to escape the confinement of stone walls still burns in us. My father would often live out here with considerably less comfort for months at a time. He would send for a woman whenever he felt like one...'

'Send for a woman...?' Faye parroted shakily.

Tariq had curved long brown fingers into the folds of the sheet she was clutching and he was almost casually tugging it back towards him inch by inch. From below the black inky luxuriance of his lashes, he glanced at her with burning amusement. 'You look so shocked. Before he married my mother, my father had at least a hundred concubines. Sex was remarkably non-pc in those days, a fact of life to my people, unworthy of any comment or indeed particular interest...'

'But not now?' Horrendously conscious that the sheet was now under slight stress as he eased it back from her, Faye splayed a hand across her ribcage to hold it in place.

'I don't have to send for you. You are here waiting for

me.' A wolfish smile played about the corners of his lips as he abandoned that idle play to loosen the sheet, the masculine gleam in his clear gaze telling her that he knew he would win any such bout with ease should he so desire. 'Some things do not change. But on this occasion, your presence here is as public as a press announcement.'

'And why is that?' At that statement, her embarrassment rose to an all-time high.

'Look to your own adventures yesterday. You can't walk the walls of the Muraaba like a trapeze artiste, borrow Omeir and force me to follow you into the teeth of a storm without rousing considerable public comment,' Tariq advised with taunting cool, watching her eyes drop and her mouth tighten and her colour rise as he spoke. 'I was angry but I am now calm. Tonight you will come to me as you should have come to me a year ago and I need practise no discretion.'

'*Come*...to you?'

'As a woman comes to a man. And *not* in a bath towel in a bedroom full of girlish fluffy toys...and *not* with a stepfather poised to interrupt with a vulgar pretence of shock and anger. Believe me, tonight there will be no interruptions from *any* source,' Tariq swore with silken satisfaction.

'But I—'

'What can you possibly find to argue about?' His golden eyes roamed over her with provocative satisfaction. 'Once you were far from shy in demonstrating your desire for me. What has changed?'

'I got older and wiser fast. I thought I loved you...you soon cured me of that—'

'And I thought I loved you too.' Releasing a derisive laugh to punctuate that startling declaration, Tariq skimmed her with a sardonic appraisal, his stubborn, passionate mouth compressed, his jawline at an aggressive slant. 'I too was cured when you lured me into your trap.'

Faye tried and failed to swallow, studying him in disbelief. *And I thought I loved you too.* No, no, a little voice screamed inside her head, no, she did not want to credit that admission for it had been so much more bearable to believe that he had never really cared about her and that she could hardly lose what, essentially, she had never had. 'You *didn't* love me—'

In a flurry of sudden movement, Tariq sprang upright, disconcerting her even more. He swung back to her and rested splintering dark eyes of condemnation on her disbelieving face. 'Do you know the moment you killed anything I still felt for you? It was when I proposed marriage the next day and you said yes without hesitation. That was what damned you…that was what convinced me that you *had* conspired with your stepfather to rip me off for whatever you could get!'

Beneath the onslaught of that blunt speech, every scrap of colour had drained from Faye's complexion. Had she been a target with a tender heart in the centre, Tariq would have hit a killing bullseye with his first dart. Furthermore he had not yet finished.

'When I asked you to marry me, you knew it was not right, you knew I was not myself, but you said nothing. By not acknowledging the true state of affairs, you let the whole sordid sham continue beneath a pretty pretence of normality…with your wedding gown and your wearing of something blue for luck. Oh, yes, I satisfied my curiosity as to the significance of the something blue in your culture. But what possible luck could you have hoped to attract when practising such blatant dishonesty?' Tariq's low-pitched drawl vibrated with his contemptuous distaste in the spreading silence.

'Tariq, please…' Faye muttered painfully, sick to the

heart to have the one sin she could not lay at the door of naivete or stupidity exposed and known by him and thrown back in her face.

'No, you will hear me out. You were only nineteen but you knew enough to know that it was not normal for a man to come to you as grave as a judge to ask you for your hand in marriage without *ever* having spoken of love or commitment!' Tariq did not conceal his scorn. 'Yet only yesterday you dared to accuse me of destroying your wedding day. As I said that day and I say now…a marriage into which a man feels forced is a charade and no true bond to be respected.'

Faye's hands trembled and she laced them tightly together, tears closing up her throat in a convulsive surge.

'I looked at my beautiful bride…and you *did* look very, very lovely, but your calculated campaign to catch me made you as soiled in my eyes as any whore is by her trade! So do not talk to me of spoiling the happiest day of your life. I at least was honest in what I was feeling that day. Angry, bitter, disappointed in you. You were not worthy of loving…I was ashamed that I had been blinded by your beauty into imagining you as perfect on the inside as you were on the outside.'

Faye was frantically fighting back the sobs welling up in her throat. She was devastated by what her own bitter recriminations the day before had unleashed on her. Not once had she allowed herself to believe that Tariq might have guessed what was in her own heart and mind that day, what she had hidden even from herself in her shameless, selfish longing to be his wife.

'And that is what I said in Arabic when I was ranting and roaring. Forgive me for feeling so much more than you were capable of feeling that I forgot to speak in English,' Tariq completed grittily.

He strode out through the curtained exit like the proud

desert warrior Percy had once labelled him. A great sob escaped Faye as she stumbled out of bed.

Shiran came running. 'My lady?'

'Is there a bathroom in this place?' Faye covered her eyes with one hand and turned away.

Mercifully there was and, in the mood that Faye was in, it was pure relief rather than a source of surprise to discover that the canopied passageway led to sanitary facilities sited behind a solid wooden door and enclosed within sturdy stone walls. Ushered into a giant marble bathroom, Faye took care of her most imminent needs and freshened up as best she could while she was still sobbing her heart out. At a sink anchored on the spread wings of a grandiose swan, she studied herself with swollen swimming eyes.

A 'calculated campaign to catch me...' She honestly thought her heart was either going to break right through or she was going to die of shame and humiliation right there and then. She did not think she would ever, ever look Tariq in the face again for there had been a dreadful mortifying truth in his every harsh word. Had she not slavishly followed her sister-in-law's every word of advice on how to keep Tariq interested? Lizzie had been so helpful on how she should behave, when to be available, when not to be, how to be a good listener, how to flatter with silence.

And although her entire relationship with Tariq had not been conducted on such superficial terms, it was horribly ironic that the one time she had strayed from Lizzie's rigid rules of dating she had wrecked everything. Lizzie had certainly *not* suggested that she invite Tariq to spend the night with her.

A frantic series of knocks was being rapped out on the door. But Faye was too distraught to open it. Sitting on the hard, cold floor, she wrapped her arms round herself and struggled to calm down. Tariq was clever and very quick off the mark. In the end, all illusions about her supposed perfection for ever buried, he had looked back and seen and recognised every single calculating move engaged to attract him. She was humiliated beyond belief and there was no hiding place.

Unlocking the door, Faye padded back to her tent room, uncaring of the massed rank of anxious female servants twittering in her wake. Slipping out of her nightdress, Faye made no demur when she was presented with a cool kaftan to don. Breakfast was brought to her in another airy section furnished with silk-upholstered low divans. Shiran watched with troubled eyes as Faye hiccuped through a piece of toast and sipped at a cup of tea both looking and feeling like tragedy personified.

'May we bring the children to see you?' the maid then enquired.

What children? Was Rafi one of them? Was she now a sight to be seen for entertainment purposes? But, not wishing to cause offence and scolding herself for doubting the courteous goodwill shown to her by everyone, Faye nodded assent. Indeed, she was surprised that there was not a distinct coolness in the air around her, for her escape attempt the day before had put Tariq in considerable danger.

Prince Rafi arrived first. Like a small adult he approached her with a stiff little face and for the first time she noted his resemblance to Tariq. 'I am sorry for upsetting you yesterday.'

'That's all right…as long as you don't do anything like that again.'

His brown eyes flooded with unexpected tears. 'I can't…they're all gone. Prince Tariq took them away.'

'They' being his retinue of slavish servants, Faye gathered, for Tariq had told her that that was what he would do. *Prince* Tariq? Was that how he had to refer to a brother old enough to be his father? Did such stifling formality in the ibn Zachir royal family exercise its rule even over little children? And, she thought sadly, yes, *yes*, it did for Tariq's hard self-discipline was the proof of it. Without even thinking about it, Faye scooped Rafi up and set him on her knee.

'I'm a big boy. Big boys don't get cuddled,' Rafi told her chokily.

'Shall I put you down again?' She wasn't teasing. She was afraid of embarrassing herself or him by doing something unacceptable.

Suddenly the little boy just pushed his head into her shoulder and sobbed out loud, clinging to her in considerable distress. She nursed him until the storm of tears was over, compassion stirred by the depth of the unhappiness he revealed. Even Tariq had called his little brother 'obnoxious', not an encouraging sign. So who did the poor child have to turn to? It was not his fault that he had been taught to behave like a little monster, but how hard it must be for Tariq, who had been raised far more strictly, to appreciate that fact.

'You like children.' Shiran wore a huge and relieved smile and she turned to address the servants waiting in the passageway.

Faye blinked in surprise as two middle-aged nursemaids hurried in with a pair of identically clad baby girls in their arms.

'Basma and Hayat,' Shiran announced.

'Twins? My goodness, what age are they?' Faye was enchanted.

'Nine months. You would like to see them closer?'

'They're only girls!' Rafi exclaimed fiercely.

Settling the little boy down on the seat beside her, Faye smiled at the twins. The little girls wore elaborate long pink satin frilly dresses with full net underskirts: so impractical and uncomfortable for babies she reflected with rueful sympathy. 'Basma and Hayat…those are pretty names—'

'I don't like them!' Rafi howled at the top of his voice.

'I don't like shouting, so please behave yourself—'

'I don't like you either!' Rafi threw himself off the divan and stormed away.

Ignoring him, Faye went on getting to know the little girls, who were easily told apart for they were not identical twins. Basma was full of confident mischief, her sister Hayat more anxious and shy.

Eventually, Rafi slunk back. 'You like them better than me.'

'Of course not,' Faye said gently. 'I like all of you.'

'Nobody likes me,' Rafi muttered fiercely and kicked at the divan base.

Faye looked down into his miserable little face and curved a wry arm round his rigid little body. 'I *do*...'

Toys were brought in then. Rafi was a pain, wanting all her attention, sulking when he couldn't have it but, between sulking and clinging, a kind of peace emerged. The morning hours passed and Faye was surprised when lunch was announced. The children were removed again to their own quarters. At the last minute, Rafi darted back. 'I see you soon...?'

'If you want.'

Some time after she had eaten, Shiran approached her to tell her that it was time for her bath. Faye frowned. 'Isn't it a little early?'

'It will take many hours to dress you for the ladies' reception tonight, my lady.'

'Oh...' Faye wasn't sure how she felt about making any form of public appearance. She still could not face the prospect of seeing Tariq again. The night he had promised her stretched before her like the worst of threats and the sweetest of dreams for the conflicting emotions dragging her first one way and then another would give her no peace.

She had only slipped into the water already drawn for her use when her maids hurried in loaded with baskets of lotions and she realised that privacy was not on offer. Rose petals were hastily scattered on the surface of the scented water and Shiran insisted on washing her hair. Such a production was made of the varying rinses that Faye sighed at the longevity of the experience.

There was washing and there was washing, but Faye felt as if she were being scrubbed within an inch of her life. Wrapped in a towel, she was urged into another room in the same block, a steam room full of billowing clouds which almost sent her to sleep, so lethargic did it leave her. Next she was persuaded to lie down on a special couch to be massaged. The rich perfume of the oil rubbed into her skin made her eyes even heavier but she enjoyed the stiffness being eased out of her muscles, the smooth feel of her own pampered skin. Tea was served in the aftermath, all the maids giggling and chattering with an informality that charmed her.

Her hair was dried and polished with a silk scarf. A manicure and a pedicure followed and a great debate opened over the shades of nail polish available. While that was going on and Faye lay back on her sofa feeling like a beauty queen, a slim leather box arrived and her companion became very excitable. With great ceremony the box was brought to Faye and opened. Within lay a note.

'Wear the anklet for me,' ran the note and it was signed by Tariq.

Anklet? Faye hooked a finger into an anklet studded with large dark blue sapphires.

'How His Royal Highness honours you!' Shiran proclaimed. 'This belonged to Prince Tariq's late mother.'

Faye wondered if a chain went with it. Since she rarely wore jewellery, it struck her as a very exotic item but she knew she was sentenced to wear it for, if she said no, she might then seem rude. A bouquet of white roses arrived an hour later. Again her companions were ravished by their admiration but Faye's heart turned as cold as the Ice Queen's. Too many memories that hurt were stirred by those pale perfect blooms.

When it was time to get dressed, she was taken aback by the fabulous outfit laid out for her perusal on the bed. But then she had nothing worthy in her case of *any* social occasion at which a sapphire anklet might be worn. Indifferent to her own appearance, she donned the gold silk strappy sheath which was worn as an underdress. Then with reverence she was inserted into an extraordinary violet-blue chiffon gown, every inch of which caught the light with exquisite gold embroidery overlaid with precious stones, and which dragged a fan-shaped train in its wake. The dress weighed a ton. Gold shoes with incredibly high heels were slipped onto her feet and she wondered how on earth she would move in so much heavy finery.

Another leather box was delivered. This time the maids whooped with unconcealed delight. Excitement was at a high. Faye undid the clasp to reveal a breathtaking diamond tiara, a pair of drop earrings and a bracelet. Why the heck was Tariq sending her such items? But the answer was writ large in the appreciative faces surrounding her. He was good as his own PR firm, she decided. His generosity in loaning her such hugely valuable articles to wear impressed everyone to death.

The tiara was slid into place, the earrings inserted, the bracelet attached to her wrist. A mirror was then carted over to her.

'You are *so* beautiful, my lady.' Shiran sighed happily.

In heels which elevated her a good few inches, Faye hardly recognised herself. Her hair had been transformed into a shining silken mane to support the tiara and fell smooth as a sheet of pale gold far below her shoulders. She glittered from head to toe like a fantastic jewellery display. In strong light, she would blind the unwary.

Led from the room, she had to walk with small shuffling steps. It was a long walk to the vast reception area thronged with women in outfits that soon gave her a different view of her own theatrical glamour. She still had the edge, but only just. Guided to a seat of honour and the cynosure of all eyes, she was introduced to one woman after another. Arabic phrases were murmured, no English was spoken. The amount of bowing and scraping she received increased her tension to the extent that she could almost have believed that she were dreaming the whole strange event.

And then the last woman approached, a flamboyant raven-haired beauty in her twenties. She was sheathed in an emerald-green gown, and her full pink mouth had a hard, sullen curve. The tension in the room was electric.

'I am Prince Tariq's first cousin, Majida. I offer you no compliments.' Her sultry eyes flared over Faye with derision. 'I say you are no virgin!'

The silence was ruptured by stricken gasps. Shocked faces were cast down, covered. An older woman rose heavily to her feet and wailed like a soul in torment. Faye's cheeks glowed red. How on earth was she supposed to meet such a very personal accusation flung at her in public? And why *should* that nasty brunette question whether she was or was not a virgin? How could such a thing be of interest to anyone?

At her feet, Shiran buried her face and moaned. 'This is a grievous insult, my lady. The woman crying is the lady Majida's mother. It is her way of expressing her shame at her daughter's behaviour.'

The wailing woman sank back down as if she had been disgraced. The food arriving was a very welcome diversion. Every dish was presented to Faye first but her appetite had died. As the lengthy meal ended, Majida approached her again and proffered a smooth apology. Feeling that the apology was as calculated as the insult, Faye responded with a tight smile of strain.

In that all female gathering, she was disconcerted when Tariq made an entrance to be greeted by a series of equally surprised but uniformly delighted cries of welcome. Looking at him, Faye drew in a sharp breath. Magnificent in silks as rich with gold decoration as her own, Tariq had never looked more exotic or more stunningly attractive. But, unable to forget the bitter anger he had shown her earlier, she stiffened and averted her attention from him to the other men filtering in behind him, some smiling, some looking a little awkward. Latif entered last, his wide smile suggesting that he was in the very best of good humour.

No fan of being ignored, Tariq took the seat beside Faye and leant towards her to murmur with the pronounced air of a male priding himself on his generosity, 'Let there be peace between us now.'

Faye compressed her generous mouth. 'I shouldn't think there's much chance of that breaking out tonight. According to you I'm so wicked, it's amazing a heavenly bolt of lightning hasn't struck me down—'

'In the name of Allah do not say such a thing even in amusement.'

'Not much amusement where I'm sitting,' Faye said stonily.

'We will exchange no more recriminations.'

'Well, you *would* be repeating yourself if you said anything more.'

'I am trying to mend bridges.'

'It's fences actually and you blew the bridges to kingdom come.' Having paraded into the centre of the room, musicians were beginning to play but it was very discordant stuff.

'It is not like western music but it is a traditional melody always played at such occasions,' Tariq volunteered, sounding just a little defensive.

A singer came on. She had a gorgeous husky voice but Faye took extreme exception to the suggestive way in which her lithe bodily undulations seemed to take place exclusively in front of Tariq. 'You're in with a good chance there,' she whispered, a poisonous, exhilarating edge to her tongue such as she had never before experienced and could not resist. 'There's a woman just gasping to get into your harem.'

'I do not have a harem,' Tariq gritted close to her ear.

'Too many women breaking out of it? Bad for the macho image?'

'One more word from you—'

'And you'll what? Have me delivered back to the airport? Well, I'll need to be carried because I'm literally weighed down by my fancy trappings. Tell me, do you only sleep with virgins?'

'What has got into you?' Tariq demanded in a shaken undertone.

'I'm coming to terms with being a concubine. Tell me, do I get sown into a sack and dropped into the Gulf when you get bored with me?'

'A sack would be very useful right now. You want me to apologise, don't you?'

'Oh, no, even you couldn't apologise for the embarrassment of a complete stranger stating that I'm *not* a virgin in front of so many people. Allow me to tell you that I found that weird and kinky and medieval—'

Both lean hands suddenly clenching on the arms of his chair, Tariq rounded on her like an erupting volcano. 'Who said that to you? Who *dared*?'

For the first time since his entrance, Faye focused on him in shock for he had not troubled to lower his voice. Outrage glittered in his flaring golden gaze, dark colour

scoring his superb cheekbones. 'For goodness' s[illegible]
down—'

'After such offence is offered to you?' Tariq growled lik[illegible] a lion ready to spring. 'What man would be calm in the face of so great an affront?'

'You're making me nervous.'

'You will tell me the name of the offender.'

'Not the way you're carrying on, I won't. There's been enough drama for one evening.'

'This hurts my honour,' Tariq informed her doggedly.

Faye closed her eyes. It had been a day in which culture shock had made itself felt on several occasions. In fact she had been in almost continual shock from the day of her arrival in Jumar for absolutely nothing seemed comprehensible to her. Not the way she was treated, not the way Tariq behaved. He reached for her hand and gripped it in emphasis. 'My honour is *your* honour.'

'But I have no honour…you've said as much.'

At that far from generous reminder, Tariq sprang upright. He lifted an imperious hand. The music stopped with a mid-chord crash. He spoke a few words in Arabic. Then he swung round and swept Faye up out of her chair and into his arms to an astonished chorus of more gasps and strode from the reception area, leaving a screaming silence in their wake.

HAPTER SIX

‘W... out over lesser insults,’ Tariq breathed with b... rkness as he strode down canopied passageways. ... do not appear to understand how high is the regard for a woman’s virtue in my culture.’

Now, had Faye been his new bride, she would have understood his fury, but she was totally bewildered by his smouldering rage on such a score when she was not his wife. She was to be his mistress and there was nothing respectable about that, was there? Indeed, in her humble opinion, it was entirely *his* fault that she had been insulted in the first place! It was madness for her to have been treated as a guest of honour in the presence of women who had to believe she was a totally wanton hussy. True, with the exception of his cousin, Majida, she had received nothing but smiling courtesy, but no doubt that was the effect of Tariq’s feudal power as a ruler. What else could it be? In fact, if his late father had once had a hundred concubines, it was quite possible his people thought having just *one* was the ultimate in self-denial and restraint on his part.

Regardless, here she was right now, being carted off very publicly to his bed, past innumerable guards saluting and standing to attention, past servants flattening themselves back out of his path. Faye was aghast. How *could* Tariq do this to her? Speeding up as he thrust his aggressive passage through a number of interconnecting tent rooms that convinced her that she would never in a million years find her way back to where she had slept the night before, Tariq finally came to a halt. He settled her down with immense and unexpected care. He smoothed down her dress where it was rumpled and stepped back from her.

'That you are *not* a virgin is my business alone,' Tariq announced, hard, stubborn jawline set like rock.

Faye reddened and attempted to walk away. It involved taking tiny, tiny steps and she wobbled on the unfamiliar heels. She was in a huge tent room, even more opulently furnished than her own and distinguished by a beautiful carved wooden bed large enough to sleep six. She studied it, butterflies suddenly flying loose in her tummy.

She flinched as about ten feet from her something metallic flew across the room and buried itself with a thud in the carved headboard of the bed. Her lips parting company, she gaped at the ornate dagger she had last noted attached to Tariq's sword belt. Now drawn from its jewel-studded sheath, the dagger was lodged halfway up to its hilt in solid wood.

'I will cut myself and smear blood on the sheet,' Tariq murmured in the most unnaturally calm tone she had ever heard. 'No more needs to be said.'

With difficulty, Faye dragged her attention from the dagger still twanging in the wood. She opened her mouth but no sound would emerge from her throat. It was finally dawning on her that virginity appeared to be a major issue on all fronts as far as he was concerned. It was medieval but there was something terribly, strangely, crazily sweet about his equally barbaric solution to this lack he believed she had. Her desert warrior was prepared to shed his own blood and mount a cover-up on her behalf.

His tawny eyes rested on her with raw intensity as if he believed she must have been distressed by the same insult which had sent him up in volatile fireworks. Finally, Faye was recognising the pronounced change in him. The angry bitterness he had revealed at the outset of the day had vanished along with the icy forbidding distance he could assume at will.

'Tariq...' she said a little shakily because, although she was embarrassed, a hysterical giggle brought on by nerves was tugging at her throat and she was terrified it would escape and cause huge offence for she could see he was trying to be diplomatic and reassuring. 'I really can't believe we're having this crazy conversation.'

'When we first met, I made the mistake of assuming that you were as innocent as you appeared.' Tariq lifted a broad shoulder in a fluid dismissive shrug. 'But that was a boy's fantasy. Many Arab men cherish similar fantasies but I am now more contemporary in my outlook.'

Contemporary? His use of that particular word absorbed Faye the most. She focused on the dagger in the headboard and skimmed her gaze away again, suddenly extraordinarily reluctant to state an opinion on that score.

Powerful emotion was welling up inside her but she could not have put a name to what she was feeling. Tariq ibn Zachir was what he was, a feudal prince. His patina of cool sophistication had once grossly misled her. Not too far below that surface was the infinitely more conservative male whose existence she had not recognised until too late. The male with the reputation of a womaniser who had, nonetheless, been shattered when she'd asked him to stay overnight.

Why? Only now could she understand why. Prior to that fatal invite, Tariq had placed her on a lofty pedestal labelled 'pure as driven snow'. And then she had so shaken his faith in his image of her that he had decided he had never known her at all. She had made it that much easier for him to credit that she had been involved in her stepfather's strenuous efforts to make money out of their relationship.

Cheeks warm, Faye plucked an imaginary piece of lint

from her sleeve. 'You seem very sure that I've had other lovers…'

'What else am I to believe after that invitation you gave me last year?'

So they were back to the catastrophic phone call during which she had virtually asked him to sleep with her and she could still only *cringe* at the mention of it. Barely twelve months had passed but the resulting fallout had ensured that she had since grown up a lot for, while she had believed she was being daring and romantic, he had believed she was being crude and cheap. While she was willing to admit to herself that she had misjudged her man and made a mistake, she was not prepared to admit that to him.

Ignoring what she saw as a most ungallant reminder of her most humiliating moment, Faye said tightly, 'What if I told you…well…er…that there hadn't been other men?'

Tariq screened his stunning golden eyes. 'I would tell you that you don't need to lie on that score.'

'But I wouldn't *be* lying if I told you that…and if you have so much respect for a woman's virtue, you should be keeping your hands off me, shouldn't you be?'

His amusement broke through to the surface in a flashing smile that disconcerted her a great deal. 'No…'

'Why not?'

'Take it from me, you are a special case…so last-ditch efforts to change my mind are destined to fail. I cannot understand why you should even attempt to change my mind. With every look you give me you let me know how much you want to feel my hands on you. I saw that at our first meeting in the Haja.'

'Really?' Her face was hotter than hell-fire. She met molten golden eyes set between lush ebony lashes. She saw the kind of absolute confidence that shook her.

'Seeing that longing in you filled me with an unholy rush of triumph…I freely admit that as a fault.' With that frank admission, Tariq strolled up to her and lifted her back into his arms with complete cool. He settled her down on the edge of the bed and removed the tiara from her hair. Long, sure fingers detached the earrings, first one, then the other before dropping to her wrist to unclasp the bracelet. It was all achieved at a leisurely pace. 'But then I was not brought up to be a good loser. I was taught to be ruthless and competitive. I was made to be strong.'

Dumbfounded by his dexterity with jewellery and that sense of being in the power of an overwhelming force, Faye watched him set the exquisite diamond set down on a silver tray on a dresser and mumbled in dazed and belated repetition. 'A fault?'

'You have already noticed the temper—'

'Rafi has it too—'

Dispensing with his sword belt and *kaffiyeh*, Tariq sent her a dark look of reproof which let her know just how much he still felt the shame of his little brother's behaviour. 'Never have I raised my hand to anyone in anger!'

'He's four and all mixed-up…you're twenty-eight and…' A slight gasp escaped her parted lips as he bent down to tug off her shoes. His proud, dark head was within reach. She curled her fingers to stop herself from stretching out a hand to touch the enticing luxuriance of his black hair.

It was really going to happen, Faye thought, swallowing hard; they were definitely about to share the bed. No sandstorm, no Percy to keep them apart. But now that they were finally at the brink, Faye just could not imagine *being* in bed with Tariq, when to date she had never so much as seen him with his shirt off…

'I'm twenty-eight *and*?' Tariq prompted.

'I've forgotten what I was about to say. You're really planning on going through with this, aren't you?'

'What do you think?'

'I just…I just can't imagine it—'

'I have more than sufficient imagination for both of us.'

'Well, I've had enough of this!' Faye threw herself off the bed with the intention of stalking away. But she had forgotten the length of the gown she wore and the train wrapped round her ankles, tripping her up. As she teetered dangerously, Tariq caught her back into his arms to steady her.

'I think I have only had enough of you talking.' Running down the zip on the gown, he eased it off her taut shoulders. The sheer weight of the embroidered fabric sent the garment sliding straight down her arms and into a heap at her feet. In speedy succession, the underdress travelled the same way.

'Tariq!' Faye, left standing in her lacy bra and panties with little warning, was paralysed by dismay and mortification.

Scanning her hot face and the self-conscious arms she folded in front of her, his gaze narrowed. 'Ignore my last comment,' he advised softly. 'I do believe you should talk some more.'

'What about?'

A sudden smile curved his wide, passionate mouth. She saw the charm, the rueful amusement which had once reduced her to a mindless level of tongue-tied longing. It did so again. As he lifted her up and settled her on the bed again, she coiled back against the crisp white pillows, conscious only of a heartbeat that seemed to be thumping madly in her eardrums rather than where it ought to have been.

In the thrumming silence, Tariq reached up and plucked the dagger from the headboard. Sheathing the blade, he tossed it aside again. Smouldering golden eyes roamed over the full swell of her breasts, the feminine curve of her hip and the slim, shapely length of her legs and then whipped back to her strongly disconcerted face.

'So…' he murmured lazily '…perhaps you would care to explain *why* a virgin would make the kind of bold invitation you made to me last year?'

Her soft mouth compressed and she jerked a shoulder, eyes veiled, chin at a mutinous angle. 'Since you didn't take me up on it, I don't think you have the right to ask that—'

'When I saw you in that towel in your bedroom, I had every intention of taking advantage of the offer,' Tariq countered in level disagreement. 'However, it seems obvious to me now that your stepfather must've *forced* you into making that distasteful phone call…'

Her lovely face taut with flushed discomfiture, Faye muttered, 'No. I can't let Percy be blamed for that. That call was entirely my own idea—'

'So even now you will not tell me the truth!' Raising a highly expressive lean hand and dropping it again in scornful dismissal, Tariq strode away from the bed, soundless and graceful as a jungle cat on the prowl.

'No,' Faye said tensely. 'I just won't tell you any more lies…no matter what the cost.'

Tariq swung back, unimpressed brilliant eyes clashing with hers.

Faye sucked in a deep breath. 'I still don't know *how* my stepfather found out that I had asked you to the house that night. Maybe it was just a horrible coincidence…him turning up when he was supposed to be in London and walking in on a situation which he thought he could use to his own advantage. But there was no set-up as far as I was concerned. I *honestly* believed we would be alone that night—'

'I do not believe in coincidences of that nature. And if you have not the courage to admit that you were involved right up to your pretty throat in your stepfather's intrigues, we have nothing more to discuss.'

'But—'

Tariq lifted his hands. 'I will not hear any more. I gave you the chance to tell me the truth and you wasted the opportunity. Your stepfather is a crook and he raised you without principles. Yet it is pointless for you to plead innocence in face of the facts as we both know them.'

Hurt resentment filled Faye. Here she was telling the truth but he would not accept it. He refused to believe that she could have had nothing to do with Percy's sudden appearance at the worst possible moment that awful evening. She was willing to admit that the facts did make it hard for her to argue a convincing case in her own defence but, nevertheless, she *was* telling the truth. Her stepfather had always insisted that his arrival that night had been pure coincidence and how was she to prove otherwise? Only Percy knew the whole story and, Percy being Percy, he was unlikely to stage a confession.

Eyes strained, Faye lifted her head again and then froze. While she had been lost in thought, Tariq had been discarding his clothes. How could she have forgotten for even *one* moment what was about to happen between them? Well, there was little chance of her forgetting a second time, she conceded in shock, violet-blue eyes now wide on the sight of Tariq shorn of his shirt.

Her shaken scrutiny roamed over his wide brown shoulders, strong arms and broad, muscular chest. A triangular haze of curling dark hair emphasised his powerful pectorals and then thinned into a silky line that arrowed down over his taut abdomen and disappeared beneath the low-slung waistband of his black briefs. Warmth prickled up from the very heart of her, making her shift on the bed and suddenly clasp her hands round her upraised knees. An enervating mix of fascination and embarrassment had her in its grip.

She watched him stroll over to the dresser and discard his watch, every movement fluid with natural grace. He had the most extraordinary predatory sex appeal. Her breathing started to seize up at source at just the thought of him getting into bed with her.

Lowering her knees again, she grabbed at the sheet already turned back in readiness for them and pulled it up over herself. Her whole being was humming with raw tension. Wanting…but still seeing what a trap the wanting was, how it would ultimately smash her pride and hurt her. Yet when she focused on the stunning lure of those hawkish tawny eyes, she could hardly breathe, much less think.

He came down on the bed, all dominant male, steely contours and hard muscle. He was very much aroused. Mouth dry, pulses racing, Faye's startled gaze skittered over him and off him again double quick. His virility was not in question. Panic and wicked excitement combined as he reached for her.

'We have all the time in the world,' Tariq asserted softly. 'I'm not a selfish lover.'

He captured her mouth with a passionate thoroughness that took her by storm, only to linger with the knowing eroticism of restraint and let his tongue delve into the tender interior and, with a smooth flicker, imitate a far more intimate penetration. She shivered with helpless anticipation, her heartbeat racing. He made her want more, with effortless ease he made her want *so* much more.

He lifted his head, his hair already tousled by her fingers. She stared up at him, wholly absorbed in the hard planes and angles of his lean, dark, devastating face. For a split second, nothing existed but the rising swell of her own unguarded emotions and her fingertips smoothed along a sculpted cheekbone, dropped to stroke in wonderment along his beautiful mouth.

'What?' Tariq husked.

'Nothing,' she framed, her voice the merest thread of sound, for in that moment she recognised the strength of her own feelings and felt terrifyingly vulnerable.

He tugged her up to him and kissed her again. Her eyes slid shut, all thought suspended for the potent hunger was more powerful. Heart hammering, her eyes flew wide as he drew back from her again, smouldering golden eyes pinned to her as he cast aside her bra. She gazed down in abstracted surprise at the swell of her own bare breasts.

'You are even more beautiful than I imagined…' Tariq curved his hand to the pouting flesh he had revealed, catching a pert pink nipple between stroking fingers, sending such a shard of sensation through her that a muffled moan was wrenched from her.

Face burning but every skin cell alive and begging for his touch, she fell back on her elbows against the pillows, one feminine part of her glorying in his unconcealed appreciation of her body, some other tiny part of her standing back in shock at the growing completeness of her own surrender. 'Tariq…'

Her voice died in her throat as he bent his arrogant dark head and teased at a prominent peak with his lips and his tongue. Seductive pleasure stopped her breathing and tensed her every muscle. He laid her down again with sure hands. As he employed greater sensual force on the tender buds, exploring the firm contours of swollen flesh, her teeth gritted and her fingers clenched, tiny cries of response escaping her parted lips. Nothing mattered but that he continue that sweet torment which was so totally addictive.

'This was meant to be,' Tariq told her with husky satisfaction. 'This was meant to be the first day I saw you. *Inshallah*, we say…as God wills.'

She collided with the burning gold of his eyes, aware of him with every thrumming skin cell in her body. There was no room for pride or principle in what he could make her feel, what he already *knew* he could make her feel. He wound long brown fingers into her tumbled pale blonde hair.

'Fate…'

'But you like to tempt fate. Why else did you run into the desert?' Tariq let the tip of his tongue trace her reddened lips, part them, dip, tease, making love to her mouth, his breath fanning her cheekbone. 'Don't you know that had you got anywhere near the airport I would have closed it and grounded every flight…don't you know that, when I set my heart on anything, I will stop at nothing until I achieve it?'

'But I didn't want this…' Even in the grip of a desperate hunger that mounted higher with his every caress, she knew that. Even as she opened her mouth, turned it under his, driven by an instinct she could not resist, she knew that. But as he drove her lips apart with electrifying passion, she refused to think.

'You do now.' Glittering golden eyes rested on her as if daring disagreement.

'Yes…'

He swept her up to him and tugged off the panties clinging to her damp skin. She trembled. He ran his hands over her, toyed with the straining sensitivity of her nipples, traced the taut curve of her quivering stomach and parted her thighs to let his expert fingers trace the infinitely more tender and private place below the soft pale curls. Her heart slammed suffocatingly fast inside her, her excitement intense. His touch controlled her, made her writhe and moan and sob for breath. She twisted her head into his shoulder, drowning in the hot male scent of him, the power of every sense heightened. Her fingers tangled with his hair, clutched restively over a brown shoulder, clenched there.

Tariq groaned something in Arabic.

'English,' she begged.

Fierce dark golden eyes held hers in an almost aggressive gaze. 'You excite me more than any woman I have ever known…'

The restive burning heat inside her was like a twisting, spiralling ache she could no longer withstand. 'Please…now.'

Without hesitation, his strong-boned face feverishly intent, he pulled her under him, pushed up her thighs and came down on her. As she felt the hard satin probe of his arousal against her softest flesh, she tensed. He smoothed her hair back from her damp brow. 'I'll try not to hurt you but you are very tight…'

And then he was there where she most ached for him to be. He eased himself just barely inside her, the sensation of his bold shaft stretching her, enthralling her, seeming to promise that nebulous fulfilment she so craved but had yet to experience. Then his hands lifted her and he tipped her back, shifting his lithe hips and thrusting deep. Sudden burning pain jolted her but almost as swiftly the hot, heady rush of pleasure returned and blanked out the memory of the first sensation.

'Assuredly paradise must be like this…' Tariq growled.

And she had no argument to make, indeed was so lost in the intoxicating world of scorching physical enjoyment, she could not have strung two sensible words together. She moved under him, skin flushed and damp, heart pounding, head thrown back, out of control and not caring as the wild surge of excitement built. She caught the age-old rhythm she had not known until he'd taught her it. She gloried in the raw dominion of his powerful body over and inside hers. She clung to him, reached a climax with a startled cry, soaring to a breathtaking peak and then writhing in the timeless ecstatic release of satiation.

Afterwards, Faye was just in shock. In shock at her own body's capacity for that much pleasure. In shock at her own hot, frenzied abandonment. In shock at the incredible sense of intimacy she felt still lying in the circle of his arms. His heart was still thumping at an accelerated rate against hers and he was struggling to catch his breath. She kept her arms wrapped round him, wanting the silence and the lack of eye contact to continue for ever, so that she could pretend that everything was bliss, everything normal…loving?

Loving? Faye stiffened at that impossibility, ironically provoking what she had wished to avoid. Tariq lifted his tousled dark head, lustrous golden eyes lingering on her as though magneticised. 'I am very pleased to be your first lover.'

Faye tensed even more and said nothing.

'But then that is justice.' With an appreciative hand, he touched the long silky streamers of her hair where it trailed across the pillow. 'Your hair is the same colour as the moonlight.'

'How romantic…' Something tight and painful knotted inside her, making her feel all kinds of a fool and she responded in a wooden tone, twisting her head away.

'Once you made me feel very romantic…'

Once. Bitterness threatened to rip Faye in two. She wanted to scream and shout. Justice that he should become her first lover? How was it justice? Wasn't it wonderful how he could seek to justify the most barbaric of bargains? His right to use her body in return for her brother's freedom. Or, as he himself had put it even more bluntly, sex in return for money, trade mark of the oldest profession in the world. She was a tramp now, she had even enjoyed being a tramp for him. She should have lain there indifferent, unresponsive, silent, maybe even smothering the occasional yawn. And what had she done? Humiliating recollections of her own begging, moaning and clinging engulfed her and she shuddered. No harem odalisque could have massaged a guy's ego more effectively than she just had!

Tariq caught her back to him so that she could no longer avoid his scrutiny. He smiled down at her with a charismatic warmth that made her feel as though he were crushing her tender heart between cruel, casual fingers and released her from his weight. 'I'm far too heavy for you…'

'As I dare say that's not the *only* drawback of being a concubine,' Faye stated in a tight little voice, face stiff as a frozen mask, 'I didn't like to complain.'

CHAPTER SEVEN

TARIQ sat up with a start. 'That joke has worn out its welcome. What is this stupid, trashy talk of being a concubine?'

'Forget it,' Faye said stonily, wrenching violently at the bedspread, hauling it round her and sliding off the bed in a series of fierce and jerky movements.

'Come back to bed,' Tariq ground out in a lethal tone of command, lean, strong face etched with cool exasperation.

Faye looked at him, all tawny and gorgeous and sexy as he was against the white bed linen, and her fury with herself, with him, with the whole wretched situation rose like a red mist in front of her. It was past time she reminded him that she was not one of his adoring subjects. 'Get stuffed!'

For the longest second of her life, Tariq simply stared at her in disbelief and then he was out of that bed faster than the jump jet her brother had once likened him to in his relations with her sex. 'Such abuse would infuriate me but for the fact that you sound like a truculent teenager…'

Shot down in flames, she conceded with infuriated acceptance, her colour rising.

'What is the matter with you?'

'The matter with *me*…?' she repeated on a rising note of volume.

Tariq stood there, naked and quite unconcerned by the fact, and focused censorious golden eyes on her. 'Tell me what is wrong.'

Wrapped in the iridescent spread, Faye flung her head high. 'Why should anything be wrong? Are you expecting me to fawn on you now like some harem slave thrilled to death by your attention?'

'Hardly,' Tariq said very drily, lean, strong features sardonic. 'Harems have been against the law in Jumar since the first year of my mother's marriage to my father.'

Confusion assailed her. 'But you *said—*'

'I was teasing you.' Taking advantage of her bemusement at that admission, Tariq lifted her up into his arms and strode, not back to the bed with her, but straight out of the room again.

'Where on earth are you taking me?' Faye gasped.

With a vibrantly amused smile at her disconcertion, Tariq strolled into a splendid green marble bathroom and shouldered shut the door. Lowering her, he extracted her from the cloaking folds of the bedspread. Before she could fully react to that new development, he had caught her up again and settled her down into the foaming waters of the Jacuzzi bath.

The water enveloped her overheated skin in an initially cooling surge that dragged a yelp from her. Then, becoming hugely conscious that she was as bare as a newborn baby and in full view of fiercely appreciative dark deep-set eyes, she sank her quivering body as far below the rippling water surface as she could.

Tariq joined her with all the cool and grace of a male to whom such inhibitions were unknown. He leant over her in a fluid arch, draping her hair over the pillowed rim so that it would stay mostly dry. Momentarily engulfed by his sheer male magneticism that close again, her instinctively raised hands accidentally brushed down over his hard male flanks as he stretched, her cheeks scorched and she dropped her hands again as if she had been burnt.

'Harems…' Tariq recalled lazily, sinking down like a lithe, tawny predator into the water to survey her highly embarrassed face. 'Although you were right in saying that

I am above the law, there would be great unease in Jumar if I was to demonstrate *any* desire to veil my woman or lock her away from all male eyes. Harems now feature only in our history books in the chapter devoted to the emancipation of women.'

'Really…?' Even to Faye's own ears, her voice sounded slightly strangled, but she had never been in a Jacuzzi in her life and was already nervously wondering what might happen next.

'In the whole of our history, our women were never veiled. Berber women do not cover their faces. The harem was a foreign concept as well, imported into Jumar by my great-grandfather, a man whose appetite for your sex is a living legend.'

'Oh…?'

'But my own father simply knew no other way of life until he met my mother, Rasmira.' Reclining opposite her in complete relaxation, Tariq looked reflective and his expressive mouth quirked. 'She was the daughter of a Lebanese diplomat, highly educated and sophisticated. She would not agree to marry my father until the royal harem had been emptied and closed. It was a long and stormy courtship.'

Her interest fairly caught now, Faye said, 'But he must have been madly in love with her—'

'She was a special woman and my father chose wisely for she had a great impact on our culture. She opened up schools for girls. She drove a car. She flew a plane. It is thanks to her influence that our society became more liberal and just.'

Faye was even more intrigued. 'So when did your mother pass away?'

His lean-boned features shadowed, his sculpted mouth tightening. 'Ten years ago. She was bitten by a rare poisonous snake. She was given the wrong antidote and by the time the mistake was recognised it was too late to save her. My father went half mad with grief.'

'How awful…' she whispered with a shaken look of sympathy for, when it came to the loss of a loved one, accidents and mistakes which might possibly have been avoided had to leave the most bitter taste of all.

'Come here…you're too far away,' Tariq urged, matching the complaint to immediate action by leaning forward and reaching for her with both hands to tug her up and across into the circle of his arms.

Faye was totally taken aback to find herself first kneeling over him and then flipped over in a careful rearrangement that left her lying on top of him and feeling very exposed. With her back turned to him, her bottom pinned between his hard thighs and her head resting back against his shoulder, she said with jerky stress in an effort to keep the conversation flowing, 'So…er…*how* many brothers and sisters do you have?'

'Only Rafi…'

'But…' She bit her lip uncertainly, concentration already challenged by the intimate contact of their bodies and the seemingly casual sweep of Tariq's hands sliding down over her smooth, taut ribcage, sending her treacherous heartbeat haywire. 'Your father…all those concubines…?'

'As a teenager, my father caught mumps. He believed he would never father a child. My arrival was greeted as being in the realms of a miracle and Rafi was conceived only with fertility assistance and my late stepmother's iron-willed determination,' Tariq admitted wryly.

'That doesn't…er…make Rafi less of a brother,' Faye said breathlessly as those lean brown hands came to rest just below the heaving swell of her breasts. She fought to keep oxygen in her lungs, sensual tension winging through her slender, trembling length like a storm warning she could not suppress. 'You should…er…think of your father when you look at him, not of your stepmother…whom I gather wasn't an awfully nice person.'

Above her head, Tariq loosed a grim laugh. 'Unhappily, Rafi is already labelled the length and the breadth of Jumar as being of a similar nature.'

'But he's still so young…how can that be?'

'His mother's unpleasant reputation went before him. She was very unpopular.' Tariq loosed a rueful sigh and let his fingers rise to cover the rosy pink nipples involuntarily straining for his attention.

As an electrified shiver of helpless response ran through Faye and her eyes squeezed shut on the intensity of the sensation, Tariq continued talking in a slightly roughened undertone. 'Were anything to happen to me in the near future, my people might not accept Rafi as my successor. For that reason and others, I will soon have to take a second wife and father a son of my own.'

Emerging from the sensual haze provoked by his most minor foray over her shamelessly wanton flesh, Faye jerked rigid when that casual announcement finally sank in. Her shaken eyes opened very wide, pain biting into her very bones without warning. *A second* wife? Did that mean that, however briefly it had lasted, their marriage had been a true marriage a year ago? But what did that matter now when Tariq had long since divorced her?

'A second wife…?' Faye parroted, although she had waged a mighty battle with her impulsive tongue and tried very hard not to comment.

'I have had enough of the water…but *not* enough of you,' Tariq countered with a ragged edge to his sexy drawl, beginning to rise from the water and carrying her with him to lift her out of the Jacuzzi again.

Dazed and devastated by the unbelievably agonising idea of Tariq marrying another woman, Faye stood there streaming with water while she was wrapped in a huge fleecy towel like a small child. There was something extremely disorientating about the way Tariq just reacted with split-second timing and switched channel and subject, something decidedly terrifying about the totally offhand manner in which he had mentioned his plans to marry again.

Here she was naked within an hour of his becoming her first lover, her body still singing under even his most light and impersonal touch, and yet here *he* was treating her like a casual bed partner, a sex object who had no value beyond the fleeting physical pleasure she might give. An object without any apparent right to have vulnerable feelings of her own. Well, a little voice said inside her head, just what did you think becoming the mistress of an Arabian prince would entail?

'Another w—?' she began shakily again, gazing up into glittering lion-gold eyes, voice failing altogether as he released his hold on the towel and let it drop round her ankles instead.

'I want you all over again,' Tariq confided thickly. 'But then that is only to be expected when it has been so long since I have been with a woman—'

'So long?'

As if that was a rather stupid question, a slight frownline furrowed his imperious brows as he drew her to him with purposeful hands. 'For the whole of the past year, I have naturally been in mourning for the tragic deaths in my family.'

His father, his stepmother, she assumed absently. Official mourning to show respect for the departed? What did she know about that? Yet she respected him for that self-denial. Or was it just that the knowledge that there had been no other woman for him since he had first met her gave her a much-needed sense of not being merely one more in a long line of available female bodies? For women, certainly in the West, would always be available to Tariq. When she had been seeing him, she had been painfully aware that he attracted her sex without even trying.

'Faye…so hungry am I for you, I could devour you where I stand,' Tariq admitted in a charged undertone.

Her lashes lifted, sensible thought snatched from her. She gazed up at him, jolted by the primal fire in his eyes, the hard male clenching of his superb bone structure. He knotted his fingers slowly into her hair, drawing her inexorably to him, anchoring her to his big, powerful frame. The hard, potent proof of his hunger brushed her quivering tummy and her legs turned hollow and her mind went blank and she could not drag her mesmerised eyes from the savage lure of his. The wanting was back with a vengeance, hotter and even less controllable than before. She could feel a damp, pulsing ache between her thighs, an ache that was becoming frighteningly familiar.

He swept her up and strode out of the bathroom. Like a doll without will or voice she didn't object but shame touched her deep for the fastest route back to the bed was all that mattered to her. Just that ragged note in his voice, just a touch, just a scorching look of raw hunger and something in her melted, reducing her to reckless, mindless surrender to his dominance, all defences forsaken. How could she fight herself?

'I meant to have you only once tonight.' Tariq groaned. 'But the once was only the breaking of a fast, not sufficient…I could have taken you in the Jacuzzi, I could have taken you on that hard floor, against the wall…the dawn is far away but it threatens me for tomorrow I must spend all day in talks with the sheikhs—'

Enervated and intimidated by that series of earthly declarations of intent, Faye mumbled shakily, 'The wall?'

Tariq gave her a shimmering smile of pure blazing assurance. 'Anywhere you want, any way you want.'

'I only know one way…'

Tariq spread her across the bed. On some dim lev awareness her nostrils flared in vague surprise at the sce of freshly laundered sheets. Evidently even in the space of their brief absence the bed had been changed.

'That was basic,' Tariq husked. 'Think steep learning curve...'

Her feverish gaze welded to him, her face hot with embarrassment but her wanton body secretly burning. She couldn't take her eyes off him. The sexual heat he emanated filled her with helpless excitement. You're going to spend the rest of your days regretting this, her conscience warned. You're going to hate yourself...

'Think pleasure beyond your wildest fantasies...' Tariq lowered himself down over her inch by sexy inch, trapping the breath in her throat, charging her quivering length with the most intense anticipation. Well, maybe she could learn not to hate herself...fate, he had called it, no point fighting fate...no point denying that that wicked smile of sensual promise slashing his lean, dark, devastating face bereft her entirely of her wits.

'Thinking...' she conceded weakly.

'Feeling...' Tariq traded, sliding between her parted thighs with the slow carnal expertise of a male who liked to tempt and incite. 'Until you don't care what day it is or what time it is and hunger and need for me controls your every thought, your every action...'

A chill of foreboding touched her deep down inside. 'You want me to love you...'

'Yes...' Tariq studied her with dark, deep-set eyes of unutterable calm.

'So that you can throw me away again,' she framed unevenly.

'If you please me enough, I may only throw you as far as my villa in France,' Tariq breathed with lazy cool. 'Then I could visit you when I wanted to and the tables would be

would be jumping every time the phone
s me and you would never ever *dare* to

genda you've got,' Faye muttered with forced amuse... 'No harem but complete enslavement.'

'The only game player would be me...'

'Well, there wouldn't really be room for anyone else with that ego of yours.'

He threw back his proud dark head and laughed with rich appreciation and then he brought his mouth down on hers and kissed her breathless. Until all she was conscious of was the feel of him, the taste of him and her own deep, endless hunger...

Faye shifted in the dawn light, waking slowly, conscious of a myriad sensations: Tariq holding her close, the weightless feel of her own limbs and a level of sweet contentment beyond anything she had ever imagined.

'Happy, *aziz*?' he murmured, easing her back into the hard heat and shelter of his lean, powerful frame, pressing his lips against a pale, slim shoulder, sending an evocative shiver winging through her awakening length.

'Blissful...' The hand he had splayed across her tummy melded her even closer and she felt his hair-roughened chest graze the skin of her back, the flex of his long, powerful thighs against her slender hips. A sheet of paper could not have squeezed between them and, at that instant, that was her definition of bliss.

Erotic images of the night they had shared assailed her mind, images that shook her but still filled her with an intoxicating heat she could not resist, any more than she could resist him. Now she understood what had once prompted her to make an utter fool of herself around him. Not just his devastating good looks or his powerful personality but the excitement, the sheer charge of physical excitement he evoked just walking into a room. That white-hot sexuality, that volatile charge of innate sensuality was as much a part of him as the cool self-discipline which cloaked it. So what was it like being an Arabian mistress? she asked herself, in a dizzy state of delight that had nothing to do with intellect. It was the passport to the sensual heaven of another world for she did not want the night to end, she did not want the light fingering through the tent room to rise to the strength of the full morning sun.

'Good…' Tariq let his hands glide up over her breasts in the lightest of caresses and she arched her spine, instinctively pushing her swelling flesh into his palms, driven by the tingling demands of her own sensitised body.

'Everything's good,' she mumbled, jolted by her own instant response, shaken by the ever-ready heat he could ignite at will, wondering for a split second if she was insatiable, wondering anxiously if it was quite normal to want any male as much as she now seemed to want him. Constantly.

'Then I'm happy too…' He let his fingers encircle the swollen prominence of her nipples, stroking, tugging, teasing the tender tips.

She jackknifed back against him, a long sobbing breath escaping her throat, and just closed her eyes tight, letting the pleasure cascade through her like a drug she craved, for long, endless moments totally lost within its grasp.

'Although "happy" is something of an understatement,' Tariq husked above her head, the dark, smouldering rasp of his voice sending tiny shivers down her taut spine. 'You are very passionate.'

She was not capable of speech. There was no yesterday, no today, no tomorrow, she told herself feverishly, no reason why she had to think if she didn't want to, for to think might be to let go of the happiness singing through her veins like a heady intoxicant.

'Indeed you might have been fashioned at birth solely for me.' A faint bitter edge harshened his tone and then he buried his mouth with sensual force in the extended length of her throat. As he hit on a tiny pulse spot with devastating accuracy, she moaned in response.

No longer did she have to tell herself not to think as the slow burn of desire flooded her with mindless heat. He was moving against her, letting her feel his hard, potent arousal, and she lay back against him, quivering, waiting, anticipating, every skin cell alight. He rearranged her with a care that was as tender as it was teasing. He pushed up her knees, drew her back again, sought with deft fingers the damp, swollen centre of her and played there until tortured moans sobbed in her throat.

'Tariq—'

'Wait—'

'I don't want to wait…I can't!' But she knew why there was the need for that slight hiatus, knew he was ensuring that their lovemaking would not result in a pregnancy.

'Yes, you can…' Tariq pulled her back to him and entered her all too willing body with surging force.

The sensation was so delicious, she arched her back in helpless pleasure. But one thing he had already taught her: there was no end to the pleasure, no boundaries either. He caught her chin and tugged her face around so that he could possess her mouth in a hot, demanding kiss that branded her. As he took her with agonisingly slow, deep thrusts, she lost herself in the rising, burning excitement of her own hunger. It was as if he were all around her for she felt totally possessed by him and she moaned his name, driven by every invasive shift of his lean, hard body to a greater height. And then the roaring in her ears came like a great wave and she felt him shuddering against her in the grip of a hungry satisfaction as powerful and uncontrollable as her own…and that was even more of a joy to her than the aching, drowning flood of her own release.

In the aftermath, Tariq rolled her back against the pillows and stared down at her. He brushed the wildly tumbled pale blonde hair from her damp brow. She noticed his hand was unsteady. Hawkish golden eyes gazed down into hers, stubborn dark-stubbled jawline clenching hard. 'Surely you are sore now…I didn't mean to take you again. Your pleasure should not be less than mine.'

Faye reddened to the roots of her hair, turned her head away, for there was no denying that after a night of constant lovemaking she was tender, but she could no more resist him than she could have resisted water after a week in the hot sun. 'It wasn't,' she mumbled.

'I don't believe you.' Long brown fingers drew her discomfited face back to his keen scrutiny. 'No woman has ever wanted me as much as you. If I keep you here, I don't believe you'll be fit to rise from this bed and walk by tomorrow, *aziz*.'

With that mortifying and earthy assurance, Tariq released her and sprang out of bed.

'So you're not keeping me here?' Faye prompted before she could bite back that startled question.

'I think it would be best if you returned to the Muraaba.'

Slight effort at diplomacy in implying she had a choice when she so evidently did not have a choice if he did not want her around. After the night they had shared, she reeled in shock from that rejection.

'In any case, I'll be engaged in talks for the next few days and too busy to give you much attention,' Tariq completed.

Attention? Like a child or a pet might hope to receive? That particular word seemed to reduce her to a very low level of importance. Super-sensitivity to his every spoken word had now afflicted Faye. The harem might have been abolished but she could not help thinking of his father who had sent for a concubine whenever he'd felt like one. After only one night, she was to be dispatched back to the palace.

'I hope you won't mind travelling back by car, rather than by air. It will be a lengthy journey.'

'And why should you spare a helicopter for little insignificant me?' Faye flipped over onto her tummy and pushed her hot, mortified face into the pillow, cringing at how immature that response had made her sound.

'It is not like that,' Tariq responded with grave quietness. 'I do not believe in unnecessary flights being made merely to save time.'

No woman has ever wanted me as much as you. She shuddered with shame that he should have recognised that and confronted her with that reality. How attractive did men really find the women who found them irresistible? A too willing woman would not challenge or excite the essential hunter in any male. She had just spent the *whole* night being overwhelmed by how fantastic he was in bed.

'Faye...you're taking this too personally.'

'Maybe you'd like to tell me how *not* to take it personally,' she said jaggedly.

'Sex is a seductive force. I walked in paradise with you last night,' Tariq murmured coolly, 'but I have other responsibilities to meet.'

That cool reminder bit like a whip into her unprotected skin. But then she already felt that during the long, passionate hours of the night she had lost an entire layer of protective flesh and somehow turned into someone else, for she no longer knew the woman she had become. He was sending her away and she was arguing about it. She could not believe that she was letting herself down to such an extent. And Tariq had a wonderfully evocative turn of phrase and tone. He had made walking in paradise sound like a giant, hugely wicked taste of the forbidden, to be treated with extreme caution, possibly even *rationed.*

'If you stay here, you would be too great a distraction. I could turn a coffee break into an excuse for a private orgy,' he murmured darkly, undertones churning up the atmosphere around him.

A distraction? Her image of herself had already sunk lower than the soles of her own feet. Numbly, she lifted her head and focused on his lithe, powerful physique in profile. The hard, clean planes of his high cheekbones were fiercely taut, the set of his strong jawline decidedly aggressive. He was pulling on riding breeches. The long brown sweep of his once satin-smooth back bore scratch marks from her nails. He had a bruise from her teeth on one muscular shoulder—maybe more than one.

Tariq looked as if he had had a run-in with a sex-starved woman, possibly even a whole bunch of them. But even unshaven and with his hair tousled by the all too frequent clutch of her greedy fingers, he was staggeringly beautiful to her stricken gaze. Her heart now felt as if it were in the palms of his lean hands, already crushed, soon to be dropped and maltreated in the worst of ways. And as she watched him dress with that easy, silent grace that was so much a part of him she could no longer pretend to herself, no longer hide from the truth of her own feelings or, even worse, her own wounding insight into his mood.

'You wish you had never set eyes on me again…' Faye said painfully.

'Do not presume to know what is in my mind,' Tariq urged with chilling immediacy, glancing up and transfixing her with brilliant golden eyes. 'Once you taught me regret but you will never do so again. Once you had the power to make me ignore common sense. *No more.*'

As a message for the immediate future it was not encouraging.

CHAPTER EIGHT

SILENCE and mute misery ruled the breakfast at which Faye shredded croissants and ate nothing for she had no appetite for food. The servants kept on bringing ever more tempting dishes to the table but she still could not eat. Soon she would be leaving the tent palace.

It was only two hours since she had woken up in Tariq's arms. Two hours since she had made the mistake of believing that she was more necessary to Tariq than she was. His seemingly insatiable hunger for her had somehow made her feel secure. But she had deceived herself into thinking what she wanted to think, she conceded strickenly. Tariq had set ruthless limits to their relationship and there was no longer any danger of her weaving fantasies. She was the light entertainment in the bedroom, nothing more.

Tears prickled at the back of her eyes. Strange how she had failed even to see that chilling single-minded ruthlessness in Tariq fourteen months ago when he had courted her with white roses and candlelit dinners. Yes, courted her, old-fashioned word that but very apt for those two months they had dated before Percy had wrecked everything. Of course, Tariq had thought he loved her back then and the officer-and-a-gentleman syndrome had ruled supreme. He hadn't tried to get her into bed, although he could have done so easily. He had not mentioned love or made any false promises.

No, even then Tariq had not asked her to love him or encouraged her to love him. But, regardless of common sense, she had fallen in love and had never stopped loving him, she now acknowledged painfully. It was impossible to continue denying the strength of her own feelings for Prince Tariq Shazad ibn Zachir. However, admitting that truth only made her feel more vulnerable than ever.

Loving Tariq put her more in his power. The guy she loved despised her yet continued to desire her. Only, now that he had slaked that hunger over and over again on her wanton and willing self, he just wanted her out of his sight. Banished to the Muraaba. How low could she sink that she should long to stay with him? Didn't she have any pride at all?

Her hands curled into tight, hurting fists. 'Sex is a seductive force,' he had said. Well, in her case, sex was a *destructive* force. With her body she had already given him eager consent to being his mistress. That was what she was…his mistress. She didn't even have the wedding ring any more. He had kept that. Yet he must have considered her as being his wife at some stage, possibly only momentarily, she reasoned, for why else would he have referred to his need to take *another* wife?

Yet even after he had told her that, she had still behaved like a lovelorn, stupid fool. She cringed, unable to credit the woman she had become during the hours of darkness. As she shifted her feet she felt the weight of the sapphire anklet which had some sort of trick lock on it that refused to be undone. She skimmed a trembling hand down her leg and wrenched at it for it suddenly seemed like a badge of servitude.

'Shiran, I want someone to speak to His Royal Highness and find out how to get this thing off me…'

The little maid departed. It was fifteen minutes before she reappeared. She got down on her knees and whispered, 'Prince Tariq says that it is his pleasure that you should wear his gift, my lady.'

His pleasure? Faye quivered with disbelief for it seemed to her that the entire country of Jumar revolved round

Prince Tariq ibn Zachir's *pleasure*. So unassailable was his status with his devoted subjects that he could even parade his foreign mistress off to bed without offending anyone's sensibilities!

'His Royal Highness also said…' Shiran visibly swallowed.

'Yes, what did he say?' Faye's charged enquiry shook.

'Please not to bother him with trivial enquiries when he is engaged in matters of state.'

As Faye plunged to her feet as though jet-propelled by that arrogant jibe, Rafi provided a distraction by bursting in on them like a missile shot out of a cannon, servants in hot pursuit. Throwing himself at Faye, he clutched at the skirt of her summer dress with frantic hands. 'You can't go away…you take me with you…you take Rafi too!'

'What on earth…?' Faye lifted the little boy in an effort to calm him down.

'Prince Rafi knows you are returning to the Muraaba.' Shiran sighed.

Rafi wrapped his arms round Faye. 'I come too…I be good…I will be really good boy.'

'Will Prince Rafi accompany us and the babies too?' her maid asked her.

'I don't have the authority to make a decision like that—'

'There is only Prince Tariq but he will be too busy for the children while he is with the sheikhs.'

'Can I come…can I come?' Rafi demanded.

Nobody else? For even little Basma and Hayat, Faye wondered in surprise. 'Surely the twins have parents?'

Shiran gazed back at her in wide-eyed surprise. 'No, my lady. All their family were lost.'

'Lost?' Faye queried.

'People go away…they die,' the little boy in her arms told her woodenly. 'Bang bang…the plane fall out of the sky…all die.'

That explanation chilled the blood in Faye's veins and she paled.

'Terrible, terrible day…' Shiran said chokily, eyes swimming.

'Prince Tariq does not cry…Prince Rafi does not cry,' Rafi chimed in, but his strained little face was dripping tears.

Her arms tightening round the child, Faye hugged him to her, her own eyes stinging. She would never have opened the subject of the whereabouts of Basma and Hayat's parents had she been aware that they were dead. 'Well, if no one minds you and I and the twins can all go back to the palace together,' she heard herself promising.

Rafi said that he would have to fetch his toys and took off at speed.

'Tell me about the plane crash,' Faye urged Shiran.

Rafi's mother, his cousin and his wife, who had been the parents of the twins, and even the twins' grandparents had all died in the same tragedy. On a flight between Jumar city and Kabeer on the Gulf coast, the plane had developed engine trouble and had attempted a crash landing which had failed. Basma and Hayat's father had entrusted his daughters to Tariq's care in his will. The poor man could never have dreamt that he might die so young and leave Tariq responsible for two babies still only months old.

In one appalling day, Tariq had lost a good number of his closest relatives. *I do not believe in unnecessary flights being made merely to save time.* Small wonder, Faye conceded sickly, sinking deep into shock.

It took four Toyota Landcruisers to transport so large a party back to the Muraaba and, during that lurching and often torturously slow drive over the desert sands, Faye had plenty of time to think over what she had learnt. She now fully understood why Tariq had spent an entire year in mourning and she felt terrible that she had not known for the tragedy must have been widely reported. However, she rarely watched television and the only newspaper she read at home was a local one which did not cover international events. Tariq, she finally grasped, had the responsibility of raising three orphaned children.

The entrance hall of the Muraaba was full of silent kneeling servants.

'Why are they doing that?' Faye whispered to Shiran in dismay. 'Who are they waiting for?'

'They are showing respect, my lady,' Shiran explained. 'Wave your hand and they will go about their duties again.'

Faye did so and passed on by. With Rafi tagging along, she was shown upstairs to a magnificent suite of rooms that rejoiced in balconies that overlooked the beautiful gardens. Signs of Tariq's occupancy were everywhere. Polo trophies, family photographs, the portrait of a gorgeous blonde woman with stunning dark eyes. His *mother*, Shiran told her with positive reverence. In another age, Tariq's late mother might have been a supermodel and no longer did Faye marvel at the surrendering of the hundred concubines.

Lunch was served to her in an imposing dining room but the presence of Rafi, Basma and Hayat made it a lively occasion. She spent the rest of the day with the children, relieved by their inability to sense the painful conflict of her warring emotions. For no sooner was she separated from Tariq than she felt empty, abandoned and miserable. She got very angry with herself and with the feelings she could not control. That evening when she had tucked the twins into their cots she read Rafi a story, but only after overcoming his temper tantrum at her refusal to allow him to share *her* bed.

By eleven, Faye was in bed reading the historical romance she had brought out to Jumar with her but hadn't got around to opening. It was a good book. Having lifted her head briefly at the noise of a helicopter landing on the palace heli-pad, she had returned her attention to her novel when the bedroom door opened.

Her head shot up. Tariq lounged in the doorway with a wolfish grin. 'I thought I would surprise you.'

Dry-mouthed, Faye stared at him. Clad in a crisp white short-sleeved shirt, open at his brown throat, and smoothly tailored cream chinos, he looked sensational. All sleek and sexy and sophisticated.

'Success…' Tariq murmured, indolently shouldering shut the door and strolling across the room. 'You look good in my bed.'

'I thought you had other responsibilities…' she said breathlessly.

'I will fly back to the talks at dawn.'

'I don't think you know what you want.'

'It is simple…*I want you.*'

Her violet-blue eyes dilated at the flashburn effect of his glittering golden gaze and the husky, intimate timbre of his dark, deep drawl. Beneath the fine cotton of her strappy nightdress, she was mortified to feel the languorous swell of her breasts and the tightening of her nipples as they pushed against the cloth.

Lean fingers twitched the book out of her nerveless grip. He studied the scantily clad Viking hero on the cover with very male amusement. 'Colourful.'

'Just something to pass the time—'

Stunning eyes glittering, Tariq studied the rising pink in her lovely face as she sat rigidly upright in the bed. 'But now I am here…'

'So?' Faye lifted her chin.

'I am much more accessible than the guy in the book…better taste in clothes too.' Sinking down on the side of the bed, Tariq closed his lean hands to her slim shoulders to tilt her forward into his arms.

I will freeze him out…I will not respond, she swore vehemently to herself.

'Ice is a challenge to those born in the desert,' Tariq breathed with audible amusement, the sun-warmed scent of him flaring her nostrils as he toyed with her tremulous lips in a provocative, darting foray. 'You know that you burn for me too.'

No more, she told herself feverishly. Ten ones are ten, she chanted inside her head as he pressed her lips apart and she quivered, suffering not only from temptation but also from the sheer weight of her anticipation. Ten twos are twenty, she continued, struggling not to lean into him, struggling not to moan as he let his tongue flick in a sexy intrusion between her parted lips. Parted lips? Close them! Think about something else, desperation urged.

Tariq laced one hand into her hair and kissed her slow and deep until the blood drumming in her veins hit fever pitch and her heart was hammering. *A second wife* hurtled up to grab her memory at the last moment, for during the afternoon she had wondered whether one of the reasons for remarrying that he had not declared was his responsibility for three young children. She jerked her head back from his, a sudden chill dousing her shameless heat and said jerkily, 'Last night, you used the expression "a second wife"…'

'Yes.'

'That suggested that you had *had* another wife…so I want to know if that was me you were sort of referring to?' Faye pressed awkwardly.

'Who else?' Tariq confirmed drily.

All of a sudden Faye had no need of multiplication tables to keep her brain focused. She drew back from him with a bewildered look. 'So you are saying that we were really married…properly married, even if it didn't last long?'

'What else?'

What else? *What else?* In complete shock as the reality that they had been truly married that day a year ago sank in, Faye snaked back from him, taut spine bracing to the banked-up pillows behind her. She studied him with huge, shaken eyes. 'But you told me that that wedding ceremony was a total sham!'

'No,' Tariq contradicted with extreme coolness. 'I told you that the essential meaning of a ceremony into which I felt forced was a sham but I never at *any* stage suggested that it was not a true marriage in the eyes of the law.'

Faye was transfixed as he made that outrageous nit-picking distinction. She just gaped at him. 'You mean I was *genuinely* your wife after that ceremony?'

'What else could you have been?' Tariq asked even more sardonically. 'You were my bride.'

'Your b-bride…?' she stammered, all wits having deserted her. 'Percy told me the ceremony could only have been some kind of Jumarian mumbo-jumbo when I told him that you had already divorced me again—'

'But I had not already divorced you and there is no mumbo-jumbo in the law of Jumar,' Tariq ground out, his dark, deep-set eyes hard with disgust. 'But how typical that offensive suggestion was of the man who made it! How could your stepfather have made that judgement when I forbade him the right to attend? Naturally it was a legal marriage and, considering that we were first wed by a Christian man of the cloth, how could *you* pretend to believe otherwise? Unlike your stepfather, I am a man of honour.'

Faye was staring at him with a heart sinking further with every second that passed and every word he spoke. 'I'm not pretending, but the Christian minister didn't use a word of English either and I wasn't sure he was what I thought he was. I only believed it was all a sham because you *said* it was… And you knew I thought that—'

'I know you say you thought that *now*. When we talked at the Haja, that is certainly the excuse you attempted to employ for your behaviour in accepting that bank draft and fleeing the embassy last year,' Tariq outlined with daunting precision. 'I soon realised that.'

'The excuse?' No matter how hard Faye tried to master the stupor of shock settling over her, she failed. Only two days back, she was recalling that when they had sheltered from the storm Tariq had made comments that had struck her as utterly incomprehensible. 'In the cave, you said something about me not having followed you back to Jumar…you said a true wife would never have left the embassy. At the time, I didn't understand because your saying that made no sense—'

'I see no point in rerunning this drama so long after the event,' Tariq spelt out coolly.

Faye studied his lean, strong face fixedly. 'But I have a right to know. Are you telling me that a year ago you would have accepted me as your wife if I had stayed or later flown out to Jumar?'

'I have no crystal ball to tell me what I might have done in a set of circumstances that did not arise…so that is a foolish question.'

'A f-foolish question,' Faye parroted but inside her had sparked a flame ready to surge into a towering inferno of incredulous raging pain. 'I didn't notice *you* trying to haul me back from running away that day—'

'Naturally not—'

'Because you couldn't get rid of me fast enough! At least, be honest about that,' she urged him bitterly.

'Understandably I was still very angry with you but I was not responsible for the decisions that you made—'

'But I didn't know I was making any decision…I thought the decision had been *made* for me! For goodness' sake, I believed that you had divorced me within minutes of our wedding, so there wasn't the slightest chance that I would have hung around, was there?' she argued with feverish emotion.

Tariq dealt her a shimmering appraisal, his lip curling. 'Perhaps you would like to be my wife now that the money I gave you then is spent—'

'I won't even dignify that with an answer!' In receipt of that ultimate put-down, Faye felt a convulsive sob clog up her throat. 'You let me walk out on our marriage and you didn't come after me—'

'Why would I have done so?' Tariq countered with sardonic bite. 'You were in the wrong…I was *not*. You made no attempt to discuss our differences or defend yourself at the time. You simply took the money and ran.'

Faye trembled. All too late she was recognising Tariq's worst flaw. A level of stubborn, unyielding pride that appalled her. He had been so stubborn and so proud that he had let her walk away from their marriage for ever, never once allowing for the fact that she might have misunderstood the situation or that she might have been innocent.

'What else would I have done when I believed you had just divorced me and I had no idea there was a bank draft in that envelope for I never opened it? You misjudged me, yet I would have forgiven you for that…' An unsteady laugh empty of humour fell from her lips. 'But you can't believe that *you* could be wrong about anything. Aside of lying about my age which is something teenagers the world over do, my only sin was just accepting your marriage proposal—'

'Faye—'

She moved a shaking hand, too wounded to look at his lean, bronzed features. 'But you were offering me what I wanted more than anything in the world. I loved you… And, yes, guilty as charged, I desperately wanted to be your wife!'

Tariq closed a strong hand over hers but his own hand was not quite steady and she was able to detach her fingers with ease. 'No one of us may change the past.'

Faye turned her back on him, bitterness enclosing her along with a mortification so deep it hurt. How could she talk as she had to him? How could she reveal so much? What was the point? He had never wanted to marry her in the first place, so naturally he was proofed against her every attempt to argue in her own defence.

'I've got only one more thing to say.' She breathed unsteadily. 'You know about as much about real love as I know about ruling Jumar so don't kid yourself that that was love you were feeling! Your horse has got more sensitivity. Percy tried to make a fool of you and that outraged you because I bet no one had ever dared to do that to you before. So you took it out on me and you're *still* taking your hurt pride out on me...'

The silence that followed seethed and sizzled.

'Are you quite finished?' Polar ice would have been warmer than that ground-out question.

She squeezed her eyes shut in misery. *Hurt pride.* Two words her macho desert warrior would never forgive her for. But then he was no good at forgiving anything, so why should she care? He thought she was a horrible little gold-digger, an inveterate liar and schemer, still set on trying to feather her own nest. But, worst of all, he had cared so little for her that he had let her leave him even though she had been his wife. *You were in the wrong...I was not.* She shuddered. No, that had not been love, not what she recognised as love, so she need not torment herself with the belief that she had lost his love, but tears still coursed silently down her cheeks.

'If I had taken my anger out on your stepfather...had I allowed myself within ten feet of him, I would have killed him with my bare hands. And not for the blackmail attempt but for turning *you* into something so much less than you might have been!'

The savage chill of sincerity in those words took her aback. In the rushing silence which followed, she listened to him undressing. She squirmed over to the far edge of her side of the bed and reached a determined resolve. From that very moment she swore she would not think again about their disastrous wedding day, their marriage which she had not even known existed in reality, or the fact that he might have divorced her since then. She had wasted a whole year of her life on endless regrets and now she had said sorry as well, so that was that. *Finito!*

The mattress gave beneath his weight. The lights went out.

A tiny betraying sniff escaped her as she opened her mouth to snatch in a ragged breath.

Tariq invaded her side of the bed without warning. 'Let me hold you—'

'No!' she snapped. 'Can't I even be miserable on my own?'

'Not when you are making me miserable too.' Tariq groaned, tugging her into his strong arms, tightening his hold on her when she made a squirming attempt to snake free. 'I will not touch you. We can be miserable together. Just lie still.'

The heat and solidarity of his big powerful frame crept into her stiffness like a sneak invasion. Slowly the tension leeched out of her. 'You know…the first I heard about that dreadful plane crash last year was today,' she heard herself whisper, for she felt that really she ought to say something on that subject.

Tariq tensed.

'I'm really sorry. Your father, your stepmother… The whole year must have been a nightmare for you to get through.'

'Surely the crash was mentioned on the British news?'

'I'm sure it was but six months ago my life was in total upheaval,' Faye confided ruefully. 'The house was being sold and I was seeing to all the packing and looking for somewhere to live. That's probably how I missed out on hearing about the crash. You mentioned your stepmother's death soon after I arrived here but I had no idea there were other relatives of yours involved—'

'Which house was being sold?' Tariq interrupted.

She frowned. 'What do you mean by *which*?'

'Your brother's home or yours?'

'Adrian lived in army quarters: he didn't own his house and when he quit the army he had to get out of it. I'm talking about the house where we grew up—'

'But why was it sold?'

Faye sighed. 'Adrian and I joint-owned it but it was too far out of London to suit Lizzie and him, so I agreed to the sale… I told you that he put the proceeds into starting up his business—'

'But I didn't realise that you had sacrificed your *own* home. How could you let your stupid brother sell the very roof over your head?' Tariq demanded rawly.

'Please don't call Adrian stupid, Tariq,' she muttered, very uncomfortably for it had occurred to her more than once over the years that her big brother, much as she loved him, was not the brightest spark on the block.

'But where have you been living since then?'

'I got a bedsit near where I work…although I don't suppose I'll have a job when I get back because I was only supposed to be away a few days—'

'What is a bedsit?'

'Are you serious?' She smiled in the darkness, thinking that there was no good reason why Tariq should understand what a bedsit was. She was probably the very first person he had met who lived at the poorest end of the rental market. She described her accommodation.

'You must share a bathroom with strangers?' Tariq demanded, aghast.

'Not all of us at the same time,' she pointed out, trying to suppress a giggle.

'I assumed you were living with your stepfather or your brother.'

'Adrian has his own family...and he came over here with them,' she reminded him. 'As for Percy, he only contacted me again when Adrian went into prison. You know it would break Percy's heart if he knew we had actually been married for real. You're lucky you divorced me...'

'Go to sleep...' A sliver of raw tension she could feel had entered Tariq's stillness but exhaustion was settling in on Faye and winding her down like a clock. Muffling a yawn, she surrendered to gravity and rested her head on his shoulder, marvelling that they were talking again and wondering if that was the result of her resolve to totally detach herself from their past.

Tariq was gone when she woke up at seven the next morning. As her seeking hand found nothing but emptiness beside her, she jerked in dismay at the sound of something moving about what sounded like *below* the bed. Sitting up with a start, she was just in time to see Rafi scramble out in his pyjamas, bounce up and shout, 'Boo! Did I scare you? Did I scare you?'

'*Yes*...what time is it?'

Rafi clambered up on the bed and landed himself on her lap. 'Can we have a picnic today?'

'Maybe.'

'I like you...'

'Please let me go back to sleep,' Faye begged.

Rafi climbed in below the sheet and snuggled up to her like a tadpole wriggling in itching powder, bony little knees and elbows jabbing in the small of her back. She swallowed a long-suffering groan. 'Did you see Tariq leaving?'

'I saw his helicopter.' Rafi imitated the noise at deafening pitch and sat up to start whirling his arms round and round at the same time. 'I won't go in a helicopter…it might fall out of the sky and go bang and die my brother—'

'Oh, Rafi…Tariq will be *fine*. Tariq is a wonderful pilot.' Faye groaned and, giving up on sleep, she flipped over and began tickling him until his giggles and hers rose to such a level that Shiran came running in to see what was happening.

She thought Tariq might come back that night but he did not. It was the afternoon of the following day before he reappeared. After enjoying a riotous couple of hours playing in the gorgeous terraced gardens that climbed the hillside, Rafi and the twins had been taken inside for a nap. Hot and sticky following such activity, Faye had taken advantage of the departure of the servants. Having kicked off her shoes, she was paddling in the wide shallow basin of a secluded fountain in a shaded arbour. The sensation of that cool water lapping her overheated skin felt like total bliss. Holding her dress up to her knees to prevent the hem from getting splashed, she kicked up water, watching the droplets sparkle in a shard of sunlight strong enough to pierce the hanging dark pink foliage of the spreading casuarina tree above her.

When she lifted her head, it was a considerable shock to see Tariq poised on the lush manicured grass only a dozen feet from her. His dark golden eyes flared over her comical look of dismay and glittered with rampant amusement. A devastatingly attractive smile flashed across his wide, sensual mouth and her heart hammered so hard in reaction to that charismatic charge, she felt dizzy and just kept on staring at him.

'You make a charming and refreshing picture,' he murmured huskily, moving forward and extending a lean hand to grasp hers and assist her back out of the basin.

'You were laughing—'

'Laughter has been painfully thin on the ground over the past thirty-six hours,' Tariq confided, retaining his hold on her slim fingers and gazing down at her with a mesmerising intensity that whipped colour into her already warm cheeks. 'I sat up half the night listening to two obstinate old men arguing about grazing rights that neither need. But now it seems worth it for I'm with you sooner than I had hoped.'

'My shoes…' Faye mumbled, her wide eyes stealing over him in greedy little bursts that she could not resist, taking in the exquisitely tailored pale beige suit that sheathed his very tall and powerful frame, lingering on the full spectacular effect of a colour that accentuated his black hair and sun-bronzed skin. It was no use. He still just took her breath away. Although she had sworn to be cooler than an ice cube, she could not shake the conviction that he was the most drop-dead gorgeous male alive.

'Never mind your shoes…although you are inconveniently small without them.' Banding both arms round her as he made that teasing comment, Tariq drew her close, lifting her up against him and draping her arms round his shoulders. 'Cling…'

'I don't cling,' she said tightly, shutting the allurement of him out with lowered eyelashes, fighting the urge to grab him and hold him tight and sink into the gloriously familiar scent and feel of him.

'Please…'

'You're wasting your time…'

He hoisted her higher with a strength that disconcerted her and bent his proud head to press his mouth against the tiny pulse beating out her tension just below her collarbone. Jolted by that unexpected approach, she let her head fall back, felt a river of liquid heat forge a path through her thrumming body and loosed a choky little moan.

'Am I?' Tariq strode over to the stone bench below the tree and sank down, keeping her trapped in his arms. He gazed down at her, a wolfish grin forming on his beautiful mouth. 'I want to spend my time with you.'

'Well, I suppose I signed up for it,' Faye muttered grudgingly, maddeningly conscious of him with every wretched fibre of her being.

'What's that supposed to mean?'

'I'm your mistress. Spending time with you is hard to avoid.'

Tariq tensed and then breathed in slowly, lean, strong features taut. 'I have considered what you said the other night. It's possible that I have misjudged you to some extent—'

'It was Percy who made off with your half million—it serves you right too!' Faye told him squarely. 'You must've made the bank draft out to him—'

'Naturally. I believed you would still be living with him and he would be taking care of your needs—'

'Look, Percy never looked after me in his life and he hardly ever lived with us either, aside of the occasional weekend. He didn't *even* look after my mother. He just paid people to do it for him—'

'This is not the picture of the happy united family you gave me when I first met you—'

'Of course it's not,' Faye agreed ruefully. 'Who do you know who drags out all the dirty washing in their family if they can avoid it? And you've got to admit that Percy is a very *big* piece of dirty washing…you think I didn't see how you avoided him? You think I don't notice how much my stepfather offends people?'

'Why on earth did your mother marry such an unpleasant man?'

'Well, if she ever regretted it, she didn't show it.' Faye sighed. 'And, to be fair, he never spoke an unkind word to her that I heard, but somehow we mysteriously went from being well off to poor during their marriage.'

'Adrian once mentioned that your own father had made some very unwise investments. Your stepfather may not be responsible for the loss in family prosperity.'

'Adrian once mentioned...? Why didn't he *ever* mention that to me?' Faye demanded in exasperation.

'I can see that I've been remiss in my responsibility towards you,' Tariq breathed flatly.

Faye stiffened. 'No, you haven't been. As far as I'm concerned, I was never your wife. In fact I don't even want to *think* about all that nonsense any more.' And with that cool assurance, she broke from the loose circle of his arms and stood up in a hurry. Having forgotten that she had no shoes on, she felt the gravel below the seat bruise the soles of her bare feet, making her gasp and jump back onto the bench beside him where she hovered, stepping off one foot on to the other. 'That hurt!'

Tariq looked up at her with a slanting smile. 'A princess would have to be very dignified.'

Faye paled and then tossed her head. 'I wish you well of one...are you going to be a gentleman and fetch my shoes?'

Tariq sprang upright and reached for her hands, enclosing them tightly in his and startling her. He crushed her soft mouth under his with a devouring hunger that splintered through her in a shockwave. Then he lifted her and settled her down on the bench. Senses reeling in the aftermath of that stormy onslaught, she watched him retrieve her shoes and return with them.

'Just like Cinderella,' Tariq murmured playfully, sunlight gleaming over his luxuriant black hair as he crouched down to slide her sandals onto her small feet.

'No, she got the fairytale prince…I got the frog of little faith.'

'I beg your pardon?'

'You heard me.'

Tariq simply laughed and closed one lean hand back over hers, walking her back down the hill towards the palace.

'You only came out here to drag me back indoors again, didn't you?'

'I only came out here to find you, but you are right. I am now taking you back to my bedroom where I intend to remove every single garment you wear as fast as I possibly can and make passionate love to you,' he admitted without skipping a beat.

'Duty calls,' Faye quipped, but she could feel herself blushing, feel the spiralling ache of the exact same hunger twisting deep down inside her. And, in her opinion, that made her not one whit better than him. Moaning about being his mistress seemed a little hypocritical when she was as keen on him as she was.

He gave her a startled glance. 'You have changed.'

'Have I?'

'Now you are joking about sharing my bed.'

'Fancy that.' She shrugged. 'Bit of a problem for you, that, isn't it? Instead of feeling punished by your revenge, I'm enjoying myself.'

'I am no longer thinking of revenge—'

'It doesn't bother me. I'm only looking on this as an extended holiday.' Unfamiliar aggression was powering through Faye. If Tariq thought he was going to hear one more time about how he had broken her poor little heart, he was in for a surprise.

'Really? I suppose I'm the holiday romance?'

'No comment.'

Ten minutes of simmering silence later, Faye kicked off

her shoes and lay down on the bed. 'Do you think you could remove this anklet now?'

Tariq nailed her with glittering golden eyes. 'I like to see you wear it.'

'All the time…everywhere? Even when I go paddling?'

He shed his jacket, jerked loose his tie in the manner of guy making a statement. Watching him, she stretched, conscious he could not take his eyes from her even though he was furious. She was thrilled by the discovery, a new sense of feminine power infiltrating her bloodstream like heady wine.

'You're fighting back…' he said softly.

'Did you expect me to stay in doormat mode for ever?'

Shedding his last garment, Tariq strolled over to the bed. Sunlight filtering in through the doors spread open on the balcony enveloped his bronzed magnificence and something caught in her throat. No today, no tomorrow, she told herself feverishly. She was living for the moment.

'You can't win.' Tariq came down on the bed one hundred per cent sexual predator. 'You are my woman, *aziz*.'

'While I still want you,' Faye heard herself point out.

His lean, sure fingers momentarily stilled on the buttons that ran down the front of her dress. Lush black lashes lifted on his stunning golden eyes and he gave her a slow-burning smile of pure sensual threat. 'I am not planning to bore you out of your mind in the near future.'

'Well, you're bound to think that…'

He spread the edges of the dress apart as thought he were unwrapping precious gold. She was not wearing a bra. 'I am not surprised that grazing rights failed to hold my attention last night,' he confided huskily, running an appreciative hand over one small pouting mound crowned by a prominent rosy peak. 'You are exquisite…'

She quivered at that glancing caress, forcing her spine back down to the bed. No need to wow him with overenthusiasm, she warned herself. 'You're bound to think that too after a year of celibacy—'

'And what would you know? Only days ago you were a virgin.' Tariq gazed down at her in exasperated challenge.

'I was only stating an opinion—'

'Don't.'

'Do you think other men would have the same opinion, then?' A little devil was dancing in Faye's head, priming her tongue.

Tariq ground out, 'Why would you ask me such an inappropriate question?'

'It's on a par with you having asked me that night how many other men I had invited to dinner and slept with.'

'I was *upset* by your behaviour—'

'Oh, were you? I thought you were just trying to make me feel cheap—'

'It was cheap.' Winding both hands into her tumbling hair as if he were imprisoning her, Tariq possessed her angrily parted lips with so much potent force, she lost her grip on her thoughts. She clutched at his shoulders, dizzy with pleasure.

But then he made the serious error of pausing to extract her from the dress. 'And you're not cheap—'

'No, indeed—to date, at my estimation, I have cost you upwards of a million pounds!'

Tariq froze at the reminder.

'Nobody could call that cheap,' Faye agreed sweetly.

Tariq glowered down at her, pale beneath his sun-darkened skin, superb cheekbones taut in his lean, strong face. 'You're worth it. Are you happy now?'

She wasn't but she nodded, wishing she had not mentioned the money: the bank draft Percy had purloined, the cost of her brother regaining his freedom.

Tariq traced her tremulous mouth with a soothing forefinger. She was blinking back tears but he didn't miss a trick and he smoothed them away. 'We are finally together. Think only of that.'

The instant he kissed her again, the hunger stormed back, intensified by her raw emotions. She loved him. She wanted him. She would not allow herself to think one step beyond those realities. A fever had got hold of her. Her hands roamed over him, adoring the flex of his hard muscles beneath his hair roughened skin. Trembling beneath her exploration, he pulled her over him, depriving her of that freedom and locking her into the hard heat of his aroused body while he plundered her lips.

'You drive me wild,' Tariq said raggedly while she struggled to catch her breath.

But even breathing was a challenge with his expert hands on her and his mouth tugging at her tender nipples. The excitement built so fast, she was lost in it, moving against him, parting her thighs with a sighing cry at his first touch. The wanting had never been so strong before, had never absorbed her so utterly. Her heart was racing, she couldn't breathe, couldn't wait, couldn't focus on anything *but*…

As Tariq sank into her in one forceful thrust, she rose against him with a driven moan of delight and what followed was the wildest pleasure she had ever known. Her heart pounding, she gave herself up to the raw excitement, wanting, needing, burning with greedy impatience and then surging so high she thought she might touch the sky in the grip of sweet ecstasy.

She surfaced back to the real world feeling glorious. Tariq was hugging her so tight, she didn't know where she began or he ended and that felt good. Even better was the way he was looking at her with tawny eyes that had a slightly dazed quality. She smiled.

'You are very special,' he murmured intently.

'So are you—'

'I might never let you go free...'

She smiled like the Sphinx, all woman and smug.

'Where do you think I am?' Tariq purred on the phone.

There was something so very sexy about Tariq on the phone, Faye reflected in a state of blissful abstraction, something so very sexy about Tariq even when he was saying the most ordinary things. He had given her the portable phone so that they could talk during the day when he had to be away from her and arrange meetings like secret lovers. It never left her side. It was her substitute for him, her instant hotline to reassurance that she was the most desirable woman in Jumar. Only two weeks ago, she had been calling him a frog, she recalled sunnily, but her frog had turned back into a prince.

'On the way home...?' she prompted eagerly.

'No.'

'How long are you going to be?' She sighed, face having fallen a mile.

'Where are you?'

'Outside...you'll have to look for me.'

'Could you doubt it?' he murmured in a husky tone of promise that sent a quiver of response down her spine.

Faye set down the phone, her attention returning to the children. It was just about nap time, she decided. Having enjoyed a long and leisurely picnic lunch, they were sitting on the carpets spread beneath the shade of the trees. Hayat clutched at Faye's arm to steady herself and planted a big soppy kiss on her cheek. Basma was already on her lap along with Rafi. When Tariq wasn't around, Faye was always with the children. She knew he spent time with them early mornings and evenings and, being painfully conscious that Basma, Hayat and Rafi were really none of her business, she never, ever intruded at those hours in the nursery section of the palace.

Indeed, she *had* wondered once or twice if Tariq had any

idea just how many hours a day she passed in their company, but as he had not chosen to open the subject she was wary of doing so herself. She could not forget the way he had cut her off the couple of times she had tried talking about Rafi, but she was sure that Rafi must have mentioned her to his big brother on at least a few occasions.

In any case, when she and Tariq were together, nothing else in the world existed. They were locked into an affair of passionate, single-minded intensity and she just felt plain and simple happy. True, if she let her mind stray in the direction of the dark cloud of future foreboding threatening in the back corner of her mind, she got scared because she was more in love with Tariq than she had ever been. But all the rest of the time, she was content to let tomorrow take care of itself.

In the dreaming mood she was in, it was a shock when the two servants clearing up the picnic debris suddenly dropped down on their knees. She glanced up and was astonished to see Tariq poised about ten feet away. He had said he wasn't on his way home but he had been teasing her, she realised. What he had not said was that he had *already* arrived.

As he took in the tableau she made with the children gathered round her, Tariq could not conceal his astonishment. He dismissed the servants from his presence with a snap of his fingers. 'Exactly when did you all become this friendly?'

Without the smallest warning, Rafi leapt off her lap and shouted something in Arabic that made Tariq freeze.

'Stop it, Rafi,' Faye urged in dismay.

Rafi flung himself back at her sobbing as if his heart were breaking.

'It would appear that you have made yourself quite indispensable,' Tariq pronounced with sardonic bite, watching the twins burst into tears in concert and clutch at Faye for security. 'Accident or design?'

And with that cutting conclusion, Tariq swung on his heel and strode off.

'What did you say, Rafi?' Faye whispered shakily.

'You're my secret mama and if he takes you away, I'm going with you!' Rafi sobbed into her shoulder, turning her face to the colour of milk.

CHAPTER NINE

FAYE found Tariq in one of the ground floor reception rooms.

'Tariq...?' she whispered apprehensively, stilling just inside the doorway.

Tariq swung round, lean, powerful face expressionless. 'Did you contrive to soothe the mass hysteria my appearance provoked?'

Faye flushed miserably. 'They're all down for a nap now. Tariq...I never dreamt that Rafi was keeping the time I've been spending with him and the twins a secret from you and certainly *not* that he's been thinking of me as his new mother.'

'I can't say I enjoyed being treated like the big bad wolf,' Tariq murmured wryly. 'Even by Basma and Hayat who usually greet me with smiles and giggles.'

'And so they would have done this afternoon if they hadn't been overtired and in the mood to be easily upset,' she assured him. 'This is all my fault.'

'That is not how I would describe the situation.' Tariq surprised her with a rueful laugh. 'I had naturally noticed the pronounced improvement in my little brother's behaviour but I had assumed it to be the result of the removal of his previous carers—'

'No, that just left him more unhappy and confused and I think that may have been why he turned to me—'

Tariq sighed. 'And then suddenly Rafi got happy and stopped his screaming tantrums and constant whinging practically overnight. To be frank, I was *so* deeply relieved by that development, I did not question the miracle. His behaviour had been a source of very real concern to me but I was hampered by the fact that he was brought up to fear me—'

'And you were always having to tell him off too...I know and I understand. But now I can see that I've been horribly thoughtless and selfish,' Faye muttered unevenly, her face taut with guilty regret. 'I've let the children become too attached to me and that wasn't fair to them.'

'It's quite amazing how well you have all bonded behind my back.' His expressive mouth quirked.

'If I've damaged your relationship with Rafi, I'm sorry.'

'No. Rafi has been much more relaxed with me since he got his hooks into his secret mama—'

'He's a very affectionate child.'

'And you're a very affectionate woman. It is just most ironic that I should have been the last to find out that you were so fond of children.'

Accident or design? he had demanded out in the gardens. But what design could she have had in befriending the children? And then her colour climbed. Did he suspect that she was angling to be considered as a wife yet again? By weaseling her sneaky way into the children's hearts and making it hard for him to end their relationship? She stiffened at that humiliating suspicion.

'Even more ironic that I would never have *dreamt* of wheeling out Rafi as he was a few weeks ago and expecting any woman to warm to him,' he commented, reaching for her curled tight hands and carefully smoothing her fingers straight to link them with his. 'In fact, most women would have run a mile at the threat of Rafi as he was then but you have great heart—'

'But not always a lot of sense...I didn't take a long-term view.'

'I don't believe you have ever taken a long-term view of anything.' Tariq stood there staring down at their linked hands as if they had become a source of deep and absorbing fascination to him. 'I, on the other hand, tend to be very decisive in most fields but most fortunately *not* when it came to divorcing you…'

'Divorcing me? When…when did you get around to it?' she muttered tightly.

Tariq breathed in very deep and then breathed out again without saying anything. She looked up at him with strained eyes, noting the line of dark colour scoring his proud cheekbones.

'Well…I actually didn't,' he finally stated curtly.

'Oh…' She was connecting with tawny eyes that could make stringing two sensible thoughts together the biggest challenge she had ever been called to meet.

'There seemed no point in telling you that three weeks ago when I still believed that I would eventually seek that divorce. At first, I thought I would be merely raising false hopes and then I thought it might distress you—'

'You actually *didn't* divorce me?' Faye was struggling a whole speech behind Tariq and a cold, clammy sensation was dampening her skin.

'You're still my wife…you have never been anything else.'

'I think I've had too much sun.' Her legs felt hollow and her tummy was churning.

Tariq urged her down onto the opulent sofa behind her. 'You've turned white.'

Word by word what he had burst upon her was sinking in, but only slowly.

'The day of the sandstorm, I agreed to a press announcement in which I claimed you as my wife. I really had very little choice. Once your presence in my life became a matter of public knowledge, I had to make a decision. Either I created a scandal that for ever soiled your reputation or I told the truth,' Tariq said, still retaining a noticeably tight hold on her now nerveless floppy fingers as he sank down beside her.

'The truth…you know, I thought you *always* told the truth,' Faye whispered, for shock was settling in on her hard.

'I have recently come to appreciate that the truth…once avoided…may be extremely hard to tell.'

Oh, how convenient, she almost said, thinking in a daze that, while her pathetic lies about her age had been held over her like the worst of sins, Tariq was now seeking to excuse himself for the same dishonesty. 'You lied to me—'

'No. I never once said that I had divorced you—'

'But you knew that I believed we were divorced—'

'Had you asked me direct, I would not have lied—'

'But you said, ''Not then'' when I questioned you in the cave,' she recalled shakily. 'How did you contrive to explain a mystery wife coming out of nowhere?'

'My family has never made our private lives a matter of public interest which is not to say that gossip, rumour and scandal do not abound,' he admitted tautly. 'However, I acknowledged that I made you my wife a year ago and it will be assumed, whether I like it or not, that I decided not to embark on our marriage while I was in mourning.'

'Should do wonders for your image with the *truly* pious.'

'That shames me.' Tariq breathed harshly. 'But it is not less than I deserve for setting in train a set of events which could only lead to disaster.'

Disaster? Of course, it was a disaster on his terms but not a disaster he would have to bear for long. Not with divorce being as easy as he had once informed her it was. All that she had not understood now became clear. 'Our marriage was being celebrated at that reception I attended in the desert…and you never uttered *one* word and neither did anyone else! How come I didn't guess?'

'My people, and that includes my relatives, would not

open a conversation with you or I unless you or I did so first. That is simply etiquette. In addition, brides do not normally exchange conversation with anyone other than their husbands. But at the outset of that day, I believed you would inevitably appreciate what was happening—'

'And, my goodness, you were angry with me, furious at the position you had put yourself in,' Faye condemned, suddenly pulling free of him and plunging upright. 'That was our wedding night but you much preferred letting me think that I was your mistress being flaunted in front of everyone!'

'To some degree that is true but common sense should have told you that I could not have behaved in such a way with any woman in Jumar *other* than my wife,' Tariq pointed out.

'Oh, I know exactly what was on your mind. You would have cut out your tongue sooner than give me the presumed satisfaction of knowing that I was your wife!' Faye whispered bitterly. 'Please take note that I am not *feeling* satisfaction.'

'Faye?' Tariq rested his hands on her shoulders and attempted to turn her back to face him.

She whirled round and shook free of him in disgust. 'What an ego you have!'

Tariq reached out and hauled her back to him. 'Stop it,' he urged. 'I have made mistakes and so have you but if you do not appreciate how much has changed between us in the last couple of weeks, I certainly do. I *want* you as my wife. I will be honoured to call you my wife—'

'Since when?' A derisive laugh was wrenched from her. She was so angry, so hurt, so bewildered, she was trembling. 'All this time I've been your wife and I was the only person who didn't know it. Once again you have made an absolute fool of me and I will never forgive you for that!'

Tariq closed both arms even tighter around her. 'Only *I* know you didn't know you were still my wife—'

'You think that makes it any better…that I can't even trust the man I've been sleeping with…that you've been playing some kind of mind games with me for your own amusement? No, I am flat out fed up with you and finished! So let go of me!'

'No, not until I have made you see reason and you are in a calmer frame of mind—'

'Calmer?' Faye swung up her hand and dealt him a ringing slap across one high cheekbone. In the aftermath as his arms fell from her and he stepped back, she was as shaken as he was. Shocked by her own loss of control and that desire to physically attack a male who was protected by the laws of Jumar from such an offence.

In electric silence, he stared at her with fathomless tawny eyes.

'So now you can have me thrown into a prison cell and be finally rid of me *for ever*!' Faye launched at him in stricken conclusion before racing out of the room.

She didn't even know where she was running for there was no place far enough where she could hide from the enormous pain he had inflicted. Blinded by tears, conscious he was following her and wanting desperately to be alone, she headed for the nearest staircase: a spiral of stone steps generally used only by the servants.

'Faye!' Tariq called from somewhere close behind her.

She half turned, forgetting she was on a spiral staircase, and suddenly one of her feet was trying to find a resting place in mid-air. With a strangled cry of fear, she tried to right her mistake but it was too late for she was already falling. Her head crashed against the wall. She felt the momentary burst of pain but it was soon swallowed up in the deep, suffocating darkness that enclosed her.

* * *

'Just a stupid bump on the head, Rafi…I was really silly to run on those steps.' Faye patted his small hand where it gripped her nightdress until she gradually felt him relax beneath her soothing. 'I'm fine and glad to be out of hospital.'

'Can I stay?'

'Faye needs to rest for a while,' Tariq murmured, bending down to scoop his little brother up into his arms. 'You will see her later…that I promise.'

Faye would not look at Tariq. Having been knocked unconscious by her fall the day before, she had started coming round in the helicopter that had taken her to hospital in Jumar City. There she had been examined by three consultants in succession and had realised by Tariq's explanation that he had broken her fall and saved her from a more serious injury.

She had not looked at him when she had had to spend the whole of the previous night under observation by both the medical staff *and* Tariq. She had not even looked at him when he had reached for her hand at some stage of that endless night and begged her for her forgiveness. In fact, not looking at Tariq and just pretending with silence that he did not exist had become a rule set in stone for her survival.

As the door closed on Rafi's reluctant exit, Tariq released his breath audibly. 'Do you want me to leave?'

She squeezed her eyes tight shut and gave a jerky nod. The door opened with a quiet click and closed again. She couldn't cry. She lay staring up at the ceiling. What did she have left to say to him? What could he have left to say to her? All that time she had been his wife but he had ignored that reality for the simple reason that he had had *no* intention of keeping her as his wife. It felt even worse for her to think that, in one sense, he had been right to do that. For what would have been the point of her knowing that she was still married to him when the divorce was still to be got through? From her point of view, it just would have meant going through the same agonies twice over.

Why on earth had he started talking nonsense about wanting her to remain his wife? That had seemed the unkindest cut of all, that he should feel *so* guilty he decided he ought to make that offer. Well, you can forget that option, Tariq ibn Zachir, she thought painfully. There was only one way out of their current predicament: divorce. No more shilly-shallying! Why the heck had he let them stay married throughout the previous year? A great emptiness spread like a dam inside her and her headache got worse but at some stage she still drifted to sleep.

When she wakened a couple of hours later, her headache had receded and she examined the blue-black bruise on her right temple. Fortunately her hair concealed the worst of it. After a bath and a late light lunch, she rifled her wardrobe for something to wear.

Her wardrobe was now gigantic: it filled an entire room. Only a week earlier, Tariq had shipped in dozens of designer outfits from abroad from which she had made selections. Dazzling, fabulous clothing such as she had only previously seen in magazines. Initially she had been hugely embarrassed by his generosity but the terrible temptation of seeing herself in such exquisite garments had overcome her finer principles. Tariq was accustomed to fashionable women who wore haute couture. What woman who loved him would have chosen to keep on appearing in the same frugal and plain clothing contained in her single small suitcase?

Vanity and the desire for him to admire her had triumphed over conscience. Reddening at that awareness, Faye would have put on her own clothes had she still had them but unfortunately she had dumped the lot. The not-thinking-of-tomorrow rule she had observed in recent weeks had made her reckless. She selected an elegant skirt suit in a rich shade of old gold. When she told Tariq that she wanted a divorce, she wanted to look good—she wanted him to feel he was losing out even if it *was* only on a convenient bed partner.

Having eased on tights beneath the sapphire anklet and put on toning high heels, Faye went downstairs, only to discover that Tariq was not at home. He was at his office in the Haja. Discovering that only made her all the more determined to confront him and discuss what had to be discussed. After an exasperating long wait at her request for transport, a limo which flew two small Jumarian flags on the bonnet finally drew up.

She was taken aback when two police outriders on motorbikes took up position in front of the limo outside the palace gates, even more uneasy when she glanced out of the rear window and saw another two cars filtering out behind them. When the cavalcade she had naively not foreseen her outing might require reached the city, red stop lights were totally ignored and traffic was held up for their benefit on every approach road. For the first time, it began to truly dawn on Faye that being married to Tariq was not quite like being married to anyone else and that even the most minor thing she might choose to do could have consequences.

Latif awaited her at the side entrance of the giant building. He was full of concern about her fall, amazed she was already up and about, and assured her that every spiral staircase in the Muraaba was now to be renovated and handrails installed for greater safety.

As Faye was shown into Tariq's office, her heart began beating very fast. Sheathed in a light grey suit, immaculate as always, he was by the window, fabulous bone structure taut, stunning dark golden eyes slamming straight into hers in a look as compelling as his touch. 'I was astonished to hear you were on your way here. You're very pale. Sit down,' he urged. 'The doctors said you should take it easy for a few days.'

'I'd prefer to stand.' Meeting the sincere concern in his gaze, feeling the instant leap of her senses to the powerful magneticism of his presence, Faye reacted in self-defence, seeking hostility rather than pleasantries. 'Just as you let me stand sweltering out in that courtyard on my first visit here a few weeks back.'

'You should know me better. My lack of courtesy was not deliberate but an oversight. I too was under strain at that interview.'

She flushed at that hint of reproach. 'It didn't show—'

'It was quite a shock for me that day to discover that my wife did not appear to have the foggiest clue that she *was* my wife,' Tariq extended with gentle irony.

'Well, all that stuff doesn't matter now and I don't know why I mentioned boiling alive in that stupid courtyard—'

Tariq drew closer with fluid grace. 'Don't you? I have a good idea of what you're thinking and feeling right now, *aziz*. Do you imagine I am not aware that you are drawing up a great long list of my every past and present sin? So that you can impose them as a barrier between us?'

Disconcerted, Faye breathed, 'I—'

'Once I went through the same process with you. Even *without* seeing you, I was able to stockpile more sins at your door. You did not even write me a letter of condolence when my father died,' Tariq pointed out. 'We were estranged but you were my wife and I was never not aware of that. I thought you were heartless—'

'I…I did *think* of writing,' muttered Faye in deep discomfiture, having turned pale as a ghost at that reference to an omission which now seemed inexcusable. 'But I didn't know what to say so…so in the end I didn't bother.'

'You didn't appreciate that you were still my wife but I

didn't know that,' Tariq reminded her. 'When that plane went down six months later and I lost my cousin, who was my closest friend from childhood...his wife and his parents, my aunt and uncle, who were all like a second family to me...what did you think I thought then of you when I *still* heard nothing?'

Feeling the tables had been turned on her with a vengeance, Faye squirmed and could no longer look at him direct, for her eyes were prickling with tears of sympathy. 'I didn't hear about the crash—'

'Yes, I am aware of that now and I am not trying to make you feel bad...'

Faye hung her head, wondering what he might achieve if he really *tried*, for she was feeling dreadful.

'I only want to illustrate how anger and hurt pride build on mistakes and misunderstandings. Don't do that to us now when we had already found our way through those barriers,' Tariq spelt out levelly.

Her tender pride took fire and she flung her head high, violet-blue eyes sparkling with angry resentment. 'Already? Where was I when this healing miracle was taking place?'

'Faye...if you love me, there *are* no true barriers and there is nothing that with time cannot be overcome.'

Rage was clawing at Faye. She had come to stage a confrontation with dignity. She had felt strong, committed to her purpose. But from the minute she had walked into his office, Tariq had been running verbal rings round her and making her cringe like an awkward schoolgirl in the presence of an adult. She could not bear to be reminded that she had gone on at such length about having been *crazy* about him only a year earlier.

'But the point is...I don't love you,' she snapped between gritted teeth. 'I discovered the joys of sex with you...that's all!'

Tariq studied her with unreadable cool but she could not

help noticing that he had lost colour at that retaliation. 'It's good to know that I excelled somewhere.'

'I came here to discuss us getting a divorce,' Faye announced.

'You could not wait an hour for me to come home?'

Her colour heightened. 'Tariq—'

'I have no intention of continuing this conversation in my office,' he murmured levelly. 'Now go home.'

At that level command, Faye sucked in such a deep and charged breath she thought her lungs might burst.

Tariq stepped past her and cast wide the door. Her trembling hands closed into furious fists. *'I—'*

'Her Royal Highness wishes to travel home before the rush hour begins, Latif.'

Faye was so dumbfounded to hear herself being referred to as 'Her Royal Highness' that she almost collided with Latif in the corridor.

The older man escorted her to a stone bench and hovered.

'Am I a princess?' The shaken enquiry just erupted from her and she went pink.

'From this moment on,' Latif informed her in a tone of great approval. 'The gift of that title is in the power of Prince Tariq alone. You are only the second princess in the history of our royal family—'

'Really?' she whispered dazedly.

Latif was now in full flood on a subject evidently close to his heart. 'Prince Tariq's lady mother first enjoyed the distinction but only on the birth of her son. However, I feel it is most appropriate that, in these more forward-thinking times, His Royal Highness should honour you early within your marriage.'

'Honour me...' Faye echoed weakly.

'It may be of interest to you to learn that you may now sit in His Royal Highness's presence in public and walk by his side as his equal without it being said that you are showing disrespect.' As Faye slowly raised her head, eyes very wide, Latif straightened his shoulders with immense satisfaction. 'Yes, we will be setting a precedent and an example in this part of the world.'

CHAPTER TEN

TARIQ did not actually return to the Muraaba until eight that evening. Having dined with the children and seen them off to bed through the usual baths, high jinks and bedside stories, Faye believed she had attained a much calmer frame of mind.

Tariq glanced into their sitting room where she was pacing the floor and flashed her a warm, appreciative smile as if everything was well between them. 'I'm going for a shower…I'll be with you soon.'

Her teeth gritted.

His brilliant golden eyes rested on her frozen face. 'You could always join me.'

Faye flew out of her seat and took the bait. 'How *dare* you suggest that?'

'Just testing the water,' Tariq murmured smooth as glass. 'No pun intended.'

She contained herself for all of ten minutes and then she headed into their bedroom. The bathroom door stood wide. Tariq was in the shower. She paced again, but the instant she heard the water switching off she lodged herself in the doorway.

'Why didn't you divorce me a year ago?' she demanded.

Tariq stepped from the shower, pushing his hair back from his brow, all bronzed masculinity and easy grace. 'Obviously because I did not want to break that final link, regardless of how tenuous that link might have appeared. And I am very much afraid that, on the subject of divorce, I have no good news to share.'

'And what's that supposed to mean?' Watching him

towel himself dry, Faye could feel familiar warmth stirring in her pelvis and she averted her eyes hurriedly.

'Some time ago, certain discreet enquiries cast that question open in a most revealing debate between the high court judges and, this evening, I learned much that I did not know. No ancestor of mine has ever applied for a divorce. There is therefore no facility for the ruler of Jumar to divorce…no case law, *no nothing*,' Tariq stated with flat emphasis.

Faye's lips parted company. 'But what about all that turning round three times and saying you divorce me stuff?'

'That must be done in a court before a high court judge and may obtain a divorce for any one of my subjects. But *not* for me. At the same time I threw those angry and foolish words at you on our wedding day, I was not aware of that. Indeed…I was so angry, I hardly knew what I was saying to you,' Tariq admitted between compressed lips.

'But you've *got* to be able to get a divorce—'

'Presumably the law would eventually work out how to allow me to divorce when I stand outside the laws of our country *but*…' Tariq rested shimmering golden eyes on her '…I don't want a divorce.'

Faye trembled. 'Yes, you do…well, you *did* when those discreet enquiries were casting open questions to some legal debate between judges!'

'No, it was my father who had those enquiries made some months before his death—'

'Your…*father*?'

'I had no idea he was considering divorcing Rafi's mother but, evidently, he was. It was Latif who enlightened me on that news this evening.' The towel draped round his lean hips, Tariq crossed the floor and rested his hands on her shoulders to stop her from spinning away out of reach. 'I will say again. I don't want a divorce…do you think you could *listen*?'

'Well, we can't stay together, so obviously I just go home and…the legal stuff can be sorted out some time later, some time never! I really don't care how or when.'

'Faye…' Tariq breathed tautly. 'Until yesterday, you were happy. There is no reason why that happiness should not be recaptured—'

'Maybe you'd like me to go on acting like your mistress!'

'Considering that believing yourself to *be* my mistress appeared to give you quite a thrill on several recent occasions, only you can answer that question.'

Her cheeks flamed at that rejoinder for there was truth in it. Pulling away, she stalked back into the bedroom.

'I care about you and I don't want to lose you but my patience is running out—'

'Just like my patience did when you were content to misjudge me for the supposed blackmail that caused all the trouble between us in the first place!'

'But I stopped judging you,' Tariq shot back at her with icy force. 'You said you wanted more than anything else in the world to be my wife because you *loved* me and, in the space of hours, I have forgiven everything and let go of every piece of my bitterness. Do you think I have no heart? Do you think I did not *feel* your sincerity?'

Faye did not want to be reminded of the more embarrassing things she had uttered in the grip of her overtaxed emotions. 'You forgave me for the blackmail…'

'As I was planning to marry you in any case before your stepfather intervened,' Tariq delivered in a velvety smooth tone, 'It was not a major problem.'

And Faye picked up on that admission and reeled in shock inwardly as he no doubt intended her to reel. Fighting Tariq was a constant debilitating struggle, she recognised in furious frustration. He was fast on his feet and kept on throwing the unexpected back at her. But Tariq had been planning to marry her even *before* Percy tried to blackmail him? Never in her life had Faye been so desperate to snatch at the carrot offered to her as a distraction. But she would not allow herself to snatch.

'But you still didn't trust my word.' She flung that promising branch on the fire with satisfaction. 'I have every right to leave you—'

'What is right? Strive to recall Rafi, whose love you have also won and who is a great deal less able than I am to cope with another major loss in his life!' Tariq ground out fiercely. 'Before you pack, you go and you tell him why you are leaving him after teaching him to love you for I will have no part of that dialogue!'

And at the exact same moment as he strode off in evident disgust with her into the room he used as a dressing room, the anger and the ferocious need to hit back every way she could fell away from Faye. She slumped back against the foot of the bed, her legs suddenly shaking beneath her.

As if she were someone waking from a dream, the previous twenty-four hours replayed within her memory and she squirmed. She recalled ignoring him all through the night while he'd sat by her bed in the private hospital room. She had acted like a huffy, ill-mannered child but he had not uttered a word of reproof. He had behaved as though her accident had been his fault. He had bowed that proud head and begged her to forgive him. And she had lain there in that bed, relishing her power like a real shrew and stoking up her resentments to new heights. Confronting him at the Haja had been even less forgivable.

She loved him. But it was as if her love had got lost for twenty-four hours, yet it was her pride Tariq had hurt more than anything else. She was his wife when all was said and done. A wife by default, though. He had not known that divorce might be a real challenge to achieve and he no longer wanted a divorce. Indeed, according to him he had *never* wanted a divorce enough to even find out how to go about getting one, even when he had believed she was heartless and mercenary. But then he also had the needs of three children to consider, children whom she had encouraged to care about her, children she had been threatening to walk out on.

'Tariq…?' she muttered unevenly.

'What?' he demanded, obviously thinking she was starting on round three and ready for her now with gloves off.

'Nothing…'

'Surely you have not run out of steam yet?' he growled.

'Pretty much. I would never hurt Rafi or Basma or Hayat,' Faye told him very quietly.

'If you are set on leaving, you should go now for, the longer you stay, the harder it will be on the children.' Tariq expelled his breath in a hiss. 'I have nothing more to say. I have said it all.'

The silence weighted Faye down with its electrifying tension. A current of fear new to her experience was infiltrating her. 'I got carried away,' she said, dry-mouthed. 'I'm sorry.'

Tariq said nothing. She watched him zip up faded denim jeans that accentuated his lithe muscular physique and pull on a dark green shirt, more casual clothing that she had ever seen him wear. He was *not* watching her any more. Indeed, he might have been on his own. All of a sudden it was as if she had become invisible. His bold profile grim, he was not ignoring her as she had ignored him; he simply seemed buried in his own thoughts.

'I'm sorry for…everything.' At that moment everything seemed to encompass so much Faye did not know where to begin.

'I'm sorry…you're sorry…the children will be sorry too.' Darkly handsome features taut and spectacular eyes cloaked, Tariq headed straight for the bedroom door.

Wide shoulders straight, he walked tall. He had magnificent carriage, she reflected numbly, and he was walking *out* on her without another word. But then she had been screaming at him like a banshee wailer. Yet he had kept his temper and explained all that he could with irreproachable honesty. Only it hadn't got him anywhere and now he appeared to have decided that her leaving was possibly for the best in the long run.

'Tariq…?' Her voice emerged all squeaky.

'I wish I could say something profound…' his lean brown hand clenched on the door knob '…but our whole relationship has been a black comedy of errors and I am out of words. *Inshallah.*'

Her throat was convulsing. Her mind was an appalling blank. She could only wish she had run out of words sooner.

He opened the door and then paused. 'What will I do with the mare?'

'What mare?'

He turned back with a frown. 'It was to be a surprise…Delilah, your mare that you had to sell last year. I had her traced and purchased from the riding school but she is in transit and, until you have stables again… Don't worry, I will deal with it.'

Faye was so shaken by that unexpected revelation and conclusion, she stood there with a dropped jaw, and by the time she unfroze and decided to chase after him he was gone. Really *gone*, for absolutely nobody seemed to have the slightest idea *where* he had gone, which dismayed her.

She phoned Latif and, after a lot of circling round the subject but somehow never actually answering her anxious questions, Latif said he would call at the Muraaba.

'There is no need for concern. Prince Tariq is quite safe,' he informed her on his arrival.

'I only want to know where he is…that's all.'

Latif sighed. 'His Royal Highness has places where he goes when he wishes to be alone. It is a great luxury for him to be alone. He might be on the beach. He might be in the desert. He might be driving himself around the city, perhaps even walking down a street somewhere as if he is an ordinary person.'

'How can he be safe if you don't even know where he is? It *can't* be safe for him to do that!'

Latif lowered his wise eyes to the exquisite Aubusson rug in silence.

'He's not alone at all…*ever*, is he?' Faye realised with initial relief and then a surge of the most powerful and guilty sympathy for Tariq. 'You still have him under security surveillance.'

'There is no reason for concern.' Latif lifted his head again. 'We understand that Prince Tariq carries huge responsibilities and endures many exasperating restrictions without complaint. Yet he is still a young man. He has never known the freedom that his father enjoyed and, sadly, he never will for the world has changed too much. But if you ask to know his whereabouts, it is, of course, my duty to tell you, Your Royal Highness.'

Faye was very pale by the end of that speech. 'No, that's all right, I no longer wish to know and, as far as I'm concerned, we never had this conversation.'

With a strained smile, Faye walked with Latif to the very doors of the palace, a courtesy which he definitely deserved for she could see she had put him in a very awkward position, not to mention dragging him out late at night.

'Last year…it was a period of almost intolerable strain,' the older man mused with his usual tact, 'but over the past weeks, the strain seemed absent.'

'It will be absent again,' Faye promised tightly.

She went to bed and lay awake. She was grateful to Latif for his advice. He had not embarrassed her but he had added a whole new and unsettling dimension to her understanding of the male she had married. Tariq only took time out when he was really at the end of his tether. Tears burned in her eyes as she remembered him admitting that he had had to acknowledge her as being his wife, just as he had once felt forced to marry her. *A black comedy of errors?* But hadn't he also said that he had been thinking of marrying her even before everything had gone wrong? So, a year ago, he had loved her and wanted her, and two days ago he had still been making mad, passionate love to her. She was not going to give up on him.

Tariq moved like a silent predator through the bedroom when he came home in the early hours. She lay still as a stone, hardly breathing. He went for a shower and she wondered if he had even noticed her presence in the bed. The curtains were not drawn and moonlight filtered over his lean bronzed length as he approached the bed and she stole a glance.

'When you're asleep, you breathe more heavily,' Tariq imparted as he slid between the sheets. 'I knew you were awake the instant I entered the room.'

'Oh…'

His hand brushed her fingertips. It might well have been accidental for he could simply have been stretching. But Faye was in no mood for subtlety and she practically threw herself across the space that separated them into his arms. Without hesitation he curved her to him.

She listened to the solid thump of his heart and slowly dared to breathe again. 'I don't need any more words.'

'We might say the wrong ones.' His strong arms tightened round her and it was more than enough. 'But curiosity is killing me. What did Latif tell you?'

She tensed. 'You *know* he was here?'

Tariq uttered a husky laugh. 'I have my own ways and means.'

'I was worried about you…stupid, really.'

'Caring,' Tariq contradicted, driving the tension back out of her again with his pronounced calm. 'I would have liked to go to the beach for a swim. But then they have to get the divers out and I am always worried that one of them will have an accident in the dark through trying so very hard not to be seen.'

'So you know you've got company?'

'I've got so much company I sometimes feel like throwing a party but it is a matter of great pride to my surveillance teams to believe they are invisible to me.'

'Only not much fun for you,' she whispered ruefully.

'But they enjoy the challenge so much.' Brushing her tumbled hair back from her cheekbones, he stared down at her, his eyes glittering like jet in the moonlight. 'I drove around half the night thinking—'

'Don't think,' she urged.

'You are staying.' It was not a question but a declaration.

'Yes.'

'A generous man would give you a choice but I can't pretend a generosity I do not feel.'

'That's OK…'

He rested back and eased her over him, shaping his hands to the feminine swell of her hips, acquainting her with the urgency of his arousal. She quivered, answering heat racing through her as if he had switched on an electric current.

'It would be cruel to sentence me to any more cold showers.'

'Agreed.'

'All of a sudden you are very amenable. But then there is true equality in the joys of sex,' Tariq commented softly.

But as her head lifted and her lips parted in dismay, he took her mouth in a hungry, seeking kiss that was quite irresistible.

CHAPTER ELEVEN

THREE days later, Faye attended her first public engagement with Tariq. A new centre for children with learning disabilities had been built and Tariq had been invited to preside over the official opening.

'But no one will be expecting me,' Faye had pointed out nervously.

'Since our marriage was announced, you have been included in all my invitations. My schedule is arranged months ahead but the organisers of every event have contacted the palace to declare that your presence would be most welcome. Indeed, extra secretarial help has had to be brought in,' Tariq revealed with some amusement.

Faye was disconcerted by that information.

'Everyone will be hoping you will make an appearance. There is great curiosity about you. However, if you prefer to keep a low profile, that is not a problem either.'

'No?'

'Your predecessor, Rafi's mother, made no public appearances. She went veiled and demanded the strictest seclusion—'

Faye grimaced. 'I'm not going to go that far—'

His vibrant smile tipped her heart over. 'She was very unpopular. Our women felt threatened by the old ways suddenly reappearing in the heart of their ruling family. In any case, I wish to show you off, not hide you away.'

In receipt of those quiet supportive words, Faye glowed and overcame her apprehension. In truth, her nerves vanished once she found that it was merely a matter of talking to people, chatting to the children present and doing a lot of smiling when the language barrier made itself felt. Photographs were taken but only after Tariq had given his permission. Only when refreshments were being served did Faye recognise Tariq's cousin, Majida, who had caused her such embarrassment at the reception held in the desert.

Her beautiful face arranged in a cloying smile, her shapely figure displayed in a cerise-pink brocade suit, Majida approached Faye while Tariq was chatting with another man several feet away.

Now very conscious that she had to lead the conversation, Faye said with a determined smile, 'How are you? I didn't see you earlier but obviously you must be involved with the learning centre.'

'I organised the fund-raising. I am well known in Jumar for my charitable endeavours.' Her dark eyes hard as nails, Majida threw her head high and, as the brunette was much taller, Faye had to resist an urge to stretch her own neck. 'May I congratulate you on your wonderfully deft touch with small children, Your Royal Highness?'

Suspecting sarcasm, Faye tensed. 'Thank you.'

'But then with three children to raise already and a pressing need for one of his own, Prince Tariq knew exactly what nursery qualities to seek in his wife,' Majida murmured sweetly. 'Rather you than me.'

As Majida dipped her head and went into instant retreat, Faye was left waxen pale. The brunette's barbs had hit a tender target. Nursery qualities? In the space of ten seconds, Faye's buoyant inner happiness just imploded into a tight little knot of hurt and pain.

For, of course, there was no arguing with what Tariq's venomous cousin had said. How might Tariq have felt about their marriage had she *not* been a success with Rafi, Basma and Hayat? Tariq had been very much taken aback by that development but had soon decided to be pleased instead. He was very anxious to do right by the children.

He took his obligations seriously and might well put their needs ahead of more personal inclinations.

In addition, Tariq might have a pressing need for a child of his own to ensure the succession, but he protected Faye from pregnancy with scrupulous care. Suddenly, even though they had only been together a few weeks, that reality made her feel even more insecure. Perhaps he didn't trust her enough yet, she decided painfully. Naturally her stridently stated apparent willingness to *leave* the children would leave its mark on his opinion of her. She had been dreadfully immature, throwing angry threats more for effect than anything else. But how was he to know that when she had not yet admitted that lowering truth? Perhaps he wanted to be sure that their marriage was going to last before discussing the matter of them having a child together.

Across the room, Faye's gaze was drawn by Tariq's proud dark head bent down to Majida's. She stiffened, uneasy at seeing him in the other woman's company. What clever remarks aimed at undermining Faye might the brunette plant without Tariq even realising it? Weren't men supposed to be vulnerable to such manipulation? By the time she got the chance to look in the same direction again, all she caught was a brief glimpse of Majida slipping out the door, her profile oddly pinched and pale.

In the limo on the drive back to the Muraaba, Tariq shook her by carrying her hand to his lips and kissing her fingers in a gesture that was both teasing and sincere. 'You were wonderful. I was very proud of you.'

She smiled, some of her tension ebbing. 'As long as people don't look to me to try and follow in your mother's footsteps. Then I'd be sure to be a disappointment.'

'Is that what made you so apprehensive?' At her reluctant nod of confirmation, Tariq released a rueful laugh. 'My mother was a very fine woman, but no saint. She was too aggressive in her support of the causes she took up and quite often offended people with her frank speech. It was her natural warmth which won her forgiveness…and you have that same special quality without the desire to change the whole world overnight.'

Touched by his honesty on her behalf and by that compliment, Faye felt her spirits rise again.

'My cousin, Majida, won't be bothering you again,' Tariq imparted with awesome casualness. 'I was very annoyed when I heard her speak to you in the manner that she did—'

Faye reddened. 'You *heard*?'

'I was listening and not by accident. I was already well aware that it could only have been Majida who insulted you on our wedding night.' His gaze gleamed with wry amusement at her look of surprise. 'I know my relatives through and through. Only Majida was likely to be unhappy with me for producing a young and beautiful wife, for the rest of my family were keen to see me married.'

'I expect she thought she would have been a better candidate.' Faye sighed.

'Marriages between first cousins are frequent in Arab countries but it was a practice always frowned on within my own family circle.'

Faye stiffened. 'So even if you had wanted to marry her, you couldn't have done—'

'No, I always had freedom of choice in that field. Majida has a great opinion of herself and she was jealous. But from now on she will be careful to treat you with proper respect.'

'You really didn't need to interfere—'

'Oh, yes, I did. When I saw you standing there like a little girl with big hurt eyes refusing to fight your own corner, I thought to myself…isn't that *just* like a woman?'

'Meaning?' Faye was stung on the raw by that description.

'You see what I mean? You're ready to shout at me

already! You have tremendous spirit yet you didn't put Majida in her place.'

Faye bristled. 'I was *trying* to be dignified.'

Tariq curved a long arm round her and pulled her close. 'I know but I was outraged to see you swallow that speech of hers. At the very least, you should have snubbed her and walked away, although I very much doubt that you will meet with such behaviour ever again. I apologise for my cousin's rudeness.'

'Not your problem,' Relaxing, Faye curved round him, tucking her head under his chin, drinking in the warm, familiar scent of him with pleasure. He might not love her but he definitely did care about her. She wondered what he had said to Majida, though, and noticed that he did not offer that information.

The car phoned buzzed. With an impatient sigh, Tariq reached for it. Faye was immediately aware of the tension that flared through his big, powerful frame and anxiety made her sit up straight.

'What's happened?' she prompted when he had set the phone down again. 'It's nothing to do with the children, is it?'

'No,' he reassured her instantly. 'But gather your inner strength and hold tight to your dignity for you will need it. It seems that this must be the chosen day for our mutual families to embarrass us.'

'Sorry, I—'

'Your stepfather awaits us at the Muraaba and Latif, who is at home with the crowned heads of Europe, sounds like he is very much in need of rescue,' Tariq told her gently.

'Percy is here in Jumar...*again*?' Faye gasped in dismay.

'What shall I do with him?' Tariq asked lazily. 'Shall I be corrupt and have him thrown into a prison cell on some trumped-up charge such as taking up too much space on the pavement? It is only what he expects of a primitive people such as he believes us to be. It seems a real shame to disappoint him.'

Faye was not soothed by his dark humour for the mere threat of Tariq being forced to have any dealings whatsoever with Percy Smythe affronted her. 'You don't need to worry. I'll get rid of him—'

'I am not worried. I am even looking forward to the encounter.' Tariq dealt her incredulous face a mocking smile. 'No, I am not planning to kill him with my bare hands. Unlike Majida, who is not a laughing matter, Percy can be richly entertaining in his own peculiar way.'

Faye was thinking that only Percy would have the neck to enter the home of a man he had once tried to blackmail. 'But what on earth does he want?'

'Perhaps your loyal and caring brother has with immense effort recalled the existence of his kid sister and has finally noted that she has gone missing.'

'That's not very kind, Tariq—'

'I don't enjoy hearing you always ask if there have been any letters or phone calls for you,' he countered. 'Your family do not deserve you.'

Faye was discomfited by the way Tariq noticed everything even if he might not choose to comment on it at the time. It had worried her that she had not heard a word from Adrian. Assuming that Adrian and his family were staying with Percy, she had phoned her stepfather's home on several occasions but, in spite of leaving messages on the answering machine, she had not been contacted. Her letter had not brought a response either.

'Adrian's never been great at keeping in touch. Men aren't,' she said defensively.

'But he owes his freedom to you—'

'Adrian doesn't know about the bargain you and I made—'

'Even the dimmest of men must have made an association by now between his own miraculous release from prison and his sister's vanishing act.'

'I'll see Percy on my own!' Outside the Muraaba, Faye tried to dive out of the limo ahead of Tariq. 'But I can't think why Latif should've brought him here to our home.'

'Only think of Percy let loose in the Haja loudly giving forth on his views of Jumar,' Tariq suggested lethally. 'He could cause a riot.'

Faye flushed and Tariq took advantage of her chagrin to close his hand over hers and walk her indoors. Latif awaited them in the entrance hall and, with a polite word of greeting and apology to Faye, turned to address Tariq in a low-pitched flood of explanatory Arabic.

An unexpected smile skimming his darkly handsome features, Tariq turned back to Faye. 'Latif tells me that Percy has come into a large amount of money.'

'Where from?'

'The British lottery had bestowed its largesse on a most undeserving man.'

Faye was shaken but she did not agree with Tariq. Percy *with* money was surely less dangerous than Percy *without* money. Her fear that her stepfather now knew that she and Tariq were husband and wife and had arrived to ask for a loan receded.

When they entered the grand drawing room, Percy was holding a very fine Minton vase upside down to peer at its base. He set it down again, quite untouched by embarrassment. 'I suppose I'm looking at the rich rewards of four hundred years of looting and plunder. No wonder your lot were always raiding each other,' Percy commented enviously.

Faye just wanted to sink through the floor at that opening speech.

'Welcome to the Muraaba, Percy,' Tariq drawled with a slow smile. 'You are quite right. My ancestors were ruthless to the extreme. They slaughtered their way to supremacy.'

Percy gave him an appreciative appraisal. 'I knew you wouldn't hold a grudge, Tariq. You're a businessman just like myself.' His small eyes flicked in his stepdaughter's direction. 'You're looking a treat, Faye. But run along, there's a good girl. I've got some private business to discuss with His Royal Highness.'

Faye folded her arms. 'I'm not going anywhere.'

Percy rolled his eyes. 'Before the day's out, you might be surprised.'

Ignoring that forecast, Faye asked, 'How is Adrian and why haven't I heard from him?'

'I sent him and Lizzie off to Spain for a fortnight with the kiddies. He still hasn't a clue you're out here. Well, I'll not beat about the bush,' her stepfather announced with the aspect of a man about to make a weighty announcement and pausing for effect. 'I'm here to fetch Faye home, Tariq.'

'I beg your pardon?' Faye whispered shakily.

Without further ado, Percy slapped down a cheque on the table beside him. 'I'm sure old Latif has brought you up to speed on my good luck in the lottery. So there you are, everything that's owed to you, including accrued interest.'

Tariq elevated a level dark brow. 'You are here to repay me for the settlement of Adrian's debts?'

'As well as the five hundred grand you shelled out to keep Faye quiet last year after that clever stunt you pulled in your London embassy.' Percy gave him an outrageous wink.

Faye could feel the cringe factor growing by the second.

'You refer, I believe, to our wedding,' Tariq said quietly.

'Whatever you want to call it, but I'll tell you one thing—I couldn't have done better myself! It's not often anyone puts one over on me but I have to confess you did all right.'

'You tried to blackmail me,' Tariq reminded the older man.

'No, I didn't try to do that, now be fair,' Percy urged with unblemished good humour. 'I only took you to one side and asked you how it would look if it got out into the newspapers that a man in your privileged position had been carrying on with a kid, Faye's age!'

'I was nineteen,' Faye gritted in disgust.

Blithely ignoring her, Percy continued, 'It was my job to look out for Faye and you can't say it wasn't.'

'You do have a point.' Faye was stunned to hear Tariq concede.

Percy beamed. 'I don't mind admitting I was gobsmacked when I lifted the phone extension and heard her offering you dinner with bed thrown in. To look at her, you'd think butter wouldn't melt in her mouth and there she was talking like a *right* little raver—'

'I appreciate your frankness,' Tariq slotted in at speed.

Face red as fire, Faye was staring into the middle distance, mortification looming so large that it did not immediately occur to her that Percy had just carelessly confirmed her own version of events that awful night a year back. But then what did he have to lose by lying now? And what on earth did he mean by slapping down a cheque and saying he was here to fetch her home like an old umbrella that had been left behind?

'I mean, I *knew* you were leading her down the old garden path—'

'How very astute,' Tariq remarked.

'You think so? It was dead simple as I saw it. In the long run, I'd be doing Faye a favour if I saw you off—'

'And you certainly achieved that,' Faye enunciated with

pronounced care, the old bitterness clawing at her for the first time in weeks.

'By the way, I invested that five hundred grand for Faye in a *family* business. So if Faye has been suggesting I ripped her off, it's just sour grapes,' Percy contended with a decided touch of aggression. 'Right, Faye…I'm sure His Royal Highness here is a busy man…isn't it time you were getting your stuff together?'

'Faye is not a commodity you may buy back,' Tariq murmured icily.

'Why would you even *want* to take me home? You don't give two hoots what happens to me,' Faye contended tightly.

'I wouldn't leave my worst enemy in this neck of the woods!' Percy declared in full self-righteous mode. 'I got robbed of my bottles of whisky just coming through the airport!'

'Our customs officials are not thieves. Visitors are not allowed to bring alcohol into Jumar but it is available in most hotels,' Tariq said drily.

'Look, Faye…I may not always have been a great stepfather,' Percy conceded with growing impatience. 'But, let's face it, you never liked me much either and there's no point you hanging on here hoping you're going to hook a wedding ring—'

'None whatsoever,' Tariq interposed in a smooth agreement that sent Faye's startled eyes flying to him in bemusement. 'My great-grandfather gave his favourite concubine a sapphire anklet which has been worn by the wife of almost every ruling prince since then in place of a ring.'

'You see what I mean?' Percy rolled his eyes in speaking appeal at Faye. 'There's nothing normal about that, is there?'

Faye tilted her head over to one side and stared down at the beautiful anklet with very wide eyes. Knowing that

Tariq found the very sight of it adorning her slim ankle incredibly sexy, she had become rather attached to the anklet once he had shown her how to undo it.

'What's that on your leg?' Percy suddenly demanded of his stepdaughter.

'Faye is my wife,' Tariq breathed wearily.

'Bloody hell...how did you manage that, Faye?' Percy studied her with beady eyes practically out on stalks.

'We've been married for over a year,' Tariq said.

'You mean—?'

'Our wedding was perfectly legal,' Faye informed her stepfather thinly.

'Well, fancy that...' In an apparent daze Percy gaped at Tariq, thunderstruck by their revelation. 'And there I was thinking you were a real sharp operator! You could have had her for nothing but you actually went and *married* her?'

Faye saw Tariq stiffen with outrage but as he took a sudden threatening step forward she grabbed the hand he had curled into a clenched fist. But Percy had already taken fright at what he had seen in Tariq's lean, strong face and he went into retreat so fast he went backwards into the table and hit the floor with a tremendous crash. Soaked by the vase of flowers he had sent flying, he lay there like a felled log, before sitting up with a groan.

'If you value your own safety, you will not attempt to enter Jumar again,' Tariq delivered stonily.

'Goodbye, Percy,' Faye said without regret.

Tariq led her back out to the hall. 'Clean out the drawing room, Latif. Have him conveyed straight to the airport and escorted onto his flight.'

'I wanted to hit him,' Tariq growled, curving a protective arm round her taut shoulders as they went upstairs together. 'My one chance and you interfered. Why?'

'He said one thing that made me feel bad. He said I never

liked him either.' Faye sighed that reminder. 'He was right and that's probably why he never took to me.'

'Even at five years old, you were a lady with good taste. He is a very crude man.'

'Never mind, he won't be back. I wonder if I will ever see Adrian again—'

'Of course you will. If necessary, I will extract your brother and his family from your stepfather's clutches,' Tariq told her soothingly.

'Percy is much more embarrassing than Majida,' she groaned.

'He asked Latif what the going rate was for a woman in Jumar,' Tariq said not quite steadily.

'He did…*what*?'

'Latif believed he was referring to either slaves or prostitutes and was offended to the extent that he could not bear to remain in the same room, but it was *you* that Percy was talking about!' Beneath her arrested gaze, Tariq threw back his head and laughed with helpless appreciation. 'You whom I would not surrender at any price!'

'I think you could have mentioned before now that the anklet was more than just a piece of jewellery,' Faye remarked.

'Ah, but I was playing it cool and there is no cool way of telling a contemporary woman that every possessive bone in your body thrills to seeing a chain round her ankle,' Tariq pointed out with a slight grimace.

She smiled. 'A chain with special family significance.'

'I must give you your ring back. It belonged to my mother.'

That he had still given her that wedding ring on that long-ago day when so much strife and misunderstanding had lain between them touched her.

'The anklet was also supposed to provide the luck of the something blue on our wedding night,' Tariq admitted.

Her eyes widened. 'You know, you're much more thoughtful than I ever give you credit for.'

'I owe you a profound apology for ever doubting your word on the score of Percy's blackmail attempt.'

Faye flushed. 'I did give you the wrong impression with that phone call I made and I suppose I ought to explain that now. You see, I hadn't the faintest idea that you were serious about me and I knew your father was dying…and I thought you were just going to vanish out of my life—'

'There was never any chance of that until my stubborn pride undermined my intelligence,' Tariq informed her darkly.

'It was a mad impulse and I thought I was being incredibly romantic and mature—'

'Well, you were certainly a lot more romantic than I was that night. I was in a rage with you because I was…*gutted* by the idea that you seemed to regard sex as something casual,' Tariq admitted, poised in the centre of their bedroom, lean, powerful face taut. 'That you might not, after all, be feeling the same special bond that I was feeling for you. That you were probably thinking of me as just another boyfriend when I was head over heels in love with you.'

'Were you really?' Faye whispered unevenly. 'Honestly?'

'And I have never been in love before. Lust, yes, but not love and it was not a grounding experience for me,' Tariq revealed with rueful dark eyes. 'Every other Western woman I had been with was only interested in fun, sex and what I could buy. But then, before I met you, fun and sex was all I wanted too, so no doubt I was only attracted to that type of woman.'

'Probably.' Faye did not really want to hear about his past.

As if he knew he had erred in being that frank, Tariq closed the distance between them and reached for her hands. 'What I am trying to explain is that, having had affairs that were nothing to be proud of…I then went on to idealise you as if you were an angel—'

'I'm not that—'

'I shouldn't have liked living with one anyway.' His breathtaking smile of innate self-mocking charm banished her tension and warmed her like the sunlight. 'I wanted to get to know you really well before I mentioned love or marriage.'

'I can understand that—'

'My father's appalling second marriage had a powerful effect on me. He was not a foolish man but he *was* fooled into making a big mistake.'

'That must have made you feel very wary—'

Dropping her hands, he raised his own to frame her cheekbones with spread fingers and a look of deep regret in his tawny eyes. 'Faye…I made an even bigger mistake. I married you still wanting you, still loving you, but my terrible pride, my even worse temper and my sheer obstinacy drove you away. I did not know a *single* moment of happiness last year but an army tank could not have dragged me back to you…'

'Percy did a lot of damage. It's not your fault—'

'It *was*,' Tariq contradicted heavily. 'Never dreaming that you believed our marriage was not a real marriage, I waited for twenty-four hours at the embassy for you to return—'

'Oh, no,' Faye mumbled tearfully.

'And then I flew home in an absolute fury and I told nobody that I had married for I *had* no wife to produce! Stop crying…I don't deserve your tears.' He groaned. 'I believed that to make the smallest approach to you would be an act of shocking weakness. Then my father died and I thought you might use his death as an excuse to contact me—'

'And I didn't do that either,' Faye muttered guiltily.

'And, for the first time, it struck me that you might really be gone, quite content to have only that money to live on—'

'I was so miserable—'

'You were left on your own without even my financial support and that shames me. I made it possible for your family to take advantage of your good nature. But I did initially believe that you cared for me and then I had to face that you did not care in any way,' Tariq related. 'When there was not even a word from you after the plane crash, I became very bitter.'

Faye rested her brow against his shirtfront and linked her arms round him. 'And then you started wanting revenge.'

'What I wanted was any excuse to get you back *without* having to admit I wanted you back. That day at the Haja, I was astonished when you informed me that you believed either that I had already divorced you or that our marriage was a sham, but it was welcome news—'

'I can't credit now that I was stupid enough to just accept that—'

'You are excused. After all, I was stupid enough to persuade myself that I could somehow have you without ever letting on to you that you were in truth my wife…and you can't get much stupider than that!' Tariq pointed out without hesitation. 'Poor Latif had to stand back aghast as I sunk deeper into this madness to have you at any cost.'

Faye spread appreciative fingers against his taut spine beneath the jacket of his suit and turned up her face. 'It's the kind of madness I like—'

'And then you frightened me out of my wits by taking off with Omeir and sanity began to return. I was so afraid that I wouldn't find you before the storm closed in that I finally admitted to myself that I was still in love with you—'

'Still in love with me…?' Relief and joy washed over her.

'Yet you only value me for my athletic performance in bed.' Tariq gazed down at her with adoring eyes full of playful reproach and swept her off her feet into his arms. 'My mistress-wife, who can insult with a compliment.'

'I'm mad about you and you know it—'

'So I had hoped, until you found out you might be tied to me for life and threw a fit.' He set her down on the bed and eased her out of her jacket.

'I was awful—'

'No, I was worse. I did not foresee how much hurt my reckless games would cause. Nor am I very good at being shouted at…I expect I'll improve with practice. I really thought you were planning to leave—'

'So you just took off and left me to it?' she complained.

'Not before ensuring that your passport was in my safe. I could not have stood by and allowed you to walk out on what we had found together…I am so incredibly happy with you.'

In receipt of that charged confession, Faye arranged herself on the bed like a very willing woman. Tariq gave her a highly appreciative perusal. 'You were made for me—'

'You were made for me first. Tell me…' Faye leant up on one elbow with newly found confidence '…when are we going to try for a baby?'

'Perhaps in a few years,' Tariq suggested. 'I am painfully conscious that I have already landed you with three children at the age of twenty.'

'I love them and I wouldn't mind having a baby—'

'But I care most about what is best for *you*.' Tariq leant over her and kissed her breathless. 'We have Rafi in reserve and no need to think further on the subject at present. I am selfish. Those first weeks when we lived only for each other and I had no idea you were seeing the children, I just didn't want to share you—'

'Is that why you never mentioned them?' Faye grinned.

'I was also afraid you would take total fright if I rolled them all out as an unavoidable extra to living with me,' Tariq admitted ruefully. 'While I am very grateful that you have room in your heart for them, that could not have made me love you or made me want to stay married to you. The night I flew home from the tribal talks because I couldn't *stand* to be separated from you, I knew I never wanted to let you go.'

'I love you so much,' she whispered dreamily, letting her fingers slide possessively into his silky hair and mess it up.

'"A frog of little faith?"' Tariq teased, sliding her out of her dress with the most deft of manoeuvres and folding her back into his arms.

'Very occasionally frogs turn into princes. I'll be sure to let you know if it ever happens.'

Eighteen months later, Faye settled her baby son into his pram in the shade of the trees.

Little Prince Asif had been something of a surprise package to his parents. They honestly had planned to wait another year but a Caribbean cruise on a private yacht the previous year had resulted in a certain recklessness. Asif stretched sleepily, big dark blue eyes flickering and then slowly sinking shut. He was a very laid-back baby.

Basma and Hayat, clad in shorts and T-shirts, were paddling in the basin of the fountain and giggling. Lifting them out at the same time as she listened to Rafi chatter about his day at school, Faye could only think how contented she was. With so many willing hands to help and acres of space, parenting four children was not the burden which Tariq had feared.

Adrian and Lizzie and their children had stayed with

them for a week only the previous month. Her brother now worked for Tariq in London in a job which had literally been tailormade for him. According to Adrian, Percy was doing very well in the field of property speculation.

Leaving the staff to preside over the nursery evening meal, Faye went for a shower. When she emerged from the bathroom, wrapped in a fleecy towel, Tariq was in the bedroom.

'You've got perfect timing.' Faye studied her tall, dark and sensationally attractive husband with bright eyes.

His tawny gaze whipped over her slim figure with molten appreciation. 'You think *this* is coincidence?'

Her cheeks warmed. 'Not when it happens for the third time in a week.'

As Tariq drew her close, he murmured huskily, 'Are you complaining?'

'What do you think?' Faye said breathlessly.

'I think, as always, we are of one mind.' He tasted her mouth with smouldering hunger and as she pushed into his hard, muscular frame he scooped her up into his arms. 'Happy?'

'Totally,' she whispered blissfully.

'You know, you never did mention when I made it out of frogdom—'

'Oh, you went from frog to prince faster than the speed of light!'

Coming down on the bed, Tariq leant over her with pure sensual threat. 'Say that again…'

'Probably when my mare, Delilah, arrived and she was the most ugly-looking horse you thought you'd ever seen but you lied to save my feelings.'

'You realised that?' Tariq was dismayed.

'Or when you fixed up that job for Adrian and he got it without realising it *had* been fixed…or when you pretended I was the sexiest woman alive when I was pregnant with

Asif…or when you put in the swimming pool so that we could have fun without divers around.'

'Anything else?' Tariq surveyed her with helplessly amused dark eyes.

Faye reckoned that she had possibly about a hundred other good reasons why she loved him more with every passing day, but she did not want to give him them all at once.

'Is it my turn? OK. You learning Arabic,' he told her.

'You not laughing at my mistakes—'

'You just being you. A wonderful wife…a terrific princess…a fabulous mother…and the mistress of my heart, *aziz*.' As every phrase was punctuated by kisses, the dialogue faltered to a halt and it was a long time until it started up again.

THE SHEIKH'S WIFE

by

Jane Porter

Jane Porter grew up on a diet of Mills& Boon® romances (reading late at night under the covers so her mother wouldn't see!). She wrote her first book at age eight and spent many of her high school and college years living abroad, immersing herself in other cultures and continuing to read voraciously. Now, Jane's settled down in rugged Seattle, Washington, with her gorgeous husband and two young sons. Jane loves to hear from her readers. You can write to her at PO Box 524, Bellevue, WA 98009, USA.

Jane Porter has a fabulous new novel available in November 2006. Look for *Hollywood Husband, Contract Wife* in Mills & Boon Modern Romance®.

CHAPTER ONE

BRYN caught a glimpse of herself in the hall mirror as she headed toward the front door, the doorbell still ringing as she padded along the carpetless hall. Sheen of white dress, brilliant blue eyes, flushed cheeks. A radiant bride. And she did feel beautiful, more beautiful than she had in years. In just seven short days she'd be a bride again. She'd be Stanley's wife.

Smiling, Bryn hummed the wedding march as she swung the front door open, late-afternoon sunlight washing over her in streaky gold waves, briefly blinding her.

Blinking, she made out broad shoulders. The high curve of cheekbone. A beautifully shaped mouth. And only one man had that mouth. Her heart staggered to a stop. "Wh...what...are you doing here?"

"Hello, darling. It's nice to see you, too."

Time stopped, changed, and for a split second she was somewhere else, spellbound. It was just like the day she met him, the day she reversed her small Volkswagen, and slammed into his silver Mercedes Benz. Her car was totaled. His was merely dinged.

Bryn felt the impact again, the air knocked out of her lungs, her lips parting in shock. *"Kahlil."*

"You remembered, good." He looked amused, but then, his gold eyes always smiled when he was angry.

Lifting a sheet of paper, he dangled it in front of her face. ''Now perhaps you'll remember this,'' he drawled softly, giving the paper a gentle shake.

Bryn stared at the paper blankly, unable to read the words. Only his voice penetrated the muddle inside her head, his voice still husky, his English formal, the same English he'd learned as a child in an English boarding school. ''What is it?''

''You don't recognize it?''

Her fingers felt nerveless as she clutched the door. ''No.''

Kahlil chuckled, the sound warm, indulgent, an indulgence he'd shown toward her early in their marriage when she'd been his prized American bride. ''It's our marriage license. The little piece of paper that legally binds us together.''

She couldn't speak, her throat swelling closed. He must be out of his mind, she thought, forcing herself to look into his face, meet his eyes.

He didn't look crazy. If anything he looked calm, perfectly controlled, as though he knew exactly what he was doing, as though he'd planned this surprise visit on purpose.

A week before her wedding…

Her thoughts spun, her brain fogged by shock and fear. What if Kahlil discovered Ben? *What if he found out about their son?*

No. She'd never go back to him. Never return to Zwar. Bryn drew herself tall, conviction making her back straight, her determination reinforcing her courage. "I don't understand what that has to do with us."

"Everything, darling." He was gazing down at her with considerable interest, thick black lashes fanning his carved cheekbones and the bronzed luster of his skin. "I've come to see why you're getting married again when you're still married to me."

Still married to him? Ridiculous. If he thought he could hoodwink her with a silly statement like that, then he had another thing coming. She wasn't eighteen anymore. She wasn't a child bride, either. "We're not married," she said crisply, disdain sharpening her voice. "We were divorced three years ago." How could he still refuse to accept their divorce? It'd been three years, more than three years. Three and a half years, actually. "I'm not in the mood for games. Perhaps in Zwar, divorces aren't permitted, but here they're perfectly legal."

"Yes, darling, I understand that much. And perhaps you've forgotten I have a law degree from Harvard, an *American* university, and despite my Arab nationality, I grasp the legality of an American divorce, but *we* were never divorced."

There was a quiet menace in his voice, a menace she heard all too clearly. Her head jerked up, her gaze clashing with his. "If this is your idea of a joke—"

"Have I ever been a comedian?"

No, she answered silently, bitterly. He was one man in desperate need of a sense of humor.

"I'm trying to prevent you further embarrassment,"

he added with the same infuriating calm. ''I considered waiting until you'd arrived at the church, the guests filling the pews. I could just picture your eager groom at the altar, standing there in his black-and-white tux—he is wearing a tuxedo, isn't he?''

She couldn't bear to be the brunt of Kahlil's scorn. She'd witness him level others in the past, but never her. Kahlil had never been anything but protective, generous, *loving.*

Her heart squeezed on the last one, pained by the unwanted memory. Their marriage had been brief. Too brief but she couldn't go back, couldn't undo the past. ''I think it's time you left.''

He put his hand in the door to keep her from shutting it in his face. ''I've tried to be polite, but perhaps it's better if I'm blunt. There will be no wedding next Saturday. And as long as I live, there will be no wedding to any man, ever.''

She ground her jaw together, struggling to contain her temper. Maybe in his country men could veil their women, tell them how to dress, what to think, where to go, but not in the United States, and not in her home. ''I don't belong to you.''

''Actually, in Zwar, you do.''

''People are not objects, Kahlil!''

Pushing the door all the way open, he picked her up, hands encircling her rib cage, thumbs splayed beneath her breasts. His fingers felt like fire against her skin, searing straight through the bodice of her gown. Her breasts tingled, her senses responding to him just as they'd always responded to him. He could turn her into puddles of need in no time flat.

Kahlil tipped her backwards just enough to knock her off her feet, and sent her heart racing. "How could you possibly think I'd let you marry another man? How could you think I'd give you up?"

"Because the divorce—" she choked, beginning to feel genuinely frightened, not by him but by the idea of still being married to him. Their marriage was over; it had to be over.

"What divorce?" he demanded.

"The divorce...our divorce."

The dark hallway threw sinister shadows across his face. "There was no divorce. You never returned the last of the paperwork, and with documents unsigned the divorce was dropped."

Her mouth dried. Her heart hammered harder. She could feel every ragged beat, every quick painful surge of blood. "Documents?" she stuttered, repeating the word as though it were foreign.

"I contested the divorce, refused to accept that you'd left me. It wasn't desertion, I told the judge, but a temporary leave of absence. The judge sent you paperwork and you never filled it out. Therefore the divorce wasn't granted."

"You bought the judge. You gave him money—"

"Don't get carried away. Your legal system isn't all that corrupt. If you want to place blame, place it on your shoulders."

He'd rendered her speechless, stole her breath, her words, her anger.

Could he be possibly right? Had she somehow let paperwork slip?

Her brain raced, struggling to remember that first year, those horrible months of struggling with the baby on her own. She'd moved a half-dozen times in as many months, did temp jobs on top of her regular job just to pay her bills. Swallowing hard Bryn found her voice. ''I didn't know you could contest a divorce in Texas.''

''In Texas, anything's possible.''

She suddenly saw him scooping Ben into his arms, boarding his private jet and taking off. He'd have Ben. She'd never see him again. The vision was so awful, so vivid and real, it felt as though he'd thrust his dagger, the one he wore beneath his robes, straight through her heart. ''Why are you doing this?''

His gold-flecked gaze slowly moved across her face, scrutinizing. ''You married me. You understand the vows. I'm keeping the vows. And so are you.''

''I'll never live with you again, Kahlil.''

''But you are my wife. You'll remain my wife.''

She crossed her arms over her chest chilled to the bone. A life tied to him. It would be a life in chains. And Ben…she closed her eyes, unable to bear the thought of Ben trapped with her.

Her lashes lifted, her gaze fixed on her husband's face. She'd once found him impossibly beautiful. Now she found him impossibly frightening. ''What do you want?''

''You.''

Her stomach fell, plummeting to her feet. *Never. Ever, ever.* She dug her fingers into her bare upper arms, fingers pressing into muscle, nails into firm flesh. ''It's not going to happen.''

He smiled, a small, hard, uncompromising smile. ''It will. I'll bet my life on it.'' Kahlil moved to the door, opened it and stepped onto the small cement porch. ''I'll send my car for you tomorrow. We'll have dinner, discuss the future.''

She lunged toward him, fists clenched. ''There is no future!''

''Oh, yes, there is. How does seven o'clock sound?''

She'd have Ben here then. It would be his bathtime, then stories and bed. She couldn't possibly go out, couldn't possibly let Kahlil return here, either. ''You can't just bully your way back into my life. If what you say is true...'' Her voice fell away. She swallowed hard, unable to fathom such a truth. After a tense silence she forced herself to continue. ''I need time. I need to make some calls, and of course, there is Stan—''

''Oh, yes, nice old Stanley Hopper. Your boss, your fiancé, your insurance agent.''

''Get out.''

Shrugging he reached for the doorknob, twisting it open. ''I'm staying at the Four Seasons. I won't leave town until we've sorted matters out.'' He leaned over, dropped a kiss on her parted lips. ''By the way, you look lovely in that dress.''

She'd forgotten all about her wedding gown. Self-consciously she pressed the skirt smooth, the silk delicate and light beneath her fingertips. She'd been trying it on, making sure it didn't need any last-minute alterations. ''I wanted to see if it fit.''

''It fits.'' He smiled, eyes glinting. ''Beautifully.''

Bryn was still shaking an hour after Kahlil finally left. She'd changed, made a cup of tea, but couldn't relax, couldn't calm down.

Kahlil was wrong, he had to be wrong. She wasn't married to him. She wasn't his wife. She *couldn't* be.

Her thoughts raced here, there, scattering in a thousand directions as she drove to Ben's preschool to pick him up.

If she were really still Kahlil's wife, then Kahlil would have a legal right to see Ben. To take Ben.

Making dinner that night Bryn battled to hide her worry from Ben. The cheerful chatter she usually enjoyed grated on her and she was relieved when he finally went to bed and she had some quiet to think.

She paced the small living room, chewing on her thumbnail. The only way she could protect Ben from danger was to keep him a secret, and she didn't know how she'd managed to hide Ben, but she had to. She just had to.

Bryn took the next day off from work and spent it making phone calls—to the courthouse, to lawyers, to anyone who might be able to help her sort out the facts regarding her divorce. With horror she heard one clerk after another explain that paperwork was indeed missing and that the divorce suit had been dropped over a year ago.

Then Kahlil was right. The marriage, *their* marriage, still existed, under Texas law.

It took her another two days to accept the terrible truth. Two days of a churning stomach, and two awful, endless, sleepless nights when she cursed herself for not being on top of details, for failing to ensure the divorce was finalized. This was her fault, her fault entirely.

Finally, heart aching, Bryn called Stan and broke the news. He immediately drove over and they talked for hours but in the end the facts remained the same and there was nothing they could do but postpone the wedding. Stan behaved like a true gentleman, offering no reproaches, just promising his full support.

But after he left, and the house was silent again, Bryn knew she had one last painful phone call to make.

She called the Four Seasons Hotel and was put through to Kahlil's presidential suite. If he sounded surprised to hear from her he gave no indication. But Bryn wasn't about to chitchat. Her voice cool, her tone formal, she suggested they meet the following night for dinner and named a popular Dallas restaurant.

Kahlil offered to send a car, she refused. She'd drive there, she told him, drive home and that would be the last time she'd see him again.

But dinner the next evening didn't start off the way she'd planned. First her car wouldn't start, and then instead of dropping Ben off at the baby-sitter's house, she had to call and ask the sitter to come for Ben. Finally she was forced to phone Kahlil and leave word at the restaurant that she'd be late due to car difficulties. Before the taxi arrived, a black limousine pulled up in front of her house. *Kahlil.* She knew it without a glimpse of him, knew it without a word from him. She felt him. Felt his strength, his anger, his conviction.

From the living-room window she saw him step out of the back and stand next to the limousine's open door. He didn't move. He didn't speak. He simply waited, and in his aggressive stance she saw ownership. He was stating his belief, that she was his, and only his.

Kahlil wasn't going to go away. He wasn't going to leave her alone.

The black limousine sailed on and off the freeway, winding through traffic but Bryn couldn't concentrate on anything. She heard Kahlil say he'd changed their dinner reservation to another restaurant, a quieter one, more conducive to conversation. He said something about taking care of unfinished business but she couldn't think about that, couldn't possibly consider anything between them unfinished. In her mind they were done. Dead. Over.

Not by her choice. It had never been her choice.

The limousine dropped them in front of an exclusive Dallas restaurant, a restaurant requiring membership, and a critical screen before a member could be accepted.

The restaurant entrance was so discreet it looked like a warehouse entrance. However, Bryn found that behind the plain concrete walls and studded steel door, the restaurant walls had been painted in gleaming shades of blue and gold and the gold-leafed ceiling glittered with dozens of extravagant crystal chandeliers.

''Hungry?'' Kahlil asked, his hand resting on the small of her back.

She felt every muscle in her tighten, her body snapping to response and Bryn jerked away from him, shocked by her sensitivity. She shouldn't still feel this way. She shouldn't still feel anything. ''No.''

The maître d' murmured polite greetings, ushering them to a curtained booth. The heavy drapes could be closed, making the table more intimate, if required.

Seated, Bryn's gaze darted to the thick purple drapes, praying they'd remain open, tied back with the gold tasseled ropes. Kahlil ordered drinks for them, and an appetizer. Her hands shook beneath the table. She struggled to breathe normally.

''Smile,'' he said, leaning back against the plush seat upholstery. ''You look like you're being tortured.''

''I am being tortured. This is torture.''

''How far we've come,'' he mocked, dark head tipping, black lashes lowering as he studied her grim expression. ''Once you would have died for me.''

I almost died living with you.

But she didn't say it. He knew nothing about her last night in Tiva, or her friendship with his cousin, a friendship that proved to be a terrible, nearly tragic mistake. ''You can't take over my life, Kahlil. It's been three years, three and a half years, since we were together. I've changed—''

''Yes, you've grown rebellious.''

"I've just grown up. I won't take orders from you anymore."

"I never had to order you to do anything. You did *everything* for me," and his accented voice caressed the word everything, "eagerly."

Her stomach clenched. She wouldn't think about the past, wouldn't think about their old relationship. "Kahlil, I want a divorce and I am going to file for one first thing in the morning. Stan knows an excellent lawyer and he and I *will* be married eventually."

Kahlil made a rude sound, deep in his throat. "I hope your Stan is a patient man because he's going to be kept waiting a very long time. I'll tie you up with every legality I can. You name it, I'll do it."

She stared at him as though he were the devil himself. "Why? What have I ever done to you?"

His golden gaze raked her bare shoulders and simple black dress. "You broke your word."

So that was it. This was just about revenge. About inflicting pain. Fear balled in her stomach and she realized yet again how dangerous this was for Ben.

The appetizer arrived, a savory baked crab dish with buttery crumbs and cheese. Bryn normally loved crab but at the moment her stomach was so queasy she could barely tolerate the smell, much less eat. Kahlil, she noticed, took none, either. "I thought you were famished."

"I am. I'm waiting for you to serve me."

As if she was one of the women from his harem! Incredible. "You are not helpless, Sheikh al-Assad!"

''But why should I serve myself when you are here to serve me?''

She glared at Kahlil, resenting his beauty, the black hair, the strong brow, the elegant sweep of cheekbone. She'd fought so hard to free herself, ripped her heart in two to escape him. It had taken her years to move forward and now that she finally was ready to marry again, he'd returned.

Treacherous man. Man that could disarm her with just a glance from his beautiful eyes. She'd loved him too much, needed more from him than he could give.

Blindly she stumbled to her feet, her long black dress tangling between her legs. His hand snaked around her wrist and drew her roughly down again. ''You are not excused.'' His dark eyes flashed at her, deep grooves etched on either side of his imperious mouth. ''You did not ask my permission to leave the table.''

''I've never asked your permission for anything and I'm not about to start now!'' Good God, who did he think he was? Bryn threw her head back, tears shimmering in her eyes. ''I can't believe I once imagined myself in love with you. What a fool I was!''

''You didn't imagine it. You did love me.''

''Did,'' she repeated bitterly, ''as in past tense. I only feel hatred for you now.''

''Love, hate, who cares? I'm more interested in ensuring you honor your vows.'' His anger emanated from him in great silent waves. ''I realize you were very young when we married but I've given you time to grow up. Three and a half years. Now I've come to bring you home.''

''Zwar is not my home!''

He snapped his fingers. ''Semantics,'' he said brusquely. ''I'm tired of debating. The fact is your place is in Tiva, at the palace, bearing my children.''

''That is one scenario which will *never* happen.''

''You think you'd be happier married to your pathetic little insurance agent? I've had my intelligence look into him and he's a man without fire, a man without drive—''

''And I love him.''

''I don't care. You can't have him.''

Anger swept through her, anger so strong that she lifted her hand and took a swing at his face. He caught her by the wrist just before she struck his cheek. ''Have you lost your mind?''

Her wrist tingled from the tightness of his grip, his fingers wrapped viselike around her fragile bones. ''Leave Stan alone. He doesn't deserve this.''

''But you do. You've insulted me, and my family. You had a responsibility—you were Princess al-Assad—and you abandoned my people.''

Her wrist began to throb. Tiny pinpricks flashed against her closed eyelids. ''Please, release me.''

''I expect an apology.''

''You're hurting me.''

His nostrils flared, his dark eyes flashing, but he opened his fingers, freeing her wrist. She drew her arm back to her lap and stared at her wrist, seeing the livid marks of his fingers against the paleness of her skin.

Kahlil dragged the heavy velvet drapes closed. The violet-purple fabric fell in deep inky folds, hiding them from the rest of the restaurant.

He was pulling her back into his world, forcing her to submit. She couldn't let him. She wasn't just his wife. She was a mother, Ben's mother.

The tears that she'd fought so hard to contain trembled on her lashes, slipping free. She pressed her lips together, fighting to keep control.

"Do not cry," he said roughly. "I won't have my wife weeping in public."

"You've drawn the drapes. No one can see."

"I can see."

Everything about him was so hard. Every word sounded harsh. She clamped her jaw shut, refusing to engage in a battle of wills with Kahlil. He was a far better debater than she. He was far better at everything than she, but that didn't make his needs more important, his feelings more correct.

Kahlil must have accepted her silence for submission as his hard expression gentled a fraction. "If you don't want a fight, don't provoke me. I didn't travel all this way to be scorned by a woman."

Had he always been so arrogant? So damned condescending? Maybe once she'd found his machismo attractive but now it filled her with terror. Terror not just for herself, but Ben, and Ben's future.

If Kahlil knew he had a son, he'd insist that Ben be raised in Zwar, his small oil-rich kingdom in the Middle

East. Zwar was beautiful but far removed from the freedom she and Ben knew in Texas.

Abruptly Kahlil leaned forward, grasped her chin, drawing her toward him. She nearly flinched, inwardly shrinking from his touch, but steeled herself outwardly, not wanting him to know how strongly he affected her.

Yet when he stroked her lips with the pad of his thumb, her whole body shuddered, a response she couldn't possibly hide from Kahlil.

"You've become quite skittish," he drawled, clearly intrigued. "Doesn't Stan ever touch you?"

"My relationship with Stan is none of your business."

"A bold answer for a woman in a precarious position."

Her lips twisted, her smile forced. She ignored the truth in this, realizing she was indeed caught, but pride overwhelmed her common sense. She couldn't back down. "I have changed, Kahlil. I'm not the girl you married."

"Good. Then we both have adjustments to make. I'm not the man you married, either." He smiled without humor, his gaze never wavering from her face. "And you have changed. You've grown more beautiful."

"Don't flatter me."

"I'm not flattering you. I've met a lot of women in my life, but I've never met another woman like you. No one with your sweetness, softness—"

"Stop."

"Your pale, flawless skin. Your eyes, the dark blue of precious sapphires. Your mouth softer than a rose."

Her spine tingled, her skin prickling. *Don't listen to this.* Don't let him get under your skin. You've survived him once. You can do it again. "You only want me because you can't have me."

His fingers opened, freeing her, and his smile remained the same. But his eyes looked harder, the glints brighter. "I can have you. I just haven't been aggressive."

No, he'd never been aggressive with her before tonight, but she suddenly knew he could be extremely ruthless, correctly reading the menace in his hard features, and danger in the crooked curve of his mouth.

His smile faded. "Does Stan know you're a flighty little wife?"

Oh, low blow. "He knows I left you."

"Did you tell him you left without leaving a note? Or giving me a kiss goodbye? He knows you just took your purse, your passport and walked?"

"He knows I took my purse and *ran.*" Her gaze locked with his. If he wanted to make it tough, she could play tough. That's all she'd been doing since leaving Zwar anyway. Cutting coupons to buy breakfast cereal. Shopping for clothes from a secondhand store. Working double shifts at the insurance agency. She'd shouldered parenthood on her own, and succeeded.

"Did Stan ever ask why you left me?"

"He knew I was unhappy, and that was enough for him."

Kahlil lifted his wine goblet, swirled the glass, ruby-red wine shimmering in the candlelight. "What an understanding man. Will he be so understanding when you toss him away, tired of that marriage, too?''

His sarcasm was as sharp as razor blades and cut deep. If she thought she could get away with it, she'd run. But she wouldn't get away from Kahlil, not like that, not this time. ''I never tossed you away.''

''No? It felt that way. It looked that way, too. The palace was wild with gossip. The scandal affected the entire kingdom. I didn't just lose face. My people lost face.''

''What scandal?''

''Rumor has it you were…unfaithful.''

CHAPTER TWO

"*NEVER.*" Color suffused her cheeks, embarrassment and surprise. How could he think such a thing? How could he think the worst?

The realization that he did, hurt far more than she'd expected.

Early on she'd hoped he'd come looking for her. She'd also hoped he'd discover Amin's treachery. Instead Kahlil accepted her betrayal, accepted her failure, accepted that she'd been unfaithful. Apparently it hadn't crossed his mind to even think otherwise.

Then he'd failed her, too. Twice.

Tears burned in her throat, unshed tears she'd never let fall.

Leaving him had nearly destroyed her. It had been the hardest thing she ever had to do. She'd nearly shattered all over again when back in Texas, she discovered she was pregnant.

It was a baby Kahlil wanted. It was a baby he'd never know. The guilt had nearly eaten her alive. Thank God for poverty. It forced her out of bed every morning, forced her to work until she dropped into bed at night, dead with fatigue.

Kahlil might mock Stan and his insurance agency, but working as a secretary at the agency probably saved her life. ''Why don't you just divorce me and get this over with?'' she said hoarsely.

''Can't do that.''

''Why not?'' Lifting her gaze, she looked at Kahlil, noting the firm set of his mouth, the intelligence in his warm golden gaze and saw her son there, the same eyes, the same nose, the same mouth. Why hadn't she ever seen it before? Ben was Kahlil in miniature.

And like that, she saw the awful truth. She and Kahlil weren't completely strangers. They did have something in common, one precious little person. *Ben.*

''Too easy,'' he answered curtly. ''Divorce might be the easiest thing, but I've never taken the easy way out.''

She knew what he was talking about, knew the reference to their marriage. He'd warned her ahead of time that their marriage would create an uproar, predicted his family's reaction, including his father's harsh disapproval. Kahlil had said there would be hell to pay and she'd shrugged it off, kissing Kahlil's lovely mouth, his cheekbone, his jaw. She'd been confident she could win his family over, so certain that Kahlil's love and approval would be enough.

And she was wrong. Very wrong.

Knots balled along her shoulder blades, her back rigid, her neck stiff. Her gaze settled on his hard profile. Once she'd love to kiss the strong angles and planes of his face. She remembered how she lavished extra kisses on the small scar near the bridge of his nose.

She could feel the heartbreak again, thick and sharp. She had loved him. Once. She'd wanted nothing but to be with him. She loved him to distraction, needed the assurance he felt the same. Instead he withdrew, his warmth disappearing behind an impersonal mask. Duty, country, business. Their worlds no longer connected, their lives ceased to touch.

"How badly do you want a divorce?"

His question sent small shock waves rippling through her middle. He was toying with her the same cruel way a cat played with a mouse just before the mouse became a feline supper.

Her spine stiff, her shoulders squared, she lifted her chin, wanting to defy him. She wouldn't dignify his games with an answer. Let him speak first. Let him be the one to grope for explanations.

But her righteous anger collapsed on itself, even as she confronted the enormity of her problem. This wasn't a small matter. Ben's whole future was at stake. Rather than provoking Kahlil, she needed to work with him, humor him. The baby-sitter, Mrs. Taylor, would be dropping Ben off at eleven, less than three hours from now. She needed to be home by then, and she had to be rid of Kahlil by then. "Badly," she choked.

"Badly enough to risk everything?"

"What do you mean by everything?"

"You'd become mine for the weekend."

She reached for her water glass, lifted it to her mouth. The rim of the chilled glass clicked against her teeth, icy water sloshing against her lips.

He leaned forward. "I want you for a weekend."

"That's your proposal?"

''I'm giving you an opportunity to take control of your life.''

''I spend a weekend with you, and you'd grant me a divorce?''

''If my terms were met.''

He made it sound so easy. Bryn stared at the water drops darkening the white cloth, her mind strangely blank. No words, no sound, no light filtering through her brain. ''And those terms…?''

''I want a long weekend with you. Four days. Three nights. City of my choosing.''

She touched one of the damp drops on the tablecloth with her finger. ''You want me to be your wife.''

''I want you to be my lover.''

Her head lifted, gaze meeting his. He smiled without a hint of warmth in the eyes. ''I want to possess you, enjoy you at my leisure, and make you mine—completely mine—again.''

Something inside her stirred, hunger, awareness. He knew how she responded to him. He knew he could seduce her at the drop of the hat. ''You don't think I have the strength to walk away from you a second time.''

He shrugged. ''Did I say that?''

''You don't have to. I know you.''

''If you please me, I shall process the divorce papers in Zwar. If you cannot fulfill the required duties to my satisfaction, you shall return to Zwar with me and take lessons from the palace concubines.''

''Either way, you win.''

He ignored that. ''You'd only sacrifice four days of your life, and surely, Stan's love is worth at least that?''

Stan's love was worth more, but Kahlil's price…

Four days in his bed. Four days making love. A vision of tangled limbs, warm bodies, damp skin flashed before her and she felt blood race to her cheeks. ''It's a humiliating proposition.''

''But it gives you possibilities. Hopes for the future.''

Hopes for the future. Ben's future.

Bryn draw a deep breath, and actually considered his offer. Just for a moment. Alone, naked, weak. He'd reduce her to hunger and fire all over again and she would need him too much, want him too much. Like before.

It was too risky. For herself, and for Ben. She felt raw, exposed, Kahlil's proposal peeling off needed protective layers that shielded her heart from the past, and the danger Kahlil still posed.

Something wonderful and awful happened when they were together. She felt more alive, more physical, more aware, but that acute awareness came at a terrible price. Kahlil made her feel emotions and desires that she couldn't control. It hurt then, it hurt now, and this feeling couldn't be natural or normal. Emotions shouldn't run so deep.

''I can't,'' she gasped, dying inside. ''There's just no way.''

His mouth curved, a crooked smile. ''You don't have to give me your answer yet. You might want to think it over a little longer. Take an hour. Take two. After all, it is your future.''

Dinner finished, Kahlil tossed a handful of bills on the table—several hundred dollars, Bryn noted woodenly, chump change to Kahlil and a small fortune to herself. Money like that would pay for new shoes for Ben. A rib roast for Sunday supper. Maybe even a night on the Gulf Coast.

Resentful tears pricked the back of her eyes as Kahlil steered her to his waiting limousine. He had no idea what it was like to struggle and worry about every purchase, every trip to the grocery store, every new month because it meant starting the vicious cycle over again—rent, gas, electric bill, car payment, and on and on until Bryn wanted to scream. It hadn't helped that Stan was always offering to ease her load, make payments for her, pick up expenses. She'd been sorely tempted but had never accepted his offers, never accepted his frequent marriage proposals, either—not until last Christmas.

She'd finally worn down resisting, reluctantly accepting that bald, bespectacled Stanley would be the right thing. Not for her. But for Ben.

Numbly Bryn slid into the back of the limousine and buckled her seat belt across her lap.

Kahlil directed the driver back to her house.

Bryn's fog of misery lifted, recognizing the peril of letting Kahlil close to her home. Ben's toys and bedroom had been packed for the move but there could be knick-knacks around the house, photos or artwork she'd overlooked. ''Why don't we go for a drive?''

''A drive?''

She ignored Kahlil's incredulity. ''Or a walk. It's a

beautiful night. Not too humid for the first time in weeks.''

Kahlil viewed her through narrowed lashes, his expression speculative. ''Who are we hiding from?''

The fact that he could read her so easily reinforced her fear, as well as her determination to be rid of him as soon as possible. Already she felt as though she was drowning, the water rising, destruction imminent. She had the agonizing suspicion that she might not be able to pull this off. Kahlil was so clever, too clever, and also too angry.

No sooner had she swallowed the sour taste of panic than she pictured Ben as he'd run out of the house earlier, eager to go with Mrs. Taylor. His small white sneakers had slapped the sidewalk, his miniature jeans rolled up at the ankle. She always bought his clothes big, trying to make them last two seasons, maybe even three.

He'd stopped at Mrs. Taylor's truck, turned around to wave and he blew her an enormous kiss. ''I love you, Mommy!''

His zest brought tears to her eyes and laughing, she'd blown him a kiss back. She'd felt a spike of worry then, the kind of worry she felt every time she kissed him good-night, what if something happened? What if there was an accident? What if she lost him? What if…

The what-ifs could drive her crazy.

Fierce love rose up within her, love, determination and conviction. She wouldn't fail Ben. She'd fight tooth and nail to protect him. He was the one perfect and true thing she'd ever known.

Bryn looked at Kahlil, gaze level, mouth smiling faintly. ''Is there something criminal in wanting to walk?''

''You never liked to walk before.''

''Of course not. I was eighteen. I preferred motorbikes and race cars and anything else that jolted my heart.'' Like you, she thought cynically. You jolted my heart a thousand times a day.

Kahlil gave the driver directions to a popular downtown park, the night quiet, the streets nearly deserted. The limousine pulled over to the curb and Kahlil and Bryn got out, to stoically circle the square.

The evening, balmy for late September, smelled sweeter than usual, the peculiar ripe fragrance of turning leaves as summer slipped away, fading into fall.

He didn't speak. She didn't try, chewing her lower lip, struggling to come up with an alternative to Kahlil's proposal, one that might meet his need for vengeance without endangering Ben. But no solutions came to mind, immediately dismissing lawsuits and threats, as well as fleeing with Ben. This time Kahlil wouldn't let her go. He'd find her, and he'd really want blood then.

They passed the fountain and large bronze statue twice with Bryn still overwhelmed with worry.

Kahlil thrust his hands into his trouser pockets. ''There's no way out,'' he said mildly, casting a curious side glance her way. ''You're not going to escape without settling the score.''

A flurry of nerves made her prickle from head to toe. How could he know exactly what she was thinking? "Score. Proposition. You're trying to humiliate me."

"Clever girl." He stopped walking, facing her, his dark features mocking. "You humiliated me before my family and my people. You're fortunate that your humiliation will be much more...private."

"What makes you think I'd agree to this plan?"

"You were once quite daring. You hungered for adventure, for travel and the unknown. Is the great unknown no longer appealing?"

No. Not since becoming a mother. She worried constantly about Ben. His safety, his security, his future. And since becoming a mother, she wondered how her own parents could have dragged her through the Middle East as a small child, living out of tents and the camper van, sleeping at desolate spots along the road. They'd led a precarious life and it had cost them all. Dearly.

Pain suffused her, time and grief blurring her parents' faces. She remembered them better by photograph than be special memories. "I prefer things simple now," she answered faintly. "My relationships uncomplicated."

"Like Stan?"

Her eyes flashed warning. "Leave him out of this."

"How can I? He's the enemy."

"Stan is not the enemy. *You're* the enemy."

He laughed, the husky sound carrying in the darkness. "Four days. Four days and you'd be free. You could marry Stan. Have a family. Get on with your life."

Oh, how like Kahlil, how clever, how manipulative. Trust the devil to suggest temptation.

But the devil knew her, she acknowledged weakly. He knew how she'd reached for him, again and again, undone by the pleasure of their bodies, so inexperienced that she couldn't be satiated, her untutored desires wanting more.

But that wasn't the kind of relationship she had with Stan. Her fault, she knew, but despite her gratitude to Stan, she didn't enjoy it when he touched her. She told herself that her feelings would change after their wedding, but would they? Could they?

Warily she glanced at Kahlil. Moonlight illuminated his profile. If she did go with him, if she did all that he asked, would he really set her free? Could she trust him to honor his word?

''You can't pick the city,'' she said, feeling trapped, the air squeezing out of her lungs. She wouldn't breathe until she was free of him. ''Four days, three nights. I pick the place, the city and the hotel.''

''The city and the hotel? Now you're sounding paranoid.''

She refused to be baited, too busy examining the proposal from every angle. A couple of nights with him in New York. How bad could it be? She'd do what he asked and then she'd have her divorce. ''New York,'' she said. ''The Ritz-Carlton Hotel.''

''Paris. The Ritz-Carlton.''

''I won't leave the States.''

''You don't trust me?''

''No.'' She lifted her chin. ''As it is you act as judge, jury and executioner. It hardly seems fair.''

He laughed without kindness. ''I guess you'd have to work very very hard at pleasing me.''

Seething, she returned to the limousine, realizing she was only wasting time—his, hers and Ben's. Kahlil might look like a modern man with his expensive clothes and gorgeous face, but his thinking was still feudal.

The limousine drew to a stop before her house and Kahlil's driver opened the back door. But before she could move, Kahlil clasped her elbow.

''It might not be safe going with me,'' he said softly, ''but it might also be the smartest thing you've ever done. Everything in life is a risk. Even your freedom.''

She didn't speak. She couldn't.

Lightly he stroked her bare arm, his touch sending shock waves through her body. ''The weekend wouldn't be without its rewards,'' he continued. ''You burn for me. You're on fire now.''

She stared at her arm in mute fascination. She did feel feverish, her skin blazing, her body melting, everything in her coming alive in response to him. He'd always made her feel like this, crazy with need. Right now her nerves throbbed, her pulse racing. He was a drug, sweetly addictive, dangerously destructive, utterly transforming. In his bed, in his arms, she would do anything for him.

Leave her home, change her name, worship at his feet. She lost control when it came to him and that loss of control completely shamed her.

She breathed deeply, dizzy, torn between wildly opposing desires. Run. Stay. Scream. Kiss.

If she went with him, she'd enjoy Kahlil's revenge. She'd welcome the humiliation as it would be at his hands, in his hands, with his body.

A woman should have more self-respect. She had none.

She could feel the press of his thigh against hers, his hips close, his warmth stealing into her. He promised intense sensual pleasure, a pleasure she'd only ever known with him.

Color banded in high hot waves across her cheekbones. Closing her eyes, she swayed, drawn to him.

He held her in his power again.

Stop it.

Wake up. You can't do this. Think about Ben. Think about the dangers in the palace. At the very least, think about Amin.

Her eyes opened, her lips parted, and reality returned. "I can't do it, Kahlil. I won't. We need to make a clean break of it." Was that her voice? High? Thin? Panicked?"

"Clean break," he mocked. "Hardly, darling. You'd remain my wife."

"That's not fair!"

"Life's not fair."

She averted her face, struggling to hide the tumultuous emotions from him. She was angry, aroused, torn. If she didn't go away with him, Kahlil would discover Ben.

But spending a weekend with Kahlil was like throwing herself in the mouth of a volcano.

It was Ben's future, or hers.

Ben's or hers.

Ben won. ''No other man would force a woman to submit,'' she said bitterly, unable to hide her anger or despair. He'd never planned on releasing her from their marriage vows. He'd given her time but not forgiveness. Space but not freedom. And without a divorce she could permanently lose Ben.

Kahlil didn't answer. He didn't need to. They both knew he wasn't just any man. He was a sheikh, his word in his country was law.

Eyes gritty and hot, she drew a short breath. ''God, I hate you.''

''I don't care. I want what's mine. And you, wife, are mine.''

He was going to kiss her. She knew it, felt it, just before his head dropped. Alarm shrieked through her, alarm because in his arms she was weak, so weak, it made her sick.

She tried to slip away but Kahlil moved even faster. He blocked the door and leveraged her backward, her spine pressed to the leather seat. ''You can't escape me,'' he murmured, his voice husky as his palm slid down her throat, spanning the column, forming a collar with his hand. ''But then, I don't think you really want to.'' And with that, his head dropped, his mouth covering hers.

His warmth caught her unawares, his skin fragrant, a

soft subtle sweet spice she couldn't place, but a fragrance that had been part of him as long as she'd known him. The very first time they'd touched she'd breathed him in, again and again, heart racing, spectacular colors and visions filling her head. She saw the full white moon above the bleached ivory sands, the grove of orange trees planted within the village walls, the warmth of the night in the darkest hour…

Kahlil.

Her lashes closed, lips parting beneath the pressure of his, welcoming him, the sweetness and the strength, the memory of their lives. She'd loved him, oh God, she'd loved him, and he'd filled her, capturing her heart and mind and soul.

Kahlil.

His tongue traced the inside of her lip, sending rivulets of feeling in her mouth, her belly, between her thighs. She tensed at the quicksilver sensation, the warmth, first hot then turning icy as he flicked his tongue across her lip again.

Helplessly she clasped his shirt, holding on to him tightly as shudders coursed down her spine. He felt so familiar, wonderfully warm, hard, real. For months she'd wept at night missing him, missing his skin, his scent, his passion for her, for their brief bittersweet year together.

The shiny green leaf of citrus, the spice of cardamom, the tangy essence of lemon…Kahlil…and her body warmed, softening for him, responding, ignoring the revolt of her mind, refusing to remember anyone or anything but the pleasure of being in his arms.

His hand slid from her throat to her breast, his touch igniting fire beneath her skin. Shuddering, she curved more closely against him, seeking more contact, more of his strength.

''Tell me,'' his voice rasped, ''is this how you respond to Stan, too?''

Bryn felt ice invade her limbs. Stiffening in horror, she pushed frantically at his chest, desperate to escape.

Kahlil laughed deep in his throat. ''Oh, don't stop making love to me, darling. I'm really rather aroused.''

Disgust, remorse, hurt shot through her like sharp arrows, piercing her conscience, reminding her who Kahlil really was. A savage. A savage from a savage land. Hurt turned to anger, the emotion blistering, and her arm swung up, fingers flexing, palm wide. She caught him square on the cheek, the slap echoing shockingly loud in the silent car.

He didn't move, but she could hear the ring of her hand against his cheek, hear it play again and again in her head. My God, what had she done? How could she have hit him of all people? ''I'm sorry.''

He didn't speak and she sat frozen on the seat, fingers pressed to her mouth, eyes wide with shock. Sick at heart, she stared at his cheek, seeing through the shadows the reddened area of his skin.

''Twice tonight you've lifted your hand against me, once you actually made contact.'' He spoke without a hint of emotion in his husky voice. ''This is not a good habit.''

She ought to apologize again but couldn't speak, too many powerful emotions swirling within her. She wanted him and hated him. Craved his touch yet longed to wound him. It was madness. Being near him was madness. How could she ever escape him again?

''This habit must be quickly broken. Do you understand, Princess al-Assad?''

''Don't call me Princess. I'm not a princess.''

''But you are. And as long as you are my wife, you are entitled to my name, my fortune, my protection.''

''No—''

''You can't escape it. Marrying me has changed your life.'' His gaze found hers, light and shadow playing across his granitelike features, even as he stepped from the car, and taking her hand in his, drew her out after him. ''Forever.''

CHAPTER THREE

THE phone was ringing inside the house. Bryn could hear it from the walkway and climbed the porch steps quickly, struggling to get the house key into the lock, but her hands shook so badly she couldn't connect.

"Need help?" Kahlil drawled, a taunt in his voice.

"No."

The phone continued to ring, the persistence of the caller creating fresh worry. What if it was Mrs. Taylor? What if something happened to Ben? Anxiously she jammed the key into the dead bolt and gave it a fierce turn. The lock gave way and she stepped inside even as the phone stopped ringing.

Kahlil must have heard the frustration in her sigh because as he brushed past her, he touched the tip of her nose with his finger. "If it's important, love, he'll call back."

Kahlil left her to wander the house, moving from the narrow dark hall into her tiny kitchen. It infuriated her that he walked right in without invitation. She followed him into the kitchen where he sucked up air and space, reducing the cramped area to nothing more than a shoebox.

Spine rigid, Bryn watched his critical gaze examine the chipped painted cupboards and worn beige linoleum.

She could tell he'd missed nothing, not even the limp dish towels hanging from the chrome bar.

"If you needed cash, you should have told me," he said at last, turning to face her, arms crossed over his chest. His folded arms accented the width of his shoulders, the tug of fabric outlined his strong biceps. Kahlil had always been built big, all hard, carved muscle, imposing even by American standards.

She drew a short, sharp breath, her head hurting, her heart hurting again. She wouldn't let him do this, wouldn't let his wealth change her feelings. This house had been home to every good memory of her life with Ben. All those wonderful firsts…his first smile, first tooth, first step, first word. Baby powder and lullabies. Mashed peas and sweet gummy kisses. A cocoon she'd spun around them, safe, fragile, wonderful. Their world had sustained her. Until now.

"I don't need your money." She choked. "I like my home. It's cozy."

"Cozy's quaint. This is decrepit."

She pressed her lips together, fighting tears of shame. Of course he'd sneer at her secondhand furniture. In Sheikh al-Assad's world, everything was the best. The best cars. The best furniture. The best jewelry. But she couldn't afford luxuries. She could barely pay her rent every month. But Ben was healthy and happy and she wouldn't trade his security for all the luxuries in the world. "I never asked you in. If you're not comfortable, see yourself out. You know where the door is."

"And what? Deprive myself of you? Oh, no, I'm staying.'' He leaned against one laminated counter, relaxed, smiling. ''However, for a Southerner, your hospitality is shocking. The proper thing would be to offer your guest some refreshment.''

She had an hour left to get rid of him, an hour before Mrs. Taylor returned with Ben. ''It's late, Kahlil.''

''Yes, and a cup of coffee would be lovely. Thank you.''

Her head began to ache, a low throbbing pain that dulled her senses. What point was there in arguing with him? He was deaf when he wanted to be, blind when he found it convenient. Which is what had drove them apart in Tiva. Kahlil immersed in palace affairs. Bryn lost and alone. She'd tried talking to him then, but he hadn't heard her, just as he wasn't listening now.

Wearily she put the kettle on the stove, still making coffee the way Kahlil had taught her, French-press style, stronger, darker, richer than American brewed coffee. Some habits, she noted dryly, were hard to break.

''As *cozy* as you find your house, I think we could do better for you.'' Kahlil's voice, emotionless, echoed in the close quarters. ''You need something more appropriate for your position. I'll hire you a housekeeper. A driver. Bodyguards.''

She didn't even turn around. ''I don't need bodyguards, or a driver. And I may be poor but I'm an excellent housekeeper. You won't find a bit of dust anywhere.''

''Just wanted to make things easier for you.''

"A divorce would make things easier. A housekeeper would merely be a nuisance."

"Don't think about the money—"

"I'm not," she interrupted curtly, gripping the quilted potholder between her hands. She was thinking of Ben, worrying about him, seeing the danger she'd unwittingly thrust him in. "You can't do this. You can't take over my life."

"I have valid concerns about your safety."

Just then the telephone rang again. Bryn tensed, shoulders knotting. Her skin prickled with dread. She didn't want to answer the phone, but couldn't ignore it, either.

Kahlil read her indecision. "Let it ring," he commanded, authoritative as ever. "It doesn't concern us."

Even from where he stood, she could feel him, catch a whiff of his cologne. Musky, rich, reminiscent of the East with cardamom, citrus, spice. It made her picture him naked in the silk sheets of his opulent bed, bronze skin covering sinewy muscle. He was built like a god. He made love like a god. She'd worshiped him.

Then he fell from the pedestal and nothing had ever been the same between them again, leaving her vulnerable to Amin's dangerous games.

The phone rang again. Four times. Five.

She moved to answer it but Kahlil stopped her, his hands coming down to rest on her shoulders. "Leave the phone. Listen to what I'm saying."

"I can't—"

"You can. You must. You've kept me waiting three

years. I think you owe me five minutes of your undivided attention.''

But she was listening to the phone, silently counting the rings. Five, six, seven. ''Please, Kahlil.''

''No.''

She closed her eyes, her body trembling, her heart barely beating. Eight, nine. And then it stopped. The phone went dead.

Brilliant red-hot pain consumed her even as she had a terrifying vision of the future, a future far from her home in Texas, a future of blistering sands and dark veils covering her from head to toe.

''You do not own me, Sheikh al-Assad, and you will not put me in another prison!'' she raged, her fury not just at him, but against his family, his customs, his inability to see her as anything but an extension of him.

''The palace was never a prison!''

''It felt like one. You left me there alone, trapped in the harem.''

''You knew in advance the wives eat, sleep, socialize in their own quarters. You were raised in the Middle East. You knew our customs.''

''But I married *you.* I expected to be with *you.*''

''And you were, at night. I had you brought to me most evenings, if I wasn't away on business, or obligated to entertain.'' He drew a deep breath, his composure also shaken. He pressed knuckles to his temple, his jaw rock-hard. ''Regardless of your feelings about the palace, we can't afford to take chances with your safety. The problem with being a princess worth millions—billions of dollars—is that people will come at you from every direction.''

''No one even knows I'm your wife!''

''They will.''

The assurance in his voice sent shivers down her spine. They will because he'd make sure people knew she belonged to him, he'd make sure no one like Stan could ever grow fond of her, make sure she remained alone in the ivory tower. ''You'll make me a prisoner in my own home.''

''The price we pay for being rich.''

Tears filled her eyes, and she averted her head.

''Your parents were killed by extremists,'' he continued more softly. ''You, of all people, should know that the world is dangerous.''

''And I've chosen to live without fear.'' Once she left Zwar she turned her back on exotic locales and wild adventure. No more nomadic travels. No more yearning for far-off places. Her parents' instability had destroyed their family. She wouldn't do that to Ben.

''I will not become someone else just to give you peace of mind,'' she added hoarsely, unwilling to remember the bomb blast at the marketplace or the horror of her parents' death. She'd been sent to Aunt Rose in Dallas, and Rose had been wonderful. Thank God for her aunt's warmth and support.

She felt rather than heard Kahlil move behind her. He walked quietly, stealthily, like a big cat. Beautiful and oh, so lethal.

''And I will not let a hair on your head be harmed,'' he murmured, reaching out and drawing her toward him.

She tensed and he kissed the back of her neck.

His lips against her skin, and it was the most amazing pleasure she could imagine.

A shudder raced through her, nipples hardening, heat filling her belly. Just a kiss and she wanted him. Just a touch and she started to melt.

Her nerves screamed. Hot tears stung her closed eyes. She wanted to feel his hand on her breasts, her stomach, her thighs.

Slowly he plucked the tortoiseshell pins from her coiled hair, combing the long tangled strands smooth. ''Not a hair,'' he repeated, lifting the light gold strands, fingers caressing the silky length. ''Despite everything, I still want you, I still want to love your body.''

''No.'' It was a desperate denial, her lips twisting as shudders of feeling traveled the length of her spine. She felt warm where she'd been cold. Soft where she ought to be hard. *Resist him. Resist him!*

''Yes. And I forgive you,'' he added, kissing her nape again, creating fresh pleasure, more intense sensation. His hands slid to her shoulders. He held her securely. ''I forgive you and want only to have you home again.''

His words cut her, deep stabbing wounds, reminding her of the secret she'd worked so hard to keep from him. She'd spent the last three years denying she'd ever been part of him, ignoring that her child, their child…

But his home would never be her home, not after what Amin had done. Not after what she had done.

Kahlil's lips moved across her nape and Bryn closed her eyes, head falling forward, caught up in the rawness of her emotions. Need flamed inside her, need to be held, touched, loved. Stan cared for her but it had never felt like this. Never had the power, or the passion.

The old kettle began to boil, the little cap whistling softly. "We have to move on," she choked, the air aching inside her lungs, her heart as fragile as a delicate glass ornament. Remembering the damage Amin had done, Kahlil would never forgive her betrayal, never understood why she turned to his cousin. "I need to put the past behind. I need to go forward."

The teakettle's whistle grew louder. "But I cannot."

"Why not? You're one of the most accomplished, educated men in the Middle East. You hold degrees from Oxford and Harvard—"

He reached past her, moved the kettle from the burner, silencing the shrill whistle. "I might have been educated in the West, but my pride, is Arabic. I am Arabic. And my pride demands justice. An eye for an eye…a tooth for a tooth…"

"A humiliation for a humiliation," she added, turning slowly, helplessly, toward him.

"Exactly."

"So until I go with you on this weekend, I will never be free."

He didn't say anything. He didn't have to.

Kahlil watched her eyes widen, the blue irises flecked with bright bits of purple and black. Anger and defiance burned in her eyes, turning the color to glowing sapphires, rich, rare, prized.

"You aren't really giving me a choice then, are you?" she demanded.

He checked the smile that curled the corners of his mouth. She looked the picture of injured innocence, eyes bright, full soft lips trembling. Oh, but didn't he know that expression? And hadn't he heard that same inflection play through his head at least a thousand times since the night she'd left him?

He found it ironic, too, that even angry, she was still prettier than a poster girl, her face all heart-shaped sweetness, her creamy skin framed by silky hair the color of citron and sunshine. He had always loved her hair, loved to run his hands through the softness and the hundred different shades of gold spill through his fingers.

He'd been furious when Amin told him about Bryn's wedding. He couldn't believe she dared to marry another man. His anger burned so hotly that he'd feared what he'd do when he arrived at her house, but when she opened the door, the violence in his heart faded, leaving only resolve. She was his. She would go home with him.

"Of course you have a choice. You can be mine, completely, for four nights, or you can be mine, in name, for the rest of your life. It's entirely up to you."

The choice obviously horrified her, and for a moment he felt almost sympathy, until he remembered how she'd walked out on him, no apology, no attempt to reconcile, nothing. She vowed to love him and she broke that vow, in less than a year.

It was time she learned the importance of a promise. In Zwar, one's life depended on one's word.

She moved away from him, filling the French press with boiling water, tightening the top, pushing the coffee through the fine grounds. He watched her hands, watched the concentration on her face.

She handed him his cup, careful to avoid touching him. "How did you know I was getting married?"

"Amin told me." He lifted his cup to his mouth, sipped the strong black liquid, noting the flicker in her eyes and the sudden press of her lips. "Your hatred for my cousin is unacceptable, and undeserved. No one has supported you more than he."

"I can imagine."

"You doubt me?"

"I doubt him." Her voice was as brittle as a branch encased in ice. "How did he find out about the wedding?"

Kahlil shrugged. "He spotted your announcement on the Internet while reading a Dallas paper."

"Don't you find that rather coincidental? Amin reading a Dallas newspaper on the Internet? Why should he care about Dallas news?"

"I have investments here. Manufacturers. Oil refineries." He watched her struggle to control her temper and he frowned. "You scorn his loyalty, but he's been more faithful than you, my young wife."

It was on the tip of her tongue to indict Amin, to blurt

the terrible truth about Kahlil's favorite cousin, but before she could speak she heard a car pull up outside, parking next to her house.

Goose bumps peppered her flesh. It couldn't be Mrs. Taylor back already, could it?

She was moving for the door, practically running. She heard Kahlil speak, something about her decision and had she made a choice, but she didn't answer, dread, fear, panic consuming her.

From the front door Bryn caught a glimpse of a truck parked at her curb. Mrs. Taylor's old Ford pickup. And next to Mrs. Taylor she spotted a small dark head. Ben.

That was the phone call. Mrs. Taylor had been ringing to let Bryn know she'd be returning Ben early. And here she was, bringing Benjamin home at the absolute worst possible time, straight into the arms of his father.

''Friends?'' Kahlil asked, appearing behind her. She couldn't see his face but she felt his tension, his gaze focused on the truck parked outside and the passengers within.

She couldn't have answered him if her life depended on it.

The truck door opened and a child tumbled out dressed in jeans, T-shirt, white sneakers.

She couldn't help it, couldn't stay in place. She was out the door and down the front steps, running toward the truck, her eyes only on Ben. Her heart felt like a mashed plum, pulpy and bruised. As she reached her son, swinging him up into her arms, she knew she'd lost.

She couldn't do anything right. Couldn't even protect Ben when she needed to most.

Cold from head to toe, Bryn began to tremble. Her arms felt like matchsticks. Her legs like feather pillows. Sinking to the ground, she collapsed onto the rough asphalt. It was over. The hiding, the running, the pretending. It was over.

She hugged Ben hard, needing him, fearing for him. Every choice in her life, every mistake she'd made, had come to this.

Kahlil's footsteps sounded behind her. The leather heels of his shoes echoing too loudly on the cracked cement walk.

Bryn closed her eyes, praying for a miracle, praying that somehow she could disappear with Ben, prevent this terrible moment from happening. Instead Kahlil came to a standstill beside her, towering above them, the legs of his dark trousers just inches from her bent head.

"Would you care to explain?" Kahlil asked quietly, his accent pronounced, his English formal, just the way they'd taught him in boarding school.

Her stomach heaved. Her teeth began to chatter.

But Ben, so young, so innocent, lifted his dark head, and stared at Kahlil, wide brown eyes fixed intently on his father's angry face. "Mommy, who is that man?"

CHAPTER FOUR

WITHIN minutes of boarding the Learjet, the engines roared to life and they were off, taxiing down the runway, lifting from the ground. The sparkling lights of Texas fell away, and the night ominously purple-black, stretched silently before them.

Bryn wrapped her arms more snugly around Ben, her nerves close to breaking. She was grateful he finally slept, his thousand questions during the drive to the airport so innocent and yet so troubling. *Where are we going, Mommy? Will we stay at a hotel? Can we go swimming?*

Can we go swimming?

Oh God, what a question! For him this was an adventure, an exciting break from the day-to-day. He was with his mommy, he was on an airplane, and he'd been given a glass of soda pop. What else could a three-year-old want?

She closed her eyes, a lump sealing her throat, tears not far off. Everything she'd fought for the last three years had been lost. Ben's safety was now in question. It all depended on Kahlil.

And Kahlil had said nothing since they boarded his plane two hours ago. But she knew him well enough to read his mood, his hard features set in sharp, tight lines, his temper barely leashed. Oh, he was angry. No, he was more than angry, he was livid.

She swallowed hard, swallowing around the lump, feeling as though she was choking, fear, panic, regret knotting inside her, making her completely crazed.

What would happen now? What would Kahlil do?

Ben stirred fretfully, protesting her tense grip. More gently she shifted him, slowly rocking in the leather lounge chair.

Ben relaxed again, his small body curling more closely against her, his soft cheek settling against her breast.

She felt his breath, and his shudder, as he sighed in his sleep. Her heart ached, her love for him almost too painful, too intense. Had her parents felt this way about her? And if so, why hadn't she known it?

She'd been without her parents now nearly as many years as she'd spent with them and their memory was blurring, not their faces as they appeared in photographs, but their voices, the inflections, the conversations they'd had with her. She remembered their love for their work, their passion for the desert and the nomadic people of the Middle East, but she couldn't recall the things they'd said to her, the little things about her interests, her needs, her dreams.

But it wasn't her needs that were important now, it was Ben. *His* interests. His needs. And she vowed now, as she had since his birth, that he'd have security. He'd be safe. He'd feel loved.

She pressed another kiss to the top of his warm brow

before smoothing a fistful of black hair back from his flushed face. He was beautiful, jet-black hair, dark eyes, perfectly made. So much like Kahlil…

"When is his birthday, Bryn?"

Kahlil knew. It was obvious Ben was his. They shared the same eyes, nose, beautiful curve of cheek and jaw. Even though Ben was young you could see the hints of the man he'd be.

Hot tears scalded her eyes. "May 8."

Kahlil didn't speak. He didn't need to. She could feel his swift mental calculations and he added it up for himself, their wedding, the months between, the birth of Ben. She'd conceived him after their honeymoon when all she wanted was to be alone and naked with Kahlil, skin on skin, fingers and lips, bodies and hunger. She'd wanted him, all of him, with passion and desperation, her heart awakening, her senses stirred. She'd never felt so alive.

"My son," Kahlil said flatly, gaze hooded, lips pressed into a fierce line.

"Yes."

Kahlil rose from his leather armchair and crossed the cabin, moving to a small table between them. He selected a piece of dried fruit from the silver tray. "You," he said quietly, "have made a terrible mistake."

Venom filled his voice. He would make her suffer.

"So silent, Princess al-Assad. An evening of protests and now silence."

She couldn't tear her gaze from the apricot in his fingers. He was squeezing it, flattening it in the press of his fingers, just as he longed to mash her, force her to submit. With an effort she dragged her gaze from the fruit to his face. ''I'm sorry.''

He popped the apricot into his mouth, chewing it slowly, swallowing after a long moment. ''You are only sorry you were caught.''

She wondered at the truth in that. Was that the only reason she felt such overwhelming sorrow?

Again she thought of her parents, their love for each other, their love for their work, very little room for her. Had she kept Ben from Kahlil out of selfishness? Had she kept Ben a secret to ensure she had someone of her own to love?

But a choice like that, selfish, blind, would have only hurt Ben. ''No. That's not true,'' she said, forcing herself to speak. ''Everything I've done has been done to protect Ben.''

''You think I'd hurt my son?'' Kahlil's tone was so cold it cut. ''Is that the kind of man you think I am?''

No, but he was blind, at least when it came to his cousin. Kahlil favored Amin. Always had, always would.

Ben could be hurt by Amin. If Amin would attack her, why would Ben be exempt?

''Your silence speaks volumes,'' Kahlil said cuttingly, fresh contempt in his voice and the hard lines of his face. His features were perfectly imperial—strong high forehead, long, straight nose, firm mouth with just a hint of sensuality and a square, stubborn chin.

"I was thinking of Ben," she answered softly, drawing him closer. "Everything is changing for him."

"As it should."

"He'll be frightened."

"He'll be fine. He has me now."

Kahlil wouldn't remove her from Ben's life, would he? He wouldn't hurt her—or Ben—like that, would he?

Brilliant pain streaked through her, her breath catching as tears burned her eyes. "I'll do anything you ask, just be gentle with him. He's still so young—"

"I can see that for myself. I can see his devotion to you, too. I would not hurt him, Bryn. I would not wound my own flesh."

She bowed her head, struggling to contain the swell of emotion. "We're going to Zwar then?"

"We should land in Tiva in six hours."

And Amin? Was he there? Would he be waiting? "Your family…do they know I'm coming?"

"My father's dead," Kkalil said shortly. "He died almost two years ago."

"I'm sorry. I didn't know."

"You don't read newspapers?"

She tried to avoid any mention of Zwar, tried to barricade her from her old life with Kahlil. "I'm sorry," she repeated helplessly.

"My cousin, Mala, the one that was about your age, she's in London now, finishing graduate school. So she won't be there. The rest are scattered."

"And Amin?"

Kahlil shot her a quick, hard glance. ''He lives abroad. Prefers Monte Carlo's nightlife to Tiva.''

Relief swept through her, wave after wave of the sweetest news she'd heard in days.

Kahlil poured himself a drink. ''Want one?'' he asked, lifting the liqueur decanter.

''No. Thank you.''

The golden liquid gleamed in the brandy glass. ''Tell me about my son.''

That's right. Kahlil was a stranger to Ben. She felt a pang of remorse. It was a terrible thing to do to him. But had there been a choice? Was there another option she hadn't thought of?

''I'd like to know him,'' Kahlil added softly, his features tightening, his expression bleak.

The pang of remorse grew, widening to grief. ''Ben is three going on eighty,'' she said carefully. ''He's what I call an old soul. One of those children that are born knowing everything already. He's very gentle, very loving. There isn't a mean bone in his body.''

''What does he like to play?''

''Cars, trucks, trains and anything to do with a ball.''

''What did he ask for at Christmas?''

Bryn's throat suddenly closed. This one she couldn't answer, not because she didn't remember but because the memory was too uncomfortable.

She'd never forget the way Ben had sat on the department store Santa's lap and asked for a daddy. Not a new car, or game, or even a puppy. But a daddy.

The Dillard department store Santa had looked at her

over the top of Ben's head and she felt like a failure. Worse yet, on Christmas morning Ben couldn't believe Santa Claus had forgotten the one thing he'd wanted—the one thing he'd asked for. Ben cried as though his heart were broken.

Ben's tears had nearly broken hers. It was then she decided to accept Stan's proposal.

"What did he want?" Kahlil persisted, unwilling to let the subject drop.

"A family," she answered softly, unable to meet his gaze.

"Why didn't you come to me?"

She shook her head, hot tears blinding her.

A minute passed before Kahlil spoke. "I don't know what makes me angrier. The fact you hid my child from me, or that you'd give him to another man."

The pain in his voice undid her, and she ached for the pain she'd unwittingly inflicted on the man she'd once loved beyond reason. She hadn't tried to give Ben away, but she could see how he'd think that.

Kahlil made a low, hoarse sound, part disgust, part despair. "You have no excuse, I see."

"None that you'd accept."

He slowly turned to look at her, his black hair hanging loose. "A real family would have been you and me, Bryn. Us together. That was the family he needed, that was the family we should have been."

Fresh tears flooded her eyes. She'd wanted a real family, too. It was the one thing she'd never had, not after her parents died, and it was her dearest wish for Ben, her greatest desire when she'd married Kahlil. But it hadn't worked out that way. Not for any of them.

Kahlil's hands clenched, muscles cording in his forearms. "I praise Allah that finally I have my son. I will make things right for him, but you...you...you're another matter entirely."

Just before takeoff he'd gone into the luxurious bedroom on the airplane and changed, removing the white linen shirt, putting on a black turtleneck and black blazer. Now, dressed in black from head to toe, he looked dark and powerful, a vengeful knight.

"Afraid, wife?" he murmured, his voice deep, threaded with warmth, curiosity, sensual huskiness.

He knew that even now, cornered, she responded to his strength, her senses alive, her emotions stirred. Heat crept to her cheeks and she ducked her head, throat working, heart racing.

And Kahlil, she knew, watched it all.

A man who had mastered sociology, anthropology, psychology before taking advance degrees in business and law, Kahlil had perfected people-watching to an art. It served him well, his powers of observation, he knew what people were feeling often before they recognized it themselves.

He knew her desire, her fear, her guilt. He knew he'd ripped her from her world and dragged her back into his. Going back to Zwar was like a time-travel into the dark ages. It was still feudal even barbaric, in its customs, particularly with regards to women. Yet Zwar was also a sensual place. A place of warmth and passion. Magic and mystery. It was the one place that felt like home. And it had been home. Until she let her insecurities pile up, until she placed her trust in the absolute wrong man.

Amin.

If only she'd gone to Kahlil with her worries, if only she'd been more patient, less…needy…

Trusting Amin had been like putting one's head in the mouth of a lion. Stupid, stupid immature decision. The lion bit. That's what lions do.

Kahlil watched the emotions flit across her face. Hope, anger, fear, despair. He had her worried now. Good. She should be worried. She should be very worried.

What was she thinking keeping his son from him? What kind of death wish did she have?

He'd fallen in love with her beauty, her laughter, her intelligence, but now he wondered if it had all been an illusion. Had his head been turned by her prettiness? Was she fair and golden without any substance beneath?

A shiny gold necklace…a gold gilding over cheap brass.

He swallowed hard, hands knotting, temper so hot he fought to keep it in check. He felt like a boiling cauldron, anger roiling, anger threatening to burn and destroy.

His gaze fell on her fair head bowed over the boy's. She held the child close to her breast, the child's cheek against her heart, his small lips parted in the bliss of sleep.

Oh, to be a child again, loved and protected, cradled against the harsh reality of life. Pain flickered briefly within, the flash of memory, another flash, this time of beautiful dark eyes, long dark hair, tears in his mother's eyes and a piercing cry as he was pulled from his mother's arms. *Mama! I want my Mama!*

He hated the memory and shoved it away, erasing all traces of a past that no longer mattered.

He'd lost his mother and survived. Ben would survive, too, if that's what fate decreed.

Yet seeing them together like this, Bryn and the boy, seeing the child's love and trust, and his wife's devotion made his chest tighten. If he came between them, it would destroy both Bryn and the boy. He'd shatter his own family, the very thing he'd vowed he'd never do.

But he wasn't the man that married Bryn. He wasn't a man who loved anymore. He wanted revenge. He wanted to punish. He wanted to break his wayward wife's spirit.

It didn't have to be like this. But she'd made her choice. Now he made his.

"Was there another man in Zwar?" he asked abruptly, turning from her, unable to look at the Madonna and child image another moment.

She would pay. Oh, how he'd make her pay.

"No." Her whispered voice reached his ears, a catch in her voice, tension in the answer.

She didn't answer with confidence. He heard the waver and the hint of guilt. Slowly he pivoted, took a step toward her. "You don't sound very sure of yourself. Would you like to think about the question a little longer?"

"I don't need to think about the question. I was faithful to you."

"Sexually?"

"Yes." Her voice hardened but red color rushed to her cheeks, heightening the blueness of her eyes, the paleness of her brow and chin. She looked like a painting, a Rueben, with the glow of red against her alabaster skin and the deep sapphire brilliance in her eyes.

"You're sure?"

"Quite sure."

"And emotionally?"

"My God, Kahlil, what kind of questions are these? If you suspect me of adultery then say so, but I won't play word games or guessing games with you. I've given you my answer and it's an honest answer. I never slept with another man while married to you. I never wanted to be with another man while married to you." The red wave of color began to recede, her cheeks turning a softer, paler pink, her lips quivering with emotion. "I just wanted you."

So why did she leave? His cold, analytical mind wanted to lacerate her tremulous words, cut through the softness to the truth. She was lying. Or she was hiding something. Either way, she'd deceived him and come precariously close to breaking his heart.

Thank God he'd recovered in time. Rifaat, his valet and personal assistant, had seen to that. Reminded Kahlil of his duties, his obligations, the future. The loss of his father helped focus him. Zwar mourned its leader and

Kahlil put his personal crisis behind him to focus on his country.

His work helped. For a time. Until he'd learned that Bryn was planning to marry again, and all the old emotions returned. The betrayal back, the pain resurfacing, the tangled emotions…anger, shock, disbelief. *I loved you. How could you walk away from me?*

It was the angry cry of a child forgotten. And he'd felt abandoned.

Kahlil despised the weakness within him, the need to love and be loved. He shouldn't feel such a need for people, or relationships. His father had never married again after his mother was gone. Why couldn't he be as strong?

''What am I doing with you here?'' he gritted. ''What am I thinking?''

She sat forward, expression brightening. ''You can turn the plane around. It's not too late. We haven't even crossed the Atlantic yet.''

Her eagerness to escape infuriated him all over again. Who was she to make decisions? She ran away. She left him. She may have even cheated on him.

''If I send you back, I send you alone.''

She looked confused, forehead furrowing and then suddenly she understood. ''And Ben?''

Kahlil felt cold, hard, strong. ''He is the crown prince. One day he will inherit my title, and position as leader of my people. He, of course, remains with me.''

She stirred, panic in her eyes, panic in her sudden restless motions. ''I'll go to the ambassador—''

"And what do you hope the ambassador will do? The child is mine. As his father, I have rights. Not even the American government will argue that point."

"They won't allow you to keep him from me!"

"Of course not. And I have no intention of keeping you and the boy apart. You are free to come and go, visiting as often as you like, but Ben will remain at the palace in Tiva."

"Without me?"

"He's young. He'd adjust." He heard the harshness in his voice and he didn't care. She'd deprived him of the first three years of his child's life. She deserved whatever she got.

"You'd break his heart."

"Hearts mend. Wounds heal. I know."

"And knowing what you know, you'd still hurt him like that?"

"You are in no position to lecture me. You were never going to let me be part of his life. You were determined to keep him to yourself." His upper lip curled, a primal snarl he couldn't conceal. "In a few years Zwar will be his home, and my people his people. Ben will love the adventure of it, and he'll be blessed with wealth, position and opportunity."

"You can't buy him, or his affections!"

He shrugged, glad to see her squirm. He'd shaken her.

"I want to call the ambassador," she demanded. "Now."

"I'm sorry. The phone isn't working."

"That's not true. You made some calls earlier."

''But that was earlier. This is now.''

''Kahlil, you have no right—''

''I have every right!''

His voice thundered, waking Ben. Bryn tried to hush her son back to sleep but Ben was definitely awake, lifting his head and sleepily gazing around the cabin.

''Are we there yet?'' he asked with a yawn, brown eyes blinking, a worried crease between his jet-black eyebrows.

''No, not yet,'' she soothed, pressing a kiss to his forehead, silently cursing Kahlil for waking Ben, and waking him in the middle of a fight. This is exactly what she wanted to protect Ben from. But Ben wasn't about to go back to sleep, not when he sensed so much tension in the air.

Tipping his head back, he stared into her face, one small hand reaching out to touch her mouth. ''Why are you yelling?''

It was on the tip of her tongue to reply that it was Kahlil yelling, Kahlil being impossible, but she couldn't say that, none of it. Whatever her feelings were for Kahlil, she couldn't allow them to influence Ben. He'd need to establish his own relationship with Kahlil, without prejudices from her.

''Was I yelling?'' she murmured, struggling to modulate her voice, and calm her racing pulse. This was a long trip, a long night, she had to get her emotions under control.

''Yes. You were yelling at that man.''

That man. Your father.

She looked up, pained, her gaze settling on Kahlil. In his black turtleneck and his blazer, Kahlil looked darkly forbidding, his beautiful features hard, his expression contemptuous.

''I'm sorry,'' she answered. ''I shouldn't yell. It hurts peoples ears, doesn't it?''

''Yes,'' Ben agreed, sitting up and wrapping his small, cool fingers around hers. ''Who is that man? Why is he with us?''

Pain tugged at her heart. She couldn't lie, couldn't ignore the question, either. Ben needed to know the truth, and he'd find out soon, if not now, then quickly after they landed. Far better to hear it from her.

''Ben, this is...your...'' Her gaze lifted, her eyes meeting Kahlil's. She found no warmth in his expression, no compassion in his golden eyes. Bryn dropped her gaze, focusing on Ben, trying to blot out the image of a seething Kahlil. ''Ben, this man, he's your...is your...''

''Daddy.''

Kahlil said it, completed the sentence, his voice crackling with anger.

It wasn't the way she wanted it said. Not with so much anger and force. Not with that kind of arrogance, either.

''Yes,'' she hurriedly agreed, hoping to soften things, ease the tension. ''He is your daddy. We were married a long time ago and lived in a beautiful desert.''

''A beautiful desert?'' Ben looked past Bryn to Kahlil. ''In a tent? With camels?''

''In a palace,'' Kahlil replied. ''But we do have camels.''

Ben sat up even straighter, using his palm to push away from her chest. ''I like camels.'' He looked so serious, his expression exactly like Kahlil's. ''I am Ben,'' he said firmly, precisely, dark eyes frowning, black eyebrows furrowed in concentration. ''That's my name. What is yours?''

''Sheikh Kahlil Hasim al-Assad.''

''That's a lot of names.''

''Not so many. Soon you will have a name like mine, too.''

''Okay.''

Okay. That was all it took. Ben accepted it, accepted the new father, the new name, the new home just like that.

Ben looked at her, touched her cheek with his fingertips. ''This is my real daddy?'' he whispered, with a swift glance at Kahlil.

''Yes.''

''The one I wanted?''

''The one you wanted, my baby.''

No one spoke. Bryn's pulse raced. She could sense Ben's struggle, his confusion and questions. Everything had changed for him just like that. Suddenly Ben thrust a hand out to Kahlil. ''I'm Ben, Daddy.''

Kahlil's features hardened, his jaw granite-tight. For a moment he didn't move, his expression closed and grim. And then slowly, very slowly he reached out with his own hand and took his son's. ''I'm pleased to meet you, Ben. It's good we're finally together.''

Ben nodded solemnly. ''It's been a long time.''

Kahlil's dark gaze lifted, his eyes met Bryn's and held. ''A very long time.''

CHAPTER FIVE

THE Learjet made its final approach and landed soundlessly on the asphalt runway. Minutes later it came to a smooth stop in front of a low, brightly lit building.

Before the jet's door opened, a grim Kahlil emerged from the private bedroom cabin, his Western clothes hidden by his robe, the *djellaba,* and a white *howli* concealing his dark hair. Bryn's stomach did somersaults and she swallowed hard, lumps swelling her throat closed.

Sheikh Kahlil al-Assad. In person.

He turned, glanced her direction, his flinty gaze inspecting her hair and dress. ''You must cover yourself.''

''It might seem strange to Ben,'' she replied, placing an uneasy hand on the top of her son's head.

His gaze met hers and held. After a tense silence, he answered. ''It will seem more strange to him if you force me to take action.''

Kahlil didn't understand. Ben might be half Arab, but he'd never been exposed to Middle Eastern customs. He didn't know anything of the language or the culture. ''Just give me a chance to explain to him first.''

Kahlil's mouth compressed, contemptuously. ''I think I should be the one to explain. After all, wearing the *djellaba* and *howli* are *my* customs. I understand far better than you.''

And he did explain, in a matter of thirty seconds, saying without apology that the robe and veil made women special, protecting pretty women and turning them into princesses. ''Would you like your mom to be a princess?''

Ben smiled, a small shy smile, and hesitantly nodded. ''Put it on, Mommy. I want to see you be a princess.''

Kahlil had trapped her. Again. She stood immobile while Kahlil unfolded a long black *djellaba* and another shorter cloth. His hands moved quickly, settling the robe across her shoulders and then the veil over her head. She felt the brush of his fingers at her temple and then against her mouth.

Fresh tears filled her eyes. She wanted him, but not like this. She wanted him when they loved only each other, believed only in the other.

Suddenly he leaned forward and pressed a kiss to her mouth, through the thin fabric of the veil. ''We're home,'' he said quietly, victorious. ''Remember where you are now. Remember who you are now.''

She couldn't speak, the air bottled in her chest and the fine hairs tingled at her nape. Fear, fatigue and anxiety overwhelmed her. She felt unbalanced, torn between her own need and Ben's needs realizing that they weren't the same and wouldn't ever be the same again.

Ben tugged at the black robe and she stepped back to see him. He wrinkled his nose as he inspected her clothes. ''She doesn't look like a princess,'' he said, disappointed, even a little disgusted. ''Princesses don't wear dresses like that.''

She'd read him too many stories, told him too many fantastic versions of Cinderella, Snow White, Sleeping Beauty. He knew princesses were soft, sweet magical creatures, nothing like the dark robed mother in front of him.

Bryn would have smiled if the situation weren't so serious. She curled an arm around his waist, and hugged him to her legs. ''It's okay,'' she answered quickly. ''The robe is to help Mommy. It's a costume, something fun and new.''

''But he said, the daddy said, you'd be a princess. I want you to look like a princess. Take it off,'' he insisted, tugging harder on the robe, trying to draw it away from her legs. ''Please, Mommy, take it off now.''

''She can't,'' Kahlil said quietly but firmly, crouching next to Ben. ''And your mommy understands. She's not upset. She knows why she needs to wear it.''

''Why?'' Tears shone in Ben's eyes, his lower lip thrust, curling with weariness and petulance.

''Because we're in my country, and it's a different country with different rules. We treat our women very special and we like to protect them. If your mommy wears this robe, she'll be safe.''

''It's magic? Like a spell?'' Kahlil had caught Ben's imagination again, and the tears dried in his eyes.

''A little like that. And she won't wear it forever, just until we reach the palace.''

''But it's not a nice color. It should be a pretty color.

Like pink, or blue. Mommy looks pretty in pink or blue.''

''Then let's pick her out a pretty dress when we reach the palace. We'll look at all the beautiful dresses and you tell me which ones would be nice on your beautiful mommy.'' Kahlil stood, extended a hand. ''Now, let's go see the palace.''

They were moving across the tarmac into the brightly lit building when sudden shouts drew a virtual army of soldiers from the building and the airport perimeter.

''What's happening?'' Bryn cried, turning to Kahlil.

He shook his head. ''I don't know,'' he replied, swinging Benjamin into his arms.

Bryn wanted Ben, needed him with her but the soldiers were converging, carrying enormous guns that filled her with terror.

One soldier approached Kahlil, bowed deeply and murmured something in Arabic.

Kahlil nodded curtly, picked up his pace and drew Ben even closer to his chest. He cast a brief glance in Bryn's direction but his expression revealed nothing.

They were practically running. She noted that the soldiers had formed a tight protective circle around Kahlil and herself and that a spotlight was sweeping the tarmac, casting a great white blinding light behind them.

Inside the building the door slammed shut and the soldiers moved, separating Bryn from Kahlil.

''Ben!'' she cried, reaching out for him, but the soldiers stepped toward her, distancing her further from Kahlil and her child.

Her mouth tasted like sawdust and she swallowed convulsively, realizing it was fear making her throat seal close. What was happening? Where were they taking her? Where were Kahlil and Ben going?

She hadn't realized she'd voiced the questions aloud until a crisp voice answered her in nearly flawless English, "No harm will come to you. Please be patient, Princess. All questions will be answered in due time."

Be patient? How? Ben was gone and soldiers were relentless, never once touching her, but moving her continually forward, leading her through an unmarked door and out into the night.

A car awaited, a black luxury-style car, a Mercedes she guessed, and the back door opened. She had no choice but to climb in and the door slammed shut, the car swiftly pulling away.

"Where are we going?" she asked the driver, hands balling in her lap.

The driver briefly glanced into the rearview mirror, dark eyes flashing, but he didn't speak, and just as swiftly his attention returned to the road.

She'd asked the question not really expecting an answer. In Zwar, men did not address strange women, especially Western women, but she'd felt compelled to assert herself, to try to make sense of the chaos at the airport.

"What happened back there?" she persisted. "Why so many soldiers?"

The driver didn't even glance into the rearview mirror this time. He simply continued driving.

Bryn leaned against the seat, fear and indignation wrestling for the upper hand. How could Kahlil do this to her? And yet thank God he had Ben. No one would touch Ben if Kahlil held him. And Kahlil would protect him, she knew that much. He might hate her, but he already loved his son.

Massive gates opened to accept the limousine, only to shut loudly after the car passed through the compound's high stone walls. Bryn felt relieved when they finally reached the palace. She wanted only to see Ben again. To know that he was safe.

Inside the palace, the guards silently handed her off to two robed servants, one which she recognized immediately as Rifaat, Kahlil's personal assistant. Part butler, part secretary, Rifaat al Surakh handled Kahlil's private affairs, business as well as personal. In the past he'd managed everything from travel arrangements to political gatherings.

Bryn felt a momentary glow, relieved to see her old friend again. ''Rifaat, how are you?''

''Well, thank you, Princess,'' he returned, bowing deeply. The son of a diplomat, he'd been educated in the West, attending prestigious Georgetown University in Washington D.C., before returning to Zwar and serving in the diplomatic corps like his father before him.

Bright, sophisticated, modern, Rifaat had always been her friend. ''Rifaat, help me, please. The soldiers at the airport, they took my baby from me. Is he here? What happened?''

Rifaat bowed again. ''I shall escort you to your rooms, Princess.''

''No, I don't want to go to my room. I must see Kahlil. He has my son. Are they here? Have they arrived?''

The second manservant silently walked away, leaving Rifaat and Bryn alone. With the second man gone, Rifaat bowed a third time. ''I am to escort you to the ladies' quarters. Your maid is waiting for you there.''

I must see Kahlil,'' she repeated firmly, squaring her shoulders. ''Please, Rifaat. My *son.*''

His eyes flashed, his gaze briefly meeting hers, before he looked away, staring at a point just past her shoulder. He didn't look at her again. He didn't intend to speak.

''Rifaat, *please.*''

''Your room has been prepared,'' he repeated woodenly, carefully keeping his gaze fixed on the marble pillar behind her. ''I hope you find it satisfactory.''

She blanched, as if he'd thrown a glass of icy cold water in her face. He didn't intend to tell her anything. Even if he knew where Kahlil was, Rifaat wouldn't share his information with her. They might have been friends five years ago but they weren't friends now.

Turning, Rifaat set off down the marble hall, his slippered feet noiseless on the gleaming black-and-white marble floor. She followed behind him, having no other choice. No one would deal with her here, not until Kahlil had given instructions.

At the elaborately carved entry to the east wing, the wing where the women lived, a veiled maid appeared and bowed to Bryn. Kahlil's valet walked away without a look back.

He'd done his duty, she thought bitterly. He'd escorted her to the harem. He could get her off his hands.

She stared after him, watching the valet's departing back. He treated her the way Kahlil had treated her—with anger, with scorn, with contempt.

She flushed faintly, the skin hot and tight across her cheekbones. Only one thing could be worse than her current situation. The return of Amin.

The young maid introduced herself as Lalia and announced that she would be the princess' personal assistant, helping with dressing and hair and happiness.

Bryn nearly smiled at the peculiar description of services to be rendered. Dressing and hair and happiness. As if life were so easy.

But Bryn didn't smile and Lalia shot a shy, nervous smile at her as she led Bryn into her private suite of rooms. "For you, my lady," Lalia said, gesturing around the spacious high-ceiling bedroom. Her English was stilted, her accent heavy. "You like, my lady?"

"Lalia," Bryn spoke gently, persuasively. "My husband, the sheikh, I must see him. He has my son, and I'm afraid."

"No fears," Lalia replied, rustling her hands like flower petals in a breeze. "Everything is lovely here. Just the way you like, yes?"

"My son—"

"This room, very pretty, yes?"

Lalia wouldn't tell her anything, either. The girl wouldn't even acknowledge Bryn's pain.

No one would.

Slowly, numbly, Bryn wandered to the middle of the room, her old room, the same one she'd had three and a half years ago, and glanced at the pale peach carpet beneath her feet.

The carpet's pattern was intricate, vines and scrolls and ornate vases, a priceless wool carpet made seven hundred years ago for a Persian queen, reputedly the most beautiful woman in the East. Kahlil had bought the carpet for her, installed it in her room. He wanted everything perfect for his bride, his future queen.

It hadn't worked out that way.

Her gaze fell on the small, elegant carved wood chest sitting next to her bed on the night table.

Her jewelry box.

Amin. The struggle. Her last night at the palace three and a half years ago.

Her heart did a ragged double-beat, revulsion radiating from her middle to her arms and legs, making her shake. She took an involuntary step backward as if she could put space between her and memories of the past.

Slowly she crossed to the nightstand and even more slowly lifted the dark heavy lid on the box. Diamonds, sapphires, rubies, emeralds sparkled in a sea of purple velvet.

Couldn't be. She'd taken it all, emptying the box into

her purse before fleeing the palace, dumping the glittering jewelry—bangles, chokers, drop earrings, a gold-and-diamond crusted tiara—all presents from Kahlil, into her handbag. She'd used the jewelry to buy her way out of Zwar, smuggling herself onto a charter flight to New York and then another flight, this one on a commercial liner to Dallas where Rose had picked her up from the airport.

But the jewels were all here, or perhaps they were merely replacements, a tiara for a tiara, gold bangles for gold bangles. Her chest tightened with sorrow and fresh pain.

He believed Amin but not her. He'd trusted Amin but not her.

Bryn lowered the jewelry box lid, the lid closing with a hollow little thud, much like her heart in her chest.

She sat down slowly on the edge of the bed, her hands braced on either side of her hips, her fingers outstretched on the smooth silk coverlet. She was stricken at the memory of her last night in the palace, in this room. Amin had trapped her here, his mouth had covered hers to stifle her scream. He'd tasted sour, of alcohol and old cigarettes, and he'd used his weight to pin her on the bed.

"My lady, this is your old room, yes? You like room, yes?"

Old room… Yes. Bryn shivered, blinked and forced herself to pull out of the past and focus on Lalia. It was her old room. A room that had given her nightmares for years.

Bryn stood up, crossed her arms over her chest. She felt disgust and fury that she was being trapped in this room—in this life—again. "I'm sorry, but I can't stay here. You'll have to tell his highness this room won't do."

Lalia opened her mouth but before she could speak, Bryn marched to the door. "Never mind, I'll tell him myself."

Bryn got nowhere. Guards outside the women's quarters wouldn't let her pass. They simply stood there, two abreast, and shook their heads. "Don't make me scream."

The guards didn't even blink.

So she screamed, loudly, shockingly loudly, screaming as though she were being hurt, even murdered, and no one came.

And the soldiers didn't move.

Only Lalia fell to Bryn's feet weeping. "Please, Princess, please, Princess, please."

"Lalia, stop!"

"Princess, you'll get me in trouble. I shall be very punished for displeasing you."

The girl was clutching Bryn's feet, pressing her lips to Bryn's ankle bones. "Lalia!"

But the girl continued to beg, muttering teary incoherent things in Arabic, speaking so rapidly that Bryn only picked up words and brief phrases. "Lalia, no one will punish you."

"His lord highness will!"

"That's not true."

Lalia cast a fearful glance at the guards. ''My lady,'' she choked, pressing her wet face against Bryn's shin, ''your last girl was sent to very bad place. Please, Princess, do not have send me away, too.''

Bryn felt a rush of remorse. Was that true? Had Adjia, her first maid, been punished? ''I must see his highness. I must,'' she said more quietly.

''And you will. His highness will call for you. I know. I am sure. Now come, Princess, have some tea.''

Kahlil had been home only three hours and already he'd received a phone call from Amin.

He slowly hung up the receiver and stared at the photograph on his office desk, a silver-framed photo Amin had given him of the two of them. The picture had been snapped after a polo match a number of years ago. Amin had his arm slung around Kahlil's neck and they were laughing at a joke Amin had made. They looked like the best of friends.

For a while Kahlil had thought they were best friends, or at least very good friends.

But that changed a long, long time ago—back before they were adults with duties. Responsibilities. Kahlil wondered when friendship had turned to envy. When genuine affection had transformed into manipulation.

During their twenties they had still laughed, continued to share a joke and spend an evening together, but it wasn't without tension. And guilt. Kahlil didn't need to be reminded that fate had treated them differently—Kahlil the crown prince. Amin, the poor relation.

And now Amin wanted to come home again, to return to Zwar for a visit. Amin had only been back once in three and a half years, and that was for an afternoon, for Kahlil's father's funeral. They hadn't even talked then. Amin acted as if the funeral was merely a government formality.

So why did Amin want to return to Tiva now? Why not six months ago? Six weeks ago? Six months from now?

It couldn't be because of Bryn, could it?

Kahlil picked up the framed photograph. He studied Amin's boyishly handsome face, the light gray eyes, the laughing mouth.

Maybe it was time he put to rest the rumors, and the speculation. If there was something between Bryn and Amin he might as well find out now.

Kahlil returned the photo to his desk and reached for the phone again. Swiftly he punched the numbers to Amin's apartment in Monte Carlo. Amin answered almost right away.

"I've thought it over," Kahlil said coolly. "You're right. It has been a long time since we've been together. Come home. Let's catch up."

Bryn watched the maid unpack the small overnight bag that managed to make the trip from Dallas.

Silently, industriously, Lalia tucked Bryn's handful of lingerie and undergarments into the clothing wardrobe. But her expression changed when she pulled the dresses and pantsuit from the bottom of the bag. ''These are not for Princess,'' she said.

But I don't want to be a princess, Bryn thought in exasperation from her perch on the foot of the bed. She just wanted to be Bryn, a twenty-four-year-old mother with a small but sincere circle of friends. She'd made a good life for herself in Texas; it might not have been fancy, and she might have lived off limited means, but it was her life and she wasn't complaining.

Lalia hung up Bryn's dresses but did so with obvious distaste. She opened up the second wardrobe door and gestured to the rainbow of color inside. Turquoise, royal-blue, violet, rose, peach, lemon-yellow, ivory, white, gold. Silks, chiffon, satin, velvets. Long gowns beaded and embroidered, jewel encrusted. ''For Princess,'' Lalia said, ''You like?''

Incredible. How long had those dresses been hanging in the closet? How much had Kahlil invested in them while waiting for her to return?

Her jewelry box was full. The wardrobe an abundance of delicate fabrics and vibrant color. Gold slippers lined on the floor.

It was how it had been before. It was how Kahlil determined it would be again. Everything had changed but nothing was different.

Incredible. Excruciating. Bryn felt a torment of guilt, realizing how hard it must have been for Kahlil to wait for her, understanding for the first time that he had never intended their marriage to end. He'd merely given her time.

He'd wanted her back.

Lalia gently closed the wardrobe doors and turned to face Bryn. "Everything is ready. Come, we shall draw your bath."

Undressing in the marble bathroom, Bryn caught a glimpse of herself in the massive gilt-framed mirror. Her long hair hung lank, blue shadows dimmed the brightness of her eyes. She felt like hell and she looked it, too.

"My lady, the bath is hot, yes, see? Please, sit." Lalia gestured to the gold sunken tub set in white marble shot with streaks of gray. The tub's faucets were gold. The sink and fixtures were gold. Marble and gold. Real gold. Solid gold. A bathroom fit for a queen.

Fragrant steam rose from the gold tub, flower petals floated on the water's surface.

Bryn dropped her towel, shy but resigned to the palace's lack of privacy. The palace maids were too well trained, too fearful of displeasing to not fulfill their duties, and their duties were many. It was their job to serve, to assist, to make the princess's life comfortable.

Suddenly Kahlil's voice grated, shattering the quiet. "Leave us," he said, voice echoing in the polished marble bath. "I wish to speak to my wife. *Alone.*"

Lalia fled the room, bowing, scraping, whimpering worshiping words that drove Bryn crazy.

Bryn's first impulse was to leap from the tub and grab a towel, but she found herself frozen, reclining beneath the rose strewn scented water in shock. ''What are you doing here? Where's Ben?''

''Which question should I answer first?''

She felt her blood begin to boil. ''Ben, please. Where is he? And what on earth happened at the airport?''

''It doesn't concern you.''

''There isn't any real threat, is there? I won't have Ben subjected to unrest or instability.''

''Your imagination runs away with you again. It was a protective measure, nothing more than that.''

''I don't like being separated from Ben and I want him back.''

He turned his face to the door. ''Unfortunately you're not getting him back.''

''Kahlil!''

''Sorry, but it's the truth. I'm removing him from your care until I know what to do.''

''About what?'' she demanded, her temper growing hotter.

''As a crown prince, the boy will need a very special education. He will require challenging coursework, intensive study of languages and exposure to European and Eastern cultures.''

''He's three. Practically a baby!''

''I was sent to England not much older than Ben is now. It's better if we begin preparing him for his duty soon—''

''No!'' The protest was wrung from her, her voice strangled. ''I will never send him away. I will not have strangers raise my son.''

Slowly he pivoted to face her, his gold gaze narrowing, black lashes lowering as he studied her reclining figure. Her knees, her pale bare thighs, her tummy, the rise of her breasts. ''The matter's out of your hands. We're in Zwar. Your opinion holds no weight.''

She sat upright, anger jackknifing in her middle. ''If you think I'll bow and scrape like Lalia then you've another think coming, Sheikh al-Assad. I might be back in Tiva, but I'm not the clinging, fragile girl you married all those years ago. I'm stronger, and this time I have a voice.''

In the hours since she and Kahlil had been parted at the airport, her husband had showered and changed, leaving Western clothes behind to dress in a traditional robe. He looked distant, detached. ''If you had a voice, wouldn't I hear it?''

Confusion made her stop and think. ''Yes…''

''Then why didn't I hear it earlier when you screamed?''

He'd heard her this afternoon, heard her cry and ignored it. Brilliant pain, hot and blinding, shot through her. Cupping a handful of water, she threw it at him, and again, liberally splashing him.

Kahlil leaned over and hauled her out of the bath onto the cool, slick marble floor. ''You've done it now.''

Goose pimples covered her flesh. ''Be mad at me, but don't take Ben away. I don't know what kind of game you're playing, but it's not fair, and it's not right.''

He dragged her against him, hip to hip, thigh to thigh,

their bodies pressed lightly. ''This isn't a game. The games are over. The consequences begin.''

Hot, cold, she felt feverish and sick. ''Punishing Ben isn't fair.''

''I'm not punishing Ben, I'm punishing you. You lied to me, deceived me, stole from me—''

Fear filled her limbs like cold wet cement. ''If you're talking about the jewelry—''

''I'm talking about my son. He is mine, isn't he?''

''Of course he's yours. Just look at him! *Your* eyes, *your* nose, *your* mouth. He's you all over.''

''Then my actions are justified.''

Closing the last bit of distance between them, he pressed her naked, shivering body more tightly to him and covered her mouth with his. It was a soul-searching kiss, drawing her breath from her lungs, drinking her protests into him.

He kissed her until her legs buckled and tiny yellow spots danced against the darkness of her mind. She was trembling, clutching his robe, feeling the rapid thud of his heart through his chest.

''I am sorry,'' he murmured, lifting his head, his golden eyes filled with a silent pain he couldn't, wouldn't articulate. ''I have to do this for my country, and my people. There is no other way.''

His body was warm, the hard planes of muscle curving tautly beneath the press of her palms. She felt him against her, felt his heat and strength and remembered what it had been like to lie with him, and love him, and be loved by him. ''If you try to take him from me,'' she choked, ''I will fight you for him, every second of every hour of every day.''

''And you will lose.''

''I have no choice but to fight. He is my hope.''

''Mine, too.''

CHAPTER SIX

BRYN couldn't stop pacing her bedroom floor, replaying the scene in the bathroom over and over in her mind, trying to forget the feel of his lips against hers, the strength of his body. He'd kissed her to punish her and yet his mouth had been anything but hard, his touch anything but unkind. She felt the old desire flicker there and burst into flame. He still wanted her but this time he wanted her for revenge.

She shivered, appalled by her response to him, and the fact that she could be attracted to a man who could wrest her son away from her. But Kahlil wasn't just any man. He was her husband. Ben's father.

Ben's father.

Oh God, what had she done? How could she have thought she'd get away with keeping Ben's parentage a secret? Kahlil was one of the wealthiest, most powerful men in the world. He was bound to find out. If not now, then later, when Ben was older and pressing to know more about his birth father. Children wanted to know these things. They had a right to know these things.

Bryn felt fresh guilt and concern. She knew instinctively that Kahlil would never hurt Ben…at least never consciously. But could he do so unconsciously? Unwittingly?

Arguing with Kahlil had always been difficult. He was intelligent, quick, eloquent. He mashed her words. Turned her arguments around so that in the end she was just contradicting herself, flustered and tongue-tied.

But now, Kahlil wouldn't even argue. He stated his opinions as facts and expected her to submit. But this wasn't the Middle Ages and she wasn't a woman raised in a harem.

She understood Kahlil's anger and frustration. She realized he needed time to sort his emotions out. But she wasn't about to allow Kahlil to strip her out of her rights.

Ben was her son. He was only three and even though he was a bright, adventurous little boy, he was also quite sensitive. He must be wondering where she was. He must be anxious to see her.

If Kahlil wouldn't bring Ben to her, then she would go to him.

The palace was dark. Serenely still. Bryn felt a thrill ripple down her spine as she tiptoed past Lalia's cot in the outer room and into the shadowy hall.

Moonlight dappled the marble floor and Bryn crept from the women's quarters to the main reception rooms and down another wing to the guest quarters. She was sure Kahlil had sent Ben there. There weren't many options. The men's quarter, the women's, the guest rooms, and then the sheikh's private suite.

She slowly opened the first door and peered into the room which was lit only by moonlight. The window was unshuttered and the large, low bed was empty.

Carefully she closed the door, moved to the next and repeated the inspection. Empty room. Empty bed.

At the third door she felt a tremor. Her senses were taut, her anxiety high. It was more frightening creeping around the palace than she'd anticipated and for a moment she had the unnerving sensation of being followed.

Ridiculous. Everybody was asleep. No one stirred.

Bryn pushed the door wider. The room looked inky and full of shadows. With the curtains drawn she could just make out a shape. She caught a sudden movement from the corner of her eye and her instincts screamed for her to run.

Lights flooded the spacious bedchamber, unusually bright lights blinding her. Hands clamped on her forearms, lifting her off her feet.

''Let me go!'' Bryn swung out with her arms and legs, kicking, elbows flying. ''Put me down!''

''Stop it, Bryn. You're only making this worse.''

With a sinking sensation in the pit of her stomach, she heard the rasp of Kahlil's voice and caught a glimpse of his profile. His jaw was shadowed with the beginnings of a beard. ''How…what…?''

''Motion detectors,'' he said shortly, making sense of her incoherence, even as he dragged her past a bevy of palace guards clustered in the doorway. Another cluster of guards stood at the far end of the marble hallway watching. ''State-of-the-art security. The moment you left your room my surveillance camera turned on.''

Mortification flooded her veins with fresh adrenaline. He'd *watched* her tiptoe through the palace. He'd watched her search through the rooms. "You're a Peeping Tom!"

"And you're a sneak," he retorted grimly, his white robe parted revealing far more skin than Bryn was comfortable with.

He looked raw and primitive and incredibly male—which is exactly what had gotten her into trouble five years ago. "I wouldn't have to sneak around if you'd just let me see my son!"

"I have never met such a disobedient woman in my life."

"I'm sorry you've been so sheltered, but I have to tell you there are hundreds—thousands—of women who are certain to be more difficult than me." Bryn yanked on her arm, struggling to free herself. "Now let me go!"

"Not an option." He swung her into his arms and clasped her firmly against his chest. "I cannot sleep with you wandering the palace, and my guards will get no rest if I return you to your room. You'll stay with me tonight. And I promise you, you'll go nowhere."

Kahlil kicked the door shut behind him. The tall tapered candles in the wall sconces flickered, casting dancing shadows on the smooth plaster walls and center columns. She shivered, feeling as though he'd carried her back in time. "Candles?"

"More restful." He dropped her on his bed, the midnight-blue velvet coverlet creasing, the dark velvet gleaming like water beneath the moon.

It crossed her mind that she was truly in trouble now.

Kahlil would never hurt her—she trusted him with her life—but being alone with him like this was incredibly dangerous. She'd never been able to resist his warmth, nor his strength.

Bryn swallowed and grabbed handfuls of the velvet coverlet, crushing the soft fabric against her skin. "What do you intend to do?"

"Lock you up."

Her heart did a painful leap, like a skydiver jumping off a cliff. "I'm serious."

"So am I." He shot her a peculiar glance as he drew a dark carved wood box from his ornate wardrobe. "Runaway wives ruin reputations."

She cast a wary look at the wood box and then up into his face. His expression was blank, frighteningly so. "You don't need to worry about my reputation. I'm fine. I'll be fine."

"It's my reputation that concerns me." He closed the wardrobe doors and turned toward her. The box in the crook of his arm was heavy enough to tense his forearm, muscles drawn, delineated, every part of him beautifully made.

"Just what is that?"

He shifted the box from his arm to the bed. "Instruments of my pleasure."

"Very funny." She stared uneasily at the lid of the box, the dark wood carved into fanciful designs; serpents encircling a tree, doves against a vine, the limbs of a man and woman intimately entwined. Not an innocent box. Not an innocent man.

''You think I'm joking?'' His black hair gleaming in the candlelight.

Maybe not. He was seriously humor-impaired, but before she could say a thing, even as she touched the tip of her tongue to her rapidly drying upper lip, he snapped the lid open, revealing the contents.

Bright gold gleamed against scarlet silk.

Bryn blinked. Thick gold bands nestled against blood-red silk. Her heart did a second, but equally painful jump. What were those? What was Kahlil planning to do?

As he leaned forward, lifting the gold bangles from the box, his robe shifted, revealing more of the hard planes of his chest, the muscles taut beneath the gleam of skin. She could just catch a whiff of the sandalwood fragrance he wore, exotic, spicy, erotic. Heat flooded her veins, her body craving his.

But the rush of desire died a quick death when Kahlil opened one of the gold bangles and snapped it shut around her slim wrist.

''You're handcuffing me?'' Her voice rose to a fevered pitch. Just who the hell did he think he was?

''I'll do what I have to do.''

''This in unacceptable, Kahlil, even from you.'' She tried to shake off the band but he'd secured it tightly, clasping it on one of the smallest locks. It pinched, too, not terribly, but just enough to remind her she was trapped.

Furious, she shook her arm again. The blasted handcuff weighed at least a pound. Had to be solid gold. No other reason for it to be so heavy.

"I had to curtail your wanderlust."

"I just wanted to see Ben."

Utterly remorseless, he opened the second gold band, this connected to the one on her wrist by a long, thick gold chain. "And I'd already told you no. What part of 'no' don't you understand?"

Tears started to her eyes, tears of shame and anger. "The part where you tell me to jump and I'm expected to do your bidding." She jerked on the chain, nearly pulling the second handcuff from his hold. "Do you enjoy degrading women?"

"Of course not, but I enjoy peace of mind, and you, woman, give me none." He snapped the second handcuff to his own wrist, linking them together.

She'd expected him to shackle her to the bed. It hadn't crossed her mind he'd lock her to him. She stared at the three-foot gold chain in alarm. Tethered. Trapped. His prisoner.

Could the punishment be worse? "I'm not going to spend the night locked up like a criminal!"

"You're lucky I haven't had you arrested. The thought has crossed my mind. Several times."

"I haven't broken any laws."

"Any? Try a half dozen. You'd be treated harshly in our court, too. We don't look kindly on rebellious women."

"So send me to prison. Explain that to Ben!"

"I wouldn't have to tell Ben you went to prison. I

could always say you chose to leave. You wanted to go home, and so you did."

"Leaving him here, without me?"

Kahlil shrugged, tightened the second shackle, and tugged on the heavy gold chain. Bryn fell forward, at the mercy of Kahlil's whim. "Mothers are human. They make mistakes. Change their minds. Run from responsibility all the time."

"Not me."

He shrugged again. "To tell you the truth, Bryn, I don't really care. I've been up over forty-eight hours without sleep, crossed the Atlantic twice, saved you from an imprudent wedding, discovered a son. I'm tired. I just want sleep."

"I'd rather be thrown into a pit of vipers!"

An eyebrow lifted. "How melodramatic, even from you."

She changed her approach, gentled her tone. She had to make him see reason. "Kahlil, you know I'm a light sleeper. How can I rest like this?"

"That's your problem, not mine. You should have thought about the consequences before you snuck out of the harem. However, what's done is done and now we'll go to bed."

"I will not sleep with you."

"*Bryn,* you are trying my patience. Can't you see I am doing my best to take care of you?"

She tugged furiously on the chain linking them. "This is your idea of taking care of me? My God, you aren't fit to be a father!"

His expression suddenly darkened, brows lowering, his features hard and cold. She'd struck a nerve. Oh, how she'd struck a nerve!

''If you want to live to see the morning, I'd lie down, and be very, very quiet. I'm tired of you making a fool out of me. I need sleep. You need supervision. I'm sorry I'm forced to treat you like a farm animal, but this is the only solution I can think of.''

''A farm animal! I'll show you a farm animal—'' She broke off to give the chain a violent yank. His arm didn't even move. He didn't even wobble. She pulled harder, with every bit of her strength, fighting to knock him off balance but Kahlil didn't budge. He simply stood there, immobile, allowing himself the smallest smile of pleasure.

Damn his six-foot-three-inch body. Damn his immense shoulders and solid thighs. Damn the muscles and skin and his incredible warm, spicy scent. ''I hate you!''

He smiled, all teeth. ''The feeling is mutual, darling. So go to bed and save us both another scene.'' And with that, he tossed back the velvet comforter, revealing dark gold satin sheets and practically threw her into bed.

Then he stripped—stripped!—peeling his white cotton trousers off his lean hips and shrugging out of the white robe.

The gold chain linking them jingled as he slid into bed next to her, the mattress giving slightly, satin sheets cool and smooth against her heated skin.

''Do you have to sleep naked?'' she gritted, trying to

block out the image of his large body stretched carelessly next to hers.

He rolled to his side, the chain between them momentarily tightening, the gold satin sheet sliding low on his waist, emphasizing his deep chest and wide shoulders. ''We're married. This is about as sexless as it gets.''

Blood rushed to her cheeks. ''What about the candles? Aren't you going to blow them out?''

''Not tonight. I'm going to need them to keep an eye on you. Besides, they'll burn out eventually. Close to morning.'' He reached out, touched a long silvery-blond strand of hair. ''And Bryn, you won't be able to break this chain. Don't try. It'll just be a waste of energy.''

She glanced at the gold chain stretched between them, still shocked he'd actually handcuff her to him. What kind of man handcuffs a woman? A medieval man. That's the kind of man, she answered herself darkly. And a man without the least bit of modesty. How could he climb into bed with her without a scrap of clothing on? For heaven's sake, the satin sheet revealed far more than it hid, outlining the hard, carved planes of his body.

''If this is the way you hope to win me over, you're wrong. Dead wrong.''

He shrugged in the semidarkness, candlelight dancing across the plastered wall, creating patterns on the stone floor. ''I don't need to win you over. I already own you.''

He touched her again, this time brushing her shoulder with the tip of his finger, his fingertip gliding across her heated skin. Bryn felt a ball of desire coil in her belly, the hunger so strong it sent a rush of blood between her thighs.

''Three years I've waited for you,'' he continued softly. ''Three years. You don't think I'm going to let you escape now?''

''Loving someone isn't about possession!''

His fingertip found her breast, slowly circled the budding nipple. ''Who said anything about love? I'm thinking retribution.'' He tweaked her pert nipple, not gently, and she gasped. ''Now sleep. I'm tired. You've made it a very long day.'' And with that he rolled over and closed his eyes. Within minutes his breathing changed, indicating he had really, truly fallen asleep.

Bryn stretched out her legs, her body aching, trembling, every muscle tight and unsatisfied. There was a special hell for men like Kahlil and Bryn wished her husband there with every beat of her heart.

Later, much later, a sinfully delicious warmth stole over her and she stirred, although only a little, unwilling to lose the pleasure. She felt wonderful, her skin felt wonderful, her body sensitive and alive. *Sleep or dream?* she asked herself, giving over to the heat and pleasure, not wanting to open her eyes in case it was just a dream.

Hands slid across her middle, over her breasts, a knee parting her own.

This was no dream. Immediately she remembered where she was, who she was with, and eyes flying open she gazed into Kahlil's gold eyes. The candles had burned low, most having extinguished themselves, and Kahlil's face was heavily shadowed.

He cupped her breast, his rough palm grazing her nipple and her lips parted, first a protest, and then a sigh.

Helplessly she arched her back, as her body stirred to life. She lifted her lashes to stare at his mouth, longing to be kissed by him again, wanting his lips against hers.

Kahlil shifted, kicking aside the satin sheet, his strong, naked thigh planting between her knees, parting her legs and moving between her thighs.

Her nightgown hiked up, tangling around her hips. She wanted nothing more than to circle his neck with her arms and draw his head down to hers. She craved his mouth, his tongue, his touch.

But instead of covering her mouth, his lips found the sensitive places on her neck, secret nerve endings that responded only to him. His tongue circled from earlobe to collarbone and she breathed faster, shallowly, head spinning with the dizzy pleasure.

Bryn worked her arms free and immediately wrapped her arms around his shoulders. They were broad, and she held him as if she were drowning. Being this close to him, being celibate so long, unleashed powerful emotions that had nothing to do with mere physical desire.

She needed him—needed to be a part of him, loved by him the way only he could love her.

"You're on fire," he whispered, his voice husky.

"I need you."

He didn't need any other encouragement. Impatiently Kahlil stripped her of her panties and slid his palm up the inside of her thigh, setting off a riot of sensation. Every place he touched burned, her skin glowing hot, then cold and hot again.

She trembled, waiting for his touch, knowing he'd touch her intimately and when he did, it would be intense, and intensely erotic.

At last his fingers cupped her mound, pressing against her heat before parting her to discover her softness and moisture. Bryn bucked, her body tense, her nerves straining. She was too excited, too aroused, finding the gentleness of his touch as painful as it was exciting.

''Please, please—'' she begged, inarticulate, her brain clouded and unable to think. All she knew was that she'd waited forever to be with him, she had dreamed of him, dreamed of this night after night, year after year, and to finally be with him and not part of him… *''Kahlil.''*

''Patience,'' he answered, easing his hand in her, over her, awakening her again, pushing her to a brittle brink.

Bryn clasped his ribs, lifting her mouth to his chest, holding him hard and close, as if she could melt into him, become one with him, escape the limitations of skin and bone.

She felt him harden, his arousal more ardent, his body tensing. She felt a smile inside of her, enjoying her own brief glimpse of power, and parting her lips, she kissed his chest, tongue teasing across the ridge of muscle, down the breastbone and across to one contracted nipple.

Subtle spice filled her nose, his warm skin fragrant, his body deliciously put together. Sucking his nipple, she heard him groan. Her small smile became a thrill of pleasure. She was exultant that she could make him ache, make him feel, make him reach for her.

His pleasure fed hers, shooting hot darts of sensation from her breast to her belly, her lower abdomen tight and heavy. She needed him inside her now.

Bryn wrapped her hands around his back and dragged him closer. She felt his erection brush against her sensitive folds. ''Now, Kahlil, please.''

He moved, parting her knees wider, sliding her feet up to create more tension. The gold chain swinging between them clinked, rattling, a stark reminder of the bitter ties binding them.

Kahlil frowned, his features dark, his expression forbidding. She felt his tension, felt the anticipation, but realized with a glance at his narrowed eyes and thin-lipped mouth that he would take her but not love her.

And still she wanted him.

Clasping her bottom, he lifted her hips higher, hesitating just a second before driving deep inside her. This was no gentle lovemaking but a statement of ownership. He was branding her his with each hard, penetrating thrust. He filled her completely, her body tender, tight stretching to accept him. She felt like a virgin, inexperienced and overwhelmed by his strength and driving passion.

She couldn't catch her breath, couldn't hold his shoulders, kiss his lips. He was taking her his way, filling her, dominating her, and she shuddered beneath him as his hips rocked against her, each deep thrust felt more raw, more intense, more powerful than the last. She felt alive, too alive, her skin, her bones, her muscles tightening, tensing, every nerve ending concentrating. Suddenly it was too strong, too real, the flood of emotion rising swiftly within her made her oblivious to all but this razor-sharp sensation.

Kahlil arched into her, straining, pushing her to the surface. That last thrust threw her from control into the wild beyond. She would have screamed if his mouth hadn't covered hers, sucking the brilliant pleasure from her lips into his mouth.

She felt utterly lost, shudder after shudder coursing through her, tears filling her eyes. She'd wanted him, she needed him…she would always need him. She could never deny him anything. Not even her heart.

Kahlil sighed, a sound of pure exasperation and Bryn felt his reluctance as he drew her close to him, forming a safe, protective circle around her with his arms.

Yet he didn't say a word. And he gave no other caress.

Tears stung the back of her eyes and she bit her lower lip, fighting to hang on to her last vestige of pride. They'd made love many, many times before, but it had never felt so empty afterward, never so naked and needy and…desperate.

Bryn longed to grab the sheet and cover them, or find a corner and hide, but the handcuff chafed her wrist, a heavy reminder that she was tied to him.

CHAPTER SEVEN

"LAST night was a mistake." Kahlil wouldn't even look at her, his back turned to her, his shadow stretching long across the sunlit courtyard. "It can't happen again, and it won't. From now on you will sleep in the women's quarters, even if I must chain you to the floor."

Making love last night had only increased the tension between them. Anger crackled from him in invisible electric waves. "You don't have to chain me to the floor. You have Ben. I'm not going anywhere."

"As if I trust anything you say."

Bryn ignored his contemptuous snort, keeping her own emotions carefully checked. It had been painful last night to be in Kahlil's bed. Realizing too late that she hadn't sufficiently hardened her heart had done nothing to assuage the aching emptiness in her heart. If this was love, she could live without it.

"You don't trust me, but you'll make love to me."

"I'm sorry. I lost control. I'll do my best to make sure it never happens again."

If he was trying to hurt her, he was succeeding. Chaining her to him wasn't punishment enough. He'd degrade her now. Humiliate her after sharing the most intimate act of all. Pain splintered within her, fresh realization at the depth of his hatred for her. "Well, I won't apologize. What happened between us was lovely.''

''It was sex.''

Her cheeks burned, heat surging to her face. She wouldn't back down. Refused to let him turn their love-making into something ugly and sordid. She'd been a willing partner last night. And so had he. ''Then it was good sex, great sex.''

He cast her a dubious glance over his shoulders, lips twisting grimly. ''You speak for me, or just yourself?''

A second surge of blood followed the first. *Stand firm,* she seethed. *Don't roll over and die.* ''Why not? You said we're still married, so why shouldn't we find comfort in each other's arms?''

''I find no comfort in sleeping with you. Just release.''

She'd vowed not to cry, and she'd meant to keep her vow, but his harshness hurt, cutting deep. She ached at the change in him, the change in them. She couldn't do this, she couldn't stay frozen emotionally. Not when he was making her feel so much and reminding her of how things had been.

Years ago when they made love, he'd murmur endearments in his native tongue, *Sweet flower of the garden; most beautiful night star; treasure of the desert.* No longer. His hatred was palpable.

If she didn't have Ben, she might have run from his anger, but she couldn't run. She needed to win Kahlil's trust, and custody of Ben. Ben needed his daddy, and she needed Kahlil, too.

Heartache gave way to action. Bryn stiffened, her

shoulders squaring. She'd do what she had to do. She'd make her marriage work, by hell or high water.

By hell or high water, she repeated silently, fiercely.

No regrets. No turning back. "Tell me what you want from me. I shall do whatever you wish. I shall be exactly as you want me to be."

"Such a change of heart."

"It's the conviction of my heart."

"You do this for me?"

"And my son."

"Ah, your son." His smile was flinty, his gold eyes icy. "I wondered when you'd return to that theme. This isn't about me, is it? It's about you, and you getting your way."

"I just want to see Ben. Even if it's just for a few minutes."

"You're in no position to make demands."

"I realize that. I'm prepared to bargain."

"Bargain or beg?"

"Either," she answered wearily. "I'll do anything to see him."

"Anything?"

The coldness in his voice stole her breath but she held her position, hands pressing together for courage. He'd push her, she realized, push her to the brink and beyond. "Anything." She clung to her resolve. It was all she had left. "I will accept whatever punishment you give me, and I will serve you in whatever capacity you request, provided you let me see my son. Soon."

"We'll see."

"Does that mean I might be able to see him today, or tonight?"

"It means I'm thinking about it."

It didn't answer the burning loneliness. "I need to know he's okay."

"He is fine."

"I don't know what fine means."

"I do, and I tell you he's fine."

"Not good enough!"

"It's all the reassurance you're getting."

She shivered inwardly, hurting in ways he couldn't imagine. He hadn't known Ben long enough to feel the intense and desperate need to love and protect one's child. Every nerve in her body screamed to bridge the distance between her and Ben, every muscle ached to just hold him against her chest. It was such a primitive instinct, but truer than anything else she'd ever felt. "Tell me what you want me to do, Kahlil, and I shall do it."

"There's nothing you can do."

"Don't say that, there must be a task, give me one, let's think of one."

"*Baraka!* Stop."

Bryn felt as though she was losing control, her emotions dangerously unhinged. "Let me prove myself, let me prove I can be trusted." She fell to her knees and clasped her hands, begging. "I will serve you, obey you—"

Kahlil hauled her to her feet, scorn blazing in his eyes. "How can I respect you, if you insist on behaving like a madwoman? I did not marry you for this, I do not desire a wife without control—''

''But you've reduced me to this! To begging, groveling, pleading. I am yours. I am no better than your handmaidens in the harem. I will do whatever I must to please you. Now let me prove it.''

A tiny muscle in his jaw popped. He reached inside his outer robe, drawing papers from a pocket sewn on the inside. ''Then sign it. Let's get this over with.''

Her fingers curled into her palm. She didn't dare touch the papers, viewing them as something inherently offensive. ''What are those?''

''Divorce papers.''

His voice shivered down her spine, his tone incredibly cold and unfeeling.

''I've been advised by my cabinet to move forward with the divorce,'' he continued. ''I've lost too much face with my people. My staff and servants know I cannot manage you. Word has spread about your disloyalty and there is no place for you here anymore.''

She didn't speak, didn't trust herself to answer. After last night, after the passion in his bed…he'd do this?

He edged towards her, the papers rustling in his hand. ''I will take care of you financially, of course.''

Chilled from head to toe, Bryn wrapped her arms around herself, gold bracelets tinkling like water splashing from the fountain. ''And Ben?'' Her voice sounded like a flutter, a whisper of wings on the sun-kissed morning.

''He'd remain with me.''

Of course.

''Sign them,'' Kahlil ruthlessly continued, ''and by this afternoon you'll be on a plane home. Free.''

Bryn heard a faint, dull buzz in her head, rather like the hum of a vacuum. She gave her head a slow shake to dislodge the buzzing noise. ''Won't sign that. Ever.''

''It's in your best interest.''

''No, *it's in yours.*'' She felt warmth bead her brow, her body growing hot where moments ago it had been cold. ''What kind of mother do you think I am, to turn my back on my child?''

''I'd arrange visits.''

''Unacceptable.''

''Mothers do it all the time.''

''Not this one. Not ever.''

''The child would adjust, better than you think.''

''*The child.*'' Fury rocketed through her. She clenched her hands, resisting the urge to lash out at him, physically and emotionally. ''Not *the child,* but Ben. Your son, my son, our son. I won't leave here without Ben.''

''And I won't let him go.''

''Then I stay.'' Shaking, she grabbed the documents from his hand, tearing them into little bits before he could stop her. ''I'll never divorce you. If you want to keep him here, then you keep me as well. It's a package deal, Kahlil. Ben and I stay together, always.''

She'd rendered him speechless. Good! Because anything he said just now would seriously push her over the edge.

The strained silence enveloped them in a cloak of

quiet that stilled the distant chirping of birds and splash of fountain.

When Kahlil finally broke the silence, his voice was quiet, almost thoughtful. "Always?"

"Yes."

"You'd do that for your son?"

He knew so little about the power of love! The papers scattered from her fingers and she threw her head back, the sun dazzling her, blinding her eyes. She couldn't see him clearly, only felt him, huge and overpowering. "I would die for him. In a heartbeat."

"Just like that?"

"No question in my mind. Is that what you want me to do? Pay the ultimate sacrifice?"

"God, no!" Kahlil visibly drew back, his expression closing, lashes lowering. He turned away to gaze across the protected courtyard. "How far we've come from what we were."

His voice, a mere whisper, wafted in the warm sunlight, wound its way into the tenderness of her heart. *How far we've come from what we were.*

Was that really regret she heard? Was that sorrow she saw in his eyes?

Her own eyes burned and a knot formed in her throat.

Kahlil turned his back to her. "I think it's best if you returned to your quarters. We'll talk later. I promise."

It wasn't the way he'd planned the meeting. He'd expected tears, yes, and angry accusations, but not her willingness to beg—beg!—at his feet, to kneel before him and offer herself, a sacrifice at the altar.

His gut burned, his eyes burned, his heart burned. Fire in his chest. Fire in his head. Fire everywhere. Kahlil swallowed with difficulty, his mouth tasting sour. He found no pleasure in his victory, no joy in his power, especially after what had taken place between them the night before. He'd wanted her, needed to feel her, touch her, taste her, but his desire infuriated him.

How could he want a woman he didn't trust? How could he desire her when she'd betrayed him both privately and publicly, breaking every sacred vow?

He'd wanted to punish her this morning, force her to submit, and yet when she did…it made him even angrier.

Kahlil slumped against the marble pillar, his head aching, his temper barely leashed. He was furious, but tonight his anger was directed entirely at himself.

Bryn had never been like the other women he'd taken to bed. From the beginning she was different, exciting, innocent, passionate, daring. She'd wanted the world and he'd been eager to give it to her. He'd thought he could give it to her. He'd failed.

A knock sounded on the outer door of his chamber. Kahlil called out, knowing it was his valet, and welcomed Rifaat to enter.

"The new papers," Rifaat said, walking the documents to Kahlil's large ornate desk in the center of the room and setting them down. "They just need your signature."

Perplexed, Kahlil stared at the sheath on his desk. He

knew what his advisors had suggested but he wasn't sure he could follow through with it. "Thank you."

"I suppose you could force her to sign."

Force, there it was again. Force her to submit, force her to bed, force her to break. The use and abuse of his position disgusted him. Why didn't revenge taste sweeter? Why didn't he relish his power? "She won't leave Ben."

The valet didn't answer and Kahlil pushed off the pillar and approached the desk, lifting the documents to read them yet again. "At least she's a better mother than a wife."

Still, Rifaat said nothing.

Wearily Kahlil tossed the papers back onto the gleaming surface of the desk. "Has my cousin arrived yet?"

"No."

"Let me know when he does. Good night."

"Good night, my lord."

Kahlil crouched next to the small bed in the nursery and gently drew the covers back. The child stirred, curling his hand more closely beneath his cheek, nestling deeper into his pillow.

Little boy, my boy. Kahlil's eyes burned, and with a hard swallow, he accepted that it could not continue like this. It would not continue like this. There ought to be a sanctuary for children, a sacred place to protect their innocence. Their tenderness.

Perhaps if he had been protected as a child he might be a different man today…he might be a different leader.

Kahlil's palm rested against his son's head. The child's hair felt silky, his scalp felt warm. Kahlil could feel his son breathe, feel his son's innate strength.

Protect the child. Protect his life.

Calmer, feeling the first hint of peace in days, Kahlil scooped Ben into his arms and stood. The boy weighed nothing but meant everything.

Footsteps sounded in her room. Bryn lifted her head, squinting in the darkness as her heart raced. Someone was in her room. Someone was moving her way.

She swung her legs out from beneath the covers and rubbed her eyes. Full of fear she was reminded of another night, another intruder.

''Bryn.''

Kahlil.

Her husband's deep voice, his English crisp, formal, echoed in the dark. ''Are you awake?''

''Yes. What's happened?''

''Nothing. Shh, he's still asleep. Don't wake him.''

Suddenly she knew. Bryn nearly lunged from bed, flinging the covers back. Kahlil had brought Ben back to her!

Kahlil placed Ben on the mattress next to her and drew the silk comforter up, covering them. Speechless, Bryn pressed the back of her hand to Ben's warm cheek. He was real. He was here.

Warmth filled her. A dizzying hope. ''Thank you,'' she choked, the words grossly inadequate. ''Thank you so much.''

Kahlil nodded, and without speaking, headed for the door.

''Kahlil, what does this mean?''

Her voice stopped him. ''I don't know.'' He hesitated, his features shadowed, his expression reserved. ''Maybe it means we call a truce. No more fighting. At least, not over our son.''

''Never again,'' she swiftly agreed. ''Kahlil, thank you again. I mean it. From the bottom of my heart—''

''I know.''

He stood framed in the doorway, the soft yellow light of the hall illuminating his height and strength and his honey-gold skin.

He looked like a prince from a medieval storybook, darkly handsome and yet so alone. She realized bleakly that he had no one, not since she had left him.

He hesitated in the doorway. She felt his tension, his silence throbbing with unspoken meaning.

The ache in her chest was so strong it made it nearly impossible to breathe. She wanted to go to him, touch him, hold him, love him. But she was afraid, so afraid of the distance between them.

''Good night, Bryn. I hope you sleep well.''

''I will now.''

''So will I.'' He turned, and left, heading off alone into the dark of the night.

Bryn cuddled Ben to her but she couldn't sleep. Minutes passed, a half hour crept by, and then finally an hour, but it wasn't a peaceful rest. She felt anything but peaceful, not when Kahlil punctuated her thoughts.

From the moment she ran into Kahlil in the Dallas parking lot, she'd felt the impact of the fender-bender accident reverberate through every part of her life.

When Kahlil climbed out of his luxury sedan, the shock wave deepened. He had said words that her mind didn't capture. She couldn't focus on his speech, only on his face. She'd known him sometime, somewhere. Recognized him from a previous life. She couldn't tear her gaze away. Entranced by the symmetry of his brow, sweep of cheekbone, the strong aquiline nose, he was the most amazing man she'd ever seen. Like Valentino from the old movies, he seemed perfect.

Kahlil had been astonished that she not only knew where Tiva was, but that she'd spent her first thirteen years in the Middle East, most in the Zwar desert. They'd gone for coffee and the one coffee became an all-night conversation.

Disarmingly honest, he told her she wasn't like most women in his country. She'd thought he meant it as a compliment. Now she knew better. Their cultural differences would destroy them, if she let it.

Kahlil needed her, but he'd never tell her. Not after she'd betrayed him, and she had betrayed him. She'd become too close to Amin, developing a friendship with an Arab man—Kahlil's first cousin, of all people!—to answer her insecurity. It hadn't been enough to be loved by Kahlil. She'd needed endless reassurance, constant proof of love.

Bryn wanted to blame her insecurity on her parents' death, and the culture shock she'd experienced moving to Aunt Rose's house in Texas, but she'd felt adrift before the market blast. Truthfully she felt adrift most of her life. She'd never felt at ease with her parents' nomadic lifestyle, nor their ability to live without friends, and worldly possessions. She wanted a bedroom of her own, pink rosebud paper on the walls, chintz curtains, lots of dolls and stuffed animals on her pillow. She wanted books on shelves, toys stacked in a closet, shoes and clothes tucked in a solid wood dresser.

Instead there had been one knapsack, a half-dozen worn dresses, a battered brown bear. Her parents meant well. They believed they were an example of good values, teaching her that things didn't matter, making it clear that too many possessions only tied one down. But Bryn wanted to be tied down and longed for the stability of a real house. It was her great childhood fantasy, waking up to discover her parents had bought a two-story house with shingles and shutters and a painted picket fence. There would be kids riding bikes on the street, and girls jumping rope or playing jacks. Bryn would go to a real school and every day she would walk home, carrying her book bag and laughing with her schoolmates.

Her parents laughed at her fantasy world, telling her it was the exact thing they'd left behind. No ordinary life for them.

Bryn had spent most of her life trying to be ordinary. Kahlil had not been ordinary. But he'd wanted what she did—stability, security, tradition. And family. They both wanted children. Desperately.

Bryn gently kissed Ben, careful not to wake him. She was grateful to hold him again, soothed by his proximity. But she couldn't sleep, not when her thoughts revolved around Kahlil.

Tonight, for the first time in years, she'd seen a chink in Kahlil's armor, and instead of moving in to wound him, she wanted only to protect him. Protect the man she'd once loved, *still loved,* when he was at his most vulnerable.

She felt a tumult of emotion, even new emotions, a combination of tenderness…forgiveness…regret. Once she and Kahlil had been so sweet together, so full of hope and love. Could they find it again? Could they ever find their way back to each other again?

Bryn slid out of bed, leaving Ben nestled in her pillows and covers, and rang for her maid. She explained that she needed to be taken to Kahlil immediately.

He was in bed, sleeping. Rifaat opened the door for her, giving her access where all else would be denied.

Bryn hadn't stopped to think, she just acted, responding to the impulse that drove her from her room to his in the dead of night.

Kahlil sat up, the satin sheet falling to his waist. Her heart did a funny double-beat. He looked shockingly sexual. Breathtakingly male, and virile.

Unlike Stan.

Unlike any other man she'd ever known.

Kahlil's gold eyes, heavily lashed and darkly brooding, met hers. ''Yes?''

As their gazes locked her heart turned over. His eyes

undid her. She wanted only to go to him, beg him to forgive her, beg him to love her. Instead she stood stiffly several feet away, feeling the chasm between them, the secrets and mistrust, the mistakes and fear.

He shifted restlessly. ''What do you want?''

Her chest constricted. ''You.''

Kahlil's forehead furrowed, an ebony lock shadowing his strong, beautiful face. Slowly he flipped back the satin sheet, making space for her next to him. It was the same thing she'd done earlier for Ben.

She ran to him, climbed into his bed, burying herself in his arms. ''Kahlil, I—''

He stopped her, silencing her words with his lips. 'No,'' he whispered. ''No talking, I don't trust words.''

His lips covered hers, and his body moved against her, the hard planes of his chest brushing the peaks of her aching breasts, his hips pressing to her belly. She felt him harden, and he moved her onto her back, his weight braced on his elbows. Fire surged within her, fire and hunger. Only one man could answer this feverish need, and that man was her first and last love, Kahlil.

CHAPTER EIGHT

SKIN still damp, desire finally satiated, Bryn gazed up at Kahlil, waiting for him to speak. She knew there was something on his mind. He had that look, the tension at his mouth, fine creases fanning from his eyes.

She wouldn't press the issue, if there was an issue. Far better to give Kahlil time. And truly, she felt deliciously relaxed, muscles weak, pulse finally slowing from its earlier furious rhythm.

Kahlil reached for her, running his callused palm across her bare midriff, over her rib cage, his fingers exploring each rib and inch of skin until he cupped one breast, and its rose-tipped peak in his hand. "You were serious yesterday, about staying?"

She stared at his hand on her breast, torn between the warmth stealing through her, the heat surging to life yet again in her belly and between her thighs, and the fear his words created.

"Bryn?"

He still wanted to send her home. Even after this, after the most intimate acts a man and woman could do together.

She closed her eyes briefly. "I won't go, if that's what you're asking."

"Is that what I'm asking?" He kicked back the sheet,

exposing both of them to light. His body was hard everywhere, his chest deep, hips narrow and hard, his thigh thickly muscled. He was still so strong. She could see the soldier in him. He'd served six years in the Zwar military. All Zwar men served their country. Ben would have to serve as well.

"Well, isn't it?" she returned, unconsciously squaring her shoulders, denying her desire to feel him again, be taken again, savored again. He made her feel like a delicacy and she loved his skill, his incredible sexual prowess.

But that wasn't the issue, she reminded herself, wondering why she'd though Kahlil would ever be anything but an adversary. Truce, indeed! He was still trying to wrest Ben from her custody. "Ben and I stay together. Always."

"No divorce?"

"Not a chance."

Abruptly Kahlil leaned forward and suckled one of her nipples. Silvery arrows of sensation shot from her nipple to her belly and she moaned a protest.

Kahlil lifted his head, smiled his satisfaction. He relished his power over her. Relished the control. "So you have no objection then to renewing our vows?"

Renewing vows. Bryn jerked, grabbed for the sheet, feeling the need for protection. "Renew vows…as in *marry* again?"

He pushed her hand away from the sheet. "Leave it. I like seeing you this way."

"I can't think naked."

''Of course you can. Concentrate.'' His gaze turned brooding. ''We were married the first time in an American courthouse. This time we'd do it here. A traditional Arab ceremony.''

Marry Kahlil again?

Her mind spun, thoughts racing, her body felt heavy, almost languid.

To be loved by Kahlil again, feel the strength and hunger of his passion not just once, but again and again, to return to his arms, his heart, his—

But he wasn't declaring love. She wasn't returning as a beloved wife, but as an object. His property. This was part of his domination, his need for control.

So? A little voice challenged deep inside her. What did it matter? She'd be with him; they'd be a family. Ben would have what he wanted and Bryn—she'd be with Kahlil again, and really, wasn't that what she wanted?

There was no reason they couldn't make it work. It had been wonderful between them in the beginning, heaven, sweet heaven before the worst hell.

A clock bonged somewhere in the palace. She felt the weight of time, the weight of the past. The last three and a half years had been so long, so incredibly difficult. She couldn't imagine going back to that kind of life again. ''If we were never divorced, why do we need to renew our vows?''

He reached out, plucked a long white-gold tendril from her shoulder, and allowed the hair to slip between his fingers. ''It's a show of faith.''

The intimacy of the touch, the ease with which he touched her, created a hunger inside of her, her belly tightening with need. If only he'd touch her again, her cheek, her breast, her belly, her thighs. She sucked in a breath, appalled by the intensity of her desire.

''Is this for Ben's b…benefit?'' she asked, curling her fingers into her palms, her limbs melting, her body melting.

''Ben, and my people.''

His people. But not her. Never her.

It stung, but better that he be honest than let her get her hopes up. This way she knew where she stood. This time she was not the beloved, but the obligation. Not the jewel in his crown but the mother of his son.

Kahlil caught her chin in his fingers and turned her head to face him. ''You have a problem marrying me again?''

''No.'' She could see nothing now but Kahlil's face. Her gaze met his and she stared into his eyes, mesmerized by gold flecks and the determination she saw there. He exuded intensity, and conviction. He was brilliant, complex, emotional. He fascinated her mind and confounded her heart.

Leaning forward Kahlil's nose briefly touched hers, his lips a breath away. ''You must be quite sure, Bryn. I won't suffer a runaway wife again.''

His lips brushed hers. A shiver raced down her spine.

''Hmm?'' he murmured, his fingers splaying against her jaw, his palm cool and strong against her throat.

She pressed her trembling lips to his. She was unable

to hold his words in her mind; her brain was lost to hunger.

His mouth, firm, cool, rasped her lips. He drew back an inch. ''I need an answer, Bryn.''

Her eyes closed. She leaned forward a hair, closing the distance between them again. ''Yes.''

''You'll marry me again?''

''Yes.''

And this time when they made love it was with hunger and intensity, a consuming desire that nearly burned them both alive. Nothing mattered, she thought blindly, nothing mattered but them, and this.

She returned to her room just before dawn, senses satiated, heart still raw. She was wrong, she acknowledged, opening her door and gazing at sleeping Ben, there were things that did matter more than making love to Kahlil.

Ben, for starters.

And earning Kahlil's love.

All the lovemaking in the world wasn't enough to ease the loneliness inside her. Kahlil touched her, tasted her, took her with passion but the emptiness in her heart, the detachment in his expression, only grew.

If only he'd utter one affectionate word, give her a sign of deeper feelings, but he kept his emotions hidden and shared with her just…skin.

His body. Her body. He was doing his best to reduce their relationship to sex.

Bryn closed her eyes, leaned against the doorframe, drawing a slow, ragged breath. She wanted Kahlil, but she wanted it the way it had once been between them. She wanted Kahlil to love her. And he didn't.

Her fear, at first small, but now growing, was that he wouldn't. Ever. But she clamped down on the fear, reducing it in size until she could breathe easier. She refused to panic, had no intention of subjecting herself—or Ben—to emotional chaos. Once she might have run away from her fears, but not anymore.

Bryn bathed and was dressed by the time Ben awoke. His delight in seeing her brought tears to her eyes. He hugged her and hugged her, holding so tightly she begged him to be gentle, to let her breathe.

"I love Mommy, I love you!"

"I love you. I missed you." She kissed his mouth, his forehead, the tip of his nose. "How are you? What have you been doing?"

He told her about his activities, chattering as she dressed him and continuing through breakfast, talking a mile a minute about everything he'd discovered since arriving in Zwar. Puppies, and miniature trains, cousins, soccer and card games. Lots to eat. Movies on videotape. Even a ride on a beautiful black pony.

"You've done all that in only two days?" Bryn said, indulgently teasing him, enjoying every breathless announcement he made.

They lingered over their breakfast in the courtyard, Ben frequently leaving his chair to creep into her lap for a snuggle.

Now with the dishes cleared away he'd begun to explore the patio garden, first poking at a pill bug he'd discovered in one of the massive clay pots and then sniffing at gardenias planted beneath a tall palm.

Footsteps echoed on the stone floor. Bryn glanced up, hoping it was Lalia with the promised coffee. Bryn had found the adjustment to mint tea impossible, but it wasn't Lalia with coffee.

It was a man. Broad-shouldered, slim-hipped, darkly handsome like Kahlil but not as tall. Amin stood before her in an expensive light gray suit, white shirt, pewter silk tie smiling. ''Hello, gorgeous.''

Bryn's arm went nerveless, her hand falling to her lap. She tried to stand but couldn't. ''What are you doing here?''

''Is that the welcome I get after all these years?'' Amin thrust a hand into his trouser pockets, head bending, dark hair cut close, accenting his beauty. And he was beautiful, more so than Kahlil, the beauty of Hollywood film stars, fine bones, perfect symmetry in his features. But now his elegance and polish repelled Bryn. His external beauty hid the heart of a snake.

''You have no business being here.''

''But I live here.'' He smiled. A thin, flat, hard smile.

''Not in this part of the palace. These are my private rooms, part of the women's quarters.'' Although that didn't stop him last time.

Amin's smooth handsome face creased before quickly clearing. He lifted a hand, gesturing to the sun and sky. ''We're outside, and all this belongs to Allah.''

Finally her legs found the strength and she pushed up

from her chair, glancing in Ben's direction where he'd followed a ladybug beneath the breakfast table. "Then we shall go inside."

"I'm surprised you're not happier to see me. We have...unfinished business."

She stiffened, her gaze locking on the curve of Ben's small back, the shape of his hand as he prodded the spotted ladybug into flight. "There is no business between us, and I will not let you ruin my life again."

Amin followed her gaze, his heavily lashed eyes narrowing as he focused on Ben. "A handsome child." He drew aside the lace tablecloth. "He looks rather like me."

Her breath caught in her throat. She couldn't believe Amin had the gall to say such a thing. "I don't see the resemblance."

But Amin was grasping Ben by the shoulders and lifting him to his feet. Bryn's heart leaped in her chest. It made her skin crawl seeing Amin put his hands on her son.

"It's there in the eyes," Amin said, roughly tilting Ben's head back, before twisting his head one way and then the other. "His nose and mouth, like mine. He could be mine, couldn't he?"

Meet fire with fire, she told herself, resisting the urge to grab Ben and run. "It's only natural for you to see a family likeness." Reaching for Ben, she firmly drew him away from Amin against her own body, shielding him within the circle of her arms. "As Sheikh al-Assad's first cousin you have many of the same characteristics."

''Yes, his first cousin.'' Amin's eyes glittered like ice. ''How lucky we are to have each other.''

''Luckier than you deserve.''

''You really shouldn't take that tone with me,'' he drawled, taking seat in the chair opposite the one she'd just vacated. He stretched out his legs and crossed his arms behind his head, revealing his solid gold Rolex watch. ''I take it you've never told him about us.''

''There is no 'us,''' she answered sharply. ''Never has been.''

''Darling Bryn, how can you say that? We were once quite close.'' His lips pursed, eyebrows rising suggestively. ''*Very, very* close.''

''Not that close.''

''You invited me to your room.''

She had, but not like that. Not the way he was making it sound. Hand shaking she reached for Ben, needing to touch him, needing to find strength. ''You know I only wanted to talk.''

''Do I?''

She felt sick, dreadfully sick, the realization that this was one nightmare that wouldn't end. Amin was evil, the worst kind of evil, and she didn't know how to deal with him.

''I'm taking my son inside.'' She clasped Ben's hand in hers and squeezed it, fearing for him, for her, for Kahlil. If she let him, Amin would destroy everything again.

''Darling, you can run, but you can't hide.'' Amin's

perfect English followed her. ''I'm back, and I'm waiting.''

Bryn pushed Ben inside the door to her bedchamber, and locked it, before sinking to the ground and covering her face with her hands. She felt hot and cold and violently ill. *Please God, no, don't let him do this to me again…*

Small hands pulled her own away from her face. ''Mommy?''

Bryn heard his voice, saw his face but felt such unspeakable horror and dread that she could only manage the briefest of smiles, her lips stiff, unyielding. ''It's okay, baby.''

But it wasn't okay. It was anything but okay.

''You can't go in there now—''

Bryn brushed past Rifaat, throwing open the doors to the suite of rooms that housed the palace office. Computers, huge color monitors, phones, faxes, file cabinets, security cameras…the office came equipped, no old world palace in this modern suite.

Two secretaries startled, covered heads lifting from their keyboards. A third assistant appeared from an inner office. All stared at Bryn.

She didn't care. ''Where is he?'' she demanded, her gaze sweeping the dark paneled walls, deep red Persian carpet, the massive oil painting depicting a feudal warlord sacking a walled city while horrified people ran from burning buildings.

''He's on a conference call,'' Rifaat answered sharply, placing his body between hers and a partially open door.

Rifaat's heroic measures were unnecessary. Kahlil, dressed in Western clothes, black turtleneck and olive-green check trousers, appeared immediately in the inner office doorway, his broad shoulders filling the narrow space.

"What's going on in here?" He held a cordless phone to his chest. His black hair was ruffled, and his deep voice crackled with impatience.

"Nice painting," she snapped, furious with Amin, Rifaat, Kahlil, all of them. She'd forgotten the politics of the palace, the sheer implausibility of getting anything accomplished...at least if you were a woman.

"You interrupted an OPEC meeting to talk about my painting?"

"No." She drew a deep breath, her confidence suddenly flagging. "Your cousin Amin is back."

"Yes, I know, and he told me he saw you in the garden today." Kahlil's brows drew together. "He said you chatted for a few minutes and introduced Ben. Is there a problem?"

The way he put it, the visit between her and Amin sounded quite amicable. He wanted it to be amicable. Amin was his cousin after all, one of his closest relations. "No," she faltered, "I just wasn't sure you knew he'd returned."

"You're pleased then? He reminded me that you two were once such good friends."

She felt sick, her skin clammy. Trust Amin to begin planting poisonous seeds! She struggled to think of something that wouldn't be incriminating. She wasn't ready to tell Kahlil about Amin's assault. She needed to think of a way to share with him her own weaknesses and failings first. ''I...yes, it's always a pleasure to see your family. I just wished you had been the one to introduce Ben.''

''We'll have dinner tonight. I'll make sure he joins us. Ben, too. I'll take care of formal introductions then.''

Alarm bells sounded in her head. She wouldn't expose Ben to Amin again. She could handle Amin, as long as Ben wasn't present, subjected to Kahlil's cousin's cruelty and games. ''I know you like to eat late. It's really too late for a little boy. What if just the three of us had dinner? Better yet, maybe you and Amin would prefer to have dinner alone tonight.''

''The three of us,'' Kahlil said firmly. ''It wouldn't be a celebration without you.''

Anxiety tangled her in knots. ''What are we celebrating?''

''All of us being together again. Just like old times.''

Lalia formed a crown on Bryn's head of silvery-blond ringlets, the blond strands smooth, gleaming with a scented pomade. She dressed her in a slim white gown with a plunging neckline, which was more daring than most and a narrow silk skirt beaded with hundreds of tiny seed pearls.

''You look like a queen,'' Lalia said admiringly, handing Bryn a mirror.

But gazing at her reflection, Bryn didn't see a queen—she saw her worry, her eyes wide, anxious, her forehead knit, her lips pressed so tightly that white lines etched on either side of her pink mouth.

She was to meet Kahlil in his dining room in half an hour. But she had to speak to him first, before Amin appeared.

Bryn appeared at Kahlil's bedroom door without invitation. He frowned at her sudden appearance but didn't rebuke her. Yet his expression darkened when she mentioned she'd rather have a quiet dinner with him without Amin being present.

"You object to my cousin?" he asked shortly, tightening the black-and-gold belt worn over his white crisp trousers, and casting a narrowed glance in her direction.

"I'm more comfortable alone with you." She squirmed at her inability to be more direct. She wanted to tell him about Amin, but needed to approach the subject carefully. She needed Kahlil's trust, first, and a stronger bond.

"But I've already asked him to join us. It would be impolite to break the engagement now. That is, unless there's a reason why he shouldn't be included." Kahlil paused, a pregnant silence. "Bryn?"

She shifted uneasily, wondering if this was some kind of a test. What did Kahlil want her to say? "I...I'm not feeling very sociable tonight, that's all."

"But you look beautiful."

The compliment was edged with savagery. Bryn swallowed nervously. Something wasn't right. Kahlil didn't seem himself, or at least, not like the man she'd woken up with this morning.

"Amin's on his way to the dining hall now. What am I to tell him?" Kahlil persisted, sliding his arms into his outer robe. "That I've changed my mind? That I'd prefer an intimate meal with my wife instead of dinner together?''

''You are the sheikh,'' she whispered.

But he didn't immediately reply, just watched her with the same hawklike wariness he revealed earlier. ''All right. Fine. I'll send word that you and I are to dine alone, but I can't get out of the evening completely. I'll invite him for an hour from now. He'll have coffee and dessert with us.''

It was better than nothing. And perhaps by some miracle, she'd find a way in the next hour to tell Kahlil exactly what had happened all those years ago.

Grilled marinated lamb, peppers, saffron rice. The meal was simple and yet delicious. They sat facing each other on the carpeted floor, pillows behind their backs, a low table placed before them. Kahlil relaxed during dinner, talking easily, telling her stories, and continuously refilling their glasses with strong, burgundy-red wine.

''No more,'' she protested laughingly, when he moved to fill her glass again. ''You'll have me doing something silly in no time.''

''Sounds interesting,'' he answered, half reclining. ''Could I make some suggestions? I recall a very erotic dance you did for me once. If I remember, it required taking off your clothes, one by one.''

She blushed. ''I don't think it's wise, especially not with your cousin coming.''

Mentioning Amin's name profoundly changed Kahlil's mood. He nearly knocked over his gold wine goblet in his haste to rise. ''Not a good idea,'' he curtly agreed, moving from her to the small sitting area furnished with large overstuffed chairs upholstered in buttery leather.

Bryn rose to gather the dishes and fill the tray.

"Leave it," he ordered, sinking into one of the massive chairs, his golden gaze hooded, his expression impossible to read. "The servants will do that. You, come sit here with me."

She wiped her hands on a damp towel and moved slowly toward him. Kahlil's good mood was gone. He exuded anger, barely leashed tension. What had she said? What had she done?

She smoothed her skirt, preparing to sit in one of the leather chairs.

"Not there. Here."

Bryn hesitated uncertainly, glancing at his long, powerful legs, the ground, the circle of chairs. "Where?"

"Here," he repeated, pointing to the carpet. "At my feet."

"On my knees?"

"Yes."

Color swept through Bryn's cheeks, humiliated by the request. She didn't move. She couldn't. She stood rooted to the spot, trembling with shame and rage.

Seconds passed, long seconds passed, one after the other. She swallowed hard. A minute must have finally squeaked by.

Kahlil pointed to the carpet at his feet.

Nerves screaming in protest, she forced herself to move, walking slowly toward him and painfully lowering herself to the floor.

''Closer,'' he commanded.

She resisted yet again, smoldering at his imperial tone. He waited. She hesitated.

''Do you have a problem doing my bidding?'' he asked softly.

''I don't know why you want me to sit on the floor when you're inviting your cousin to join us. A chair would be more appropriate, don't you think?''

''It strikes me you're more interested in pleasing Amin than in pleasing me.''

''That's not so—'' She broke off at the sound of footsteps echoing on polished marble.

Amin had arrived. Kahlil gestured for him to come forward.

''Please let me up,'' she softly pleaded.

''No.'' Kahlil gazed down at her, utterly expressionless. ''Stay where you are.''

''You're unfair.''

''One more word and I shall use you as a footstool!''

Blushing furiously, she slowly sank down, her white silk skirt beaded with pearls billowing gently.

''Closer.''

Blood surging from her neck to her hairline, Bryn slid forward on her knees. Kahlil pointed to the navy cushion decorated with immense gold tassels wedged between his feet. ''Here.''

She cast an indignant glance at the pillow. Not just at his feet, she noted, clamping her jaw tightly together, but between his feet, like a dog panting for his master. Kahlil really was taking this king role to an extreme!

Her hesitation didn't go unnoticed. Bending down,

Kahlil tapped the pillow twice, a wordless command. All in front of Amin.

It was like pouring salt in tender wounds.

Her flashing blue eyes met Kahlil's and his thick black eyebrow lifted, *I'm waiting,* he seemed to say.

His dominance mortified her. She couldn't believe he was forcing her to submit in front of Amin. Torture, that's what this was, torture.

Irritably, her temper barely controlled, she scooted forward until she finally knelt between his legs, her hands balled in her silk-covered lap.

''That's better.''

''For whom?'' she gritted.

''Shh,'' he replied, pressing a finger to her lips. ''You don't want me to enforce my threat, do you? Because surely, *laeela,* you'd feel even more inelegant as a footstool.''

Amin laughed.

My God, he laughed.

She closed her eyes, held her breath and prayed for the ground to open.

It did not.

CHAPTER NINE

COFFEE was poured by a servant, desserts were passed, and Bryn sat during the boring conversation staring at the carpet in front of her. Amin droned on about his life in Monte Carlo: girls, cars, gambling in the glittering casinos. But finally conversation dwindled and Kahlil eventually bade Amin good-night.

As the door closed behind Amin, Bryn jumped to her feet, her legs stiff, her knees aching. ''Well, that was quite impressive! Amin must be amazed by your mastery.''

''Mastery of...?''

''Me,'' she snapped, banging her thumb into her chest.

Kahlil leaned back in his chair, tapping a finger to his lips. ''Do I have mastery over you?''

''That's not my point—''

''It's exactly my point,'' he interrupted. ''You promised me you'd change, assured me of your loyalty. Tonight was a test. I wanted to see how you'd behave around Amin.''

''Did I pass?''

''Yes. Beautifully.''

''Next time, tell me your intentions. I might be able to fulfil your imperial expectations.''

''Why tell you? So you can play a little game, pretend to obey? *Laeela,* I don't want pretense. I want the real thing.''

''Obedience.''

''Surrender.''

She shrugged impatiently. ''I've given you my body. I've agreed to renew our vows. What else can you want? What other proof do you need?''

''Yet you're angry.''

''Yes, I'm angry. I'm angry you think so little of me that you find it necessary to make me sit there like a lapdog, panting at your feet.''

His golden eyes suddenly gleamed, otherwise his expression remained neutral. ''One wouldn't have known you objected to my attentions—''

''*In*attention.'' She interrupted, correcting him with a scowl. ''I wasn't part of the conversation. You didn't once look at me.''

He reached out, caught her hands in his, brought one wrist to his lips, kissing the tender skin on the inside. ''I'm paying attention to you now.''

''I don't want the attention now!''

A small muscle pulled in his jaw. ''Strangely, darling, your behavior leads me to believe otherwise. Your color is high. Your breathing quick, your lovely lips parted. Truthfully you appear…exhilarated.''

Truthfully she felt overwrought. She was torn between excitement and anger, her skin acutely sensitive to him, her nerves too taut. Just the press of his lips to her wrist sent shiver after shiver streaking down her spine. And now, just like every other time, his touch undid her, her mind going blank, her body throbbing to life.

Dragging her gaze up, her eyes met his. His eyes, amber and flecked with bits of pale gold, glowed. She imagined she could see the fire behind the gold, the passion simmering within. He'd taught her everything about making love, made her body an instrument of pleasure…hers and his. She blushed, heat scorching through her skin, heightening the color in her cheeks.

He kissed her wrist again, his lips lingering against the slender bones, before linking her fingers in his. "We'll marry," he said quietly. "We'll try again to make our marriage work. But first, I think we should discuss a few things, air grievances, wipe the slate clean. Let's start with you. Why did you leave me three years ago?"

Did they have to do this now? It had to be close to midnight, she was dead on her feet and wanted nothing more than to creep into bed. "Can this wait, Kahlil? I'm exhausted. I haven't slept well in days."

"We can't start a marriage with ghosts hanging over our heads."

"Perhaps then, we should take some time to explore this, but not so late at night after the most impossibly long couple of days, and not after your cousin has spent two hours bragging about his gambling debts!" She felt her cheeks burn, her temper close to erupting. "Why do you tolerate him away? He's a leech, Kahlil, he doesn't even work."

Kahlil's jaw tightened, a small muscle popping close

to his ear. ''He lives off his trust fund. It's his fund, his choice.''

''You set up the trust fund. Not your father. That was your doing.''

''And if it was?''

She missed the raspy pitch, his deepening inflection, too caught up in her own emotions to read Kahlil properly. Because if she had heard the caustic note in Kahlil's voice, she would have immediately known she was entering very dangerous territory.

''Kahlil, I understand the blood is thicker than water part, but he's not good for you. He's not loyal—''

''He'd said you'd say this. He bet me a thousand sterling pounds that you'd attack his loyalty, and his integrity. I owe him.''

Bryn swallowed hard. ''When did he say this?''

''Earlier. In my office. Before I went to change for dinner.''

So Amin had approached Kahlil privately, rushing to reach him when she wasn't around. What a snake, what a cruel, poisonous snake. ''He's a liar, Kahlil.''

Kahlil sat forward, weight resting on his elbows, robe parting at the chest, displaying the bronzed plane of muscle. ''Tell me, did anything happen between you two? Anything unflattering…anything possibly incriminating?''

She felt chilled to the bone. My God, *what* had Amin told Kahlil? ''No! No. I can't stand him. He makes my skin crawl.''

''Two lies, Bryn, two lies tonight. How can I possibly ever trust you?''

Bryn stood frozen, stunned. Her mouth worked, lips quivering, her brain struggling to sift through the truths and motivation. ''I don't know what lies you're talking about.''

''Lie number one—I asked you earlier if you had a problem with Amin and you said no. Lie number two—I asked you moments ago if something had happened between you and my cousin, and you said no.'' His eyes were riveted on her face, no mercy in his harsh expression. ''Amin told me about your little...infatuation. It's been three years, enough time has passed, why can't we discuss it?''

She went to him, knelt before him, placed her hands on his knees. ''Kahlil, I'll tell you why I don't like Amin. He destroys people, destroys the truth. I've never known anyone to twist the truth the way he does. I thought he was my friend but he's not. I confided in him, and spent time with him, but there was no sordid relationship.''

''No kiss?''

''No. Never.'' She rose up higher on her knees, begging him to listen, to understand. ''I wasn't attracted to him. I had you. But it made him angry. He wants to punish us—''

''Why would he do that?'' Kahlil barked.

Gently she reached up, touched his jaw, pained by the way he flinched from her touch. Yet she didn't draw her hand away, she continued to caress his chin and the warmth of his mouth. ''Maybe because he envies our happiness.''

Kahlil caught her hand in his, holding it immobile. His gold eyes pierced her, searching for the truth. ''If he betrayed me, I want to know. If he took advantage of you, he will be punished. Is there something else I should be aware of?''

What was she to accuse Amin of? Assault? Rape? She'd sent him a note, asking him to meet her. It was essentially at her invitation that he came to her room. How could she explain Amin's threatening behaviour and still justify her own?

She couldn't.

''No,'' she said at length, sitting back slowly on her heels. ''There is nothing else.''

''I do not want you and Amin to be alone again. No more confidential talks. No more cups of tea or whatever you used to do. My wife must be above reproach. My wife must conduct herself in a manner befitting a princess. Understand?''

''Yes.''

''In one week we say our vows,'' Kahlil said slowly, enunciating clearly, ''and this time, no secrets, no lies. No runaway brides.''

The week passed with unusual swiftness. Bryn spent her days with Ben, nights with Kahlil, and saw virtually nothing of Amin. In fact, after going three days without a single glimpse of Kahlil's cousin, Bryn wondered if perhaps Amin had returned to Monte Carlo. She grinned, liking the thought. No more Amin, no more of his threats, no more worrying about his twisted intentions.

Amin, however, only got passing attention. Kahlil dominated her thoughts. It was almost as if he was superimposing himself on her life. He had moved her permanently into his room at night, located Ben's nursery in a nearby suite and took most meals with Bryn, and whenever possible, with his son also.

At night Kahlil loved to undress her, seduce her, savor her. He made love so thoroughly that when she finally slept, she drifted off into deep, dreamless slumber. Sometimes he'd wake her in the night to claim her again, but always by morning, he'd be gone, dressed, in his office, conducting business and meetings.

She overheard Kahlil on the phone once. It seemed he was required to participate in a conference, but Kahlil was giving his apologies, explaining he couldn't go, that leaving Tiva wasn't an option at the moment.

He wouldn't leave her alone, she realized, more unsettled than reassured. He didn't trust her.

She tried asking him about the conference over dinner, attempting to give him reassurance that things would be fine in the palace if he needed to attend. Kahlil nearly snapped her head off. "I will not leave you here alone."

His voice echoed, his tone razor-sharp. "But I wouldn't be alone," she answered mildly. "Rifaat, Lalia, the castle guards, Ben."

"I'm not going. End of discussion."

He didn't touch her that night in bed, and Bryn fell

asleep, huddled in a little ball, feeling like a stranger sleeping in Kahlil's bed but not part of his heart.

Would things never be the same between them again?

The next time he reached for her, he made love with an intensity that left her breathless and dizzy. It was as if he was reclaiming her, branding her, reminding her of possession. She was his. She belonged to him. But he didn't, wouldn't, love her.

The morning of the wedding arrived. In her old suite of rooms, Lalia attended Bryn, drawing a bath, then drying her with scrupulous care before applying a perfumed oil to her skin.

Lalia sang as she helped Bryn dress, her dark eyes lit with excitement. "This is a happy day, yes? You marry the Sheikh al-Assad here, nice traditional ceremony, and everyone be very happy."

Except for Bryn. She wanted Kahlil to show her some sign of affection, some hint that he might have deeper emotions, but he kept everything hidden. Their conversations were banal. The only time they were close was at night in his bed. Otherwise they were practically strangers, distant and detached.

A knock sounded on the door and Lalia went to answer it. She returned with a folded sheet of paper.

Bryn stared at the scrap of paper, darts of anxiety pricking her spine. Only one person had ever passed notes in the palace. Only one person would dare send her a note in the women's quarters.

Slowly she unfolded the sheet of paper. *I must see*

you. Immediately. No name, but she didn't need one. She knew the handwriting. Amin.

For a second she couldn't breathe and then, when feeling returned, she fiercely squeezed her hand closed, crumpling the note. She wouldn't answer him. He didn't deserve an answer. He shouldn't even be here. What was he doing in the palace on her wedding day? Shouldn't he be back in Monte Carlo, gambling and partying?

Bryn was tempted to send for Kahlil, to confess everything once and for all. Better face the music, get the whole episode with Amin put behind them before they renewed their vows. But she hesitated, feeling the wadded note in the palm of her hand.

Would Kahlil understand if she told him? Would he realize why she'd allowed herself to trust a man like Amin?

No. Kahlil needed no one. He didn't like weakness in others. He despised it in himself. No matter what she said about Amin, the fact was that he and Kahlil were once inseparable, practically brothers.

Amin had her backed into a corner and he knew it. But she wouldn't give in, and she wouldn't give up. This was her home now, her family. Perhaps she couldn't speak against Amin, but she didn't have to play his game, either.

The wedding gown was a pale shade of gold encrusted with precious jewels. It clung elegantly to her slender frame, catching the light as she moved beneath crystal chandeliers and passed ornate wall mirrors. The wedding party was waiting for her outside. Lalia led the way, brimming with excitement. Suddenly a hand clamped around her upper arm and dragged her to a step. ''What is that American expression? 'You can run, but you can't hide?' ''

Bryn watched Lalia continue walking. Her heart raced uncomfortably fast. ''You've watched too many movies, Amin. Let go of me.''

''We need to talk.''

''There's nothing to discuss.'' But he ignored her, forcibly dragging her down the hall to a discreet door tucked between oversize gilt mirrors.

Amin pulled her into a broom closet and shut the narrow door behind them. ''I can make your life hell, if that's what I choose.''

''You only think you can.'' She bristled, furious that he'd try something like this minutes before the ceremony. She wasn't afraid. More irritated than anything. Why didn't Kahlil realize Amin was an underhanded sneak? How could Kahlil tolerate such a person in his life? ''You're a fake, and a phony, and if you continue to make threats I will tell Kahlil *everything* about you.''

''Don't push me, Miss America.''

''And don't you push me! I'm not the naïve bride of five years ago, and I've had more than enough of your sordid little games. You attacked me that night in my room, you were going to rape me—''

He caught her by the upper arm, his fingers digging hard into her flesh, hurting her. ''You wanted it. You wanted *me*.''

''Want you? I despise you! And if you don't let go I will scream bloody murder.''

She reached for the doorknob but he stopped her, pressing himself against the length of her, his hand covering her mouth, another arm around her throat. ''I wouldn't scream, and I wouldn't go to Kahlil if I were you because he won't understand. He's a sheikh, an Eastern man with Eastern thinking. He won't forgive a wife that's betrayed him. He won't forgive you. Ever.''

Bryn bit his fingers and swung out from beneath his arm. ''Stay away from me!'' she cried, flinging the door open.

Her legs shook as she walked down the hall toward the open doorway where everyone was gathered. She saw the clustered servants but couldn't think clearly, thoughts tangled, emotions wild, tears pricking her eyes. Amin muddled truth and lies better than anyone she knew.

He also knew her fears, which gave him a horrible amount of power over her. He knew she was afraid of being abandoned. Knew she was terrified of being thrown out and separated from her beloved Ben.

With a trembling hand she smoothed her wrinkled shirt and adjusted her headpiece. Her heart continued to pump wildly and she couldn't silence Amin's voice, his words echoing around and around in her head. *Kahlil's a sheikh, he's Eastern and his thinking is Eastern…*

Bryn silently cursed herself, hating that she'd ever shared so much of her feelings with Amin. Amin knew she used to be insecure. He knew she probably still fought that same insecurity now. It didn't take much to topple one's confidence. The right words, the right accusations, the right seeds planted…

"No!" She wouldn't—couldn't—let Amin do this to them again. He'd come between her and Kahlil once before and he'd destroyed their marriage, but she refused to allow it to happen again. She was stronger this time. More confident. She knew what she wanted and it was Kahlil.

This was her wedding day. She wasn't about to let anyone—much less Amin—ruin it.

Outside sunshine poured across the smooth tiles and Bryn drew a deep breath, calmer, more focused. Quiet laughter and eager voices surged around her. Everyone was excited about the festivities. She was excited. This was the start to a brand-new life for her and Ben, a brand-new future.

Rifaat and Lalia were waiting for her just outside the door. "Was there a problem?" Rifaat asked, his gaze moving past her, searching the long dark hall.

Bryn forced a smile to her lips, her body still cold but the trembling less obvious. "Everything's fine."

Rifaat's brows knotted, dark slashes above gray eyes. "I thought I saw his highness' cousin—"

"Yes, you did. I passed Amin in the hall. He was just heading to his room."

Rifaat's gaze swept the hall once more before turning to her, surveying her pale composed face. She saw his eyes focus on her neck. His eyebrows flattened. Self-consciously she reached up, touched the spot where he was staring. The skin felt tender. Amin might have bruised her. Her stomach flip-flopped and yet she couldn't do anything about it now. This was a happy day, a day she'd waited years for. She wasn't going to let Amin spoil another moment. "Are we ready?" she asked.

"Yes, Princess," Lalia answered, reaching up to cover Bryn's mouth and nose with the filmy scrap of fabric. "Time to go. His highness is waiting."

She joined Kahlil at the palace gate, butterflies replacing her fear, anticipation making her warm, almost too eager. She felt like a real bride—felt jittery and anxious, happy and a little tearful. To become Kahlil's wife in Kahlil's country. To marry in his sacred ceremony. To exchange vows in his language.

It felt right. Felt perfect. But her idea of perfection disappeared when Kahlil stepped aside and she caught a whiff of her least favorite mode of transportation. "A camel, Kahlil?"

Faint creases fanned from the corners of his eyes as he took her hand in his and kissed her fingers. "It's custom."

She balked beneath the ornate arch festooned with boughs of flowers. "You know how I feel about camels."

"You had one bad experience, *laeela.* This one hasn't bitten anyone in months."

She glared at Kahlil, giving him the full weight of her disapproval. They were newlyweds when they'd taken that last camel ride. Kahlil's camel behaved beautifully.

Hers dumped her. Flat on her backside and then had the gall to take a bite.

And from Kahlil's expression she could see he remembered, too. He'd picked the camels on purpose. It was his way of linking her—today—to the past. "As long as he doesn't spit, too. I don't want to ruin my hair. Lalia spent two and a half hours making it look like this."

"On my honor, I won't let this one spit."

Her lips twitched. "You can do something about prices of oil, Sheikh al-Assad, but even you can't control a camel."

And yet, looking at him now, seeing him dressed in the traditional wedding *djellaba,* the *howli* on his head, he never looked more fierce, more Arabic, and more sensual than now. Truthfully, she would have ridden beneath the camel's belly if he'd asked her.

But he didn't ask her, thank goodness. He smiled at her, his golden gaze locking with hers. "You look beautiful, have I told you that yet?"

Blood rushed to her cheeks, making her skin hot and tingly. "No."

"I've never met a more beautiful woman in my life. I'm honored you've consented to be my wife."

She couldn't speak for a moment, couldn't even swallow, her heart thudding hard, her chest tender with love. She'd never loved any other man the way she loved him. He made her feel real—complete. "I want to make you happy," she whispered, not trusting her voice.

"You have."

And for a split second they were the only two alive, the only two breathing, thinking, feeling. She felt the world wrap around them, snug, vivid, perfect. If only it could always be this way.

"Come," he said, taking her hand, "your camel awaits. And so does our son. My cousin Mala has flown in from London with her children. She's taken Ben to the ceremony with them and they're waiting, impatiently, I imagine."

Once seated on the kneeling camel, house servants crowded behind, filling the courtyard. Lalia rushed forward to adjust Bryn's elaborate gown. The servants cheered as Kahlil took his camel and the cheer turned into music once his camel arose. With flower petals cascading, and the hauntingly evocative music echoing, the camels set off. Bryn lifted her hand, waved to the crowd behind, and caught a tender pink petal in her hand. Her heart beat quickly. This time, she silently vowed, she and Kahlil would last forever.

CHAPTER TEN

THE scene was just like a set from an old movie studio: enormous white tent, tethered camels, luxurious ruby-red Persian carpets lining the shady tent interior. Music and palms, enormous fronds swaying with the late-afternoon breeze. The sun was just setting, as Kahlil had predicted, painting the creamy dunes of sand red, peach, gold.

The ceremony, beautiful as it was, passed in a blur of prayers, blessings, and the joining of their hands. Then it was over and Kahlil was guiding her to the helicopter that had just touched down, Kahlil's hand in the small of her back, his warmth doing something crazy to her senses.

''Where are we going?'' she asked, buckling her seat belt and glancing out the open door to catch a glimpse of Ben. Kahlil had already told her that Ben would be staying at the palace while they were gone, taken care of by the palace nanny and Kahlil's cousin Mala who had two little boys of her own. Ben was thrilled at the chance to play with other children and yet it was always hard for Bryn to leave him.

But Ben, catching her eye, grinned and waved and she waved back. At least he wasn't worried about her going away with Kahlil for a few days. He was so confident. So much like his father.

She looked at Kahlil and he met her gaze. "We're going to a special place of mine," he said. "A place you've never been before."

"Is it far?" she asked.

She caught the wry curve of his mouth, his expression was boyish, almost exultant. He looked as though the weight of the world had been pulled from his shoulders. "Not unless one's traveling by camel."

It was dark when the helicopter landed. The sky was the darkest of purple with pinpricks of light and the ground below was a deep shadow, no glow of street lamps, no hint of civilization.

In this shapeless, formless nowhere the helicopter began to descend, lowering straight down into a sea of black. This meant they were either landing in the middle of an ocean or a sea of sand.

Bryn heard the helicopter pilot speak, giving directions into his headset. She frowned as the helicopter lowered, then caught small points of light, shimmering light, like miniature flames. And as the helicopter touched ground, Bryn realized the shimmering light was actually flames, burning torches set in a large circle around the helicopter pad.

"Where are we?" she whispered.

"My hideaway." He took her hand, and ducking beneath the still whirring blades, they ran through ancient stone arches into a very old fortress that had to date back at least a thousand years.

"This is yours?" she said, still breathless from the dash into the palace. Kahlil had swung her into his arms at the last moment before entering a high-ceiling bedchamber with silk pillows strewn across the floor and candles burning in rugged wall sconces. ''Ah, and more candles. Didn't realize you loved firelight so much.''

''No electricity,'' he answered, drawing her down on the low mattress. ''I don't have a choice. If we didn't have candles, I couldn't see you, and believe me, I want to see you.''

She felt heat creep into her cheeks, her limbs suddenly weak. ''You do?''

He reclined backward. ''Yes, very much so. I'm actually dying to get you naked.'' His voice lowered, turned husky. ''Strip for me.''

''Wh...what?''

''I want to watch you undress and then inspect my wife.''

She was shocked, and yet strangely aroused.

''You said you'd obey me,'' he quietly chided, reminding her of her promises. ''You said we'd have a real relationship.''

''Yes, but...''

His eyebrow cocked. He simply looked at her, waiting.

Blood flooding her cheeks, fingers trembling, she reached for the narrow zipper at the side of her gown. Kahlil leaned back on the bed, watching. With short, nervous tugs, she worked the zipper down and then carefully stepped out of the lavishly embroidered dress.

Next came the narrow silk straps of her bustier. She

pushed the satin fabric down, toward her waist, exposing her breasts.

''Ah.''

Bryn swayed beneath the intense scrutiny, feeling Kahlil's heat and interest, aware of his gaze as he drank in her bared breasts, the pale skin taut, the pink nipples hard, aching, like the ache between the thighs.

''The rest, please.''

He sounded completely indifferent but he wasn't; he was a study of concentration. Shyly she tugged her satin panties over her hips, to her knees, and pulled them from her ankles. Completely naked, except for the gold jewel-studded crown she still wore in her hair, she blushed, warm color rushing from her toes to her head.

Wordlessly Kahlil rose, drew her to him, pressing her naked length to his. He was hard everywhere, his chest, his abdomen, his thighs, but it was his erection that generated more heat in her, his own hunger throbbing at the V of her thighs.

His arms encircled her, his hands cupped her bare bottom, the curve of her derriere in each of his palms. He lifted her slightly, drawing her closer, pressing her against the thrust of his desire. Her inner thighs clenched. Her belly tightened. She felt empty inside, empty and deprived.

''You're so warm,'' he murmured in her ear, his voice rich, seductive. ''You feel like heaven.''

''I think it feels like hell,'' she protested, shiver after shiver racing through her, his chest brushing against her aching nipples, intensifying her sensitivity.

"You just need to learn patience."

"I'm trying." Bryn rose on her tip toes, slowly circling his neck with one arm, and then the other, drawing their bodies even closer. His chest crushed the bare fullness of her breasts. Her calves balled into hard knots of muscle and her abdomen stretched, long, lean.

"Lovely," he murmured, fingers caressing the curve of her spine, then rising to play each vertebrae in her back.

She liked it better with his hand in her lower back, his hard length tight against her mound, her body desperately drinking him in. Feverish, Bryn nipped his beard-roughened chin and then his mouth. "Kiss me back," she begged. "Kiss me like you used to."

In response he swung her into his arms and carried her to the bed covered in luxurious silks and satin. She smelled his signature fragrance of sandalwood and citrus and cupping his face in her hands, kissed him deeply even as she tugged at his robe.

There were no more formalities, no more foreplay. It wasn't long before both were swept away, carried to the highest peak of pleasure. And for the first time since returning to Zwar, she felt a wall come down between them, some invisible barrier breaking and Kahlil held her, kissed her, loved her with profound tenderness.

Warm tears pricked the back of her eyes but these were tears of hope. They would make this work. They would find happiness after all.

Shudders still coursing through her, Kahlil shifted Bryn in his arms, drawing her down to the mattress beside him. "You are mine, do you understand? Mine, all mine."

"Yes, master."

His eyes glinted, and smiling faintly he kissed the corner of her mouth, and then the soft full lower lip still throbbing with blood and passion. "I like the sound of that," he murmured.

"I know you do."

"Are you sure you're not just humoring me?"

"Could I be any more obedient?"

"That's different from a surrender." But he laughed, the sound rich, deep, husky. "And I'll just have to step up my training."

Still smiling, he kissed her again, his laughter warming her mouth, stealing her breath. She felt tingles rush through her, pleasure and happiness. If Kahlil was letting down his guard enough to laugh with her, she knew she'd found her way back into his heart. He might not tell her in words he loved her, but the tenderness was there, hidden within him. She'd just give him time. Lavish him with love. It was all they needed—time and love.

He kissed her neck, and the hollow beneath her ear. She felt heat explode inside her, her desire for his insatiable. "Don't start anything you're not prepared to finish," she softly teased, locking her hands behind his neck and drawing his mouth down to hers.

"Oh, I'm prepared," he answered, shifting his weight, settling between her thighs, and from all impressive evidence, he most certainly was. He nipped at her lip, teeth sharp, hunger barely restrained. ''You do know I've cheated to get you back, don't you? I told a little lie—''

Bryn's hands flew to his shoulders and pushed him back. ''What?''

''It's not a big deal. Practically a white lie.''

White lie? Kahlil? ''And just what was this *white lie?*''

He kissed her again, ignoring her attempts to evade his mouth, and finally she melted beneath him, resistance fading. He smiled against her lips, acknowledging her feeble defense. ''Well, I did pay a certain official to destroy a certain piece of paper. That document you never signed? My fault. I made sure it never reached you.''

''Kahlil!''

He clasped her face in his hands, kissed her fiercely. ''I wasn't going to lose you. I never wanted to lose you.''

Suddenly they were interrupted by a pounding on the bedroom door. ''Go away,'' Kahlil shouted, smiling wickedly at Bryn, his hand moving across her belly to her thighs. ''I'm busy.''

''Forgive me, your highness,'' the voice answered from the far side of the door. ''But this is an emergency.''

Kahlil was gone less than five minutes. ''A problem has come up in Tiva,'' he said, returning to the bedchamber and flinging a shirt over his shoulders. ''It's urgent. I must return to the palace immediately.''

He was dressing in Western clothes. His brow furrowed deeply, his expression was nothing but grim. "I'll be back as soon as I can."

Something in his expression unnerved her. Bryn sat up in bed. "What kind of problem?"

"Can't discuss it just yet. But I'll send the helicopter for you first chance I get."

"You're going to leave me here, in the middle of nowhere?"

"It's safe. It's my home. I want you here."

It was a no-argument tone, one of his submit-and-surrender expressions.

"At least tell me what you do know."

"Bryn, I wish I could. I don't have all the facts."

"But something at the palace?" Immediately her thoughts turned to Ben. He was there. He was there without her. "Has there been an uprising?"

"No, nothing like that."

"Then what? My God, Kahlil, the baby—"

"I know." He clasped her hard by the shoulders, kissed her forehead, his mouth a brief imprint of heat against her skin. "Be patient. I'll learn more soon."

He released her, grabbed an overcoat and swung toward the door.

Sixteen hours later Kahlil reappeared. He'd only just returned to the crumbling fortress. Bryn could still hear the rotary whir of the helicopter blades.

"It's Ben," Kahlil said sharply, without preamble. His complexion looked ashen, deep purple shadows beneath his bloodshot eyes. "He's gone."

Ben. Gone. Impossible. But that's what Kahlil had said.

Through a narrow window Bryn saw clouds of red-gold spiral, desert sand swirling furiously. Her mind was like that, swirling, dizzying. "What do you mean gone? Gone where?"

"We don't know."

You don't know? An irrational voice screamed inside her head. *You're the sheikh. The king. You must know.* She wrapped her arms across her chest, lifted her chin, fighting for calm. "Did he run away?"

"No."

"Then what? Are you telling me someone *kidnapped* Ben?"

"Yes."

She staggered backward, eyes widening. Her mouth felt dry, her tongue like lead. Disbelief surged through her veins. "Who?" Her voice came out a whisper, airless, powerless, a flutter of sound.

"Amin."

She took another half step backward and Kahlil's shoulders shifted, an uneasy gesture that revealed more than his words could. "I have every resource working on this, Bryn. We will find them. That's a promise."

She felt as though she'd plunged into an icy river and her body was shutting down, legs numb, muscles numb, heart freezing.

This was her fault.

She hadn't protected Ben, hadn't confided her fears in Kahlil. She'd felt strong, impervious to Amin. She'd even challenged him, taunted him that he couldn't hurt her, that he wasn't powerful enough. My God. What had she done?

Helplessly she crunched her fingers to her palms, folded her arms against her breasts, fighting to stay warm. She felt cold, desperately cold, and desperately afraid. "What do you know right now? What are your leads?"

"Ben was taken last night after the ceremony. The maid was drawing his bath, had her back turned while filling the tub. When she went to fetch Ben, he was gone."

Gone. The word conjured terror. Puff, gone. Puff, lost. Puff, her heart broken.

She pressed the tip of her tongue to the roof of her mouth but her mind went blank. What could she say? Nothing. Nothing. Finally, after long, impenetrable seconds, she stuttered, "How do you know Amin took him? How do you know he didn't wander off? That he didn't get out through an open door?"

"We have evidence."

"What evidence?" She refused to be thwarted. This wasn't a lost set of car keys, for God's sake, but their *child!*

"Amin left a note." Deep grooves formed on either side of Kahlil's mouth. "It was cryptic. Didn't really make sense. We just need to be patient and let my men continue their investigation."

If he'd hoped to calm her, he'd failed. His words only

incited greater alarm. Her stomach heaved. ''Tell me, Kahlil. I want to know. I *need* to know.''

''The note was short. And as I've said, cryptic. Amin wrote that he was taking what was his. That's all he said.''

Relief washed over her. ''So we don't know that Amin has Ben. We have two missing people. We don't know they're together.''

''But we do.'' Kahlil's lips compressed, the lines near his mouth almost white. ''We have it on videotape, Amin bundling Ben up and carrying him from the nursery.''

''No! Not like that, he didn't do that, tell me, Kahlil—''

Kahlil caught Bryn in his arms and drew her close, cradling her against her chest. ''Shh, *laeela,* we'll find them. We'll have our son home soon. I swear.''

The helicopter returned them to Tiva, landing in the gated palace courtyard. The whirring blades blew the palms, creating a swish of green against the white plaster walls.

A scarlet-throat hummingbird buzzed past their heads, flitting to one of the pots of coral-red hibiscus flanking the door. Bryn paused for a split second to watch the emerald-green bird dive into the petals. That is how she'd been with Kahlil, the hummingbird unable to resist the nectar.

And look what her desire, her intense love, had done to them. Secrets, lies, a kidnapped baby.

It was almost too much to bear.

Kahlil gently touched her spine, prompting Bryn through the enormous door. He walked her to her suite of rooms, stopping outside the harem entrance. With a kiss on her upturned lips, he promised, "I'll send word as soon as I hear something."

He felt warm and solid, and she found comfort in his proximity. It was easier facing the future with Kahlil at her side. "I don't want to be alone," she pleaded, fingers grappling, tangling in his robe. "Let me stay with you."

"This is a high-level security matter. I'll be meeting with my advisors. It's better if you stay here."

"It's not better for me. I'm scared."

"Bryn, trust me." He plucked her hands from his robe, gave her an encouraging smile, although the deep lines fanning from his eyes told another story. "I promise I'll let you know as developments occur. Now try to rest. You need it."

Lalia ordered a small dinner tray that Bryn didn't touch. She didn't want food. She wanted Ben home.

Minutes turned to hours. The wait grew intolerable. Two hours. Three. Her back ached, her head hurt. Her eyes felt like small rough pebbles, too dry from so little sleep.

Four hours passed. Bryn began to shake, the after shocks of adrenaline. Too little sleep. Too much anxiety. She felt as if she were turned inside out and about to break.

"You must sleep, my lady," Lalia soothed, drawing down the cool sheets, dimming the bedside lamp. "Lie down. Rest."

But Bryn couldn't sleep, and she spent the night sitting against the wall of her bedroom, her gaze fixed on the distant horizon.

Amin was evil, the worst kind of evil, but not even he would actually hurt Ben, would he?

She tried to imagine where Amin had taken Ben, wondering if it was very dark, and if Ben was frightened. But her mind shied away from a morbid scenario. She had to remain positive, had to believe that Ben was fine and that Amin would be kind.

Comforted somewhat, Bryn watched the moon shift in the sky, arcing slowly through the night, the stars growing whiter, brighter, only to dim again, until at last the purple faded to violet and then to lavender.

The morning sun rose and Bryn still sat, her back against the wall, her arms encircling her knees.

The maid reappeared, shrouded in filmy veils. She, too, looked tired, as though she hadn't slept. ''Breakfast, Princess,'' she said, delivering a tray with sweet breads, fresh fruit and hot mint tea.

''I can't eat. Not until Ben's home.''

''The sheikh will bring him home. The sheikh is all-powerful.''

All-powerful. If only it were true! Bryn sipped her tea but didn't touch the food, staring at the sliced mango on the tray, the fruit's vivid flesh ripe and juicy. She wondered what Ben would have for breakfast. She prayed Amin would give him breakfast. If Ben were even still alive… No! You can't think like that. Of course he's alive. Amin is cruel and selfish, but he wouldn't hurt a child.

Tears filled her eyes and she bit her knuckles, determined not to cry, not to give in to useless emotion. Tears wouldn't help Ben.

A rustle of fabric, Lalia in the doorway. Her features were drawn. ''My lady, Sheikh al-Assad is waiting in the main reception room. Please, I dress you quickly.'

Bryn fidgeted as Lalia dressed her in a simple apricot chiffon gown. ''You must be brave, Princess,'' Lalia urged, combing Bryn's hair smooth and tying it with an apricot ribbon.

''I am very brave,'' Bryn answered grimly. She wanted nothing so much as to be with Kahlil and to discover his news. She could only pray that he'd located Ben.

Rifaat waited for her at the entrance to the women's quarters. ''Good morning, Princess al-Assad.''

Bryn had grown so accustomed to his silence that his greeting startled her. ''Good morning, Rifaat.''

''You look very tired. Are you not sleeping?''

How could she? How could anyone sleep when a three-year-old was missing? ''Has his highness heard anything?''

''That I do not know.''

Her eyebrows arched, impatience, frustration balling into one. ''Why must we play these games, Rifaat? You know everything that happens in this place. You're Kahlil's secret ears. You're privy to all the servants' gossip. You often know things before Kahlil!''

Rifaat almost smiled, but the expression in his deep brown eyes was infinitely sad. ‘‘A blessing, and a curse, my lady. Sometimes it is better not to know.’’ And with another slight bow he led the way through the gleaming marble hall, past the center pavilion and down another breezeway.

Bryn immediately spotted Kahlil at the far end of the reception room. He stood at an open window overlooking the private patio. Soft gold light washed the windowsill, the sky still the fairy-tale pink of early morning.

Kahlil was the only one in the room. He slowly turned from the window and moved to a massive chair with burgundy cushions and sat down even more slowly.

He didn't make eye contact. He didn't even look at her.

Bryn's stomach dropped. This was bad. Very, very bad. Something terrible had happened to Ben.

CHAPTER ELEVEN

''TELL me,'' she whispered. ''Tell me what's happened.''

''Come closer.''

She was frozen, petrified of what he might say. ''Tell me first. Just get it over with.''

His dark head lifted, his eyes, brilliant with emotion, met hers. ''I've heard nothing about Ben. This has to do with you.''

She shuffled forward, one step, and then another, adrenaline still surging, too much tension and exhaustion for her to think clearly. ''Me?''

''Yes, my dutiful wife, you.''

''What have you heard? What's this about?''

''What have you heard?'' He repeated her words, enunciating the consonants as though they were sharp things in his mouth. ''Oh, I've learned quite a bit, read quite a bit, too.''

''I don't understand.''

''You bluff, Princess.'' He rose from his chair and descended the dais. His feet were bare, his robe open, revealing long white trousers and the bronze of his chest. ''Sit down.''

She sank to the cushion in front of her, a burgundy

silk embroidered with gold thread. ''You've totally confused me. I have no idea what you're talking about.''

''None?''

She leaned away from Kahlil as he marched a circle around her, scowling, his hands knotted behind his back. He wasn't making sense. She'd been nowhere, gone nowhere. How could she have displeased him? ''What does any of this have to do with *Ben?*''

''The correct question should be, what does any of this have to do with *Amin?*''

The sinking feeling returned. Kahlil had obviously heard something, learned something. Had Amin made a threat? Told stories? How had he incriminated her now?

''Well?'' Kahlil stopped in front of her, rocked back on his heels. ''You're not going to defend yourself?''

Beads of perspiration formed across her forehead and on her nape. ''I can't defend myself if I do not know the charge.''

''I want to know about your affair with Amin.''

Her skin felt clammy and cold despite the warm morning and the moisture on her brow. ''There was no affair.''

''That's not what the videotape shows.''

''There is no videotape of Amin and I together—''

''There is plenty of video tape of you two together.''

''But not of us having sex.''

''Tell me, was he, or was he not in your room?''

Dear God, how did he know that? It must have been Amin. Amin must have confessed. ''He was, but nothing like that happened.''

"Yet you ran away. Perhaps because you felt guilty?"

She couldn't believe he'd do this now, when Ben was missing. "We had no affair. We never had sex. Look at your videotape for proof!"

"There's no surveillance camera in the harem. The camera stops at the door."

"How convenient!"

"But this wasn't a one-night stand. You have been passing love letters for months."

"They weren't love letters, they were notes, very childish notes—"

"I don't think they're all that childish," he ground out, drawing slips of paper from a pocket in his robe. *"Amin, you've been too wonderful. I don't know what I'd do without you."* He unfolded another. "*I must see you tonight. When can we meet?* Or, how about this one? *You're an angel. I adore you.*" Kahlil's dark head lifted. "I adore you? What the hell does that mean?"

"It means nothing, it meant nothing. They were schoolgirl notes. I was eighteen!"

"And married to me."

"I know it looks bad—"

"Looks bad? It *is* bad. What the hell were you doing writing love letters?"

"They weren't love letters, they were messages between friends. Amin was giving me advice—"

"I bet he was."

She flinched at the snarl in his voice. "It's not like that, Kahlil. Please try to understand. We'd returned to Zwar and you immediately buried yourself in work. I was lonely, overwhelmed, I felt totally out of my element.''

''So you turned to Amin.''

''For friendship, and friendship only. He once was very kind to me. He listened to me, encouraged me, made me believe that everything would soon be better between you and me.''

''So I'm at fault? I was a lousy husband?''

''No, Kahlil, please try to understand. When we were dating you were so attentive, you made me feel special, and very loved. Maybe I was spoiled—''

''Maybe?''

''All right, I was spoiled, and immature, but the fact is when we returned here, you buried yourself in work and you had so little time for me. Amin befriended me. He realized I was lonely, lacking confidence, and he made me believe everything would be okay.''

''You don't tell another man you are lonely and lacking confidence. You tell me. You don't turn to another man for comfort, you turn to me.''

The savagery in his voice ripped through her. His features contorted, a dark violence in his expression, a bitterness she'd never seen before.

''Kahlil, please forgive me. I beg you.''

''Spare me the apology, Bryn, it's a little late for that, don't you think?''

''I never meant to hurt you. I love you. I've always loved you.''

He made a rude sound. ''Amin says Ben is his.'' His voice whipped her again. ''If that's so, Amin has every right to take the boy. I have no legal or moral reason to recover him for you."

"No!"

"The search has been called off."

She nearly screamed in protest. Hands outstretched. "My God, Kahlil, you can't mean it. Ben's a baby. He must be terrified."

"Amin can handle it."

"Amin isn't Ben's father. *You are.* And I've never been with another man, so even if you're angry, don't punish Ben. He doesn't even know Amin!"

"It's not my problem anymore."

"Not your problem? You're the sheikh of Zwar. Your cousin has kidnapped your child. You say it's not your problem? Who runs this bloody country anyway?"

Kahlil grabbed her wrist and swung her against his chest, slamming the air from her lungs. "Do you know who you're speaking to?"

"My husband!" Tears rushed to her eyes. "My arrogant, prideful pigheaded husband. You know why I turned to Amin all those years ago? Because you shut me out. You stopped seeing me, hearing me, talking to me. I was lonely and I wasn't very good at being lonely, but I never slept with Amin and if you dare risk your child's safety out of pride—" she drew a deep, staggering breath "—I swear, Kahlil, I'll..."

"What will you do?"

"I'll search for them myself. I won't eat, sleep, rest until I find them."

"You're a woman in the Middle East. You have no

money, no transportation, no friends. You'll never find them.''

Her heart was breaking. ''Why do you hate me so much? Is it because I'm weak? Because I have needs?''

''Your needs drove you into my brother's arms.'' He released her swiftly, his scathing tone blistering, drawing blood to her cheeks. ''You make me sick.''

She didn't hear the last part, just the first part and it echoed in her head. His brother? ''You mean *cousin's* arms.''

''Amin is my brother.'' He swallowed, his jaw thickening. ''My half brother. My mother's bastard son.''

Stunned, Bryn held her breath. She felt the blackness of Kahlil's mood, his confession wrung in pain and anger. ''I thought your mother died after you were born.''

''She didn't die. Not until I was in high school. When my father discovered her affair with his best friend, he exiled her from Zwar.'' His lashes lowered, accenting the harsh sweep of his prominent cheekbones. ''My father was kind. Under our law, she could have been killed.''

''If your father was truly kind, he wouldn't have deprived you of your mother!''

''My mother chose to betray the marriage vow. She paid the consequence.''

''No, *you* paid the consequence! She made a mistake and you suffered for it. Just like you want Ben to suffer for my mistake, but that's not fair.''

''Life isn't fair, Bryn. It's never been fair. Ben might as well learn that now.''

''You can't mean that.''

''I do. Life's full of hard knocks. I was lonely as a child. I suffered, too, but I'm here, stronger for it.''

''Knowing that you suffered, remembering the pain, you'd inflict that on your own son?''

''I don't even know that he is my son.''

''Yes, you do. He's you, he's yours. You might be angry with me, but you can't deny your own child.''

''Did you sleep with him, Bryn?''

He'd changed the conversation, switched the focus in a split second, but she followed the leap, and her emotions swung from rage to pity to helplessness. ''No, Kahlil, *no.* I'm not attracted to Amin. I've never been attracted to Amin.''

''But these notes, his visit to your room, they clearly show that there was more than a friendship between you.''

''Not on my part. I never wanted him, never imagined more. I can see how the notes could be misinterpreted, and I realize now how immature I sounded, but truly, Kahlil, there was no affair, no desire, no physical relationship.''

His lashes lifted again, revealing the brittle glitter in the golden depths. ''Just an emotional one.''

He wasn't going to go, wasn't going to help with the rescue, but when word came that Amin had been located, Kahlil didn't even hesitate. He might be furious with Bryn, but he'd never make the boy suffer. Without changing clothes, he dashed to the waiting limousine, settling into the back seat although his hands itched to take the steering wheel himself. He still couldn't fathom how Amin could take a child—not just his child, but *any* child. How could a man stoop so low?

As the limousine sped through the city Kahlil rubbed his temple, fingers massaging, but the tension didn't lift. It was time peace was restored to the palace. And time to exert some order. It had been so long since Kahlil felt in control. So long since he felt easy in his own home.

Bryn was going to have to go.

Kahlil closed his eyes and gritted his jaw against the livid thrust of pain. He barely felt the car jolt as it hit a deep pothole in the road, his emotions running hot and wild, a black violence he fought desperately to suppress.

He loved her. No doubt about it. He'd once worshiped her, too, but that was before she shattered his trust, never mind his heart.

For long moments he saw nothing, heard nothing, felt nothing but a raging grief—half anger, half sorrow—the same irrational emotion a young child would feel. Knuckles pressed to squeezed eyelids he forced the scalding tears back. No crying over spilt milk. He couldn't change what had happened, and life moved on.

Move on.

Move on, Kahlil, move on for God's sake.

Long minutes later he dropped his hands, and gazed blankly out the limousine window. White bleached dunes swirled up around the sides of the road. Finally he could draw a breath without wanting to scream. He'd been through worse pain before; he'd survive losing

Bryn. He'd survive losing all of them. He was Sheikh Kahlil al-Assad and his word was law.

In the palace Lalia was doing her best to calm the princess, wringing out a damp scented cloth and placing it on Bryn's forehead. "Shh, my lady, you mustn't cry like that. You'll make yourself sick."

Bryn turned her head away, knocking off the cloth Lalia had pressed to her forehead. She didn't want a cool, damp cloth, mint tea, or conversation. She just wanted Kahlil, and Ben. She just wanted her family together again.

Bryn awoke with a start. Voices outside were shouting and an engine roared close to the palace entrance.

She'd fallen asleep while the sun was still bright, but now her bedroom was bathed in the lavender of twilight, the interior space violet, gray and cool.

Even as she sleepily stumbled to her feet, her bedroom door burst open. Dirty, bloodied, Kahlil marched toward the bed.

"Get up," he demanded. "We'll have this out. Once and for all."

A scarlet slash marred his forehead and his jaw was swollen. Another gash streaked his cheekbone. "You're hurt!"

He ignored her concern. "We have Ben, he appears fine, but I'm having my doctor see to him anyway. You will join him shortly."

"Thank God." She flung herself at Kahlil, wrapped her arms around his waist and held tight. "I knew you wouldn't leave him like that. I knew you'd find him."

He stood stiffly. ''I did it for him, not for you.''

She felt his rigid muscles, the tightening of his limbs. He was grinding his teeth, enduring the embrace. She could feel his anger and apathy, and his revulsion terrified her. What if he'd never forgive her? What if he couldn't forgive her? How would she live without him? ''Kahlil, I love you. I have always loved you and—''

He dragged her arms from him and pushed her away. ''I don't want to hear this.''

''But you must—''

''*No.* It's too late. Too late for any of this.'' With a hoarse sound, he pushed her away once again, holding himself stiffly. ''Amin waits for us. Let us get this over with.''

It was madness, what Kahlil was asking of her. Did he want her to confess to adultery, betrayal, to crimes she hadn't committed? Bryn refused to confess to anything other than failing to trust Kahlil when she was a new bride, but the rest she refuted verbally, and physically, with adamant shakes of her head.

Not Amin. He talked, or more accurately, smirked and talked, indicting her in his twisted fantasy. He insisted on clinging to his outrageous story, enlarging on it as the evening passed. He called her hot, passionate, insatiable.

Bryn shuddered as Amin elaborated, his lies making her skin crawl, his remembrances destroying her innocence, making her trust in him appear sordid.

Kahlil didn't look at Bryn as Amin talked. He stood before his ornate chair, arms crossed, expression blank.

And Bryn, knowing how his mother had failed him, knowing how he'd never felt secure in his father's love, realized she, too, had failed him. If Kahlil had wanted to torture her, he couldn't have picked a better punishment.

She saw Rifaat from the corner of her eye and the man stared off into space, silent, invisible. She shuddered, wondering what he must be thinking, what he must feel for a disloyal bride.

She'd failed them all.

Next time she'd do it differently. Next time she'd be stronger, tougher, braver. Next time she'd speak her mind early and ask the right questions and not hang on to grudges. Next time she'd be quick to forgive and even quicker to forget. Next time…

She closed her eyes, trying to keep the tears from falling but they gathered on her lashes and trembled there, against the curve of her cheek.

Kahlil. I love you, Kahlil. Forgive me, Kahlil. You are my sun and my moon and everything…

Kahlil's fingers snapped, loudly, too sharply. She opened her eyes to spot Kahlil marching toward Amin. ''Enough, I've heard more than enough. The police are waiting outside, and somehow I think prison won't be as comfortable as your apartment in Monte Carlo.''

''As if you ever cared,'' Amin snarled.

''I cared. You are my brother. You are my blood.''

His mouth worked, his Adam's apple bobbed. ''Blood? Since when? I've been nothing but your obligation, your charity case.''

"I've shared with you everything."

Bryn shuddered at the rawness in Kahlil's voice. He sounded utterly bewildered.

"You shared with me nothing. You took my mother—"

"I lost her, too!" Kahlil interrupted hoarsely. "When my father sent her from Zwar, it broke me, too."

"But you recovered, crown prince of Zwar, you had all the opportunities, every advantage. Boarding schools in England. Graduate school in the U.S. Money, power. You had it all. I just wanted my share."

"My wife wasn't an option."

Suddenly Amin laughed, a high, hysterical pitch. "Wasn't she?"

Bryn covered her face with her hands. She couldn't bear it. She could hear the guards drag Amin from the room but didn't watch, didn't even look up until the heavy doors banged shut. But Amin wasn't the only one gone. Kahlil had left, too.

Bryn sat still for an agonizing moment, nervously rubbing the silky skirt of her gown. Rifaat remained in the room but he didn't speak to her. Finally, unable to bear the silence another moment, she blurted, "When is he coming back?"

Rifaat didn't immediately reply. She turned, glanced at him, noted his peculiar expression. "He is coming back, isn't he?"

"No, my lady."

She wasn't sure she'd heard correct. She bent her head. "But later, he'll send for me."

"I am to take you to your car. It's out front, waiting."

"And...Ben?"

"He's already in the car. With your things. Your servant has packed everything."

Bryn didn't understand, felt stupid for not understanding but it was all the excitement and the late hour and the fear of losing her baby. Now if only Rifaat would speak more slowly, explain it all again. "Why is Ben in the car? Where are we going?"

"Home."

But this was home. Kahlil and Bryn and the baby. This was where they belonged. So why was Ben in the car by himself? What was Kahlil doing putting Ben in the car by himself? How could Kahlil do that, how could he be so cruel? She jumped to her feet, her throat threatening to seal closed. "Where is Kahlil?"

"I know this is difficult, Princess, but perhaps his highness is correct. It would be wise to make a clean break. I am sure the crown prince is probably asleep in the limousine, and once you're on the plane, you will sleep, too. Soon this will just be a memory—"

"*No.* No, no, no." Kahlil couldn't do this. He had no right, not after dragging them here and putting them through hell. He'd awakened her heart, revived their love. He couldn't throw it back at her now! "I must see him."

"You can not, Princess—"

Bryn didn't wait to hear the rest, running from the royal chamber, racing down the long palace corridors, feet echoing against gleaming marble. She slipped past a pair of guards too startled to stop her, bursting into Kahlil's office suite but the rooms were dark, no one was there.

From a distance she heard Rifaat call her name but she ignored him, running on, racing toward Kahlil's bedroom. The door was shut. She tried the handle. It was locked and soft gold light poured from beneath the door.

"Kahlil!" She cried his name, frantically pounding on the door, sensing Rifaat behind her. "Listen to me. I understand you're angry, and you have every right. But don't punish the baby. Fight me, but not him! He loves you. He needs you. *I* need you." Her throat ached, her heart hurt, she shivered from head to toe. "Dammit, Kahlil, how can we ever make this work if we won't ever talk to each other? Open the door, *please!*"

She wouldn't let Kahlil do this, couldn't let him shut her out again. She knew he loved her, deep down, somewhere in his hard, imperial heart. "Oh, Kahlil, talk to me. You can't just put the baby and me on a plane and not say goodbye. What will we do without you? Where will we go? How can I raise Ben without you? If you're going to send me away at least give me some help—answers, advice, something Kahlil, please!"

Rifaat reached her, his hands closing on her shoulders as he attempted to pull her away from the sheikh's door. "My lady, come, don't make me call the guards."

Bryn broke free, pounding wildly against the door, desperation making her faint. "Kahlil, help me." The door rattled beneath her pounding fist. "They're going to take me away. You can stop them. You must stop them!''

Rifaat's hands settled again on her shoulders, gently this time, kindly. ''Please, Bryn,'' he spoke softly, urgently, using her name for the first time since she returned, ''you don't want to be carried out in disgrace. Go with dignity, I beg of you. For Ben's sake if nothing else.''

But she was fighting for Ben's sake, fighting for all their sakes. Kahlil needed them, just as much as she and Ben needed him. ''I will not go!'' she cried, pressing her forehead against the door, fingertips glued to the wood as if she could become one with the door and melt through. ''I will not.''

Rifaat applied more pressure to her shoulders, hands firm. ''I must see you to the car. Come with me, Bryn, don't make this harder than it already is.''

Salty tears raced down her cheek, streaking the door. ''Kahlil.'' She choked, breaking down, her vocal cords closing, shut down by her sobs.

The light beneath the door flickered casting a shadow on the other side. Hope returned, hope and anguish. ''In all my life, Kahlil, I've only loved you.''

Bryn could sense Kahlil on the other side of the door. She knew he must be there and she imagined she could feel his heart beat, feel his warmth and his sinewy strength. Closing her eyes she pressed her palm where she thought his chest must be. She needed to reach out to touch his heart. His anger pulsated through her palm. She felt his anger, his indecision and his pride. Before he could walk away, she knelt down and slid her fingers beneath the door, entreating, "I would walk to the ends of the earth for you. I would give up my heart if you demanded it. Kahlil—" and suddenly his shadow receded. She felt him move away from her. Physically. Emotionally. He was shutting her out. Moving on. *Kahlil!*

Rifaat and a guard hauled her to her feet. She didn't have the strength to resist, all air sucked from her lungs in numb disbelief.

It was over. Kahlil didn't want her. Kahlil didn't want Ben. He'd made the decision and he wasn't going to change his mind.

Outside the driver waited in the limousine, behind the steering wheel. The back door to the black limousine stood open and Bryn spotted Ben, curled up on the back seat, beneath a soft blanket, sound asleep, his small arm clutching a stuffed blue elephant.

Trembling, she stooped down to lightly touch Ben, her fingers gentle against his brow. Her baby. Kahlil's baby. "I can't believe it's going to end like this."

Rifaat placed his hand on the top of the car door, stared down at her. "I am sorry, my lady."

Bryn couldn't speak.

"I know what he did, my lady, the sheikh's brother. I was there that night he attacked you in your room."

Her head jerked up, but still her voice failed her. Rifaat shook his own head once, slowly, wearily. "The surveillance cameras picked up that he'd entered the women's quarters. I didn't know what to do but then I heard you scream. I went into your room, and you were struggling, reaching for the jewelry box.''

Suddenly aspects of that night fell into place for Bryn, pieces of a difficult puzzle coming together. She'd wondered how she'd managed, how she'd escaped. ''I didn't knock him out. You did.''

''It had to be done.''

''Then you dragged Amin away.''

''I saw you leave the palace. I didn't stop you.'' Rifaat tapped the car door and stepped away. ''I've thought many times I should have told his highness about that night, but you'd run away, and Amin remained close with Kahlil. How to tell a sheikh that his brother is a fraud?''

It dawned on her then that Kahlil would always be vulnerable. Everyone wanted a piece of him. Everyone expected something. She felt Kahlil's impossible burden, and her chest squeezed tight. ''You can't,'' she said softly. ''You don't.''

''I'll talk to him now if you want.''

''And what? Turn Kahlil against you, too? I don't think so. I love him too much to have him live without at least one true friend, and you are his friend, Rifaat.''

''If I don't go to him, you'll lose him.''

''I've already lost him.'' She tried to smile but failed. ''Tell Kahlil—'' She stopped, cast a last lingering glance at the shuttered palace. ''Never mind. I better go before Ben wakes.''

CHAPTER TWELVE

ONLY two weeks ago she had sat in this very soft, leather seat in the luxurious jet cabin, cradling her sleeping son. Now here she was again, returning to Texas, but Dallas was no longer home. Home was with Kahlil. Home was the three of them together.

The plane vibrated, engines on, noise unnervingly loud. She could smell a whiff of the fuel, and the green and white lights of the runway twinkled in the distance. They'd leave the gate any second now. Tears burned the back of her eyes, her throat raw and swollen from too much emotion.

How could it all end like this? For one night, that one blissful night of their second honeymoon, there'd been such hope. Instead it had all come apart—and she didn't know how to ever explain the truth to Kahlil, how to make him understand that her love for him was greater than her shortcomings, greater than her insecurities, greater than anything else in the world. Real love wasn't just passion, but faith. And yet Kahlil had no faith in her. No trust, either.

The engines thrust forward. The plane pulled away from the gate. Lights flickered, overhead lamps turning down.

It hurt, wild, raw, unjustly, that she lost him not just

once, but twice. She wanted to weep with the loss but knew if she let a single tear fall, she'd lose all control.

"If you go," a deep male voice rasped from the back of the cabin, "you must take me."

Kahlil?

Slowly, afraid to discover his voice was a figment of her imagination, she turned in her seat.

Kahlil stood in the back of the cabin, faded jeans, T-shirt. Red-rimmed eyes, hair disheveled, his face washed but bruised. "Don't go. Not without me."

She couldn't speak, a lump the size of Kentucky prevented her from uttering a word. Hot, gritty tears burned her eyes and she simply shook her head, unable to believe he was here, on the plane, even after everything that had happened.

"I can't do it," he added roughly. "I can't do this without you."

Her lips parted, her mouth trembled. She forced sound through her throat. "Do what?"

"Rule Zwar, or lead my people." His voice broke and he shoved his hand through his hair. "I don't know if I can even live, feeling like this."

"No—"

And still he hung back, in the soft shadows of the cabin. "I'm no better than my father. He said he always acted for the good of his people, but I don't know if that's true. He said rules—order—must always come first, but I've tried to live like that and it's unbearable. My life is unbearable."

She struggled to rise, wanting to go to him but she

still held Ben and at the moment her legs weren't strong enough to fully support both of them. ''It can't be unbearable, not when people love you as much as we do.''

Kahlil jerked forward. ''So why do I have to hurt you? Why have I put us through this hell?''

''I don't know, but there's a reason, I'm sure.''

''No, there's never a reason for being deliberately cruel.'' He stopped a foot away, his golden eyes haunted, his expression bleak. ''I can't hurt you anymore. I have to stop, and I have to stop now.''

''You're here now, that's what counts.'' She fought to swallow, the tumult of emotions almost overwhelming. She didn't know whether to be happy or angry that Rifaat had broken his word and gone to Kahlil. ''Rifaat told you, then? I asked him not to.''

Kahlil frowned. ''Rifaat told me what?'' His expression revealed his confusion. ''Has something happened? Something to Ben?''

''No, nothing like that.'' She hesitated, realizing Kahlil obviously had no idea what she was talking about. So Rifaat didn't go to him…which meant Kahlil had come here on his own. For a moment she didn't know what to think, feel, and then suddenly something powerful in her heart broke loose and Bryn felt an intense wave of joy.

''How is he?'' Kahlil asked, indicating Ben, moving forward to take him from her arms.

''Good. He's been asleep most the time.''

''Poor little man.'' Kahlil cradled Ben close against his chest, muscles in his arms cording as he hugged his son. ''Does he know what I did? Does Ben know I was sending you away?''

''He woke up earlier when we boarded the plane, but I didn't tell him where we were going. I just said we were taking a ride.''

Kahlil's jaw jutted as he swallowed hard. ''I don't know what I was thinking—I don't know how I could send you away like that. I was there on the other side of the door, listening to you cry.'' His sober gaze met hers. ''I felt your hand on the door—there was heat, and pain—and yet instead of opening the door, I ignored you. I pretended you didn't exist.'' His mouth twisted, his expression raw. ''It makes me sick. How could I do that to you? How could I do that to my family?''

''Probably some coping mechanism left over from your childhood,'' she answered faintly.

''Doesn't make it right. I'm sorry. Forgive me.''

''There's nothing to forgive.''

''There's plenty. We al-Assads are notoriously hard on our women.''

Tears, gritty tears, pricked her eyes. She reached up to touch his face, moving her fingers down from his beautiful cheek to his angular jaw. ''I love you.''

''I know. And I know nothing happened between you and my brother. You're not that kind of a woman. Your heart is too pure. Besides, I know my brother. He's spent his life manipulating me, playing me. I can only imagine the hell he put you through.''

''It's over now. We have Ben back, and I have you.''

Abruptly Kahlil looked away, his jaw tightening.

"Tonight, when you screamed my name, it was the same way my mother had cried out for me. I didn't know then why she was being taken away, I just knew something awful was happening. I never saw her again."

He drew a deep painful breath, features contorted. "I had the chance once, when I was a teenager, visiting the States. But I refused to see her." He made a rough sound in the back of his throat. "She died less than a year later. Cancer."

"You didn't know."

"Refusing to see her was one of the worst mistakes I ever made. But I came close tonight to making another one." His head jerked around, his eyes bored into hers, searching, needing to know. "Your home is in Tiva with me, and I want you here with me. *If* that's what you want."

"I want," she whispered, fighting tears.

"I can't keep losing you."

"I've never wanted to go."

"Life is very hard—"

"I know. I want to spend forever with you. I want us to be together, for Ben, for each other."

"Good. Because I don't want Ben pulled between us. I couldn't bear for him to know what I've known." He drew a ragged breath. "The suffering did not make me stronger. It made me cruel. Please still love me."

"Oh, Kahlil, I do. I swear I do."

"No more separate rooms, no more harem and women's quarters. I just want you with me."

"Like a real couple?"

He nodded grimly, determined. ''A normal couple, so we can do our best to give Ben a normal family. It's what he deserves, what every child deserves, and it's what I want most.''

Her heart ached, tinged by bittersweet joy. ''I love you.''

''I love you more—''

''You can't!''

''I can. I'm the Sheikh Kahlil Hasim al-Assad, ruler of Zwar, leader of my people. Whatever I say goes.'' And leaning forward, Ben still tucked safely against his chest, he kissed her, tenderly. Reverently. ''You can't fight it, love. You're not going to win.''

These were the sweetest words in the world. Smiling through a blur of tears, Bryn threw up her hands. ''Fine. I surrender!''

LOOK OUT...

...for this month's special product offer.
It can be found in the envelope containing your invoice.

Special offers are exclusively for Reader Service™ members.

You will benefit from:

- Free books & discounts
- Free gifts
- Free delivery to your door
- No purchase obligation – 14 day trial
- Free prize draws

THE LIST IS ENDLESS!!

***So what are you waiting for — take a look* NOW!**

DM/OFFER V2